ACCLAIM FOR *WAKING HOURS*

"... an exciting faith-based series that skillfully blends romantic tension, gripping supernatural suspense, and a brutal crime."

—*LIBRARY JOURNAL*, STARRED
REVIEW OF *WAKING HOURS*

"Wiehl's latest is a truly creepy story with supernatural undertones that seems eerily real."

—*ROMANTIC TIMES* REVIEW
OF *WAKING HOURS*

"... a truly chilling predator and some great snappy, funny dialogue will keep readers engaged."

—*PUBLISHERS WEEKLY*
REVIEW OF *WAKING HOURS*

"This smart, spooky, high-stakes mystery engaged my mind and my spirit. Tommy and Dani's battle against the seen and unseen forces rising in East Salem has only just begun, but I'm fully invested in their journey."

—ERIN HEALY, AUTHOR OF *THE PROMISES
SHE KEEPS* AND *THE BAKER'S WIFE*

"A strong debut full of suspense, romance and supernatural mystery. A fine start to the series."

—ANDREW KLAVAN, BEST-SELLING AUTHOR OF
TRUE CRIME AND THE HOMELANDERS SERIES

"One word describes *Waking Hours* by Wiehl and Nelson—WOW! A gut-wrenching ride of supernatural suspense that left me breathless and wanting more. The book was a reminder that the battle between God and Satan is not over. Highly recommended!"

—COLLEEN COBLE, BEST-SELLING
AUTHOR OF *LONESTAR ANGEL* AND
THE ROCK HARBOR SERIES

"A gripping plot, intriguing characters, supernatural underpinnings, and a splash of romance make *Waking Hours* a fast-paced and thoroughly enjoyable read. I want the next book in the series now!"

—JAMES L. RUBART, AWARD-
WINNING AUTHOR OF *ROOMS*

ACCLAIM FOR LIS WIEHL'S
TRIPLE THREAT SERIES

"Only a brilliant lawyer, prosecutor, and journalist like Lis Wiehl could put together a mystery this thrilling! The incredible characters and nonstop twists will leave you mesmerized. Open [*Face of Betrayal*] and find a comfortable seat because you won't want to put it down!"

—E. D. HILL, FOX NEWS ANCHOR

"Three smart women crack the big cases! Makes perfect sense to me. [*Face of Betrayal*] blew me away!"

—JEANINE PIRRO, FORMER DA; HOST OF THE CW'S DAYTIME
COURT TELEVISION REALITY SHOW *JUDGE JEANINE PIRRO*

"Who killed loudmouth radio guy Jim Fate? The game is afoot! *Hand of Fate* is a fun thriller, taking you inside the media world and the justice system—scary places to be!"

—BILL O'REILLY, FOX TV
AND RADIO ANCHOR

"As a television crime writer and producer, I expect novels to deliver pulsepounding tales with major twists. *Hand of Fate* delivers big time."

—PAM VEASEY, WRITER AND
EXECUTIVE PRODUCER OF *CSI: NY*

"Book three in the wonderful Triple Threat series is a fast-paced thriller full of twists and turns that will keep you guessing until the end. What makes these books stand out for me is my ability to identify so easily with Allison, Nic and Cassidy. I truly care about what happens to each of them, and the challenges they face this time are heart-wrenching and realistic. I highly recommend!"

—DEBORAH SINCLAIRE, EDITOR-IN-
CHIEF, BOOK-OF-THE-MONTH CLUB
AND THE STEPHEN KING LIBRARY

"Beautiful, successful and charismatic on the outside but underneath a twisted killer. She's brilliant and crazy and comes racing at the reader with knives and a smile. The most chilling villain you'll meet . . . because she could live next door to you."

—DR. DALE ARCHER, CLINICAL
PSYCHIATRIST, REGARDING *HEART OF ICE*

DARKNESS
RISING

DARKNESS RISING

THE EAST SALEM TRILOGY
BOOK TWO

LIS WIEHL
WITH PETE NELSON

THOMAS NELSON
Since 1798

NASHVILLE   DALLAS   MEXICO CITY   RIO DE JANEIRO

Published in Nashville, Tennessee by Thomas Nelson. Thomas Nelson is a registered trademark of Thomas Nelson, Inc.

Page design by Mandi Cofer.

Thomas Nelson, Inc., books may be purchased in bulk for educational, business, fund-raising, or sales promotional use. For information, please e-mail SpecialMarkets@ ThomasNelson.com.

Scripture quotations are taken from the KING JAMES VERSION of the Bible as well as the NEW AMERICAN STANDARD BIBLE®, © The Lockman Foundation 1960, 1962, 1963, 1968, 1971, 1972, 1973, 1975, 1977, 1995. Used by permission.

Publisher's Note: This novel is a work of fiction. Names, characters, places, and incidents are either products of the author's imagination or used fictitiously. All characters are fictional, and any similarity to people living or dead is purely coincidental.

ISBN 978-1-40168-786-1 (IE)

Library of Congress Cataloging-in-Publication Data

Wiehl, Lis W.
  Darkness rising / Lis Wiehl with Pete Nelson.
    p. cm. -- (The East Salem trilogy ; bk. 2)
  ISBN 978-1-59554-943-3
1. Paranormal fiction. 2. Murder--Fiction. 3. Forensic psychiatrists--Fiction. 4. High school students--Fiction. 5. Faith--Fiction. I. Nelson, Peter, 1953- II. Title.
  PS3623.I382D37 2012
  813'.6--dc23

                                  2012022633

Printed in the United States of America

12 13 14 15 16 17 QG 6 5 4 3 2

For my loving mom, Inga Wiehl. And for Dani and Jacob, from your loving mom.

1.

Abbie Gardener could remember sitting on the back of a very broad, gray, docile plow horse named Bob. She loved Bob.

"You are a very special girl," her father had told her, but she knew fathers always told their little girls they were special.

"Why?" she said.

"Because Jesus loves you. Do you believe Jesus loves you?"

"Yes, Papa."

"Did you say your prayers last night?"

"Yes, Papa."

"Did you say your prayers this morning?"

"Yes, Papa."

"That's a very good girl. You must say your prayers every morning and every evening before bed, and the Lord will protect you and keep you safe."

And she had done so for many, many years. But lately she couldn't remember if she'd prayed or not. It troubled her greatly. She was often certain that she had, but the next minute she wasn't sure, and two minutes after that she'd forgotten what it was she was trying to remember.

Bob pulled a plow. He was a good horse. I used to feed him green apples.

She suddenly realized where she was. She was not a little girl. She was very old. She was in the same town where she'd lived her whole life. East

1

Salem, New York. But she was not in her home. She was not on her farm. She was in a nursing home.

Why am I here?

It was dark outside. The clock on the bed stand had jumped ahead again. Beside the clock there was a small paper cup with two pills in it and a glass of water. She'd promised the girl in the blue jacket she'd take the pills before she went to bed, but she hadn't.

Because it was coming.

It was coming soon, she knew, because it knew she couldn't fight it any longer.

She went to the window in her nightgown and looked out. She looked at the floodlight in the parking lot and saw that it was raining.

"Of all the gifts in God's domain, I think the most sublime is rain," she sang. She could only remember the hymns she'd learned as a little girl. There were so many more, she knew, but she couldn't remember them. Only fragments. "A mighty fortress is our God . . ." She suddenly realized that she needed to lock the windows.

She tried to find the button to call the girl in the blue jacket to tell her she must lock the windows. Where was the button? Was it a blue jacket? Was it green?

She wanted to lock the door, but there wasn't a lock to lock.

The bracelet on her ankle itched. She wanted to take it off. If she didn't remove the bracelet, the thing that was coming would use it to find her.

Bob pulled a plow. He was a good horse.

She went to the window. It was still raining.

"When God first saw the world in pain, I think he wept and called it rain . . ."

She thought she saw something moving on the lawn, in the shadows just beyond the light in the parking lot. Had she said her prayers tonight? Perhaps she should say them again, just to be safe.

"Our Father, who art in heaven . . ."

How did it go? Why couldn't she remember?

"Our Father, who art in heaven . . . "

"Our Father . . . "

"It will come for you one day," her father had told her. But it wasn't her father. It was another man. The banker? "You have been chosen. You have been given gifts, and you will fight and be strong, but you will live to be very old and too weak to fight, and then one day . . ."

She looked out the window and saw a shape in the rain, or rather a hole in the night where rain was supposed to be. It moved slowly, deliberately, wending its way toward her.

Where was the button to call the girl?

But when she checked, the windows were already locked. Good.

It drew closer.

She looked around the room for anything she might use to defend herself. The chair was too heavy for her to lift. Her umbrella was one of those short, collapsible ones, not the long kind with a sharp point that might have been useful. She would fight it even though she could not win.

She moved behind the bed.

The thing was outside her window now. She saw it rise up, translucent at first, or made from darkness, absorbing light. She could see through it to the parking lot beyond.

Then it came through the window.

She could smell it before she could see it, a stench like rotten eggs, fetid and metallic—she could taste it at the back of her throat, harsh and revolting.

The entity began to take solid form, drawing molecules from the air and the walls and the floor. She saw its heart first, black and horned, sprouting arteries and veins like vines, wrapping around stone-gray bones. As it grew, it gradually stood upright, the vertebrae of its long neck like a string of black beads. "You'll know it by the form it takes," the man had told her. "In the olden times, brave men fought it and called it a dragon, but it's a demon by any name or shape."

Scales great and small covered its skin. Unsightly blisters spread across the underbelly. The room turned cold. A month ago they'd killed the girl. Abbie had tried to warn the girl, but she was too old.

"What a friend we have in Jesus," the old woman sang. "All our sins and griefs to bear . . ."

Fully formed now, the thing tossed the bed aside and stepped toward her. The room was dark. It looked like some kind of animal, but nothing she'd ever seen before.

"What a privilege to carry . . . ," she sang, louder now.

"WHERE IS IT? WHERE'S THE BOOK?" it said, commanding her not with sounds her ears could hear but with words that impaled her thoughts. A month ago they'd killed the girl because they knew her father was the one. The next. The girl, Julie, had tried to find him, and they killed her. Then they burned down the girl's house to kill her mother and sister. Had they killed her father too? If so, the book was the only hope left, the only thing standing in their way. Abbie tried to remember where she'd hidden it, then laughed, because she couldn't remember. What better hiding place was there than one the hider couldn't find?

"Get thee behind me," she answered.

"WHERE'S THE BOOK?"

"Is this the book you mean?" she shouted as she grabbed the Bible from the shelf next to the bed and held it up like a shield.

The beast cried out and slapped the Holy Book from her hand, sending it sailing across the room. It stepped closer, reached out, and pressed a bony finger to her lips. She struggled, lashed out at it, but couldn't back away. She felt all the air inside her being sucked out. As the air left her lungs, the air outside her body pressed in. She was being crushed beneath an invisible weight.

The demon lifted its finger from her lips, and she could breathe again, gasping.

"WHERE IS THE BOOK?"

She looked at him defiantly and spat in his face.

"The Lord is my shepherd, I shall not want," she said. "He maketh me to lie down in green pastures; he leadeth me beside—"

The beast again pressed its finger against her lips, and the air rushed out of her. She was unable to breathe, her vision dimming. Slowly, life left her body as the room and the sky and the world pressed down on her. She heard her bones cracking but she felt no pain, no fear, and she was able to finish the psalm silently, reciting the words in her head as she died: *Surely goodness and mercy shall follow me all the days of my life: and I will dwell in the house of the Lord forever . . .*

Then darkness.

Then light . . .

2.

"Into the lions' den," Dani said.

"Danielle and the lions," Tommy said. "That has a ring to it. Hopefully we'll get the same kind of help he had."

"Hopefully we won't need it," Dani said.

"We're here."

Tommy put the Jaguar in neutral, handed his keys to the parking valet, a boy who didn't look old enough to drive, walked around the front of the car, and opened the door for Dani. Couples waiting to enter had gathered on the patio outside the art museum, men in tuxedos and cashmere overcoats, women accessorized in pearls and gold and diamond chandelier earrings.

The last time Dani Harris, a forensic psychiatrist, and Tommy Gunderson, her "assistant," had visited St. Adrian's Academy for Boys, it had been to question a boy they'd suspected of murdering a girl named Julie Leonard at a place called Bull's Rock Hill. Dani's employer, Ralston-Foley Behavioral Consulting, had been hired to consult with the district attorney's office. Although the DA had officially closed the case, as far as Dani and Tommy were concerned, it wasn't over. And though Dani was technically on leave of absence to deal with any post-traumatic stress disorders she might be experiencing, she knew there was no time to waste.

"Ready when you are," Tommy said. In his pocket he had a device he'd purchased on the Internet, an electronic bug in the form of a coil of wire with what looked like a small black transformer on one end and a USB jack on the other. It could be plugged into a free USB port in the back of any computer, where its presence would go unnoticed, hidden in plain sight in the nest of wires and cords most people had connecting their peripheral devices. Once programmed and in place, it would use the Internet to transfer all the host-computer's hard drive and keystroke data to a second monitoring computer, in this case, Tommy's. They'd come to plant the bug or die trying, though dying wasn't part of the plan, exactly.

"Onward," Dani replied, offering Tommy her elbow.

The art museum was a brightly lit modern building with straight, clean lines and white surfaces on an ancient campus where the dormitories, halls, administration building, and student commons favored stone or red brick covered with ivy, slate roofs, garrets, balconies, leaded windows, bell towers, sloping dormers, marble cornices, and chimneys capped in wrought iron.

The occasion was an exhibition marking the first time the major works of Dutch renaissance painter Hieronymus Bosch had been shown in America. The show included his mysterious triptych *Garden of Earthly Delights*, on loan from the Prado in Madrid but owned by St. Adrian's alumnus Udo Bauer, a German multibillionaire whose family owned Linz Pharmazeutika. Dani's boss had received an invitation but had a prior commitment and couldn't attend. Dani had said she'd be happy to go in her stead, though "happy" wasn't the right word, because she didn't know how to be happy and scared at the same time.

Inside, Tommy steered Dani to the coatroom off the entry hall.

"Quite the turnout," Dani said. "A Who's Who of East Salem."

The reception was in the atrium. Boys in black pants, white shirts, and black bow ties circulated bearing silver trays of canapés or glasses of wine. Dani accepted a tomato and basil bruschetta as Tommy surveyed the room.

"Keep an eye out for anything that isn't human," he said. "And make allowances for bad plastic surgery."

They passed two women in conversation, both of whom looked like their faces had been shrink-wrapped in cellophane. A student string ensemble in the corner provided chamber music. They played well, Dani thought, but mechanically and without much feeling. There was, she noted, a kind of flattened affect to many of the boys in attendance, a palpable stiffness. They were all polite but unsmiling, slightly robotic. Her evaluation of the St. Adrian's student they'd suspected, Amos Kasden, had been that he'd suffered from a dissociative identity disorder. His mind had become disconnected from his body and nothing seemed real to him, emotions reduced to ideas, and confusing ones at that. Zero empathy. Somewhere in the computer belonging to Dr. Adolf Ghieri, the school psychologist, there had to be a file on Amos. What it would tell them, they could only guess, but that was the computer they were targeting.

"You're rocking the room, by the way," Tommy said. "You're what women who have plastic surgery wish they looked like."

Dani was wearing a sleeveless black Carmen Marc Valvo cocktail dress she'd picked up at a sample sale, with black and tan ribbing at the bodice above a taffeta skirt, accessorized with silver earrings, a silver evening bag, and a pair of Prada knockoff shoes she'd picked up at T.J. Maxx for $25. Tommy wore the black Armani tuxedo he'd purchased the first time he'd accepted the ESPY award as NFL Defensive Player of the Year, tailored to allow extra room for his broad shoulders and less for his tapered waist.

"Thanks," Dani said. "I assume you mean that as a compliment."

He touched her arm and gestured toward a group of men standing near a statue of a figure Tommy guessed was St. Adrian, the school's namesake.

"There's Wharton," he said.

Dr. John Adams Wharton, the headmaster, was shaking hands and greeting guests. He wore a black tux, his position of authority marked only by the boutonniere in the school colors of purple and red pinned to his lapel. His long, thinning white hair was brushed straight back.

"Where's Ghieri?" Dani said. The school psychologist had seemed menacing and defensive when they'd questioned Amos Kasden. Something about him exuded evil. Dani couldn't put her finger on it, but Tommy had told her to trust her feelings, comparing it to the way people instinctively fear snakes.

Then they saw him, balding and stout, standing between two men they didn't recognize. One was in his seventies, with unkempt frizzy white hair, a white moustache, and round wire-rimmed eyeglasses. The other man was tall, fair-haired, and too tan for November; in his forties, with a long neck and a narrow head that reminded Tommy of a ferret. His expression was pinched and annoyed, as if he'd just caught a whiff of something foul.

"I bet the tall one is Bauer," Dani said. "He looks very German. And very rich."

Tommy surveyed the room and noticed that all the exits were guarded by young men in black shirts with walkie-talkies and earpieces.

"I know these paintings are valuable, but am I the only one who thinks there's more security than they need?"

"Should we wait for a better time?" Dani asked.

"No," Tommy said. "As long as they're concentrating on the paintings and not on Ghieri's office, this could work in our favor. Plus, when are we going to get another invitation? Let's chat 'em up and see if they recognize us. I'll take Ghieri. See if you can get a rise out of Wharton."

"By doing what?"

"I don't know. Flirt with him."

"Not in my skill set," Dani said. "My sister says I must have skipped class the day they covered that in Girl School."

"Don't overthink it. Just pretend you care. Laugh at his jokes. If a guy thinks a pretty woman is interested in him, he'll change the litter in her

9

cat's litter box," Tommy said. "Which reminds me—I changed the litter in Arlo's litter box."

"Thank you," Dani said.

"Don't underestimate yourself. Text me if you need me." Tommy patted the phone in his breast pocket.

Dani furrowed her brow. "Be careful," she said.

"You know me."

"That's why I said 'Be careful.'"

She straightened his bow tie and brushed a bit of lint from his shoulder, then moved left, accepting a glass of chardonnay from one of the waiters. Then she set it down, found her phone, and entered SOS in a text message for Tommy's mobile number, ready to send just in case.

She paused to chat with two women from her book club. They were reading *War and Peace*, having recently finished *Moby Dick*. "We really need to pick thinner books," one said. Dani nodded and kept moving.

She had no problem engaging strangers at dinner parties, looking judges or attorneys in the eye, teaching classes at John Jay College of Criminal Justice, or speaking at conferences, but idle chitchat was a challenge for her. Dani knew men found submissive women attractive because it made them feel powerful, but how did one fake "submissive"?

Dr. Wharton, the German, the man with the moustache, and a fourth man were standing by a framed Albrecht Dürer sketch of a rhinoceros. The older man, the one with the moustache, seemed to be explaining something to the others as Dani approached.

"Dr. Wharton," she said. "I'm Dani Harris. Irene Scotto asked me to give you her regrets. She had a conference in Washington, so she sent me here to represent the district attorney's office."

"Yes," Wharton said, giving no sign that he remembered meeting Dani or cared whom she might be representing. "I'm pleased you could attend."

Dani remembered Tommy's advice, but there was nothing funny in the words *I'm pleased you could attend*. She thought of how idiotic it would be to laugh, and she must have made a face, because Wharton looked at her as if she were utterly demented. So much for flirting.

"If you'll excuse me," he said with a polite bow and a puzzled expression, moving on to greet another guest.

"Miss Harris," the fair-haired man said, without a hint of a German accent. "Are you here by yourself?"

"I came with someone from my office," she said, holding up her glass. "He's probably looking for me—"

"Udo Bauer," the man said, extending his hand. She took it, half expecting him to click his heels together. "Let me introduce my friends. Dr. Julian Villanegre. Dr. Peter Guryakin. Dr. Villanegre is here to oversee the installation. Dr. Guryakin works for me."

Dani shook hands with the white-haired Villanegre and then with Guryakin, whose name rang a bell.

"And what do you do, Miss Harris?" Dr. Villanegre said, surprising her with his British accent.

"I work at Northern Westchester Hospital." She had visitation privileges there but rarely used them.

"You're a nurse?" Bauer said.

"A doctor."

"My apologies," Bauer said. "My personal physician is a fat old man with liver spots on his liver spots. I can't picture doctors any other way."

"I also consult with the DA's office as a forensic psychiatrist," she added, looking for a reaction. Usually when she told people her job title, they asked her what it meant, and she'd explain that she evaluated suspects and witnesses for competency and testified in court as to the emotional or mental state of the accused.

"I was just explaining to my friends what an astonishing anatomist Dürer was," Villanegre said, pointing at the drawing mounted on the wall. "He drew his rhinoceros based entirely on a description a friend gave him of an animal being exhibited in Lisbon. The friend said the animal wore armor, so the artist took the liberty of adding rivets. Other than that, I think he got it right."

In her peripheral vision, Dani saw Bauer peeking down the bodice of her dress.

"You're an art historian?" she said to Villanegre. "Professional or amateur?"

"I curate for the Ashmolean in Oxford, but Mr. Bauer asked me to supervise the shipping of the works. Have you seen *The Garden of Earthly Delights*?"

"Not yet," Dani said. She turned to the shorter man. "Dr. Guryakin, you work for Herr Bauer—may I ask in what capacity?"

"Yes," he said, nodding politely. Dani watched as he touched his nose and folded his arms across his chest. When he spoke, his lower lip pulled to the left. She'd been trained to recognize signs that a suspect was lying, and Guryakin had just hit the trifecta. "I work in marketing," he said. His accent was Russian.

"You're a charming young woman, and it's been a pleasure meeting you," Villanegre said, "but I'm afraid I have to go prepare for my little talk. If you'll excuse me . . ."

Dani smiled and nodded. Then Villanegre stopped and looked her in the eyes as if he recognized something. His face a foot from hers, he studied her, as if unaware that she was looking back, and then he seemed to nod to himself. Dani had no idea what it meant, but she felt as if she'd been caught at something.

Tommy had trouble moving through the crowd. He'd played in the NFL for eight years, was a six-time Pro Bowler when he walked away from the game after killing an opposing player on the field—a clean hit, it was

12

ruled, but a tragic accident. He didn't care what the league called it; he only knew it wasn't going to happen again. His picture still ended up in the tabloids from time to time. He'd learned that men from the highest social circles and men who raked leaves for a living and preferred Budweiser over Chateau Lafite Rothschild often had in common a love of football. This usually served Tommy well, but made it hard to walk through a party without shaking a hundred hands.

He kept moving, chatting people up. The fact that a teenage girl had been murdered by a St. Adrian's student less than a month before did little to dampen the party mood on campus tonight. He made small talk but kept Ghieri in his sights, working to get closer. But every time Tommy moved, Ghieri moved too.

He gave up trying to catch the man alone when the doors to the main gallery swung open and the crowd filtered in. He found Dani by the statue of St. Adrian.

"Any luck?" she said.

"Not much. I learned you can't teach here unless you're a graduate," he said.

"Hence the term 'Old Boy Network.'"

"You?"

"I was right about Bauer. The man with the Albert Einstein hair and the moustache is an art historian. The other guy works for Bauer. Dr. Peter Guryakin. When I asked him what he did, he lied and said he was in marketing. I Googled his name."

"And?"

"Nothing."

"Who gets zero hits on Google?"

"That's what I thought," Dani said. "Unless somebody scrubbed the databases. Shall we go in and have a look at the painting?"

"If I get a chance to slip out—" Tommy began, then stopped, momentarily distracted by the statue. "That's odd."

"What is?"

"This is St. Adrian," he said. "The guy they named the school after, right?"

"And?"

"He was the abbot of St. Augustine's Abbey in Canterbury around 700 AD."

"So what's odd?"

"He's not wearing a cross," Tommy said. "You'd think he'd have one. So why doesn't he?"

"Good question," Dani said. She stepped closer and examined the figure's hands.

"What?"

"Look at the marks on his fingers, here and here." She pointed for Tommy's sake but tried not to draw attention. "The statue looks like it was weathered everywhere except there. As though he *was* holding a cross, until someone removed it. Why? Someone stole it because it was valuable?"

"Maybe it was just something the administration didn't want the student body exposed to," Tommy said. "They might get ideas."

3.

There were rows of folding chairs in the main gallery, but not enough for all the guests. Dani and Tommy stood on the side with their backs to the windows, close to the door. Behind a portable podium at the far end of the room they could see a curtain concealing what Dani assumed was the main attraction, the painting known as *The Garden of Earthly Delights*.

The headmaster took the podium.

After a few seconds of polite applause, Wharton glanced briefly at his notes, then removed his reading glasses to speak from memory.

"We are all here," he began, "because of a gift. The paintings and drawings you see on the walls around you, or will see when the lights come up, and in particular the special painting behind this curtain"—he gestured over his shoulder—"are of course not gifts. Would that they were . . ."

"I'll never understand how Americans like Orson Welles or William F. Buckley or this guy end up with British accents," Tommy whispered.

"They have been generously loaned to us," Wharton continued, "by one of our most esteemed alumni, Herr Udo Bauer. His continued support for St. Adrian's Academy and its mission has been a precious gift indeed."

"Esteemed?" Tommy said to Dani over another round of applause. "He's forgetting the part where Bauer's grandfather tested his drugs in Nazi concentration camps."

"Allegedly," Dani said. The research they'd done before the exhibition had turned up a few accusations but nothing conclusive.

"Right," Tommy said. "And the sun 'allegedly' rose in the east this morning."

"I had in mind," Wharton said, "to ask Udo, class of '77, to say a few words tonight, but he's far too modest and asked that I not force him to speak. I will instead announce, on his behalf, that in addition to loaning the paintings from his family's collection, he has also seen fit to make a contribution to the school's development fund for a new science facility. It will be, simply, the finest of any preparatory school in the world."

"What's wrong with the one they have?" Dani asked Tommy over the next round of applause. "I thought they just built one ten years ago."

"Toward that end," Wharton continued, "fifteen minutes ago, Udo Bauer handed me a check. This one . . ." He pulled a check from his shirt pocket and held it up. "For the sum of . . ." He paused for effect. "One hundred million dollars."

There was a collective gasp, then thunderous applause that didn't stop until Bauer stood and nodded to the crowd.

"That's going to buy a lot of frogs to dissect," Tommy said.

"We will, of course, keep our alumni informed as the building progresses," Wharton said once the applause died away. "Now, to tell you about the paintings you are about to see, I give you the distinguished art historian, antiquities curator at the Ashmolean Museum in Oxford, England, don emeritus of Trinity College, University of Oxford, and the world's leading authority on Heironymus Bosch—ladies and gentlemen, Dr. Julian Villanegre."

As the crowd welcomed Dr. Villanegre, a large screen lowered from the ceiling and the lights came down even further, save for a spotlight on the podium. Julian Villanegre smiled broadly, adjusting the microphone and thanking the headmaster. He paused, waiting for the audience's complete attention. Dani thought again of how he'd looked at her.

16

Something about him defied understanding, something . . . mystical? Was that the word?

"For the first time," he began, "one of the world's most breathtaking—and most misunderstood—paintings has come to America. Heironymus Bosch, born 1450, died 1516 . . ."

A self-portrait of the artist appeared on the screen. He looked kind, avuncular. He'd grown up in the town of Hertogenbosch, Villanegre said, in the Duchy of Brabant, a region that today would include parts of Holland and Belgium.

"Hertogenbosch, we note, burned to the ground in 1463. The artist, who would have been about thirteen, was suspected of setting the fires. It's thought that his famous 'hellscapes' may have been his way of imaginatively revisiting the scene of the crime."

"Sounds a lot like Amos Kasden," Tommy whispered.

The slide of the artist faded to black, and then a slide of *The Garden of Earthly Delights* faded in.

Villanegre paused to let the image of the painting register. The room fell silent.

Dani listened closely as Villanegre briefly reviewed the function of paintings in the Renaissance, before movies, television, or photography. *The Garden of Earthly Delights* was a triptych, with the two outer rectangular panels hinged to fold over the square center panel like shutters. *The Garden of Earthly Delights*, or *The Millennium*, as it was also known, was, like most altarpieces, intended to be a pedagogic tool mounted above the altar in a church to illustrate spiritual texts, usually Bible stories.

"But that's where the enigma begins," Villanegre said, "because it's difficult to imagine what kind of church might have commissioned this one. One cannot say with certainty whom Bosch was working for when he created his extraordinary vision. He left no written record of his thoughts regarding the painting. The work must speak for itself. But what does it say?"

He explained that altarpieces were meant to be read from left to right. In *The Millennium*, the left panel depicted the Garden of Eden, the middle panel represented life on Earth, and the right-hand panel depicted hell. Villanegre directed the audience to the center of the left panel, where God presented Eve to Adam.

"Adam has an astonished expression, as one might expect," Villanegre said, using his laser pointer to circle Adam's face. "And yet even in paradise, things have begun to go wrong. We see the snake, familiar to readers of Genesis, but also a two-legged dog . . . a three-headed salamander . . . here a duck with teeth . . . and here a duck reading a book. Given that Eden is where man was born, we may consider these to prefigure knowledge of birth defects . . ."

"Or genetic disorders," Dani whispered to Tommy.

"The center panel teems with Adam-and-Eve-like figures, cavorting in twos and threes and fours, engaged in a variety of sexualized behaviors." Villanegre continued to use the laser to highlight people on the screen behind him. "Here . . . here . . . and here . . . We note that in each group, one man has some sort of oversized piece of fruit on his head, symbolic of organic or natural wisdom. The ones with fruit on their heads are the instructors. But nothing in the painting is simple. You'll see that the creatures in the panel are hybrids, blending animal, vegetable, and mineral. The architecture is also hybrid, where man-made constructions look like caves and boats are half fish. All is in flux, midtransformation, with opposites in union.

"The question over the centuries," Villanegre continued, "has been whether the artist is condoning or condemning these behaviors. Is it a portrait of paradise on earth, where man has returned to an antelapsarian state of grace? Or is it a scathing depiction of human folly, where man, exalting himself above God, lives purely for the pleasures of the flesh? Ecstatic utopian vision, or nightmarish phantasmagoria? In the hellscape, filling the right-most panel, we see how God will punish those committing the seven deadly sins, with gluttony represented by this figure here, condemned to an eternity of dyspepsia . . . and sloth . . . and avarice . . ."

"Wait here," Tommy whispered. "I should be back in ten or fifteen minutes."

"I'm coming with you," Dani said.

"Bad idea. If they catch me, I'm just another dumb jock with a sense of entitlement who's had too much to drink. It's the 98 percent of all jocks who give the other 2 percent a bad name."

Dani smiled, even though she'd come to understand something about Tommy Gunderson: he made jokes when he was afraid.

"I'll be back in ten. Fifteen tops. If I'm not . . ."

"What?"

"I don't know. Pull the fire alarm or something. And then go home. One of us has to make it out of here. Don't come looking for me. Promise?"

"Promise," she said, then watched as he sidled toward the door.

⁂

"The key," Villanegre was saying, "may be deciphering this figure in the lower right-hand corner of the center panel." The laser pointer circled a man who appeared to be emerging from a cave. "This area, we know, is where artists of the period commonly inserted cameos of their patrons. One of the more compelling theories comes from the Swiss historian Viktor Friedrichs, who makes a strong case that the painting was commissioned by a pagan cult led by the Duke of Ghent, a patron of the arts who was later put to death for heresy. The provenance of the painting is not known, but it is believed to have hung in the duke's private chapel."

Villanegre let his laser pointer pause on a vaguely defined man beside the duke. Dani tried to concentrate on the lecture, which she found fascinating despite the odd, even sinister circumstances of the painting's arrival. She tapped the screen on her phone, went to her apps and then to her stopwatch application. She'd give Tommy fifteen minutes, and then she was going to look for him despite her promise.

"Even more mysterious is this fellow here," Villanegre said, "lurking in the shadows. He appears to be whispering something in the other man's ear, serving as either a friendly advisor or, according to Friedrichs, as his Rasputin, his dark priest."

Dani studied the projection of the painting. They'd come to look for anything out of the ordinary, and Heironymus Bosch's painting was as far from "ordinary" as anything she could think of. A celebration of evil, a nightmarish vision of psychotic content, and clearly, in any day or age, the product of a profoundly disturbed imagination. This was a "pedagogic tool"?

Was that why it had been brought here? To be used, once more, to teach?

Tommy held up his cell phone to the man at the door to indicate he had an important call to make. "My dad isn't well," he whispered. That much was the truth. He closed the door noiselessly behind him and stepped out onto the patio, where he pretended to make a call, aware that the man at the door was watching him through the window. He looked up at the sky, then held his phone out at arm's length, pantomiming that he was unable to find a spot with adequate cell tower coverage. It was a common problem in East Salem, where no one wanted a cell tower in his own backyard. Holding his phone out in front of him, he wandered away from the museum and into the darkness. When he glanced behind him, he saw he was no longer being observed.

He moved quickly now, crossing the quad to the main building, where he found a door at the west end. The door was locked, opening only with a key card. Part of Tommy's training to become a private detective included private lessons in lock picking with an ex-con he'd met through his talent agency, but the lessons hadn't covered electronic card locks. He moved to the rear of the building, staying in the shadows. The lights were out in the library wing, the stacks lined up inside like black tombstones. The back door accessing the rear parking lot was locked as well. The windows seemed formidable. The basement window wells had iron bars over them. The only way in was through the front door.

Tommy was prepared to say he was looking for the men's room, but discovered on entering the foyer and the domed great hall that no one was around. He listened, thinking there would at least be a switchboard operator or a night watchman afoot. His luck held. Everyone seemed to be at the museum. The soft rubber soles of his black cross-trainers, which he was wearing only because at the time he was dressing he couldn't find his one pair of dress shoes, made his footsteps silent on the parquet floor.

He walked quickly down the hall, past the library, and made his way to the school psychologist's office. He listened. Nothing. The door to the waiting room was unlocked. When he closed the door behind him, the windowless room was plunged into total darkness.

Tommy tapped on his phone for his flashlight app.

He crossed to Ghieri's office door. This one was locked, the mechanism again controlled with a magnetic key card. Breaking either the lock or the door or both was not an option, assuming it was even possible.

He draped the listening device around his neck to free his hands, opened his phone's slide-out keyboard, and went to the Google search box, where he typed *How can you pick an electronic keycard lock?* He'd just reached the results screen when the lights came on.

Adolf Ghieri stood by the door, his hand on the light switch.

"Oh, *that's* where the switch was," Tommy said. "I couldn't find it. I'm glad you're here—"

Dr. Ghieri blocked the exit. "What are you doing?" he said coldly.

"As I was about to explain," Tommy said, slurring his words, "I was looking for a computer. I can't get Wi-Fi, so I gotta hardwire to a computer to download a file from my accountant because apparently the underwriters are having some sort of conniption fit that has to be straightened out before the IPO next month . . ."

"What are you doing?" Ghieri repeated.

"As I was saying," Tommy said, smiling as he held up the USB jack to the listening device draped around his neck, "I didn't think you'd mind, but . . . you guys really need to get a Wi-Fi setup if you—"

Ghieri stepped forward and grabbed Tommy by the throat. His grip was like iron as his hand closed around Tommy's windpipe and lifted him off the ground.

Tommy weighed 220 pounds, but the man raised him as if he were holding up a dandelion to blow away the seeds. Tommy tried in vain to pry the smaller man's hand from his throat.

Ghieri grabbed the wire around Tommy's neck, examined it for a moment, then snapped it as easily as breaking a dry spaghetti noodle. He pulled Tommy closer until their faces were inches apart. His breath smelled sulfurous and putrid. His eyes were penetrating and blank, windows not into a soul but into the absence of one.

Tommy struggled to free himself.

Ghieri heard something.

Startled, he spun around, lifting Tommy even higher. Pinning him against the wall with one hand, Ghieri listened. Tommy couldn't breathe.

Then Ghieri simply wasn't there anymore.

Tommy dropped to the floor.

He rubbed his throat and gasped desperately for air, coughing. He managed to rise to one knee.

Something picked him up and gently lifted him to his feet.

He turned to see a burly man in a tuxedo, with a close-cropped beard and long hair pulled back in a ponytail. He wore an earring in his left ear and had a tattoo of a cross on the back of his right hand. Tommy had last seen this man the night he'd gone to Bull's Rock Hill hoping to find out why Julie Leonard had been murdered—only that night the man had been dressed in biker attire. The "biker" had revealed himself to be an angel and said his name was Charlie.

"Are you all right?" Charlie asked.

"I'm okay." Tommy rubbed his throat. He looked around. "Where did he go?"

"That's not a question I can answer, but he'll be back. I thought you could use some help."

Tommy saw a small red object, marked by a white cross, in Charlie's hand. "From a Swiss Army knife?"

"It has multiple attachments."

Standing this close to the angel, Tommy couldn't think of what to say. The air had a kind of excitement to it, an ozone smell, as if lightning had just struck, or would any second.

"I know," Tommy said. "I have one."

"Can it do this?" the angel said. He opened a small blade and pointed it toward the ceiling. As Tommy watched, it transformed into a large sword, radiating a bright white light that forced Tommy to shield his eyes with his hand.

The light became flame, swirling toward the ceiling in beautiful, flickering tongues. Then, just as suddenly as it appeared, the flames were extinguished. The light went out and the blade shrank back into the angel's hand.

"No," Tommy said. "Mine can't do that."

He knew somehow that what the angel had chosen to show him was only a partial display, a hint at the full extent of his power.

There were a hundred questions Tommy wanted to ask, but this wasn't the time. He had to get back to Dani. Knowing her, she'd be looking for him. The bug he'd hoped to plant was useless, but he shoved the pieces into his pocket lest someone find them and take a closer look.

"What should I do if he comes back?"

"When a demon is in physical form, it feels pain," the angel said. "You can't kill them—humans can't—but you can drive them off. They operate in the shadows. The pure light of God is harsh to them. It burns them. And they don't like to draw attention because they know we might come to defeat them. I have to go. But you're on the right track."

Tommy blinked, and the angel was gone.

Next time, he told himself, *don't blink*.

4.

Dani was shocked when she read a text message from Carl Thorstein telling her Abbie Gardener had passed away in the night. Carl was a friend of Tommy's, a theologian and scholar who'd counseled Tommy after that tragic accident convinced him to do something other than play football. Carl often visited residents at High Ridge Manor, the nursing home where Abbie had been a resident. According to Carl, Abbie had been alive during a routine bed check at ten and dead at the next check at two.

Dani put a kettle of water on the stove for tea, then texted Tommy the news. He instantly texted her back: I HEARD. INTERESTING TIMING.

She'd been thinking the same thing. She typed back: FIGURED HE TOLD YOU. NATURAL CAUSES, RIGHT? CARL SAID IN HER SLEEP.

She'd barely set the phone back down when Tommy's response popped onto her screen: IN THE NIGHT. BIG DIFFERENCE.

Dani reread Carl's text and realized Tommy was right. She sent him one more: I'LL MAKE SOME CALLS.

Dani had questioned Tommy's run-in with Dr. Ghieri because she was skeptical by nature. When he'd told her Ghieri had lifted him off the ground, she reasoned that Ghieri was a strong man temporarily assisted by a jolt of adrenaline. She thought it more likely the guidance counselor had "vanished" simply by running from the room while Tommy was still on the floor, recovering from being choked. Charlie wasn't an angel; he was simply a guest at the opening who had appeared to help Tommy because he'd heard the scuffle. She didn't believe in prophecies or premonitions—she knew that if you had a thousand premonitions a day, you'd only pay attention to the one that came true and forget the other nine hundred and ninety-nine.

But when Tommy told her Charlie had produced a flaming sword and provided a demonstration of its power, she did not doubt him but sought corroboration. After he dropped her off at home, she'd researched the notion of angels wielding swords and had found plenty of references in the Bible and in noncanonical texts.

"You *should* be asking questions," Tommy had said. "God wants you to ask questions—he wants you to be *you*, and to use all your scientific training. Test your hypotheses and don't take things at face value. That's what you do, and you're good at it."

Following Tommy's line of thinking, however, required a leap of faith. Dani had made the leap when she realized science couldn't explain the things that were happening. On the night Julie Leonard was killed, Dani had begun having troubling dreams that woke her at exactly 2:13 night after night. Then Tommy reported having the exact same dream she'd had, an apocalyptic nightmare where millions of people were fleeing a flooded city and jumping to their deaths from tall white buildings. Then an angel had spoken to her—in a dream, but she knew it was real. He'd said, "Go ahead and jump—I'm here to catch you if you need me." The angel had spoken to Tommy too, and told him to look in the book of Revelation, chapter 2, verse 13: *"I know where you dwell, where Satan's throne is; and you hold fast My name . . . My witness, My faithful one, who was killed among you, where Satan dwells."*

Tommy's conclusion was that God wanted them to be together. He'd sent them an angel to tell them Satan was at work somewhere in the town where they lived, East Salem, and God wanted them to do something about it. Dani couldn't argue.

She and Tommy had decided to do what each did best, a kind of division of labor. God had brought them back together and given them an assignment, a part to play in a spiritual war, the breadth and scope of which were beyond their knowing. They agreed that Dani would approach things scientifically, using her medical training and psychiatric expertise, while Tommy would pursue the more spiritual lines of inquiry.

She sat down at her kitchen table to sip her tea and think.

Tommy was right about the timing. Abbie Gardener died the very night the Bosch exhibition opened at St. Adrian's. After all the strange things that had happened in East Salem recently, Dani was inclined to believe that if something seemed suspicious or evil, it probably was.

Why that night? For over a century, before succumbing to Alzheimer's, Abbie had lived on a 150-acre farm that included half a mile of frontage on Lake Atticus. Abbie drove her own car, worked in the town archives, and stayed active until she was 100, declining an invitation from the mayor for a town-wide birthday party. Her son, George, brought her to High Ridge Manor at the age of 101, when he'd realized she was failing and he could no longer keep her from wandering off the property. If she'd lived so long, why die the very night the painting came to town? What was the connection?

Dani went to her study and looked on the shelves where she kept books she'd treasured as a child. Among them she found what she was looking for, a slender volume entitled *The Witches of East Salem* by Abigail Gardener. She leafed through it but found nothing remarkable save the title page, where the author had written during a visit to Dani's fourth-grade class, *You are special.*

Tommy and Dani still wondered if Abbie was somehow connected to the murder on Bull's Rock Hill. The night Julie Leonard died, Abbie had wandered away from the nursing home and managed to set off the alarm on Tommy's property at two in the morning. Tommy found her by his pond, where she insisted on showing him a dead frog she held in her hands. "These are the first," she'd told Tommy. "You'll be the last." She'd seemed incoherent, rambling about luck's fairy, they thought, until Carl Thorstein realized she'd been speaking Latin. "Luck's fairy" was in fact *lux ferre*, which translated as "light-bringer," the Latin root for the name Lucifer.

It placed her in proximity to the killing, if nothing else.

Tommy had met with Abbie in the nursing home a few days later, hoping she'd seen something the night Julie died. He'd had Carl record the interview, which hadn't gone well—a few semi-cogent responses, and then the old woman transitioned into a psychogenic fugue.

Dani looked out the window of her study. The morning sky was dark gray and heavy with the promise of rain. With the leaves all down on an overcast November day, the town of East Salem took on a sepulchral tone, the massive homes and mansions suddenly visible through the naked trees, and they looked gloomy and lonely, isolated from each other. Once the Christmas lights went up in December, things would be cheerier, assuming the town could shake the additional pall cast by the recent tragedies. People were still on edge. Parents hugged their kids just a little harder, tucked them in just a little tighter, checked to make sure the doors and windows were all locked before going to bed.

Dani picked up the phone to call Stuart Metz, the assistant DA. She'd dialed the first three numbers when her cell phone rang. She glanced at her caller ID.

"Stuart," she said. "I was just about to call you."

"You heard?" Metz said.

"About Abbie Gardener?" Dani said.

"They took the body straight to the medical examiner. He said he's never seen anything like it."

"What does that mean?"

"I don't know. Just telling you what Banerjee said. How soon can you be there?"

"They need me?"

"Casey asked for you," Metz said. Detective Philip Casey had been the lead detective on the Leonard murder. "If you're feeling up to it. I know you're still on leave, but this is just a little consulting. I think he has some questions about Alzheimer's."

"I never evaluated Abbie," Dani said. "There must be someone at the nursing home who knows more about her condition."

"Yeah, but you're on the payroll."

"I'll be there in thirty minutes. Forty with traffic."

The county medical examiner had never seen anything like it? Baldev Banerjee had seen a great deal. Dani wasn't sure she wanted to see what had happened to Abigail Gardener. She'd been a brave soul who deserved a peaceful ending. Dani doubted she'd gotten one.

5.

Tommy drove his father, Arnie, and his father's caregiver, Lucius Mills, to the airport and put them on a plane for Texas to stay with Tommy's Uncle Sid, Arnie's kid brother. Tommy's Aunt Ruth, the middle child, was the East Salem librarian. Arnie suffered from a kind of cognitive impairment called Lewy Body Dementia. He had good days and bad days, more bad than good lately, and Tommy was concerned about having to keep one eye on his dad with everything else that was going on.

When he returned home from the airport, he punched in the code on his security keypad, drove through the gate, and was glad to see Carl Thorstein's motorcycle parked in the courtyard. Tommy put his Jeep in the garage and greeted his friend who, in addition to knowing the code to open the gate, had his own key to the house. He was sitting on the back steps. He'd been a kind of second father to Tommy—not a substitute, Tommy liked to say, but a close second.

"Feel like riding?" Carl said.

"Where to?"

"Does it matter?"

"Might rain."

"Might."

Carl, a die-hard enthusiast who rode year-round and wore a snowmobile suit to keep warm during the winter months, rode his motorcycle for some of the same reasons Tommy turned to exercise. It was where he got his best thinking done. He rode when he was troubled or sad. He'd ridden to Mexico after his daughter, Esme, drowned in a boating accident. Today Tommy knew Carl was thinking about Abbie.

Tommy had three motorcycles: a Harley-Davidson 883 Sportster for light riding, a more muscular black Harley-Davidson Night Rod Special for longer highway trips, and a white BMW R1200 GS for going off-road. He rolled the Night Rod out of the garage and followed Carl's chrome yellow Fat Boy west on 35 to the Taconic Parkway and then north to Taconic State Park and Copake Falls, where they stopped to stretch their legs.

The only other visitor at the park was an older man in a trench coat and black beret, walking a large black poodle. Tommy and Carl were looking at the falls when the rain started. They rode their motorcycles under a nearby picnic pavilion and sat on a table. Tommy thought about the first time he'd put his arms around Dani, waiting out a thunderstorm beneath a bridge.

"Bad for us but good for the waterfall," Carl said, taking off his gloves. Sections of an old *New York Times* sat on the picnic table next to a can of lighter fluid, near a blackened charcoal grill and beside a box of dry kindling. Carl slid the sports page across the table to Tommy, who glanced at a story about one of his former teammates demanding to be traded to a championship team and then pushed it aside.

"Are you sad about Abbie?" he asked.

"I shouldn't be, right?" Carl said. "It's not like her life was cut tragically short at 102. Tough old bird—isn't that what they say? I'm sure the Lord was glad to finally meet her face-to-face."

"And vice versa."

Esme had been seventeen when she died, several years before Tommy had met Carl. "*You don't get over it,*" Carl had told him. "*You move on, and you keep living, but you carry it with you forever.*" Carl had dedicated his life to helping others and had thrown himself into his work as a way to cope with his loss, but Tommy knew the pain came back from time to time, particularly when the days grew short and the nights grew longer.

"Your text said you had something to tell me," Carl said.

"I do," Tommy said. "About what happened last night at the exhibition."

"Did you see the painting?"

"Up close."

The old man and the poodle were making no effort to get out of the rain, the man throwing a stick, the dog joyously chasing it. Tommy wondered if the old man had a wife. Perhaps the dog was his sole companion.

"Do you see that guy?" Tommy asked. "Do you think he has a guardian angel?"

"Sure," Carl said.

"What do you know about angels?"

Carl considered his answer. "Personally?"

"Yeah. Have you ever seen one?"

"Never been so lucky," Carl said. "I can think of times when I would have loved to. One time in particular."

Tommy knew Carl was referencing the day he'd lost Esme. "*Why take her and not me?*" he'd said. "*That just never made any sense. But not everything makes sense, I guess.*"

"What do they do?" Tommy asked. "I mean, I know the stories in the Bible. I know about Daniel, and the angel that rolled away the stone from Jesus's tomb . . ."

"Boulder," Carl corrected. "Big one."

Tommy nodded. "I mean recently. What do you know about what angels are doing now? Today?"

"Hard to say. Most of the time they work unseen. Billy Graham called them 'God's secret agents.' But there are plenty of stories."

"About what?"

"Angels helping man," Carl said. "People have seen angels carrying children from burning buildings. I read about a platoon during World War I that got lost in no-man's-land in the fog of battle, and an angel showed them the way back to their line."

"Why?" Tommy said. "I mean, why save those men and not others? A lot of platoons probably got lost in no-man's-land."

"God's purpose regarding who receives help isn't something we can know, except that each man in that platoon was served in a way unique to him."

"Are they born?"

"Angels? No. But they're created by God."

"Can they be killed?"

"No."

"Are they omniscient? Like God?"

"No. They certainly know more than you or I do. But they're not lesser or miniature versions of God. We don't worship them or pray to them."

"And they can take human form, right?"

"All the time."

The man with the dog walked slowly toward the only car in the parking lot, a black Mercedes Benz coupe.

"So that guy could be an angel and we wouldn't know it."

"I suppose," Carl said. "Though I'm not sure an angel would put a wet dog in a CL600."

"Do they feel what we feel?"

"By the way," Carl said, climbing down from the table to stretch his back, "I'm telling you what I've heard and read and what I believe, but I'm not going to pretend I'm the ultimate authority on the subject."

"I know," Tommy said, "but I value your opinion."

"I think angels have feelings," Carl said. "They weep. They even eat—Genesis talks about three angels sitting down to break bread with Abraham. I'd like to think they can laugh too. And they love—they love God. And they love us. Not all of us, of course—First Chronicles tells of a single angel who destroyed Jerusalem when David defied God's command. If they're sent to carry out God's punishment, that's what they do."

"But mostly they help, right?"

"That appears to be true," Carl said. "Deliver messages. Offer guidance. Give us a gentle nudge when we need it—or a stern warning. The Bible says people tremble in fear at the sight of them. More like awe."

He sat down on the picnic bench and leaned back against the tabletop. Tommy moved to the table opposite and sat facing him.

"And demons are fallen angels, right?"

"Right."

"And they can take human form too? Does that mean they can be killed? Though if you killed one, where would it go? It's already in hell."

"Maybe someplace worse," Carl said.

"Like Winnepeg?"

"Possibly," Carl said, leaning back and crossing his legs. "I know there's a reason why you're asking me all these questions."

"I'm trying to decide something."

"What?"

"If I tell you what it is, you can't go back to not knowing," Tommy said. "And if you know, your life could be in danger. The same way Abbie's was. So do you want to know?"

"Is your life in danger?"

"Maybe," Tommy said. "Dani's too."

"If you need my help, count me in," Carl said. "Is this about the angel you saw when Abbie came to your house? The one who looked like a biker?"

Tommy nodded. "He was there last night, at the exhibit."

"You talked to him?"

"I did," Tommy said. "I'll tell you what happened, but first I need to tell you a story. Dani and I discussed it last night, and we decided we'd ask you to join us. You know about the Julie Leonard murder, right?"

"Amos Kasden," Carl said. "I know what you told me."

"Part of it we haven't told anybody, because most people would think we're off our rockers. Something's going on in East Salem, Carl. Something really big, maybe as big as it gets. Which is about all we know for sure. And we could use your help figuring out what's going on."

"I'm all yours," Carl said. He gazed out at the sky and the rain. "It doesn't look like we're going anywhere anytime soon."

"Do you remember me telling you," Tommy began, "that Dani kept waking up from her dreams night after night at exactly 2:13? And the dreams were about blood and water?"

"I do," Carl said.

"Make yourself comfortable," Tommy said, "because this is going to take awhile."

〰〰〰

Dani drove through town, stopping briefly at her office on Main Street to check her mail. The shops were open but no one seemed to be shopping. The gazebo in the middle of the green was still decorated for Halloween; rotting old pumpkins had faces curling in on themselves like old men with their dentures out, and soggy black-and-orange crepe paper streamers clung to the pillars and balusters. She saw Eddie, the owner of the Miss Salem Diner, coming out of the hardware store with a pair of eight-foot-long fluorescent lightbulbs over his shoulder, finally replacing the two that had burned out two or three years ago, if she remembered correctly. Eddie had told Dani his motto back when she waitressed at the diner in high school: If it ain't broke, don't fix it, and if it is broke, don't fix it.

She took the Saw Mill Parkway to the Sprain Brook Parkway and parked in the DA's reserved space outside the medical examiner's office on the New York Medical College's Valhalla campus. The building was non-descript. The ME was not. Dr. Baldev Banerjee was a British ex-pat with an Oxbridge accent and a Monty-Pythonesque sense of humor, dark and

35

often absurdist. He stood six foot two, with dark skin and jet-black hair. His dark brown eyes seemed to drill deep, but his most startling feature was the crescent-shaped scar on his cheek, which he'd told Dani in jest was a dueling scar. Metz had told Dani the real story, that Banerjee, who'd grown up in the Upton Park section of East London, had been hit with a beer bottle in high school after taking on a group of skinheads after they'd called him a Paki.

"He's pretty tough, for a doctor," Metz had said.

It was raining hard by the time Dani arrived, so she ran from the car to the entrance. In the hall outside the ME's office Metz greeted her with a venti vanilla soy latte. He was Dani's age, with a keen legal mind and an underdeveloped social intelligence. Detective Casey was checking something on his phone. He was sixty, with a gray flattop and a brusque approach that concealed a heart that was equally brusque. Where Dani and Stuart were Starbucks people, Casey was Dunkin Donuts all the way. He logged off his phone and nodded to Dani.

"Good morning, Detective," she said. Casey smiled grimly. "Can you give me an idea of why I'm here?"

"We may be looking at a homicide. You knew Abigail Gardener?"

"I met her once, in the fourth grade. Tommy knew her."

Banerjee waved them in before the detective could ask any more questions.

The medical examiner's office was the size of a high school classroom, with multiple workstations and four five-foot-long lab tables with stainless steel legs and black chemical-resistant epoxy tops on a clean bare linoleum floor.

Banerjee greeted Dani with a smile. Today he was wearing a gray cardigan sweater over gray pants, a blue oxford shirt, and a pale yellow tie.

"Nice to see you, Dani," he said. "I missed you last night."

"You were at the opening?"

"My wife and I arrived late."

"And we left early."

"It was an interesting talk," Banerjee said. "If you can give me a minute, we'll be meeting in autopsy. I just have to print something out first."

The autopsy room contained a single stainless steel dissection table in the middle of the room. The table had side drains and a stainless steel catch basin at the head, with rinse and suction hoses cradled by their nozzles above the basin. A stainless steel cart next to the table supported a tray of dissecting tools, a saw, shears, scalpels, and forceps. The transport cart had been pushed against the wall, where Dani saw shelves of glass sample jars filled with formalin. The fixtures in the ceiling provided a cold, washed-out, neutral light, supplemented by a pair of movable lamps, one ultraviolet and the other incandescent, suspended from armatures fixed to the ceiling. The body on the table was covered by a sterile white evidence sheet.

Banerjee snapped on a pair of latex gloves and turned on the ventilation fan. As he took hold of the sheet, he advised Dani, Metz, and Casey to step back. "This may be more unpleasant than usual," he said, "but I wanted to show you something."

He pulled the sheet away from the body. Dani saw the familiar cuts, a V-shaped incision starting at the top of the shoulders and meeting at the sternum, a T-shaped cut from the shoulders to the breastbone, and a vertical cut from the neck to the pubic bone. The body had been reconstituted, organs restored minus the usual histology samples, skin flaps back in place. The legs and arms were blue and bruised everywhere, the torso as well, as if the poor woman had been beaten from every angle. Dani was shocked at how loose the skin seemed, as if the body inside it had shrunk.

"I had to work quickly because of advanced cell deterioration," Banerjee said, moving around the body and occasionally referring to his clipboard. "External and internal. Decedent ate a meal at six o'clock, so by the progress of the stomach contents, I would place the time of death between eleven and twelve. Cause or causes of death may include hypovolemic shock, a collapsed airway and suffocation, and/or compression fractures of the vertebrae and skull. I anticipated advanced osteoporosis in a woman this old but found only the expected loss of bone mass. Structural damage is severe, with a qualification that I will explain in a minute."

Banerjee glanced briefly at his clipboard. Dani heard thunder rumble through the walls. With the body on the table and the storm outside, she thought of old black-and-white horror movies and mad scientists reanimating corpses.

"My preliminary blood work," Banerjee said, looking up from his clipboard. "I've sent samples to FBI serology; I'll let you know when I hear from them." He read from the clipboard. "Elevated electrolytes, myoglobin metabolites, elevated potassium and phosphate ions, and uric acid released by damaged muscle cells. Histology indicates high methohemoglobin infarction, excess lactic acid . . . Her bladder was empty."

He pulled the sheet down again to cover her and faced them.

"Questions so far?"

"Can we get that translated into English?" Casey said.

"I'll cut to the chase," Banerjee said. "I called my sister Nalini to confirm. She's a thoracic surgeon and a very good one. She flew down to Haiti after the earthquake, where she treated a number of people for traumatic rhabdomyolysis, which is another way of saying they were—"

"Crushed," Dani said. She couldn't remember where she'd heard the word, but she knew what it meant.

"Abbie was crushed?" Metz said. "By what?"

"Before I speculate, I want to show you something," the medical examiner said. "As you know, the body's failure after death to release myosin and actin results in muscle contraction—"

"Rigor mortis," Casey said.

"Yes. Maximizing about twelve hours after death and dissipating at about seventy-two. It has been less than twelve hours since TOD. She ought to be stiff as the proverbial board. And yet . . ."

He walked to the end of the table, pulled the sheet back briefly, and lifted one of Abbie's legs by the toe. Instead of being rigid, the leg rose the way a rope would, limp and flexible.

He set the leg down and replaced the sheet.

"Rigor is incomplete because she's lost skeletal integrity. Her bones have been more or less pulverized. Multiple fractures and splintering. The skull's spherical configuration resisted compression but the rest . . ." Banerjee made fists and then exploded his fingers. "But not from concussion. She was not hit. She was squeezed. The result is something like what happens when you suck the air out of an empty plastic soda bottle to create a vacuum. The bottle collapses under atmospheric pressure."

"How?" Metz said.

"I don't know." Banerjee tucked the clipboard under his arm and put his hands in the pockets of his sweater.

"Would it be possible," Casey said, raising a finger, "and I'm just thinking out loud here, but would it be possible for someone to . . . This is going to sound crazy."

"Crazy might be the right way to sound," Dani said.

"Could somebody have put some sort of plastic bag around the body, maybe after she was dead, and then sucked all the air out of it?"

Dani's thoughts led to an explanation she didn't dare voice. She didn't know how or why, but Abbie was clearly an enemy of evil and somehow engaged in thwarting whatever was going on at St. Adrian's. If she was a threat to them, it made sense that they would have wanted to eliminate the threat, though Dani couldn't very well raise her hand and say, "Have you considered the possibility of a demonic assault?"

"If that were the method," Banerjee said, nodding toward Casey, "we would still need the means. Do we have any evidence of human-sized vacuum bags or massive air pumps?"

"No," Casey said.

"What *do* we have?" Dani said.

"We have her," Casey said, gesturing toward Abbie Gardener's body.

"Found in a room with the windows locked from the inside, and the only other entrance is the door to the hallway."

"And the hallway was under video surveillance," Metz said, raising his hands to his eyes as if using binoculars.

"The videos don't show anybody entering her room?" Dani said.

Metz shook his head.

For a long time nobody spoke, each of them trying to think of an explanation. Tommy had said *Interesting timing.* For Dani the question was again not, *Why now?* It was, *Why not before?* If it was a homicide, and someone or something wanted her dead, why wait until she was 102?

"I have two other findings," Banerjee said. "But they're not going to be of much help, I'm afraid."

He moved to the head of the dissection table and pulled back the sheet covering Abbie Gardener's face, which was as bruised and blue as her body. Dani moved around to the far side of the table for a closer look. Banerjee pointed to Abbie's mouth, to a black blotch at the center of both her upper and lower lips, which were otherwise purple.

"What is that?" Casey said.

"Frostbite," Banerjee said. "Fourth degree. No other indications anywhere else on the body."

"What would make it this localized?" Dani said.

Banerjee laid his finger over Abbie's lips to cover the blotches, though his finger wasn't wide enough to cover them perfectly. "A few things," he said. "Exposure to liquid nitrogen or liquid helium."

"She was trying to drink it?" Metz said. "Or she was forced to?"

"Either seems unlikely," Banerjee said.

Dani heard thunder again. "You said you had two more findings," she said. "What's the second one?"

The medical examiner covered the body again and turned off the fan. He removed his gloves and threw them in the wastebasket, then gestured for Dani, Metz, and Casey to follow him.

In his office he turned on a stereomicroscope and invited them to have a look. The specimen on the slide appeared to be a sample from a pine-cone. When Dani looked up from her turn at the microscope, Banerjee, anticipating her request, handed her a pair of tweezers. She flipped the sample over and refocused the scope. She stared intently into the eyepieces. Whatever it was seemed translucent, pointed at one end and rounded at the other. Finally she leaned back.

"I give up," she said.

"We found this under a fingernail," Banerjee said. "She had rather long fingernails. Apparently she didn't like to have them trimmed. We also found a more complete sample on the floor near her bed. I've sent that to the FBI lab for DNA."

"What is it?" Casey said impatiently.

"Well," Banerjee said, drawing a deep breath and then sighing. "It seems to be a scale of some sort."

"Fish?" Dani asked.

"No."

"Reptile?" Metz said.

"Probably."

"Snake?" Casey said.

"A giant anaconda might explain the compression fractures, but I don't think so. The formation is keeled, indicated by the ridge on the top, and there's a dermal papilla on the reverse, which makes me think this may be an epidermal component with an osteoderm beneath it."

He saw the confused look on Casey's face.

"The osteoderm is the layer of skin beneath the epidermis," Banerjee said. "The epiderm would be like having an outer layer of, well, armor."

"Armor? Found on?"

"There are different kinds of armor. Turtles, rhinoceroses. In this case, lizards. Judging from the size of the scale, big ones. Did Ms. Gardener, by any chance, keep a Komodo dragon as a pet?"

6.

Dani had supper that night at her sister's house. Beth and Gary lived just three miles away on a cul-de-sac in a subdivision called Willow Pond Estates, where Dani saw teams of Spanish-speaking landscapers readying properties for winter, wielding leaf blowers and rakes. Dani was long overdue for a visit and in great need of a little face time with her nieces, Emily and Isabelle. After dinner she played Yahtzee with them, and when it was time for bed, they asked Aunt Dani to tuck them in.

"What kind of bedtime story do you want?" she asked.

"Something embarrassing about Mommy!" they chimed in unison.

So Dani told them how Beth once bought a new jacket for an important job interview and did the whole interview with a large price tag dangling from the cuff of her sleeve. The girls howled with delight.

Dani joined them as they said their evening prayers: "Now I lay me down to sleep, I pray the Lord my soul to keep; if I should die before I wake, I pray the Lord my soul to take." She pulled the covers up and kissed them each on the forehead.

"And a hug," demanded Emily, who was ten.

"And make sure the closet door is shut tight," added Isabelle. "'Cause there's a brain-eating monster in there, but he can't get out if the door is closed."

"Sounds like he needs to eat a few more brains," Dani joked as she closed the closet door.

She recalled her own recent nightmares, the ones that woke her up night after night at exactly 2:13. They made a brain-eater in the closet appealing.

She joined Beth in the kitchen, where she'd just finished loading the dishwasher. Beth made two cups of tea and the sisters sat down in the breakfast nook. Dani's brother-in-law, Gary, was in the den watching a Knicks game on the television.

"So tell me about Tommy Gunderson," Beth said. "You two have been spending a lot of time together lately."

Beth, of course, knew the first part of the story. Dani and Tommy had first met in grade school, when boys and girls were sworn enemies. In high school they'd been elected homecoming king and queen, but he'd been the super jock and she the academic overachiever. "Princess and the Pea-brain," someone had joked. Dani had dreaded their first duty as newly crowned high school royalty, the prom's first dance together, because Tommy was "the boy no girl could resist." She'd been determined not to fall under his spell.

"It's nice," Dani said, smiling. "He's a lot different from what I remembered. I mean, we all are, but I was wrong about him."

"Wrong how?"

"There's more to him. I thought he was just . . ."

"Incredibly handsome? Built like a Greek statue?"

"Beth, please," Dani said. "I'm entirely impervious to that sort of thing."

"Oh, right. So why does he want to be a private detective? His fitness center isn't making any money?"

"The gym is doing fine. He said when he was a kid he wanted to be either a professional football player or a private eye. He did the football thing and now he's following his other dream."

"And you hired him?"

"Not exactly. I mean technically, legally, yes. I'm paying him. One dollar a year."

"Wow," Beth said. "I'll bet he could get twice that. So what's going on between you? And don't say it's nice. I know it's more than that."

"It's good."

"Good? That's all you're going to give me?"

"I think he's . . ." Dani tried to think of the word.

"Oh my gosh," Beth said. "You're in love. Did I call it or what?" She called to the den, "Gary—what did I tell you?"

"Beth—"

"Don't pretend."

"I won't pretend," Dani said. "Let's just say: to be continued . . ."

"I can't believe it," Beth said. "You're not worried that he's on the rebound from America's sweetheart?"

She was referring to Tommy's well-publicized engagement to—and breakup with—the actress Cassandra Morton. After leaving pro football, Tommy had been a favorite of the tabloids, portrayed after the end of "Tomsandra" as a bad boy dating starlets and supermodels while poor Cassandra wept and wasted away from a broken heart.

Tommy had told Dani the truth, that beneath Cassandra's absurdly beautiful façade and the romantic comedy roles she'd used to perfect her image as the girl next door with the heart of gold and the total-package body, the real Cassandra Morton was deeply troubled. She was an abuse victim still struggling to cope, making meaningful intimate relationships hard to establish, her doubts self-sabotaging and in the end tragic. Her entire life, men had wanted things from her, promised her things, only to break their promises. Tommy hadn't broken up with her—she'd broken up with him, repeatedly, and he'd finally agreed to play the part of the cad to protect her image. In the end they'd wished each other well, and he'd prayed that she might learn from the experience and break out of the pattern that entrapped her.

"There's more to that story," was all Dani told Beth. "Don't believe everything you read in *Us Weekly*."

"I don't believe anything I read in *Us Weekly*," Beth said. "So it can't possibly be true Cassandra Morton is dating the soccer player recently voted Sexiest Man Alive. Can it?"

"I wouldn't know. Tommy's not in touch with her these days."

"I certainly hope not," Beth said. "For your sake. Oh gosh—that didn't come out right."

Dani smiled.

"I just mean I'm happy for you," Beth said. "So when are you going to bring him over for dinner? Gary would die. He still has a Tommy Gunderson jersey in his closet."

"I'll bring him along next time. Just make sure Gary doesn't wear the jersey. That would be awkward."

When she got home that night, Dani parked her car in the garage, closed the garage door, and let herself in through the back door. She flipped on the kitchen lights and saw a man standing in the middle of the room.

Without another thought she reached for a kitchen knife, but then the man smiled, and she realized she knew him.

Charlie.

"Sorry," he said. "I didn't mean to startle you."

The angel was dressed the way she'd seen him in her dream—and the way Tommy had described him—black boots, jeans, black T-shirt and black leather jacket, one earring, and a ponytail. He looked around the room as if he'd never seen a kitchen before.

"Can I get you anything?" she said. It was, she realized, a stupid question to ask an angel, but she had been brought up to be hospitable.

She was a little surprised when he said, "What have you got?"

"I'm not sure. Lemme look in the fridge."

As she opened the refrigerator door, she wondered exactly what an angel would eat. She could just hear Tommy saying *"Angel food cake, obviously,"*

45

but she didn't have any of that. Or much of anything. A few sodas, some cheese, a little tub of ice cream . . .

"Would you like a root beer float?"

"I don't know," he said. "I've never had one."

She grabbed a can of root beer and the ice cream. Charlie stepped aside when she opened a drawer and started digging around for her scoop.

"Have you been waiting long?" she said as she dug into the ice cream.

"What would you consider long?"

"I don't know—twenty minutes?"

"Not long," he replied.

She handed him the float, along with a long-stemmed iced-tea spoon and a straw. He took a sip, and Dani saw the angel's eyebrows rise in surprise.

"That's *very* good."

"They're even better on warm summer nights, sitting on the porch," she said. Everything that came out of her mouth seemed stupid and inadequate.

"I'll bet," he said as he worked the straw. "You have a lovely home."

"I inherited it from my parents. They died in a plane crash."

"I know."

Of course you do, she thought. Something about him seemed to change as she looked at him. It was as if he flickered in and out of focus, but at the same time was entirely present. He seemed kind and patient.

"You remind me of someone," she said.

"Who?"

"My father. A little."

He set the empty glass on the counter. "I have a message for you," he said.

"What?"

"Someone is going to betray you. Someone you trust."

"Someone I trust . . ." She hesitated, unsure how to respond.

"How you handle it," he said, "will make all the difference."

She wanted to say, "All the difference in what?" but before she could get the words out, he was gone.

She went to the counter and picked up the empty glass. She held it up to the light, wondering if angels had fingerprints.

—————

Both the cardio and weight rooms at the All-Fit Sports, Health, and Fitness Center of Northern Westchester were filled to capacity with men and women working out. Tommy welcomed the newcomers and greeted the regulars, including a man the staff had dubbed The Poser because he was always pacing intensely and shaking his limbs and stretching as if he'd just finished a set of repetitions or was just about to begin one, but no one had ever seen him actually lifting weights. Tommy, who'd built the center after retiring from professional football, had gone to the gym to plow through some paperwork he'd been putting off, and because he needed to work out. He did his best thinking when he wasn't trying to think. If he exercised, answers came to him, sometimes to questions he hadn't even asked. He'd read enough scientific papers to know that when you are in the middle of a workout, the brain sometimes transitions into a wakeful, dream-like state, generating theta waves, akin to what happens during REM sleep. For him it was the right blend of conscious and unconscious thinking, a way to keep his body occupied while his mind was free to wander.

Dani had sent him a text that afternoon: ABBIE'S DEATH SUSPECTED HOMICIDE. BODY FOUND IN LOCKED ROOM. As he pushed through his reps, he tried to think of why anybody would bother to kill a 102-year-old woman. The first thing that occurred to him was that her property was one of the most coveted pieces of real estate on the East Coast. It was possible somebody wanted her out of the way in order to acquire the farm—it sounded far-fetched, but he'd heard scarier stories concerning choice bits of land in Westchester County. The second thing that occurred to him: was it possible Abbie knew something about Julie Leonard's murder? Maybe someone still wanted to stop her from talking.

He quickly showered and hurried to his car, eager to take a second look at the video he'd shot of his interview with Abbie in the nursing home. The roads were slick with wet leaves and strewn rotting shells of smashed Halloween pumpkins.

Ten minutes later he was home. He paused outside his gates to retrieve a package from his mailbox, an item he'd ordered online after the Leonard case was closed.

He set the package on the food island in his kitchen, grabbed a carving knife, and sliced open the box. He knew Dani would make fun of him for buying yet another gadget, but he really needed this one. Unlike, for example, the Locator, a device that used microchips to help you find your keys or your sunglasses—which would probably have worked fine, if he could remember where he had put the Locator.

He inserted batteries in the handheld infrared thermal imager, flipped open the video screen, turned the device on, and pointed it at his refrigerator. His $10,000 Sub-Zero was supposed to have a perfect seal around its door gaskets, but the image on the screen showed a blue spot at the top of the freezer where the seal leaked, as well as heat from the condenser coils venting out the toe-plate and around the sides. Things that were hot registered from yellow to orange to red, and things that were cold went in the opposite direction, registering from green to purple to blue. When he swung the imager around to scan his kitchen, he saw cold air coming in from a window he'd left open a crack, and orange heat radiating from the lights above the sink.

When he pointed the imager toward the back door to see if any cold air was leaking in, he saw the outline of a man radiating a shimmering white aura.

He looked up to see Charlie, who had changed out of his tuxedo from the night before and was now wearing his customary black boots, jeans, and leather jacket.

"What's that?" the angel asked.

"An infrared imager," Tommy said.

"What's it for?"

"Well . . . ," Tommy said. He again felt a deep sense of awe and wonder, but at the same time the angel seemed approachable. "It measures heat. People use it to check their homes, to find places where they can be more energy efficient. For a better planet."

Charlie seemed to be waiting for further explanation, so Tommy handed him the device and helped him point it toward the refrigerator.

"Cool," the angel said, handing it back.

"I know," Tommy said. "It's a RAZ-IR PRO. It even has an optical lens so that—"

"I meant the air leaking from your freezer is cool," Charlie said.

"Oh. Yeah," Tommy said. "I should fix that."

"Do you like root beer floats?" Charlie said.

"I do, though I eat sugar-free ice cream, which doesn't work as well. But I like root beer floats."

"Particularly on summer nights when you're sitting on the porch," the angel said.

"Exactly," Tommy said, puzzled.

"Why are you trying to be energy efficient?"

"We all should be," Tommy said, "but that's not why I bought it. I'll show you."

He turned on the computer in his kitchen, logged in to his security system, then switched views from video feeds to infrared. Charlie watched over his shoulder.

"The guy I bought the house from installed this system," Tommy said. "I recorded this one night about a month ago. I couldn't even see it until I slowed the video down thirty times. Anything generating heat shows up as yellow, orange, or red. Things that are cold show up as green, blue, or deep blue-violet."

He clicked on a file that showed something, an entity of some sort, registering deep blue, moving from the woods to the edge of Tommy's house. Then it passed through the wall, exiting a moment later.

"Not sure what it was doing here. Maybe just trying to scare us."

"What did you think it was?"

"Dani and I think it was a demon," Tommy said, looking to the angel for confirmation. "The handheld infrared seemed like a good way to detect the presence of a demon."

"Sounds about right," the angel said. "But doesn't your heart tell you when evil is present?"

"Yeah, but it's hard to be certain sometimes," Tommy said. "There's so much of it around."

"Tell me about it," Charlie said.

"Can I ask you a question?"

"Sure," the angel said, glancing briefly at the sports page lying on Tommy's food island. Tommy had grabbed the newspaper from the picnic pavilion where he'd spoken with Carl, intending to read it later.

"I used to play with him," Tommy said, realizing Charlie was looking at the photograph of Tommy's former teammate. "You follow football?"

"A little," Charlie said.

Tommy usually knew when somebody wanted to talk football. This didn't feel like one of those times.

"Why are you here?"

"I'm here to help you."

"Help me how? I mean *us*. Help *us* how?"

"It depends on the situation," Charlie said.

"So you can't say? Or you don't know?"

The angel nodded enigmatically. "This is my first time."

"Your first time what?"

"Here," Charlie said. "On Earth. I came here tonight to tell you something. Someone you trust will betray you."

"Who?"

"That's all that I know. But how you handle it will be critical."

"Okay, but—"

"And tell your friend he should try to sign with the Patriots," Charlie said.

"Do you know who's going to win the Super Bowl?"

The angel shook his head. "No. We just like Bill Belichick."

"Huh," Tommy said. "That explains a lot."

He glanced down at the sports page. When he looked up, Charlie was gone.

Tommy picked up his RAZ-IR PRO infrared thermal camera, went out to the back porch, and scanned the forest behind his house. The woods were cool, greens and blues, save the yellow outline of a small raccoon lurking in the underbrush, waiting for his chance to raid Tommy's garbage cans. He scanned the ground, hoping to find a set of warm footprints leading away from his house. Nothing. When he pointed the sensor toward the heavens, he saw an array of stars, orange points of light against a blue background, which was odd because the sensor wasn't able to read the heat from stars in space. It could have been something other than angels he'd detected in the sky above him, but he doubted it.

※

The phone rang and Dani answered.

"What's up?" she heard Tommy say.

"Nothing much. I ate at my sister's. She wants me to bring you over some night for dinner."

"I'd like that."

She wasn't sure why, but she decided not to tell him what the angel had said to her, not until she'd had time to give it more thought.

"What are you doing tomorrow?" Tommy asked.

"I want to have a look at the brain tissue analysis on Amos Kasden. The ME ordered a full workup."

"Okay."

"I also need to tell you what I learned today when we viewed Abbie Gardener's body."

"And I want to have another look at the interview we did with her," Tommy said. "Oh, and I told Carl everything. He's in."

"That's good," she said. "Call you tomorrow?"

Tommy agreed and hung up. He'd called to tell her about the warning Charlie had given him and to set up a time to show her what he'd recorded on his new thermal imager, but something odd—a hesitation in her voice, as if there were something she wasn't telling him—had stopped him.

He shrugged it off and decided he'd tell her tomorrow.

7.

Banerjee told Dani he had an early appointment in Chappaqua and suggested that she meet him afterward at the district attorney's Mt. Kisco office, where they could use the flat screen in the conference room to go over the postmortem lab report on Amos Kasden. The day was overcast and blustery. Dani wore her black North Face down parka and was glad that the BMW she'd inherited from her father had heated seats.

The leaves had fallen and the branches were bare, which meant that as she drove the winding road to Mt. Kisco she could see the grand houses and estates that the foliage hid from view during the summer. East Salem, New York, in northern Westchester County, was where the Department of Public Works had dammed up streams and rivers in the early 1800s to create reservoirs to supply the great metropolis of New York City with drinking water. The hills remained forested, by zoning code, to protect the reservoirs from soil erosion, creating a pristine wilderness just an hour north of Manhattan, overrun by deer and the predators that fed on them, coyotes and bobcats and even a mountain lion, according to reports. Northern Westchester was where celebrities and CEOs and mutual-fund managers built their mansions and their horse farms, but it was also home to automobile mechanics, single moms, nurses, and landscaping crews.

The medical examiner was wearing blue jeans, cowboy boots, and a black turtleneck sweater. He apologized in advance for slurring his words, explaining that he'd just come from his dentist and the Novocain had yet to wear off.

She waited while he established a Wi-Fi link and then connected his laptop to the large monitor on the wall. Irene Scotto was still out of town, which left the DA's office uncharacteristically serene. Stuart Metz was in court and the holding cells on the ground floor were empty. Dani briefly wondered if Baldev Banerjee was the one the angel had said would betray her, but dismissed the thought—what possible reason could he have?

"Here we are," Banerjee said when the file he'd been searching for came up on the monitor. "Would you mind?"

Dani dimmed the lights and sat opposite the ME at the conference table.

"I apologize for making you come this far, but they won't let me send my files to unsecured computers," he said. "Have to keep it in the house." He clicked on the file and opened it. "Given what we knew about Amos Kasden's talent for pharmaceutical experimentation, my first thought was simply to get his serum toxicology to see if he was drinking the same punch he'd given his friends."

Amos Kasden had drugged not only his victim but a half dozen other East Salem teenagers who'd attended what they'd believed would be a "passage party"—a chance to enter a controlled, drug-induced near-death state that would, they believed, afford them a glimpse of what was beyond death. It was one of those idiotic things teenagers believed in, but Amos had used this allure to get them to drink a cocktail that combined the date-rape drugs gamma-hydroxy-butyric acid (GHBA) and Rohypnol ("roofies") with an amnesia-producing drug called Versad, used by children's dentists to help kids forget traumatizing experiences in the chair. Kasden's father was a pediatric dentist and he'd stolen the drug from his father's supplies. None of the teens Kasden had doped could remember what happened, but all of them thought they'd helped him kill Julie.

"I'm gonna go out on a limb and guess Amos Kasden was drug-free," Dani said.

"He was. And as you know, he had rather long hair, so we were able to test hair samples going back at least a year, maybe a year and a half. No indication of marijuana use, no cocaine, no methamphetamines or hallucinogens. His liver was clear, so I don't think he even drank alcohol."

"A real all-American boy," Dani said.

Amos had been adopted from a Russian orphanage that had failed to disclose why he'd been sent there—he'd killed his abusive, alcoholic father. With an ax. When he was five. His adoptive American parents had him in public schools until he was ten, but sent him to St. Adrian's Academy at eleven when he'd begun to develop emotional problems. The school had a reputation for teaching "troubled" kids. As far as Dani could tell, it taught them how to be even more troubled.

"That was simple toxicology," Banerjee said, clicking on a link to a large table of numerical values. "I asked the FBI lab for the works, partly to see what they could find. They did a complete proteome analysis, liquid chromatography, catecholamine assay, and shotgun mass spectroscopy. I was hoping to find protein biomarkers for schizophrenia, but no luck."

"I wouldn't have thought so," Dani said.

"You knew the boy, did you not?"

"I spoke to him twice." She still had a hard time talking about it.

"And your impression was?"

"I was leaning toward a dissociative identity disorder. DSM-IV code 300.14. Dead inside, emotionally."

"These are his postmortem homeostatic levels," Banerjee said. He gave her a moment to consider the chart. The numerical values represented the relative concentrations of hormones and neurotransmitters in Amos

Kasden's cerebrospinal fluids. Studying it reminded Dani that it had been a long time since she had taken a class in neurochemistry. She'd done well in the subject but had decided to focus her studies on the behavioral side of cognitive disorders.

"Did you look for tumors on the adrenal medulla?" she said.

"Ah," Banerjee said, glad to see that she'd zeroed in on the same anomaly he had spotted. "I did not, but I did run a cranial MRI. No catecholamine-secreting tumors on the adrenal medulla to explain the discrepancies."

Catecholamines were essential hormones synthesized by the nerve synapses in the brain and used to communicate between neural cells. They included dopamine, sometimes called the "pleasure molecule"; adrenaline; and noradrenaline. Amos's dopamine levels were lower than anything Dani had ever seen. His adrenaline and noradrenaline levels, on the other hand, were extremely high.

"But look at this," Banerjee said, clicking to a different table that gave values for a postmortem urine analysis. "Urine levels for vanillylmandelic acid are significantly disproportional to catecholamine plasma levels. Almost negligible."

Dani recalled that after adrenaline and norepinephrine crossed the nerve synapses in the brain to transmit messages, they were not reabsorbed; instead they were metabolized. The metabolites should have been excreted as vanillylmandelic acid.

"How can there be high plasma levels but low urine levels?" she said. "It's gotta go somewhere."

"Something is blocking it?" Banerjee said. "In other words, I have no idea."

He clicked back to the previous screen. "Note the serotonin levels as well. This is not my field, but as I understand it, after the synapses release serotonin, half of it is reabsorbed."

"Ten percent is lost," Dani said. "Ninety percent is reabsorbed."

"Which is why serotonin reuptake inhibitors have proven effective as antidepressants," Banerjee said. "They prevent the transporters from reabsorbing serotonin, resulting in higher homeostatic levels. Flip that around and low levels—"

"Cause depression," Dani finished.

"It appears that something in this poor boy was enhancing serotonin reuptake, rather than inhibiting it. You said in your report that he was being treated? At the school?"

"I don't know what they were doing for him. Or to him. They claimed *in loco parentis* on top of doctor-patient and refused to release his medical records. But they confirmed that he was in treatment."

"I wonder if Amos was on some kind of medication that could explain these results. Hard to imagine we'd get a proteomic profile like this on someone who was getting professional care."

"It would be nice if we had a baseline," Dani said.

"We need to get a good neurochemist to look at this," Banerjee said. "It's beyond my ken. Do you know anyone?"

"Yes," Dani said.

Banerjee noticed the dubious look on her face. "There's a problem?"

"The one I know," she said, "used to be my fiancé. Sort of. We were never in the same place at the same time long enough to talk about it. We were both working in Africa for Doctors Without Borders. He's quite brilliant. In a flaky sort of way."

"Who broke off the engagement?"

"Nobody. We weren't even sure it was an engagement. Then my parents died and I came home. I doubt he's even in the country."

"But you think he could help?"

"Definitely."

Banerjee saved the Amos Kasden file to the district attorney's secured hard drive, told Dani she was free to use it in the office, and departed. After wandering the halls for a few minutes, she found an open terminal in Stuart Metz's office and entered the name *Quinn McKellen* in the Google search box. Links to articles on neurochemistry McKellen had published in scholarly journals appeared first. Then she spotted a link telling her Quinn was speaking tomorrow night at a conference at Columbia, delivering a paper entitled "An Immunoradiometric Study of Hyperandrogeny and Autism." Linz Pharmazeutika was listed as one of the sponsors.

When she clicked on the link to Linz, it took her to a page advertising a new drug called Provivilan, promoted as the first effective prophylactic vaccine against depression. She knew how to read between the lines of pharmaceutical ad copy, written to give care providers the information they needed while seducing the general population—always overpromising and underdelivering. Dani had heard numerous stories from colleagues about patients telling their doctors what antidepressants they wanted to try based on TV ads showing happy people picking flowers and tousling the hair of small children. "Make me like the people in the ad," they demanded.

Provivilan had been originally developed to treat autism in children, she read—that was the connection to the conference—by inhibiting serotonin reuptake in a specific set of receptors affected by growth hormones. Collateral studies suggested Provivilan was also effective against depression when taken by adults. It was also, according to the ad copy, safe to take during pregnancy, and significantly improved cognitive function and school performance in children who took it on a low daily maintenance dosage. *We're changing the world, one child at a time*, the slogan in a larger font at the bottom of the page promised.

The Food and Drug Administration regulated what drug ads could and couldn't say, and required them to list any potentially harmful side effects. Provivilan had remarkably few of those. Saying your product was going to "change the world one child at a time" was too general a statement to measure by any FDA standard for truthfulness, but it was exactly the kind of assertion that would make any concerned parent eager to try it.

She needed help. In this case, help was just around the corner, in a hotel room in Manhattan, where Quinn McKellen was preparing his speech.

Or was he the one who was going to betray her?

He'd done it once before.

8.

Tommy asked Carl to meet him at the East Salem library. He'd called Dani too but got her voice mail. He'd also called ahead to make sure the library's media room wasn't in use. His Aunt Ruth told him it was available, and added that since he'd donated the money to buy all the equipment in it, including a dozen new computers, an HD projector, and a Smart Board, he was welcome to use the room anytime.

The library, one of the oldest buildings in town, sat on the square and shared a parking lot with the Grange Hall, where the town meetings took place. The building was Greek revival, with white pillars out front and white siding, and it had served as a kind of daycare center for Tommy when his mother would drop him off to spend afternoons loosely supervised by his aunt. Tommy had read all the books he could find on sports first, and made many great discoveries, including the disappointment in sixth grade that a *National Geographic* story about the Bikini Islands was not actually about a place where ladies wore revealing two-piece bathing suits.

Aunt Ruth smiled and came out from behind the reference desk when she saw him push open the back door. She was wearing one of the cable-knit sweaters she made herself. Tommy could remember many nights when she'd babysat him, and how the sound of her knitting needles clicking together had comforted him when he was young and afraid of the dark.

"Is that your friend I hear?" she said, referring to the sound of a loud motorcycle pulling up outside.

"I still think you should bake him a pie or something," Tommy said. "He's too shy to ask you out and you're too stubborn to make it easy for him. Somebody's gotta break the logjam."

"I'm not baking a man a pie just to get him to ask me out."

"Then bake *me* one and I'll see that he gets it," Tommy said as Carl strode through the library's automatic front doors. He took his helmet off and tucked it under his arm as he removed his gloves.

"Carl," Ruth said in a measured tone.

"Ruth," Carl said. "How are you?"

She said, "Very well, thank you," and returned to the reference desk.

"Why does she hate me?" Carl said to Tommy.

"She doesn't hate you. That's Scandinavian reserve. Saying, 'Very well, thank you,' is the Norwegian way of flirting. It's actually almost lewd. Do you like strawberry-rhubarb pie?"

"It's my favorite. Why?"

"Not important," Tommy said, gesturing toward the media room. "We can talk in there."

When they got inside, Carl took off his leather jacket and the down vest he wore beneath it and set them both over the back of a chair, then placed his helmet carefully on the seat. Tommy closed the door, turned on one of the computers, plugged an SD card into it, then turned on the projector and used the Smart Board as a video screen. Ruth had used the room for everything from toddler Music Together classes to senior citizen *Thin Man* movie marathons, though for the senior citizens a marathon meant four p.m. to nine p.m. Tommy had decided that his next donation would be a grand piano for the music series.

"You said this has to do with Abbie Gardener?" Carl said while Tommy fiddled with the computer. "Do they know more about how she died?"

"Dani was going to fill me in, but she hasn't called yet. Usually she's good about checking in. I left her a message to meet us here."

"I'm sure she just got busy with something."

"Probably," Tommy said, turning down the lights. "Remember when we interviewed Abbie at the nursing home?"

"Who could forget?" Carl said. They'd found the old woman in the lounge watching *Jeopardy*. She'd been engrossed in the show, in which the moderator, Alex Trebek, gives contestants answers and they have to come up with the proper questions. Abbie had seemed confused, unable to tell where the TV show ended and real life began.

"We thought she was ranting, right?" Tommy said.

"As far as I could tell."

"Then she got really upset."

"I believe 'disinhibited' is the term."

"What if she wasn't ranting? What if she was trying to tell us something?"

"Why didn't she just say it straight out?"

"Maybe she couldn't," Tommy said. "Just hear me out. Assuming her brain was scrambled—"

"Not sure 'scrambled brain' is the technical term, but go on."

"As I understand it, sometimes people with Alzheimer's have trouble saying the right words. They want to say *table*, but what comes out of their mouth is *watermelon*. Right?"

"Okay . . ."

"So maybe she had to find a way around what she was actually trying to say. But she was trying to tell us something important. Something she'd tried to tell us before. I don't think she just accidentally showed up at my house the night Julie Leonard was killed. I think she came to me on purpose."

"Because she needed to tell you something," Carl said.

"Yes. I don't know why she needed to tell me, specifically, and not somebody else, but for right now let's assume she came to my house for the same reason the angel did—to deliver a message."

"Can you assume that? You think God was speaking through her?"

"Maybe not directly," Tommy said. "I mean, she was the one talking, but the words weren't coming out right. Maybe God spoke to her at some point in either the recent or distant past, and she wanted to tell me about it but her mouth just couldn't produce the proper words."

"With you so far."

"So when we visited her in the nursing home, the same thing happened. Maybe she saw it as a second chance to tell us something important."

"Maybe," Carl said.

"I was up late editing the recording we made and transcribing what she said," Tommy told his friend. "I think the first part is relatively easy to figure out, but the second part is harder. I'll play it for you and you tell me what you think."

Tommy clicked on the Windows Media Player and opened the file on his SD card containing the interview with Abbie that Carl had recorded using Tommy's phone. On the screen, they saw Abbie in her wheelchair with a housecoat over her nightgown.

"I'll skip the preliminary stuff," Tommy said. "She started out reasonably lucid, if you'll recall. She recognized us, I think. And she remembered her son, George. Then she started to overheat."

He advanced the video and turned up the volume.

World Religions for six hundred . . . The Beast and the antichrist. The false prophet and the false teacher. You'd better be on your toes, Alex. They stand on their heads by the crossroads at the foot of Mt. Maggedo with the 999 and think they're fooling us! They think we don't know the war has already started! That the Tribulation is just the school of hard knocks! Ha!

You'd think we would have done away with human sacrifice by now. After all, we're not Aztecs. We don't eat the hearts of those we capture—though we might poison them just a little bit.

Tommy hit the pause button.

"Now you know why we used to call her the Witch Lady when we were kids," he said. "Nobody dared go to her place on Halloween."

"I'll bet she had a big bowl of candy ready anyway."

"So what do you think?"

"Well," Carl said, "she's warning us about Satan, clearly, and the end times. A lot of what she's saying we could find references to in Revelation. Armageddon and the sign of the Beast, 666, which is 999 upside down if you stand on your head, in her words. Which is what she told you the night she came to your pond, right?"

"Pretty much," Tommy said. "The thing with the frogs and predicting the future by examining dead animal entrails. What else do you get from it?"

"I'm not sure," Carl said.

"Well, humor me for a second," Tommy said. "Suppose Abbie knew something about St. Adrian's. She was the town historian. Suppose she was digging around and she found something. Revelation talks about the false teacher. St. Adrian's is a school. It could be full of false teachers. She's talking about human sacrifice—"

"Which was how Julie Leonard was killed, apparently," Carl said.

"Yes. But then Abbie says, 'We don't eat their hearts, but we might poison them a little.' I think she was trying to warn us about the school. She's talking about 'the hearts of those we capture.' Students are captive, in a way."

"So when she says, 'They think we don't know the war has already started,' she's talking about Wharton and Ghieri?"

"Maybe. So that's number one." Tommy wrote on the Smart Board with the tip of his finger: *#1. Abbie knows about the school.* "So how does she know about the school?"

Carl shrugged. "Town histories? Archives? Old newspapers? All of the above?"

Tommy wrote: *Question #1: How does Abbie know about the school?*

"What's next?" Carl asked.

"Now it gets weird."

World Religions for a thousand, Alex! Anyone for a little game of
dodge ball? Dodge one, Dajjal . . .

"Dodge one, dodge all," Tommy echoed.

"Dodge what?"

"A ball," Tommy said. "Those soft red playground balls they gave you
in gym class, with the pebbled surface, about the size of a basketball. That
used to be my best sport."

"She wanted you to throw a ball at somebody?"

"That makes no sense."

"No, it doesn't," Carl agreed.

Tommy wrote: *Question #2: Dodge ball? What?*

"What else did she say?" Carl asked.

"Here's the last bit, before the men in the white coats came to take her
away. Literally."

World Religions for a thousand, Alex! It's both the question and
the answer, Alex. The beginning and the end—what more do you
need to know?

Potpourri for one hundred, Alex—this common element is
something you pass, but that's asking a lot . . . Make your way
with all haste and look not behind you, 'cause you never know
what's sneaking up on you, Satchel Paige! Baseball for two hundred, Alex—this Sultan of Swat is the boy's best chance! Native
Americans for five hundred, Alex—this Native American sorcerer's
black magic killed the daughters of Hiawatha . . .

Tommy paused the video on the image of Abbie being wheeled away,
reaching up with one frail arm to grab the sleeve of one of the orderlies.

He minimized the screen and opened a text document in which he'd transcribed what she'd said.

"This one goes by pretty fast, so I typed it out. 'The question and the answer . . .' The beginning and the end is alpha and omega."

"Don't forget the symbol Julie Leonard drew on her stomach," Carl said. "The letter *Z* in the Cyrillic alphabet. Omega."

"The question and the answer are the same thing," Tommy said, tapping the words with his finger. "The beginning is the question and the ending is the answer, and they're the same thing. I'm getting a headache."

"A circle? A circle begins and ends at the same place."

"A circle doesn't have a beginning or an end," Tommy said. "That's why they call it a circle."

"An orbit has a beginning and an end," Carl said. "Maybe it means something that repeats, like a year on the calendar."

"We begin the way we end," Tommy said. "With a party in Times Square with drunk people throwing up."

"We end the way we began?" Carl said. "Flip them around because it's the same thing."

"Which is what?"

"We're born helpless infants who need to be taken care of by our parents, and we end as infirm old parents who have to be taken care of by our children. Like the old riddle—what has four legs in the morning, two in the afternoon, and three in the evening? A man who crawls on all fours as a baby, walks on two as an adult, and ends up with a cane. The diaperer becomes the diapered."

"Not helping," Tommy said. He wrote, *Question #3: Beginning-end, question-answer, same thing?*

"You could have been a schoolteacher," Carl said. "You have excellent handwriting."

Tommy ignored the joke.

"What about 'This common element is something you pass, but that's asking a lot. Make your way with all haste and look not behind you, 'cause you never know what's sneaking up on you, Satchel Paige.' What do you make of that?"

Carl thought a moment. "'Common element we pass' could be . . . water? But that's not quite an element. What else do we pass?"

"Gas," Tommy said, and as Carl grimaced, he quickly added, "stations. We often pass gas stations."

"I doubt that's what she meant."

"You can take the boy out of the locker room, but you can't take the locker room out of the boy," Tommy said. "Maybe *pass* means miss? Something we walk right by without noticing it. And *element* is like the weather. The elements. What weather don't we notice? Or take for granted?"

"We definitely notice the weather when it's bad," Carl said. "When it storms. So what's the opposite? When it's nice out? The absence of bad?"

"Now I'm *really* getting a headache," Tommy said.

He wrote, *Question #4: What common element do we pass?*

"Next one: 'Don't look back because something might be gaining on you' is a quote from Satchel Paige," he told Carl.

"He said that in reference to what?"

"I don't know. Growing old, I think."

Carl stood suddenly and moved to the screen, where he used his finger to draw a circle around the last word of the previous sentence and the word *lot*.

"Salt," Carl said, tapping the screen. "The common element we pass is salt. It's not *a* lot. It's *Lot*, nephew of Abraham. Genesis 19, I believe it is. Lot fled from Sodom with the help of an angel when the city was destroyed by fire and brimstone. The angel told Lot his wife could escape too, on the condition that she not look back at the burning city. But she did and turned into a pillar of salt."

"Abbie was trying to warn us about too much salt in our diet?" Tommy said.

"Or not enough. Though that seems pretty unlikely, given the American diet."

Tommy clicked the eraser icon and used the side of his hand to erase Question #4, then wrote: *Question #4: What about salt?*

"Why 'Don't look back'?"

"She wants us to flee the city?" Carl said. "Don't look back or we'll turn into pillars of salt? I'm not ruling it out, but there's not a lot of that going around these days."

"Dani and I both had a dream about people fleeing the city. There was a flood."

"Flee East Salem?"

Tommy wrote, *Question #5: What does "Don't look back" mean?*

"Next one is easier. 'This Sultan of Swat is the boy's best chance,'" Tommy said. "The Sultan of Swat was Babe Ruth."

"Who's the boy?" Carl said. "The kid in the hospital who Babe Ruth promised he'd hit a home run for?"

"Hang on," Tommy said. He grabbed his phone and tapped his Google app. "Johnny Sylvester from Essex Falls, New Jersey. Died January 11, 1990, at the age of seventy-four. Oh wow. You're not going to believe this."

"What?" Carl said.

"It says here," Tommy read from his phone, "that it happened in the seventh game of the World Series. The Yankees were trailing 3–2 in the ninth, but the game ended when Babe Ruth got thrown out stealing second."

"Maybe we should try to focus on the task at hand," Carl suggested.

"Oh, right," Tommy said, putting his phone away. "Sorry. 'This Sultan of Swat is the boy's best chance.' Probably not Johnny Sylvester."

"Amos Kasden?"

"Maybe."

"But why would Babe Ruth be Amos Kasden's best chance? Babe Ruth is dead, so he's not going to help us," Carl said. "We're all out of Babe Ruths. Unless she meant the candy bar."

Tommy wrote, *Question #6: Babe Ruth?*

There was a knock on the door and then Tommy's aunt entered carrying a plate of brownies. "I had a few left over from story hour this morning—thought you boys might be hungry."

Tommy shot Carl a look as he said, "Speaking of babes named Ruth . . ."

"Maybe she's the one Abbie meant," Carl said. Tommy shrugged to say, *Anything's possible.*

"She's right here and she can hear you," Ruth said. "May I ask what you're doing?"

"May I ask why you're snooping?" Tommy said. "We're trying to figure out what Abbie Gardener was saying when we talked to her at the nursing home."

"There isn't anything . . . suspicious?"

"No," Tommy said. "I just wondered what Carl thought. What do you know about this, Aunt Ruth? 'This Native American sorcerer's black magic killed the daughters of Hiawatha'?"

"I'm old enough to remember when we had to read *The Song of Hiawatha* by Longfellow," she said. "People used to consider him America's greatest poet. Today nobody's heard of him."

"I'm old enough too," Carl said. "I don't recall any black sorcerers in the poem. I don't think Longfellow was writing about vampires and zombies and the things kids are reading these days."

"Maybe he should have," Aunt Ruth said. "Then people would remember him. Why don't I look into it for you? That's what a reference librarian does, you know. People ask me to help them with questions all the time. Just this morning, that English art historian was in here asking me about old maps."

"Old maps of what?" Tommy asked.

"Of the town," she said. "Who owned what, when."

"Did he say why?"

"He's a historian. That's what historians do," she said. "I'll look into

Hiawatha and tell you what I can find out. Actually, I came in to tell you Dani called. She said she sent you a text but she didn't hear back. She'll be here in—oh, there she is now."

Tommy saw Dani wave to him from the reference desk.

He held the door for her and then opened his arms to hug her. She hugged him back, gave him a quick kiss, and then gave Carl a brief hug.

"Sorry I'm late," she said, smiling apologetically. "I had to meet with the medical examiner. I have a number of very strange things to tell you."

"We'll match you strange for strange," Tommy said, pulling out a chair for her. "Let's get everything we know so far on the table."

She glanced at the words he'd written on the Smart Board and the six questions they'd come up with.

"Good idea," Dani said. "And if we're talking about everything we don't know, we're going to need a bigger table."

Once Ruth was out of earshot, she turned to Carl. "I'm really glad to have you on the bus."

"Bound for glory." Carl smiled. "One way or another."

9.

After they'd debriefed each other for another hour, Tommy suggested they all get dinner somewhere. Carl begged off, his body language conveying a you-two-lovebirds-probably-want-to-be-alone message. He headed over to the nursing home, saying maybe there was something he could find out about the circumstances of Abbie's death that Detective Casey had missed.

"I feel like sushi," Tommy told Dani. "There's a new restaurant just across the state line in Ridgefield—want to try it?"

"I feel like a wet noodle," Dani said. "But if they don't have that, sushi's fine."

At the restaurant a waitress in a black kimono took their order quickly and left them with a pot of tea and two small cups. Dani wrapped both hands around her cup as she sipped.

"I just can't get warm today," she said. "Did playing in cold weather ever bother you?"

"I never noticed," Tommy said. "If you keep your body temperature up on the sidelines by jumping around or riding a stationary bike, it cancels out the cold. It's like jumping out of a sauna into a frozen lake."

"You've done that?"

"Even better—I'm a member of the 300 Club."

"What's that?"

"There's a sauna at McMurdo Station, Antarctica, where the research scientists set the sauna 300 degrees higher than whatever it is outside. So if it's 83 below, they set the sauna to 217, and then once you're so hot you can't stand it, you run out from the sauna around a flagpole fifty yards away and then back into the sauna. If you make it, you're a member of the 300 Club."

"What if you don't?"

"You freeze to death."

"Who says scientists don't have any fun?"

"So far everybody's made it. The cold is very motivating."

"When were you in Antarctica?"

"A couple years ago."

She saw that her question had made Tommy uncomfortable.

"Look—I went with Cassandra," he said.

Now Dani felt uncomfortable. She trusted Tommy's affections completely, but that didn't mean she enjoyed hearing about Cassandra.

"*Why* did you go to Antarctica?"

"I'd promised I'd take her someplace she'd never been before," he said. "Which wasn't easy. She'd already been to St. Tropez and Thailand and all the usual places celebrities go when they want to pretend they don't want to be recognized."

"Is she a member of the 300 Club?"

"Dani, I'm okay talking about this if you really want to, but I'm sorry if it makes you feel as weird as it makes me feel. The past has passed."

"Agreed," she said, smiling and taking his hand. "In which case, you won't mind me telling you that I'm driving down to Columbia tomorrow to see Quinn McKellen. He's delivering a paper at a conference, and I think he might be able to help us figure some of this out."

Tommy squeezed her hand, then leaned back in his chair. A distancing gesture, Dani thought, something suspects did as a kind of unconscious admission of guilt. A sign that tells trained interrogators they're on the right track.

"He lives in the city now?"

"I don't know where he lives," Dani said. "I just sent him a text that I'd be coming and hoped we could have coffee, and he texted back suggesting we have lunch."

"Why do you want to talk to him? I just mean, how do you think he can help us?"

"He understands brain chemistry better than anyone I know," Dani said.

"Probably because his own brain is so gigantic," Tommy said. He didn't intend to sound defensive and hoped his comment would pass for humor, but Dani wasn't laughing. To his relief, the waitress appeared then with their dinner.

"Are you going to tell him the whole story?" Tommy said after the waitress had left them alone.

"Oh no, no, no," Dani said. "If you think I'm a skeptic, I'm nothing compared to Quinn. Sometimes I think that what makes him a brilliant scientist is the same thing that makes him a less-than-brilliant human being."

"You can be both, you know," Tommy said. "You can have questions and be a believer too."

"I know. I just want Quinn to tell me what was going on in Amos Kasden's skull." Her phone chirped. She made a face that said, *It's always something* and reached into her coat pocket.

Tommy couldn't resist peeking at her phone, trying to read the text upside down. Dani had never said much about her relationship with Quinn McKellen, other than that he was a nice guy who was very smart but . . . what was the word she used? Hopeless. The fact that she said so little about him made Tommy wonder if there was still something between them she wasn't telling him.

"This is interesting," she said, showing Tommy the message.

WERE YOU INVESTIGATING THE MURDER MY FRIEND AMOS COMMITTED?

"Who do you think it is?" Tommy said.

"Number's blocked. What should I say?"

"Say yes. Ask him who he is. Or who she is. I didn't think Amos had any friends."

Tommy moved around to the other side of the table so that he could read the conversation. Dani typed quickly.

YES. WHO R U?

NOBODY.

DO YOU HAVE A NAME?

NO.

HOW DID U KNOW AMOS?

I'M A STUDENT AT ST. ADRIAN.

"Wow," Tommy said. "This is good. Ask him what he knows about Amos."

"If I push, he may bolt," Dani said. "Trust me."

"I trust you."

DO U LIKE IT THERE?

NO.

Y NOT?

STUFF.

DID AMOS LIKE IT THERE?

YES.

HOW DID U KNOW HIM?

STUDY GROUP.

WHAT WERE U STUDYING?

NO.

NO WHAT?

WE WEREN'T STUDYING ANYTHING. THEY WERE STUDYING US.

WHO IS THEY?

IT WAS A TEST.

OF WHAT?

4 PSYCH DEPT.

WHAT WERE THEY TESTING?

DRUGS.

WHERE ARE U?

STARBUCKS.

STARBUCKS WHERE?

Tommy was already handing the waitress a fistful of money as he pulled Dani's chair out. He led her to the door as she kept an eye on her phone. They got in his car and he started it up, looking to her to tell him where to go.

RIDGEFIELD.

"Main Street. Across from Stop & Shop," Dani said as Tommy backed out quickly and then punched the gas.

WHAT KIND OF DRUGS?

DON'T KNOW.

WHAT WERE THEY SUPPOSED TO DO?

MAKE U FEEL BETTER.

DID THEY?

DID THEY WHAT?

MAKE YOU FEEL BETTER?

DON'T KNOW. DIDN'T TAKE THEM.

Y?

I ALREADY FELT BETTER.

THAT'S GOOD.

I PRETENDED 2 TAKE THEM.

"I think we may have a spy from the school," Dani told Tommy.

"What do you mean? What's he saying?"

"He was part of a test group. The psychology department was testing a drug on some students, but he refused to take it. He pretended to take it."

"Why?"

"I don't know. Hang on."

Y?

BECAUSE I WOULD GET IN TROUBLE IF THEY KNEW I DIDN'T TAKE THEM.

WHAT KIND OF TROUBLE?

BIG :(

Tommy sped up to beat a yellow light, and the car bounced hard as it went over a speed bump.

DID AMOS TAKE THE DRUG?

YES.

HOW MANY OF U?

10.

DID ANYBODY ELSE NOT TAKE THE DRUG?

DOUBT IT.

DID IT MAKE THEM FEEL BETTER?

I GUESS.

DID IT MAKE AMOS FEEL BETTER?

APPARENTLY NOT.

DO U KNOW Y HE KILLED JULIE?

NO.

DID HE TALK ABOUT IT?

NOT WITH ME.

WITH ANYBODY ELSE?

DON'T THINK SO.

CAN I BUY U A COFFEE?

NO.

PLEASE. I CAN HELP U.

NO.

OK.

"He desperately wants to tell us something," Dani told Tommy. "Why else would he contact me?"

"I thought your number wasn't listed."

"I gave it to Ghieri when we interviewed Amos," Dani said. "Maybe Amos got it from Ghieri's computer, and whoever this is got it from Amos."

"Maybe Ghieri is actually the person texting you," Tommy said.

"I don't think so," Dani said. "Don't ask me why. This is real. This kid wants to blow the whistle."

DID U SAVE THE PILLS?

YES.

DO U STILL HAVE THEM? Then, "Oh, nuts!" Dani yelled as she slapped the dash of Tommy's car.

"What! What!"

"No service. I hope he doesn't think I cut him off."

"This area is always a dead zone," Tommy said, still speeding through downtown Ridgefield. "Your texts will go through as soon as we get closer to town. Hang on. Almost there. And don't hit my car."

At the bottom of the hill he turned right into the Starbucks lot and parked around the side, where customers wouldn't see them.

"Wait outside and keep texting him," Tommy said. "I'll see if I can spot him. He might recognize you."

"Recognize *me*?" Dani said. "Tommy—people recognize you everywhere you go around here. People recognize you in China."

"Tell you what—I'll go in the back door and you stand out front. If he recognizes me, he'll run toward you."

"Just order a cup of coffee and sit down," Dani said. "Keep it simple. I'll join you in a minute."

"Excellent," Tommy said. "I'll order a coffee and sit down, and you join me in a minute."

U STILL THERE? she texted. She waited for a response, then shook her phone, as if jarring it would summon a response.

While Tommy waited in line for coffee, he discreetly scanned the crowd as he put his phone on vibrate. A poster on a bulletin board by the door listed a support group for families still dealing with the Julie Leonard murder. Next to it was a small photograph of Julie above the words WE MISS YOU!

During the day the place was generally full of female real estate agents and retired bankers reading the *Wall Street Journal* and young moms having coffee while their kids ran amok. At night it was a teen hangout. Tommy had hoped to spot one sending text messages. That was simple. All of them were sending text messages, poking at their handheld phones with their thumbs without speaking or even looking at each other. A kid could spontaneously combust in the middle of the room and none of the others would look up from their smartphones.

Dani stood in the dark outside the window looking in. There were a dozen boys and twice that many girls, middle schoolers and high schoolers. She knew the parents of three of the girls, including one whose mother would have been shocked to see the skimpy outfit her daughter was wearing. Some kids had their laptops out and were trying to study. Many more had their laptops out to make it *look* like they were trying to study as they played video games and updated their Facebook pages.

Tommy's phone buzzed in his pocket.

"He stopped texting me," Dani said. "I've got nothing."

"I haven't spotted him. Maybe the kid in the black hoodie?"

"I've seen him before somewhere," Dani said. "I think he might be a bag boy at Stop & Shop. I'm still outside. Can you see me?"

"Yes," Tommy said. "And I don't want you to freak out, but there's someone behind you who looks like he wants to talk to you. Just pretend to hang up but don't—let your screen time out and I can listen in. Say the word . . . *elephant* and I'll come running."

10.

The person behind Dani said, "Dr. Harris?"

She spun around to see Julian Villanegre, the art historian, smiling.

"So good to see you again," the white-haired gentleman said warmly. "I know these Starbucks places make a fine cup of coffee, but I came tonight to see what they do to a cup of tea. Would you care to join me?"

"That would be nice," she said.

Villanegre held the door open for her. On their way in they passed Tommy sitting on a stool at the front window counter, his cell phone pressed to his ear. Dani briefly made eye contact while Villanegre found two empty seats. Dani set her phone down on the table, screen side up.

"This must be my treat. What would you like?"

"Oh, thank you," said Dani. "A venti vanilla soy latte."

As the Englishman stood in line, Dani again made momentary eye contact with Tommy, who nodded to tell her he could hear the conversation.

Villanegre returned a few minutes later with their drinks. She thanked him as he took a sip of his tea.

"Does it measure up?" she asked, thinking that the old man did not, tonight at least, seem as threatening as she'd first thought.

"It will do just fine," Villanegre said.

"Do you have Starbucks in England?"

"Oh yes. Not quite as ubiquitous as here, though."

"Where in England do you live?"

"Morningside, Hinksey Hill. A little place south of Oxford. It's been in the family awhile."

"I'm picturing a castle with a moat."

"Well, you're right about the castle, but we had to fill in the moat when we started getting water in the basement. That's the problem with moats."

"I'll remember that the next time I buy a castle. What do you think of the McMansions of East Salem?"

"Lovely little town. I like it very much. We're having the painting scanned in a high-definition digital format, which is a slow, laborious process, so I'm here until that's completed." He took another sip of tea. "You said you're a forensic psychiatrist—tell me more about that. What is it you do day to day?"

"I work with the district attorney," Dani said. "When there's a suspect or a witness whose mental state may be called into question during a criminal proceeding, they need an expert who can evaluate that individual and speak with authority in court."

"So when someone declares innocence by reason of insanity, are you the one who determines if they're insane?"

"No. The jury or the judge decides that, but I testify on behalf of the prosecution. The defense calls their own expert witnesses."

"I have to wonder where one draws the line. Can a person who intentionally kills another human being ever be considered wholly sane? Are you insane if you chop the body up into little pieces, but sane if you don't? What distinctions can possibly be made?"

"There's a lot of work being done on that," Dani said. "But you're right. I wonder all the time about where we draw the line."

"I find this fascinating," Villanegre said. "I hope that doesn't make me seem ghoulish. Though working with a painting like *The Garden of Earthly Delights* could make anybody a bit ghoulish, I suppose. Now tell me—as a forensic psychiatrist, suppose you had a man in jail, and your district attorney showed you *The Garden of Earthly Delights* and told you the man in jail painted it. Could you make a determination as to whether or not that man was insane?"

"Well," Dani said, considering again the very question she'd asked herself the night she and Tommy had attended the exhibition, "I would ask how the painting might express his interior landscape."

"And?"

"I'd note that the artist pays considerable attention to detail in a way that suggests a mentality on the lookout for things it's afraid of. Constantly searching or sweeping the spectrum of experience, like a police scanner or an early-warning system, hoping to spot the smallest clues or the hidden signs of things that threaten him. That suggests a paranoid or obsessive-compulsive personality, as opposed to the kind that doesn't want to see and looks away, eyes closed, head in the sand, the way a hysterical personality might cope."

"Intriguing. What else?"

"If I were a Freudian, I might want to look for divisions between id, ego, and superego," she said. "The trios in the center panel where one figure has authority over the other two might be interpreted as the superego struggling for control over the more dangerous male id and the more vulnerable female ego."

"But you're not a Freudian?"

"I think his work was groundbreaking, but as a clinician I'm not sure I'd call myself a Freudian. There's been a lot of excellent work done since then."

"I knew his grandson, Clement Freud," Villanegre said. "Terribly quick wit. He was on a game show in Britain, and when a fellow panelist asked him why he was so fat, he said, 'It's because every time I sleep with your wife, she gives me a biscuit.' What do you think Clement's grandfather would have said about Bosch's hellish dreamscape in the right-hand panel?"

"I think I'd be more interested in what Jung would have to say about the archetypal symbology and the integrated opposites. You called them 'hybrids' in your lecture."

"Indeed I did. So you think Jerry Bosch was a madman? Hieronymus is the Middle Dutch form of Jerome."

"You're more the expert here than I am. Do *you* think he was?"

"By today's standards?"

Dani nodded.

"Oh, quite," Villanegre said, chuckling. "Quite so. But I think he fell under someone's sway. Someone truly evil. Like your infamous California madman, Charles Manson. Were his followers insane when they carried out his orders to commit murder? The man who gave the orders surely was. Can you be insane by proxy?"

"Another good question," Dani said. "You have a gift for asking them."

His questions reminded her that she and Tommy had concluded Amos Kasden acted alone, but at the behest or under the guidance of someone else. *Who?* was one of the central questions they were trying to answer. One of the girls who'd been at the "passage party" the night Julie was killed had asked Dani, "Would it be possible for someone to give you a post-hypnotic suggestion that could make you kill someone?"

Dani had said no, it wasn't possible. The girl had been convinced, but Dani was not.

"And you have a knack for dodging them," Villanegre said. "I asked you if you thought someone could be insane by proxy."

"Not insane by proxy, but evil by proxy," she said. "Evil can be taught. Insanity is more organic."

"Have you taught, Dr. Harris? If you haven't, you should. I wasn't very good at it at first. I'd ask my students a question, and when they didn't answer, I'd answer it for them. But I learned to wait them out. That's how I met Udo Bauer, you know. He was my pupil at Oxford. After he'd finished at St. Adrian's."

"Was he a good student?"

"He was. Surprising, considering his family had so much money that he didn't have to apply himself. I think he concentrated on art history because of his family's collection."

"He didn't study pharmacology?"

"Oh no—why would he? Business administration. Biology too. Had the most extraordinary collection of poisonous tree frogs. How is it that God gave the most beautiful colors and patterns to his deadliest creations?"

Dani gave Tommy a quick look. Abbie Gardener had handed him a dead frog that night in his yard, and the frog had dissolved when he threw it back into the pond. *These are the first, you'll be the last,* Abbie had said. He'd later found a frog in a pond on the St. Adrian's campus that didn't try to jump away when he reached for it; it just sat calmly in his hand.

"One of Udo's associates told me studying frog toxins has been lead-ing into some very promising medical applications," Villanegre said. "Dr. Guryakin. Did you meet him?"

"Briefly. What does Dr. Guryakin do for Mr. Bauer?"

"He's the head of research at Linz, I believe. Intelligent enough chap, but I don't know what he was doing at the exhibition. No particular grasp of the subject as far as I could tell."

"Perhaps he was there to learn."

"Perhaps," Villanegre said. "We were all there to learn something. If I may ask—are you married, Dr. Harris?"

"I am not, Dr. Villanegre."

"Julian," he said. "Please call me Julian."

"Only if you call me Dani."

"Agreed, Dani. So is there someone special in your life?"

"There is," Dani said. "Quite special."

"Then I suggest," Villanegre said, rising to his feet, "you avoid the young gentleman by the door who has been staring at you this entire time.

Unless, of course, he's the special one. Good night, Dani. Very nice chatting with you."

Once the art historian was out of sight, Tommy joined Dani. "What?" he said as he sat down. "I was being inconspicuous."

"Obviously not inconspicuous enough."

"Next time I'll cut a pair of eyeholes in a newspaper, like in *The Three Stooges.* So what do you think?"

"About Villanegre?"

"Please, call him Julian."

"What do *you* think?"

"I'm not sure," Tommy said. "At first I thought he was one of them, but now . . ."

"I agree," Dani said. "In all my years—well, okay, it hasn't been that many years—*during the time* I've worked with the criminal element, I've had one criterion that has yet to steer me wrong."

"Which is?"

"I like him. I've never liked someone who was guilty. Though I've disliked plenty who were innocent."

She was about to say something more when her phone chirped. She opened her message screen. LOOK BEHIND THE SWT'N LOW.

She quickly scanned the room as she showed Tommy the message. She saw nothing unusual. No one was looking at her.

Tommy jumped up and walked to the coffee station, where he reached behind the small pink packages of artificial sweeteners. He probed until he felt a small capsule. It was pale blue and about a half-inch long with no markings. He pocketed the capsule and rushed through the front door, looking both ways in the parking lot, hoping to see if someone was fleeing, but the lot was empty.

He returned to the table and set the capsule in front of Dani. She picked it up and examined it.

"Can you tell what it is?" he asked.

"Not by looking at it. But I know someone who can figure out what's inside it."

"Quinn?"

"Uh-huh."

"When are you going to see him?"

"Tomorrow. Would you like to come?"

"I would, but I asked Carl if he wanted to run over to the Gardener farm tomorrow to talk to George. Do you mind going alone?"

"I don't mind."

In fact, she was relieved. Seeing Quinn with Tommy present would have been awkward. She couldn't help but wonder if she was making the same mistake she made with Quinn . . . letting too many things go unsaid.

11.

"My name is Ben Whitehorse, and I saw you in a sacred vision. I'd like to talk to you."

The voice on the intercom was strong but calm. It was seven in the morning, and Tommy was just finishing up his morning workout when his security system alerted him to a visitor at the gates.

Tommy had found the system useful over the years. Occasionally autograph-seeking football fans appeared on his video monitor standing at the end of his driveway with Sharpie in hand, but it was rare for someone to press the call button. Even rarer that someone said they had seen him in a sacred vision. He considered his options. Would pure evil just ring your doorbell at seven a.m. and ask to come in? Probably not.

Tommy pushed the intercom button. "How can I help you?"

"I just need a few minutes. I don't want to intrude, if you'd rather meet me out here."

Tommy studied the image on the monitor. The man was dressed in blue jeans, suede cowboy boots, and a khaki-colored barn coat over a plaid shirt. He wore tan buckskin work gloves and a black cowboy hat, and his gray hair fell in a braided ponytail halfway down his back. He appeared to be in his late sixties or early seventies, a Native American who gave no evidence that he was uncomfortable even though the thermometer said the temperature was only forty degrees. The man's breath made clouds of steam that rolled out from beneath the brim of his black hat.

"I'll buzz you in," Tommy said. "You must be freezing."

"Thank you. I'm not cold, but I appreciate your concern."

Tommy's morning workout, on easy days, consisted of a five-mile run, a hundred push-ups, and a hundred sit-ups. He'd just finished and needed a shower. He looked out the window where the old man was walking slowly up the driveway, still a quarter mile away, then went upstairs to his dresser, opened the top drawer, grabbed his .45 Taurus 1911SS automatic, and stuffed it into the pouch of his sweatshirt. The sweatshirt was the same lucky one he'd worn in high school. Dani had teased him about being superstitious, even though he'd explained to her that professional athletes considered it bad luck to be superstitious.

The man in the black cowboy hat was wiping his feet on the bristle mat on the back porch when Tommy opened the door.

"Ben Whitehorse," the man said, extending his gloved hand. Tommy shook it. The man's grip was firm despite his advanced years.

"Come on in and have a seat," Tommy said, closing the door behind him. The older man was several inches shorter than Tommy but firmly built, with a barrel torso, as if he were wearing a baseball umpire's chest protector beneath his coat. He took his gloves off but kept his coat and hat on as he sat down at Tommy's kitchen table.

"Can I get you anything to warm you up?" Tommy said. "Coffee or tea or cocoa or something?"

"I would love a cup of cocoa."

"Do you take marshmallows with that?" Tommy said, putting a kettle of water on one of the front burners of his six-burner Viking gas stove.

"Is that good? I've never tried it that way."

"It's very good," Tommy said, emptying two packs of Swiss Miss cocoa mix into a mug and then fishing in the back of one of his cupboards for the bag of marshmallows. He added hot water, gave the cup a quick stir, and handed it to his visitor.

"You have a very nice house," Whitehorse said, sipping the cocoa. "Do you live here alone?"

"I live with my dad. I moved him in after he started failing. His caretaker stays with us sometimes, but they're both down in Texas right now visiting my uncle."

"Old people can have a lot of trouble with cold weather," Whitehorse said, still looking around the kitchen.

"Where'd you come from?" Tommy said.

"You used to play professional football," Whitehorse said. He seemed not to have heard Tommy's question.

"I did."

"Why did you quit?"

"The joy came at too high a cost."

The old man slurped up the last of his marshmallows.

"Would you like more?" Tommy said. The old man nodded and handed Tommy his mug. "So you had a vision about me?"

"I will tell you about that," Ben Whitehorse said. "But before I do, tell me why you have a gun in the pouch of your sweatshirt. Are you going to shoot me?"

"No," Tommy said. "I just thought I'd be careful." With an apologetic shrug he laid the gun on the counter.

"You have no reason to be afraid of me," Ben Whitehorse said.

"I can see that now," Tommy said, refilling the old man's mug and adding an extra marshmallow. "There've been a lot of strange things happening around here lately."

"I think I know why that might be," Whitehorse said. "Do you know what the Europeans said to the Native Americans when they landed in North America?"

"'Stick 'em up'?" Tommy said, handing the man his cocoa.

Whitehorse smiled. "No, they wanted to buy the land. But the people who already lived here couldn't imagine buying or selling the land any more than they could imagine buying the ocean or selling the clouds in the sky. If somebody offered you $28 for a cloud, you'd take it, right?"

"Probably."

Tommy sat down at the table.

"The Europeans said to the people who already lived here, 'Who is your leader?' It was a difficult question to answer because in many tribes, the people who already lived here didn't have any one single leader. So the Europeans tried again; they said, 'Take me to the person who speaks for you.' And when the people who already lived here translated that request, they brought out their storyteller, and then the Europeans asked the story-teller to sign some papers, and he thought, *Well, why not? You can't buy a cloud anyway.* And then the Europeans took the land because the storyteller signed the papers."

"My ancestors just stopped in for a visit," Tommy said with an apologetic shrug.

"The Vikings? Yes, that's true." The old man swirled the cocoa in his mug. "Do you know the biggest advantage the Europeans had over the people who already lived here?"

"Guns?" Tommy said, nodding at the Taurus automatic on the counter.

"No. Paper. They could write their stories down and make copies so that everybody could have their own collection of the important sto-ries. The Native Americans didn't have paper, so they depended on the storytellers to keep their history and their wisdom alive, and they could only do that by speaking to a group that had gathered to listen. I'm tell-ing you this because I want you to know who I am. I am a follower of Jesus Christ, but I'm also one of those storytellers . . . one of those story-keepers."

"Okay," Tommy said, more than a little intrigued. He thought about Abbie Gardener's reference to Hiawatha. It had seemed random at the time. He wondered if his aunt had learned anything. "And you saw me in a dream?"

"It wasn't a dream. I wasn't asleep. It was a picture that I received in my mind. You probably think I saw your picture in the newspaper sports section, but that isn't true. But I knew who you were and I knew where you lived and I knew that I had to come see you."

"Why?"

"I need to warn you. Do you know anything about demons?"

Tommy sat up.

"A little."

"Well, I know a lot," Whitehorse said. "This is what I came to tell you. The people who already lived here before the Europeans arrived formed many tribes, Mohegans and Pequots and Ojibwa and Cree. About a thousand years ago, they started to tell a new story about a demon called the Wendigo." Whitehorse paused to sip his cocoa.

The kitchen was unusually quiet, Tommy thought. He could hear the hands of the clock on the wall turning, and the sound of the far-off furnace pushing heat through the pipes.

"The Wendigo was a terrible demon," Whitehorse said in almost a whisper. "The people who already lived here didn't know the power of Jesus, so they had no defenses against it. The Wendigo changed the people who came into contact with it. They began to eat the flesh of other human beings, and they were always hungry and needed more and more. They knew things they'd never known before, like greed and gluttony and wastefulness. Before the Wendigo came, they never killed more than they could eat, but after the Wendigo, they killed just because they could. It gave them pleasure to destroy things. And they became murderous toward each other, even toward members of their own families. The Wendigo took many shapes and had many different names—"

"Paykak?" Tommy interrupted.

"That's one," Whitehorse said, nodding. "How did you know that?"

"My scoutmaster used to tell us stories to scare us. Campfire stuff."

"The stories have stayed alive that way," Whitehorse said. "The problem is that children can't tell the difference anymore between what's entertainment and what's true. They think they're just stories. The demon has had many names. Paykak. Da'anabe. Ashnabeg. The Wendigo can move through the air without being seen, faster than a bird can fly, or it can take on a physical form. But when it does, it smells like death. Like things that are unclean and rotting and decaying. It can come inside a person or it can stay outside of them. But either way your scoutmaster was right. You should be afraid of it. You won't see it until it's on top of you. It's a terrible demon."

"Where does it come from?"

"It comes from the devil himself," Whitehorse said. "Satan sends it out to do his work. You can't defeat it. Only an angel of the Lord can do that."

"Why are you telling me this?"

"Because it's here," Whitehorse said. "The Wendigo is in East Salem."

"Here? Why?"

"That, I don't know. I just know that I needed to tell you," Whitehorse said. "Sacred visions come from God. He wanted me to tell you. This thing is bad. It shouldn't be here. It's stronger than it's ever been. You need to do something."

"Me? Do what?"

"I don't know, but you can start by giving me a ride to the Peter Keeler Inn. I left my bag on their porch because they weren't awake when I got there this morning. I need to check in."

"You're staying in town?"

The old man nodded.

"How long?"

"As long as you need me."

12.

VERY INTERESTING DEVELOPMENT. CALL ME.

Dani looked at her watch, then her phone.

OKAY. NOT SURE WHEN. ASAP

Quinn McKellen was late. He was always late and he always had a good excuse. She was waiting in a restaurant called Andante on Manhattan's Upper West Side, a place Quinn had picked because it was close to his hotel. Finally, just as she was about to call his cell, he plopped down across from her, blustering in the way a newspaper blows down an alley and comes to rest pressed against a fence.

"Hello, Harris," he said. "I know you're asking yourself why I'm always late, but I met the most interesting man on my way here who invited me to join him on a fascinating project. I don't think I will, but he's been running EEGs on epileptics to see what lights up during seizures and collaterally located a part of the amygdule that activates in the presence of another animal—spiders, snakes, whatever—you know how we jump away from a snake long before we consciously process the threat? Snake-venom-danger-flee, but the precognitive response is more like flee-danger-venom-snake. He's found specific neurons triggered by biological stimuli that cue an instantaneous affective response. You work with deviants who like to torture animals, don't you? Could be why. Digging deep to see if they can kick-start the emotional engine. To no avail, I'm sure. How are you, by the way?"

Dani felt like she needed to take a deep breath just to keep listening. Quinn had always talked fast, his mind jumping from one idea to another and making connections that seemed obvious to him but weren't readily apparent to anyone else. He took medication for attention-deficit disorder, a condition he was diagnosed with when he was twenty-five. The medication made him less forgetful and slowed him down a bit but not enough.

"I'm good," Dani said. "You're not going to work on the project?"

"Nah," Quinn said, picking up a menu. "I have way too much on my plate as it is. Speaking of plates, what's good here? Oh, right—I picked the restaurant. Do you remember what I like to eat? I don't."

He'd always been thin, but he seemed even thinner than she remembered. He was six foot four with black hair always in need of combing. He shaved once a week because he couldn't bear to waste the time it took to shave every day. His auto-tinting wire-rimmed glasses never cleared all the way, even at night, which made him look a bit like a rock star. He was wearing black corduroy pants, a white shirt, a narrow black tie, and a black blazer that made him seem more like an English schoolboy.

"What I remember is that you don't like to eat," Dani said. "You never had time."

"At these prices, I'm still having a few misgivings," he said.

When the waiter came, Dani ordered a salad and he ordered coffee and a side order of garlic bread.

"Do you come into the city much?" Quinn asked. "You're up in Westchester, aren't you?"

"Just when I teach," Dani said. "John Jay College of Criminal Justice."

"What are you teaching? It's really good to see you, Dani."

"It's good to see you too."

"Listen, before we go any further, let's just say that whatever was going on between us in Africa, we blew it, or I blew it, if you need me to take 100 percent of the blame, because that's fine with me. And probably accurate. I blew it, it's over, no regrets, moving on, all's forgiven, still friends—okay? I wanted to get that out, straight off."

"Okay," Dani said, both startled and comforted by his directness.

"I trust you've moved on and are seeing somebody?"

"I am," Dani said.

"I'd say tell me about him, but it's none of my business. I've been too busy to date. But that's not what I should be telling you—your e-mail asked if I could help you with something, and I'm making it sound like I couldn't possibly find the time. Which I can't, but for you, I will tell somebody else to go—I will tell them my dog deleted my homework. I got a dog—did I tell you I got a dog? A bloodhound. I call him Otto. I'm trying to train him to sniff out depression."

"Vanillylmandelic acid?"

"Well done!" Quinn said. "This is why we had such a good time together. My friends say I should just let him be a dog, but he's a bloodhound—he *wants* to sniff things out. It's incredible, what he can do. What did you say you were teaching?"

"You didn't give me a chance," Dani said. The waiter brought their food, and as they ate, Dani told him about the teaching she'd been doing, classes in criminal psychopathology, character evaluation methodologies for noncooperative subjects, forensic psychiatry in the courtroom. She told him about her job in general terms. When he wasn't talking nonstop, Quinn could be a very good listener. When she'd finished, Dani thought it only fair that he have the floor to update her on his recent activities.

"What's the paper you're delivering about?" she said. "'An Immunoradiometric Study of Hyperandrogenism and Autism'?"

"Well, it's kind of a spin-off from the work I'd been doing on neurotransmitters of the frontal cortex—"

"Impulse control?"

"Exactly. The original work was with dopamine dysregulation syndrome and Parkinson's and Tourette's, and then we went longitudinal and started asking what happens to autistic children when they hit puberty. You're aware of the effect of hyperandrogeny on teens in the A-A spectrum?"

"Not the way you are, evidently," Dani said, "but sure. Kids with autism who already have a hard enough time coping with emotions have an even harder time when they reach puberty and become flooded with testosterone or estrogen. They get completely overstimulated."

"And when they can't take it anymore, they explode with anger," Quinn said, fishing for his wallet to hand the waiter the money to cover the bill. He hadn't touched his coffee or his garlic bread. "Sometimes. Not every time. Walk me back to my hotel?"

They headed north on Broadway.

"What do you know about Provivilan?" Dani said as they dodged pedestrians approaching from the opposite direction.

"Not a thing, thank you very much," Quinn said.

"Isn't Linz Pharm one of the conference sponsors?"

"Indeed they are. Provivilan is the new miracle drug. If memory serves, one of those comes along every 2.5 years. Actually, I haven't really dug in. Though I should. They offered me a job. Just last summer. In fact, this invitation to speak may be part of an ongoing wooing process. I could have made more money than Croesus."

"Maybe you should have listened," Dani said. "You could have funded your research for years. No more grants to write."

"Yes, but they would have told me what to work on," Quinn said. "I'm not cut out for that. I'm better off following my own path. If my life is ever going to amount to anything, I think that's the way I have to go."

Dani thought it was odd to hear him sounding so fatalistic. When they'd first met, the sky was the limit and he spoke as if nothing would ever stop him. Now he seemed aware that the clock was ticking. Perhaps that was the curse that came with winning awards and scholarships at an early age—the gnawing sense you're not living up to your potential.

"Did the name Peter Guryakin come up when they offered you the job? I met him at an art opening in East Salem."

"It did not, but it probably would have if I hadn't turned them down. He's one of the research directors, right?"

Dani smiled. "He told me he was in marketing."

"Perhaps he was just being humble. Or lying outright, which would not surprise me. The word on the grapevine is that he was running a KGB weapons program. Weren't they trying to use their mental powers to make goats explode back then, or was that just a Hollywood movie?"

"That was a movie. And I think the CIA tried that, not the KGB."

"Either way, the whole thing sounded unsavory," Quinn said, craning his neck to look up at a tall glass building. He folded his hands together behind his back and rocked on his heels. "This is my hotel. We've had a snack and a walk, and you still haven't told me how I can help you."

"I have a favor to ask," Dani said. "Actually, two. We tested a boy, post-mortem, who killed a young woman in a rather terrible way. I diagnosed him as having dissociative identity disorder, but that wasn't with a full intake. His proteomics were all over the map. I was hoping you could explain the find-ings. The only catch is that I can't send you the file. You'd have to come up."

"I don't have a car. Can I take the train?"

"Take Metro North to Katonah and I'll meet you at the station. Can you do it?"

"I deliver my paper this afternoon, but I'm free after that. This is good—it gets me out of dinner. What's the other favor?"

"The boy was supposedly in treatment, in a drug trial of some sort. I don't know who was sponsoring the trial or even running it, but I think this is what they were testing."

She handed him a small zip-locked baggie with the blue capsule Tommy had found behind the Sweet'N Low at Starbucks. Quinn held it up to the light to look at it.

"And you want me to find out what this is?"

"Can you do it?"

"I can, but I'll need a lab. I know someone at Columbia. It's not Provivilan, is it?"

"I don't know," Dani said. "I didn't exactly get it from my pharmacist."

"Did you steal it?" Quinn said, smiling mischievously.

"No," Dani said. "One of the boys in the trial gave it to me."

"But you think it's an SSRI?"

"Or something related."

"To treat depression?"

"Possibly."

"I'll have a look. Which of the two favors has the higher priority?"

"If you can assay the pill first, it may help explain the proteomics."

"I'll get right on it," Quinn said. "I assume this is the only sample you have."

"It is."

Across the street a woman was already decorating a shop window for Christmas. Quinn put the baggie into his pocket and patted it.

"Then I'll be very careful," he said. "Maybe when I come up, you'll introduce me to whoever it is you're in love with. I'd like to meet him. He's lucky to have you."

"I didn't say anything about—"

"You said everything but," Quinn said. "I'm not a behaviorist, but some things are obvious. I'm glad for you. I really am."

"It's good to see you, Quinn."

"It's good to see you too," he said. "I worried about you."

"I'm strong," she said. "And getting stronger all the time. You know me."

"Not sure that I really do," he said. "Or ever did. But that's my loss. I'll call you when I know something."

She liked that he'd said *when* he knew something, and decided she'd been wrong to worry that it would have been awkward to introduce him to Tommy. She was certain Tommy would like him.

A new worry occurred to her. She was involving Quinn in something that could be dangerous. Was that fair? She wondered if she should have laid all her cards on the table instead of keeping a few in the hole. But in a way, she thought, the less Quinn knew, the safer he would be. Unless his curiosity led him into dangerous territory. And she knew there was no stopping his curiosity.

13.

By talking to the staff at the High Ridge Manor nursing home that morning, Carl had at first learned little more than the police already knew—that the windows of Abbie's room were locked from the inside, and that the surveillance videos didn't show anybody going in or out of her room in the hour prior to when her body was found. Her physician told Carl that the progression of her illness had been slow but steady. The candy striper, a girl of sixteen named Amber who'd helped box up Abbie's personal effects, said the clothing in her drawers had not been as neatly folded as Abbie usually kept it, but nothing was missing as far as she could tell. Carl found nothing unusual in Abbie's stuff, save that the spine of her well-thumbed Bible had been cracked and partially torn.

He was about to leave when Amber asked if he knew where Abbie's son, George, was. "We've been trying to reach him," she said. "He was here to visit that morning."

"Didn't someone go to the house to tell him the news in person?" Carl said.

Amber nodded and said with a shrug, "Nobody was home."

Tommy was also looking for George. He wanted to run some of Abbie's comments by her son to see if he could shed any light, so he and Carl drove to the Gardener farm. As he drove, Tommy told Carl about the visit earlier from Ben Whitehorse. Carl wasn't sure what to say, other than they needed all the help they could get.

When they reached the farm, they paused at the long gravel drive. The hayfields beyond the low stone walls were brown, and they could see the slate-gray waters of Lake Atticus. Tommy turned down the drive slowly, honking his horn three times and turning his headlights on and off to let anyone in the house know they were coming. He parked in the circular drive in front of the house and shut the motor off.

The large old house was a Queen Anne, with a stone foundation, a wraparound porch, corner turrets and gables and reddish-brown siding, black shutters and black gingerbread trim, and thick climbers of dark green English ivy rising up and over the trellises. Tommy remembered that when Abbie was healthy, the gardens and the decorative shrubs around the house were pruned and weeded, but it had all gone to seed in her absence. In the fading late-afternoon light, a month shy of winter solstice, the house looked not just dark but dead, as if no one lived there now or ever had.

They got out of the car and without speaking split up to circle the house, looking in the windows to see if there was anyone inside. The day was getting colder and darker. Tommy turned up the collar of his navy peacoat against the wind and tugged down the brim of his Irish newsboy cap.

They met up behind the house on a broad lawn leading down to the lake. A gas grill on the back patio was covered with a large garbage bag. On the lakeshore, an Alumicraft rowboat was docked.

"That oughtta be turned over if they're done for the season," Carl said. "If George went to Miami to lie on the beach for the winter, he would have taken care of that. Is there a car in the garage?"

"First there'd have to be a garage," Tommy said, heading for the barn.

"What does George drive?" Carl asked, following him.

"I've seen him driving into town to pick up stuff at the hardware store in an old green Ford F150 with rusted fenders," Tommy said. "I don't know if he has any other vehicle."

"Didn't Abbie have a car?"

"A Dodge Dart. With a slant six. Those things were good for 300,000 miles."

"So was the driver," Carl said.

Tommy slid the barn's great door open and saw both the Dodge Dart and the F150 parked inside, but with enough room left in front for a third vehicle. He paused to use the infrared handheld to scan the building. Carl looked over his shoulder.

"Heat camera," Tommy explained. "I spotted something on my property that registered extremely cold."

The floor of the landing above them glowed with warmth.

"What's that?" Tommy said, wary.

"Just the hay," Carl said. "If the bales are put up damp and packed tightly enough, you get fermentation inside, and it generates heat. Plus, it insulates. A good barn full of hay will stay warm all winter."

They checked the machine shed where they found a new John Deere tractor and the implements needed to mow, rake, bale, and transport hay, as well as a workbench and the tools needed to service the machinery. Tommy found an old boom box on a shelf above the workbench and turned it on. The radio was tuned to the local NPR station, and there was a Rolling Stones tape in the cassette deck. He turned it off.

"I would have thought country and western," he said.

He moved to a bookshelf of greasy, well-worn service manuals and tipped them out one at a time as he read the titles.

"What are you looking for?" Carl said.

"This," Tommy said, holding up a manual for a 2004 Honda CRV. "He fixes his own vehicles. He's got a manual for the Dodge and the Ford, so I'm thinking this is the car that's missing."

Standing by his Jeep again, Tommy used the infrared camera to scan the house but found nothing unusual. The windows appeared to be the same color as the siding, indicating that the furnace inside either wasn't working or the thermostat had been turned down low. Carl asked if the coast was clear.

"I don't even know for sure if this thing works," Tommy said. "I'm pretty sure nobody's home, but why don't you go around back and see if the back door is locked. I'll try the front."

As Carl walked around the house, Tommy climbed the steps of the front porch and peered into the front windows. The house was dark and nothing stirred. He went to the front door and pulled the brass knocker back to rap against the plate. When he did, a business card that had been pinned by the knocker fluttered to the deck. He picked it up.

The card belonged to Julian Villanegre, Morningside, Hinksey Hill, Oxford, England, and listed an eleven-digit cell phone number. Tommy flipped the card over and saw, written by hand:

I'll be happy to appraise your collection. I'm staying at the Peter Keeler Inn. Please give me a call.

He knocked on the door, first with his knuckles. There was no response. He tried again with the knocker, louder this time. He heard something and then realized it was Carl knocking on the back door. A moment later Carl came around the corner of the house and held his hands out, empty. Tommy showed the card to Carl, put it back where he'd found it, then called Dani to tell her they'd struck out. George Gardener was not home, and it didn't look like he'd been home for a while.

"Casey's been trying to contact him," Dani said. "So's Banerjee. Next of kin. Where are you?" She was on the Saw Mill Parkway and heading home after saying good-bye to Quinn.

"Right now I'm standing on George Gardener's front porch with Carl," Tommy said. "We're thinking he's driving a 2004 Honda CRV. What does Casey want with him?"

"He was the last visitor Abbie had before her death," Dani said. "Or rather, the second to last, not counting a candy striper who checked on her after dinner. We've been trying to reach him for two days."

"Can you track his license plates through the tollbooth cameras or figure out where he's using his credit cards?"

"I can't make that happen, but Casey can," Dani said. "He might have thought of it already. Do you think George is on the run?"

"From what?" Tommy said. "Unless you think he's guilty of something."

"We're all guilty of *something*," Dani said. "I'm meeting Quinn's train in Katonah later tonight. Do you remember my grandfather's friend from the State Department?"

"Ed Somebody?"

"Stanley."

"I thought it was Ed. Oh, wait—Stanley's his last name. He was stationed in . . ."

"Moscow. I sent him an e-mail. Quinn said he'd heard gossip in the neuroscience community about Guryakin working for some Soviet weapons program. Ed Stanley might know somebody who can find out if it's true. Worth a shot. Where are you going next?"

"Library. My aunt said she has some information for us."

"I'm about twenty minutes away. I'll meet you there," Dani said and hung up.

She had wanted to say more. She had wanted to say, "When this is all over, why don't we go somewhere, just the two of us, and fall in love the way everybody else does, instead of . . ." But that was being selfish, she thought. And off task. Not possible, not right now, anyway.

From the hayloft of the barn, the thing watched as the two men drove off in the car, staying low behind the insulating hay in case the younger one turned his scanner on to look behind him one last time.

When the car was far enough away, the beast leapt down from the hayloft and bolted along the ground, unable to use the atrophied wings on its back but running fast enough to keep up with the car, sometimes overtaking it and crouching in the branches of a tree by the side of the road to wait like a buzzard, watching them as they passed.

It stayed in the shadows, leaping from rooftop to rooftop. Finally it came to rest high on the roof of the Grange Hall, where it looked down as Tommy parked in the lot next to the stone building that housed the East Salem Library and watched as Tommy and Carl got out of the car and entered the building.

It looked down on the town green, the gazebo in the middle, the row of shops, and at the opposite end of the green, a white church with a tall steeple and a gold cross mounted atop the steeple. The thing hated everything it saw. It felt scorn for the way these humans lived, and looked forward to the time when it would destroy the people who had just gone into the library, as easily as squashing bugs. It looked forward to the time when all of this would end, and there would be nothing left but the rats and the cockroaches and the flies swarming over the carcasses and the offal.

From the roof of the Grange Hall, next to the library, it waited, watching.

14.

"Tommy—that strange man has been here since lunchtime, and we close at six tonight," Ruth said. "He's very nice, but he's making me nervous."

"I'll have a word with him."

Tommy went to the carrel where Ben Whitehorse sat, surrounded by a half dozen volumes of local history books, including two by Abigail Gardener—*The Witches of East Salem* and *History of Ghosts in East Salem*. Ben looked up from the *Atlas of the Colonial Era* when he saw Tommy.

"You wouldn't be following me, would you?" Tommy said, hoping he sounded friendly.

"I'm a good tracker," Ben said, "but even I'm not good enough to follow someone and get there before they do."

"Good point. Did my aunt help you find what you were looking for?"

"If that woman over there is your aunt, then the answer is yes," Ben said. "I was very happy when I saw that there was a library so close to the inn. Whenever I get to a new town, I like to read up on the local history. Do you remember what I was telling you about paper?"

"That it was the biggest advantage the Europeans had when they arrived in North America?"

"Correct. Most of the work I do is with oral histories, but I love paper histories too. Did you know that these days you can get a book and listen to it on a CD player? It's quite amazing. Though I wish they wouldn't let Hollywood actors do the reading. They ham it up too much. A good story should speak for itself."

"So to speak," Tommy said. "I did know that. Listen, I'm actually here to have a discussion about history that you might be interested in. Would you care to join us?"

"I would like that," Ben said, closing the books in the carrel and straightening them before picking up his hat and following Tommy.

Tommy paused briefly to peruse the community bulletin board—advertisements for tag sales and yoga classes and pictures of lost cats. It had been an early morning yoga class on their way to perform a Salutation to the Sun on Bull's Rock Hill that discovered Julie Leonard's body.

He showed Ben the way to the media room, pleased when he saw Dani push through the door. He waved to her. Carl and Aunt Ruth were setting up the projector and logging into the proper files. Dani threw her coat over the back of a chair. Tommy was about to comment on how nice she looked—a sleeveless black dress with a Mandarin collar, accessorized by small gold hoop earrings—when he remembered that she'd had lunch with Quinn. It was perfectly natural to want to look nice for an old friend you hadn't seen in years.

"How was lunch?" he asked.

"Good," Dani said. "Fill you in later. Quinn's coming up on the train tonight."

"Dani, this is Ben Whitehorse, the man I told you about. Ben, this is Dani—uh, Dr. Danielle Harris."

The old man shook her hand and said, "Dr. Harris, it's a pleasure to meet you. May I ask you—what kind of doctor are you?"

"I'm a psychiatrist."

"I admire psychiatrists very much. I sometimes think of them as spiritual healers of a different kind. A person's heavenly spirit can only be healed by prayer and by the grace of our Lord Jesus Christ, but people have a body spirit too. When that is sick, it makes people terribly sad or gives them an anger they can't get rid of. The body is God's temple, and you're the electrician for the temple. You make sure all the lightbulbs work."

"Thanks," Dani said. "I never quite thought of it that way. Where are you from, Ben?"

"Oh, I'm sort of from all over the place. I travel a lot."

It was closing time for the library, so rather than bother his aunt, who seemed to be getting along cordially with Carl, Tommy locked the front door for her and turned off some of the lights. Dani introduced Ben to Carl and Ruth, who set a platter of marshmallow Rice Krispy treats that had survived that day's story hour on the table. The Smart Board displayed a Thanksgiving mural the children had drawn that morning. Ben examined it closely.

"Ben's visiting from . . ."

"The Midwest," he said, smiling.

"I was just asking Carl if he had any plans for Thanksgiving," Ruth said to Ben, exchanging a brief glance with her nephew. "If you're in town over the holiday and have nowhere else to go, perhaps you'd care to join us? We'll be having all the traditional foods."

"Eel?" he said.

"Well, no," Ruth said. "Turkey. Stuffing. Cranberry sauce."

"At the first Thanksgiving, they ate eel," Ben said. "It was very plentiful in this part of the world back then."

"I can make eel if you'd like . . ."

"No, turkey will be fine," he said, admiring the mural. "Your children are very artistic."

"I was hoping Tommy and Dani would join us too," she said, looking to her nephew for a reply. Tommy saw Carl nodding urgently to him, as if he were too shy to be alone with Ruth for more than a few minutes.

"We'd love to," Dani said.

"Now that *that's* settled," Tommy said, taking the floor. He explained that the reason they'd gathered was to help decode something Abbie Gardener had said. He described the circumstances of the interview he and Carl had conducted with her and then logged out of the Smart Board's Thanksgiving mural. In its place he posted his transcription of the interview and the questions he and Carl had written down after going through it the day before.

"We know she was talking about Satan, and we're pretty sure she was telling us something was, or still is, going on at St. Adrian's," Tommy said, turning to Ben. "That's a local private school. So here's what we're left with . . ."

World Religions for a thousand, Alex! Anyone for a little game of dodge ball? Dodge one, dodge all . . .

   World Religions for a thousand, Alex! It's both the question and the answer, Alex. The beginning and the end—what more do you need to know? Potpourri for one hundred, Alex—this common element is something you pass, but that's asking a lot. Make your way with all haste and look not behind you, 'cause you never know what's sneaking up on you, Satchel Paige! Baseball for two hundred, Alex—this Sultan of Swat is the boy's best chance! Native Americans for five hundred, Alex—this Native American sorcerer's black magic killed the daughters of Hiawatha.

   Question #1: How does Abbie know about the school?
   Question #2: Dodge ball? What?
   Question #3: Beginning/end, question/answer, same thing?
   Question #4: What about salt?
   Question #5: What does "Don't look back" mean?
   Question #6: Babe Ruth?
   Question #7: Who is the Native American sorcerer?

Tommy gave them all time to read the statement and the questions.

"This is better than paper," Ben said of the Smart Board. "I liked that drawing the children did better, though."

"It's saved," Tommy reassured him. "I think we can probably just think about questions one through six. Ruth said she had some information about number seven?"

"Well," his aunt said, moving to the computer and resting her hand gently on the mouse. "I have to say, I feel a bit odd talking about Native American history with an expert like Mr. Whitehorse here. Maybe he should be the one telling us about Hiawatha."

"You go ahead," Ben said, "and if I have anything to add, I'll jump in."

"I can't say I know how this applies to poor Abbie," Ruth said, "but I can tell you a little bit about Hiawatha. For starters, let's throw out anything you knew based on the poem by Longfellow. I don't know where that man got his information, but I think he made a lot of it up."

"I think so too," Ben said.

"My primary sources were a book called *Ancient Society* by Lewis Henry Morgan, published in 1877, and a book that's more local, *The History of Cortland County, New York* by H. P. Smith, published in 1885."

Ben suddenly sat up straight.

"Is everything okay?" Ruth said.

"Yes," Ben said. "I'm sorry. I thought I heard something."

"What I can't seem to find out is whether or not Hiawatha was a real person," Ruth continued. "I have various sources placing him in the tenth century, the twelfth, the fourteenth, and the fifteenth. Neither Morgan nor Smith is able to say for certain whether or not Hiawatha was a legendary human or simply a legend. Ben, would you know?"

"Yes," he said, smiling. Ruth waited but Ben remained silent.

"At any rate, the historical Hiawatha is credited with uniting the Iroquois Nation in this part of North America, which is something New York children study in fourth grade, so I'm sure Thomas can recall. Thomas? Can you name the five tribes of the Iroquois Confederacy?"

"Oh man," Tommy said. "If I knew you were going to call on me, I would have sat in the back row."

"Mohawk, Oneida, Onondaga, Cayuga, and Seneca," Dani said. She offered Tommy a mock *So there!* smile.

"I knew that," he mumbled.

Ruth clicked on a link to a map of New York State prior to the arrival of Europeans, with an estimation of how far the Iroquois Nation had spread.

"But Hiawatha didn't do it alone," Ruth said. "He had help from a man named Deganawida. Did I pronounce that correctly, Ben?"

"The *g* sounds a bit like a *k* in Iroquois," Ben said.

"Well, this is about all I have," Ruth said. On the screen they saw an ancient Indian pictograph, the photograph taken in Leatherman's Cave in a state park called the Ward Pound Ridge Reservation about five miles west of East Salem. The drawing showed, at the bottom, five groups of people in a line from left to right, each paired with some sort of designating totem, and above them two human stick figures holding hands.

"The Leatherman was an early nineteenth-century hermit," Tommy explained to Ben. "Nobody knows much about him, other than that he dressed in hides and lived in a cave. They don't even know his real name. He was a white man. I've done a trail run past his cave."

"At first they thought he'd done the drawings in the cave," Ruth said, "but they brought in some experts who established that the pictograph was definitely pre-Columbian. They can't say for certain, but they think it was done somewhere from 1000 to 1200 AD."

"Every year they have a 10K race in the park called the Leatherman's Loop," Dani told Ben, "where you run through mud and across freezing streams and up rocky trails. You have to be completely insane to run it."

"Tommy ran it three times," Carl said. "He won it twice."

"You don't have to be *completely* insane, but it helps," Tommy said. "You were saying, Ruth?"

"Deganawida was also called the Great Peacemaker or the Man of the North," she said. "Deganawida means 'Two River Currents Flowing Together.'"

"Sken-nen-RA-ha-wi in Mohawk," Ben said.

"Thank you. Apparently he came from somewhere north of the Great Lakes. Hiawatha and Deganawida are credited with forging an alliance among the five tribes that lasted for hundreds of years. It had a stable agricultural economic base, shared defense, and limited representational government—rather advanced for pre-Columbian North America."

"What's the reference Abbie Gardener made to the 'black sorcerer who killed Hiawatha's daughters'?" Carl said. "Isn't that what she was trying to warn us about?"

"Well, again," Ruth said, "I'm not going to be able to separate fact from fiction, but according to the legend, the black sorcerer who killed Hiawatha's daughter was a fellow named Thadodaho. His name translates as 'entangled.' He was an Onondaga chief, apparently, said to be deformed, with gnarled arms and legs and snakes in his hair. Like Medusa, I suppose. He led his people into cannibalism and self-destruction. But I think maybe Mr. Whitehorse would know more about him than I do. Ben?"

Ben studied the picture for a moment, then took his hat off, smoothed his hair back with one hand, and replaced the hat.

"I can tell you the real story," he said. "What you've been able to learn is very good, Ruth Gunderson. I'm impressed. Tommy, I think your aunt is the answer to question number six. She's the Ruth the old woman was directing you to. The knowledge contained in a library is the boy's best chance. And I think you're the boy."

"I can go with that," Tommy said.

"Most of what the books say is true, as far as it goes. How do you think it could be possible for a man to have snakes for hair?"

"I assumed that was figurative," Ruth said.

"Why did you assume that?"

111

"Well . . ."

"You're right, of course, that it's not possible for a man to have snakes for hair, but if I heard a story about a man with snakes for hair, I would assume that he was not a man."

"Thadodaho wasn't a man?" Tommy said.

"I think he may have been a man at some point, but then he chose not to be a man," Ben said. "If he let the Wendigo into his heart, he would have been driven by something that wasn't human."

"What do you mean?" Dani said.

"I've heard it said that he was Onondaga originally," Ben said. "But the people he led were not the Onondaga that we think of today. They were cannibals. They decorated their lodges with the heads of their victims. For hundreds of years they ruled that part of the world because of their violence and their brutality and hatred. Other people fled to be as far away from them as they could get. They had no idea of goodness until Hiawatha showed it to them after he defeated Thadodaho."

"Hiawatha and Deganawida," Carl added.

"Yes," Ben said. "And it was Deganawida who taught Hiawatha the ways of peace. Then Hiawatha taught the others."

"He was a Huron?" Dani said. "Why did they call him the Man of the North?"

"That was where he was from, but he wasn't Huron," Ben said. "He was from farther north."

"He was an Eskimo?" Tommy said.

"Not that far," Ben said, "but you're getting warmer. I think you probably know a name for other men who came from the north. Some of them may be your relatives."

"Norsemen?" Ruth said. "Do you mean Vikings?"

Ben nodded.

"That's . . ." Dani couldn't think of the word. She needed one that combined *ridiculous* and *obvious*, so she said, "That's interesting."

"You can look all this up," Ben said. "The Vikings sailed to America in the year 1002."

"Leif Erikson, right?" Carl said. "They found some archaeological proof of a Viking settlement in North America. They called it Vinland."

"*Leifsbudir*," Ben said. "That was the village they created. He was an outlaw, but when he went back to Norway for a visit, he became a Christian. He made all the men on his ship become Christians too. By the end of the first millennium, Christianity had spread to Norway. Before they became Christians, the Vikings were not very nice people. No offense."

"None taken," Tommy said.

"Christianity was the end of the Vikings," Ben explained. "Leif Erikson was still a Viking and an explorer, and he wanted to see the country to the west. So he set sail from Greenland with thirty-five men and explored America, including the St. Lawrence River and Lake Ontario and Lake Erie. But when he got back to Iceland, he only had thirty-four men with him. It's in the records."

"One died?" Dani guessed.

"Nobody died," Ben said. "They kept very good records. They had paper to write on. I was telling Tommy what a great thing paper is. Erikson left one man behind."

"Deganawida," Carl said.

"That's what the people who already lived here called him. He stayed behind to spread the Word of God and to bring the salvation of Christ to the people he met and to tell them the stories. The Man of the North was the first missionary to the New World, centuries ahead of the others who came later."

"Two River Currents Flowing Together," Tommy said.

"And the man he met who helped him was Hiawatha," Dani said. "You're saying the Iroquois Confederacy was a Christian movement?"

Ben Whitehorse stood and walked to the Smart Board, which was still showing the pictograph.

"He converted Hiawatha to Christianity. You can see in this pictograph the five tribes," Ben said. "This box with the sun on the left is the Seneca. They were the Keepers of the Western Door. This turtle represents the Cayuga, the People of the Swamp. These flames are the Onondaga, the Keepers of the Fire. This stone is the Oneida, the People of the Standing Stone. And this box with the sun on the right stands for the Mohawk, the Keepers of the Eastern Door."

Ben stepped back for a moment to let his lesson sink in.

"Thadodaho sought to destroy the alliance to protect his power. There was a great battle, but in the end, Thadodaho was driven away. Before he left, though, he summoned the Wendigo to kill Hiawatha's daughter."

Tommy saw Carl grimace at the idea of a man losing his daughter.

"'Suddenly, with a mighty swoop,'" Ruth read from a book she held open, "'a huge bird, with long and distended wings and a pointed beak, came down and crushed the beautiful child to the earth. Despairing and desolate, Hiawatha remained for three days prostrate upon his face on the ground. Everyone present shared the old man's grief.' That's from H. P. Smith's *The History of Cortland County, New York*."

She stopped and they all looked up when they heard a noise, a scurrying and scraping of nails or claws above them.

"Oh my," Ruth said. "I think we've got squirrels in the attic again. I don't mean that as a euphemism. This time of year, as soon as it gets cold out, they start looking for a warm place to spend the winter. Mice too."

"What happened to Hiawatha and Deganawida?" Carl said. "I guess what I'm asking is, what happened to the Word they were preaching?"

"Thadodaho gave them a disease before he was driven away," Ben said. "I think it might have been smallpox. They knew that if they didn't quarantine themselves, they'd give all the people the disease, so the two of them went away."

"What happened to Thadodaho?" Tommy asked. "And the Wendigo?"

"Demons don't die," Ben said. "You can damage the corporeal forms they take but not the spirit that animates them. Only angels can do that. I'm sure that when the body Thadodaho was possessing died, he found another one to occupy. He went into hiding after he was driven away and didn't come out again until he thought it was safe."

Dani looked uncomfortable. "I have to ask," she said, "are these just stories, mythologies that tell a fiction, or are you saying they're true? Is what you've said one out of several possible explanations?"

Ben smiled. "I can tell you're the kind of person who needs proof," he said. He turned to Tommy. "Is it possible to enlarge the pictograph for a closeup? This area here."

He drew a circle around the two figures at the top of the pictograph representing Hiawatha and the Man of the North. Tommy zoomed in until the designated area filled the Smart Board.

"Can you see what Hiawatha is wearing around his neck here?" Ben asked Dani.

"A cross," she said.

"And here on the Man of the North, you can see the symbol of the horned helmet that the Vikings wore. In native tongue we could say it was his totem. His version of the cross."

He circled the symbol.

It was the same 𝔚 they'd found drawn in blood on the body of Julie Leonard.

And the same symbol Tommy and Dani had found mysteriously drawn in the cremated remains of Amos Kasden.

Dani and Tommy shared a glance. Julie had drawn the symbol on her own body, to send a message. Now they knew what the message was. The question remained as to whom it was directed. How the symbol appeared in Amos Kasden's ashes was still unclear, but now both Tommy and Dani understood that if the symbol represented Christ, Amos wasn't the one who'd tried to tell them something.

15.

In a small private library adjacent to the headmaster's office at St. Adrian's Academy, Dr. John Adams Wharton poured two glasses of sherry and handed one to Dr. Adolf Ghieri, then took the other and sat in a leather easy chair in front of the fireplace, where a small blaze warmed the room. Ghieri set his glass of sherry down, used his thumb to tamp down the tobacco in his pipe, took a long wooden match from a brass container on the hearth, leaned over to place the head of the match in the flames, and once it ignited, used the match to light his pipe. He sucked on the stem of the pipe three times, the bowl hissing to life, and puffed smoke from the corner of his mouth before tossing the match into the fire.

"I think it's a problem," Wharton said. "They grow in number. Sometimes there's strength in that."

"I think you're right," Ghieri said. "Though the greater the numbers, the greater the opportunity to sow discord."

"I'd hoped we could deter them when it was just the girl and that idiot athlete."

"I'd hoped so too."

"Frankly, I didn't think she'd be so easily persuaded by his simple-minded piety," Wharton said. "Not that I expected anything else from him, but from her, yes. I misread her."

"Agreed."

Wharton picked up a cast-iron poker and stirred the fire.

"We're too close to completion to let anything get in the way now," he said. "The next few weeks are critical."

"Obviously."

"It's equally obvious that you should not have left things to the boy," Wharton scolded. "He wasn't ready to improvise."

"Amos was a capable child," Ghieri said. "He tested very high."

"Your tests are dubious at best. He was still a child. There was far too much emphasis on public display. We can't afford to make that mistake again."

"No."

"They're growing stronger," Wharton said. "I'd like to know how much they know."

Ghieri sucked on his pipe, then blew smoke toward the hearth, where the draft pulled it under the lintel and up the flue. "Do you think they know where the book is?" he said.

"I'm not willing to rely on guesswork," Wharton said. "We need to get someone inside their circle."

"I have an idea," Ghieri said. "I think one of them is weaker than the rest. Angrier. We can use that."

"Maybe it would be simpler just to destroy them all."

"Not yet. The information we need might be lost. I know which one is weak, and I know whom to send."

Wharton held up his glass to see how the crystal and the brown liquid refracted the light from the fire. He studied the flames.

"If we can separate the two," Ghieri continued, "the girl and her fawning little puppy, we may not need to worry about the others. They're holding the whole thing together. The others follow them."

"What about the angel? Do you intend to underestimate him too?"

"I underestimate no one," Ghieri said. "He's obviously fallible; he's already missed some opportunities. We can't let him affect us either way. We've dealt with angels before."

"Your hubris is unearned. Do what you have to do," Wharton said, rising from his chair. "Keep me informed. Apparently I have to supervise everything. Now if you'll excuse me, I have work to do."

Once Wharton left the room, Ghieri put both of his hands deep into the fire, not to warm them, for he had no need of that, but only to draw energy from the flames and bring it into his body. Wharton was still useful, Ghieri thought, but it would not be long before his usefulness ended. Wharton was a slug too stupid to know he was a slug. Ghieri looked forward to the moment when he could crush that slug under his boot.

Dani was waiting at the curb, her view of the train pulling into the Katonah station obscured by a row of pine trees and sumac. On the town bulletin board by the stairs she saw a flier for Julie Leonard's memorial service that someone had forgotten to take down. She saw a policeman on foot patrol beneath the streetlight at the corner where flashing red lights marked the railroad crossing, the bulge of his service automatic visible in silhouette. Before they'd caught Julie's killer, the police had increased their presence on the street. After the case was closed, the increased presence remained, because people were still scared. Dani knew one or two policemen with guns would be to no avail in confronting the evil they faced, but if it helped people sleep . . .

The train squealed to a stop. Passengers disembarked, climbed the central staircase from the platform to a bridge over the tracks, then descended. Dani could see first legs, bags, and briefcases descending the stairs to where she waited in a line of cars, mostly women picking up their weary husbands after a long day in the city. She watched the steady parade of stockbrokers and lawyers and investment bankers in trench coats and Burberry scarves, checking their cell phones as they chucked their *Wall Street Journals* into the waste bins at the bottom of the stairs. Some businesswomen too, but not as numerous as the men.

She'd just started to worry that Quinn had missed his train when she saw him. But before she saw him, she saw the nose and the front paws and then the rest of a massive dog that dragged him down the stairs, a giant brown-and-black bloodhound with drooping flews and ears that almost swept the ground. Quinn wore the same black coat and pants he'd worn that morning, but with a black turtleneck sweater.

He smiled when Dani rolled down the window. "This is Otto," he said. "I told you about him, didn't I?"

"You did, but you didn't say you were going to bring him."

"Didn't have a choice," Quinn said. "I had a dog sitter lined up, but it fell through. I couldn't very well leave Otto if I wasn't sure how long I'd be gone. Is it okay?"

The massive dog put his nose up to Dani's open window and sniffed her.

"How'd you get him on the train?"

"I told them he was my smelling-nose dog," Quinn said. "Said I was epileptic and he warns me when I am about to have a seizure. They can do that, you know."

"I know," Dani said. "But I'm pretty sure the Peter Keeler isn't going to let you have him in your room. It's a fairly posh inn."

"Hmm," Quinn said. "Well, I suppose I could always—"

"He can stay at my house," Dani said. "Though I'm not sure what my cat will think. He's housebroken, isn't he?"

"Oh yes. I've got some food for him in my suitcase, but I'll have to get more tomorrow."

"I didn't know bloodhounds could be so—"

"Huge?" Quinn said. "He's well above average for size. Are you sure you don't mind?"

"What would you do if I did?"

"Beg?"

She popped the trunk open so that Quinn could throw his bag in. The dog filled the backseat, but he was well mannered and didn't drool or smell bad. When he sat upright, his head brushed the roof of the car.

As Dani drove, Quinn told her he'd given the pill sample to a lab technician at Columbia who'd promised to have results tomorrow. "I said it was something my mother was taking and I wanted to check to make sure she was getting the real thing—did I tell you she's been making runs up to Canada to get her prescriptions filled because it's so much cheaper there? She's doing much better. The only side effect is that now she watches a lot of hockey."

Dani remembered Quinn's endless descriptions of his mother's maladies, real and imagined.

"Am I going to meet the lucky man in your life?" Quinn said.

"Maybe tomorrow," Dani said. "You probably know him. Tommy Gunderson."

Quinn shrugged, clueless.

"The football player."

"American football or soccer?"

"American," Dani said. "This is going to be interesting."

At the Peter Keeler Inn, a fire blazed in the fireplace in the lobby. On the walls hung framed portraits of three of the inn's most famous guests, General George Washington, General Horatio Gates, and Mark Twain. Dani helped Quinn check in, then said she'd call him tomorrow when she knew what time she'd have access to the file, either at the medical examiner's office or the district attorney's.

"It sounds exciting," Quinn said. "Like one of those television shows in which the forensic scientists sit around in exotically lit high-tech laboratories solving crimes between witticisms. You don't carry a gun, do you?"

"I'm an officer of the court, not a policeman," Dani said. "Any special instructions for Bluto?"

"Otto. Just keep his dishes full. And when you take him out for a potty stop, don't let him off the leash because if he gets a scent, he will take off after it. They say his sense of smell is 100,000 times better than humans', but I'm inclined to think that's a low estimate."

Back in the car, Dani had to push the dog to one side to see around him as she backed up. Fortunately, he was as gentle as he was large. Before she put the car into first gear, she unlocked and opened the glove compartment. She checked to make sure the Beretta 3032 Tomcat .32 caliber automatic Tommy had bought her, a "purse pistol" he called it, was loaded, with the safety on. She'd been reluctant to accept the gift, even though Stuart Metz and Detective Casey had both suggested, independently of each other, that it might be a good idea to protect herself. After Amos Kasden had invaded her kitchen, she was less reluctant.

"Between you and *that*," she said to the dog, looking at him in her rearview mirror as she closed the glove box, "I pity the fool who tries to mess with us, to quote Mr. T. You know who Mr. T is? Of course you don't. When I was really little . . . Look at me. I'm talking to a dog. I suppose it's okay as long as you don't talk back."

After bidding Ruth a good evening, Tommy walked Ben Whitehorse across the town green to the inn. Carl said he thought he might go for a ride before going home. Ben was oddly interested in the roofs of the buildings on the square, the church steeple across the way, the clerestory of the Grange Hall, the town hall's clock tower. Perhaps he was a bird watcher, Tommy thought—though he believed that was more of a daytime activity. He pointed out the gazebo and told Ben that during the summer they had band concerts there, and families brought picnic baskets or bought ice cream from a truck parked in front of the library.

"It sounds like a nice little town," Ben said.

"We had a pretty gruesome crime here last month. People are still checking to make sure their doors are locked. It doesn't seem like the kind of place that Satan would pick to hang out in," Tommy said.

"What do you mean, 'hang out'?" Ben said.

"We were told this town was the seat of Satan's throne," Tommy said. "Maybe not this town but this general area."

"Who told you that?"

"An angel."

"Then you should believe it."

"I do," Tommy said. "You said the Wendigo came from the devil, but that nobody was telling stories about him until about a thousand years ago. When Hiawatha and Deganawida were fighting Thadodaho."

"Yes."

"So where was the Wendigo before he was here? He existed before they started telling the stories about him, right?"

"Yes."

"And he still exists, right?"

"He does."

"So where was he before he was here?" Tommy asked again.

"He was wherever someone called him to be. Demons will come if you invite them in by name."

"So who summoned him here? How could the Native—how could the people who lived here already summon him, if they didn't know his name?"

"That's a good question."

"So how? Was he summoned by someone from somewhere else?"

"I think so."

"Where did Thadodaho come from? You said he was an Onondaga chief—was he possessed by a demon? By the Wendigo?"

"No. The Wendigo has its own form. Some said it was like a bird or a dragon. But there could have been other demons. Scripture indicates that perhaps a third of all the angels sided with Satan and were cast out. That's a lot of demons."

"But who? Who was summoning them?"

"I don't know," Ben said. "But I think you're asking the right questions, Thomas. Good night. I'll see you tomorrow."

"I look forward to it," Tommy said as he watched Ben climb the front stairs of the inn.

Look forward . . . Tommy considered what Abbie had been trying to say when she said, "Don't look back." Did she mean the opposite? *Look forward—be optimistic?* Probably not. Another interpretation would be *Look toward the future.*

He thought of a riddle he'd learned in Boy Scouts. A man is standing on the ground floor of a house next to three wall switches. One of them turns on a lightbulb in a windowless closet in the attic, and there's no way to tell from the ground floor if the light is on in the attic. You're allowed to turn the switches on or off in any combination, as many times as you want, but you can only go up to check once to see if the light is on. How do you solve the problem?

He'd raised his hand almost immediately, and afterward the scoutmaster said he'd never known anyone who could solve the riddle so quickly. You turned the first switch on, left it on for ten minutes, then turned it off, turned the second switch on, and ran up to check. If the light was on, it was the second switch. If the light was off *but it was still warm*, it was the first. If it was off and it was cold, it was the third.

"That's very intuitive, Tommy," the scoutmaster had said. Tommy'd had to look up the word *intuitive* when he got home, but he liked the sound of it.

Look to the future. How far? Who knew? *But think in four dimensions, not three*, he told himself.

⁓

Ruth Gunderson decided that before she closed up the library for the night, she'd check in the attic to see if the squirrels had gnawed on any of the books in storage. The attic of the old brick library was used to house the town's historical archives and collections that had been donated or bequeathed to the library—but no one had bequeathed enough shelf space to hold all the extra books, so they sat in the attic in boxes. There'd been talk for years of expanding the building, but East Salem was not a town where anything got done quickly.

She climbed the steep steps leading up to the attic, but when she got to the top and tried the light switch, nothing happened. There were only two bare lightbulbs illuminating the space, one directly above the stairs and a second at the far end of the room. She thought it odd that the two bulbs had burned out at the same time, and wondered if the squirrels had been nibbling on the wires. That could be a fire hazard.

She had a small LED light on her key chain. The battery was low and the light was weak, but she could still see ten or fifteen feet in front of her. She shone the light into the darkness and saw the shapes of a few cartons and containers in what felt like an infinite void.

She sniffed and detected a pungent, horrible smell, as if something dead and rotting was up there. She recalled asking Leon, the custodian, to set some Havahart traps last fall, when they'd last had a problem with squirrels. Perhaps he'd caught one but forgotten to remove the carcass.

She moved farther down the aisle, between stacks of cardboard boxes stuffed with papers and books. She'd closed the door behind her when she'd ascended the stairs, lest some sort of furry critter run out and lodge itself in the stacks downstairs, but now it occurred to her that if something happened to her up here, a broken leg or a heart attack . . .

But she was being a timid old woman to think that way. She scolded herself for being so nervous. It was time to leave anyway—there was little she could do tonight without proper lighting. As she turned for the stairs, the battery gave out in her key chain and her tiny light died. She was in total darkness.

"*Fand!*" she said, an expression her little Norwegian grandmother had been fond of saying, when *Uff-da!* wasn't strong enough. She knew the stairway had to be just twenty or thirty feet in front of her, but without any way to judge the distance, she worried that she might accidentally step wrong and fall down the stairs.

Then she heard something, a scratching sound, coming from somewhere to her left. The sound they'd all heard earlier, but much louder now. And the animal making it seemed much bigger than a squirrel.

"Who's there?" she said.

No answer.

She heard it again.

Darn squirrels! she thought.

"I'll give you three days to leave, and then I'm telling Leon to take care of it," she said into the darkness. Her heart beat faster, but she was being foolish again, she thought, scared of the dark like a child.

She felt her way forward, tapping the floor in front of her with her toe before she stepped. Finally she found the top of the stairs and the railing.

Back on the second-floor landing, Ruth closed the door leading to the attic. And locked it. At the reception desk she wrote herself a note to tell Leon to change the lightbulbs in the attic and to find whatever it was that was making that smell.

Carl nudged the gear lever up with his left boot toe to shift the motorcycle into fifth and rolled the throttle back with his right hand as he sped onto the Taconic at 80 mph. He rode north at a speed well over the legal limit because he didn't care if he got a ticket, and he didn't care if he had an accident, and he didn't care about anything at all. He tried to let the deep thrum of the engine and the roar of the wind and the fierce vibration of the machine nullify the many sad and dark things he felt inside. He turned into Taconic State Park and paused, idling at the waterfall, where he remembered the man with the poodle, the man Tommy thought could be an angel. When Carl remembered him, he saw only a man who was pathetic and alone except for a dog, a man who'd settled for something far less than what was possible, and then Carl hated the man with the dog, which made no sense, he knew. What Carl hated was himself. That made sense.

When Carl returned to his house, he took off his coat, then went to the cupboard above his refrigerator, where he found a bottle of bourbon toward the back of the cupboard. Carl generally never drank to excess, but tonight seemed like a good night to make an exception. Tonight he had a secret that he'd kept from Tommy and the others. The story of Hiawatha losing his daughter had served to make the pain all the more acute. Today was Esme's birthday. She would have been twenty-six, an elegant young woman, possibly with a family of her own. No. *Would have been* was wrong. *Should have been* was more like it.

He found a rocks glass in the cabinet, opened the bottle, filled his glass with ice and bourbon, and took a sip. The sip was good. If the sip was good, the gulp would be better, and if a gulp was good—it was—several gulps would be exquisite. He refilled his glass and emptied it again just as quickly, feeling the alcohol burn and glow inside, coating him with a false warmth, because inside he felt empty, dead, like the cast-iron woodstove in his living room that he knew he probably should fill with a couple of fat pieces of hardwood that would burn all night. Instead, feeling frivolous, he loaded the stove with split birch, tossed in some kindling, and struck a match.

He opened his mouth to sing "Happy birthday to you, happy birthday to you," but no sound came out.

The birch quickly jumped to life and gave off a sharp dry heat and a golden light that made the shadows dance. Carl pulled his chair in front of the stove and refilled his glass. This time he sipped more slowly. The house was small, but tonight it felt like an enormous cavern, too large for one man to live in or, more accurately, too large for half a man to live in.

He sipped and briefly thought that tonight might be the night he would go upstairs and open the door to the room down the hall from his, a door he had not opened in ten years.

The room was probably a mess, with the bed half made and a basket of dirty laundry on the closet floor, with a few items on the floor that had not made it all the way into the basket. Resting against the pillows would be a well-used stuffed bear named Figaro with one eye coming loose. The left one or the right one? He couldn't recall, though he could remember promising Esme he'd fix it for her, and saying her mother was the one who knew how to sew and fix things like that, but now that Mom was gone and it was just the two of them . . .

There would be a picture in a frame on her desk, somewhere amid the books and drawings, of a boy named Louis. Esme had just started dating and Louis was a nice boy. Carl had gotten a Christmas card from him last year. He'd probably get another this year. The last time Carl had opened the door to Esme's room, he'd seen the photograph of Louis, and he'd told himself he really needed to have The Talk about sex with Esme, even though he was certain she would roll her eyes and say, "I know, Daddy, I *know!*"

He sipped and then gulped. He'd already had too much to drink. But so what? It took so much effort to maintain the positive façade that other people saw, when he knew how he really felt inside. For one night he could let go. Collapse. Tomorrow he would rally, the way he always did.

He thought about the long summer afternoons when, starting in first grade, he'd meet Esme at the town park at three o'clock after her day camp was over. It was his job, because his wife had a nine-to-five job, to keep Esme happy and occupied until dinner. She'd insist that they go to the pool. She'd change into her suit in the girls' locker room—first she'd hold up a finger and tell him, "Daddies are *not* allowed"—and then she'd jump bravely into the water, without testing it first by dipping a toe. Carl always tested the water first, and then he had to count to three, sometimes more than once, while Esme treaded water and called out, "Come on, Daddy!"

Then they'd play a game she'd invented called Cherry-on-Top, in which they'd pretend he had a cherry on the top of his head and it was Esme's task to pluck it off and eat it. First he'd try to fend her off with one arm, then one arm and one leg, then two arms, then two arms and two legs, and finally the last level when he was free to run around in the pool and fend her off in any way he could while she swam after him. If her feet ever touched the bottom, or if he was able to shake her loose once she'd latched onto him, it was a fail and she had to start the level over. They'd spent long hours playing the game, but then one day he'd realized that she'd gotten older, her body filling the bathing suit with curves and bumps, and he'd told her they couldn't play the game anymore.

For a while he'd missed the little girl who had burst into the house one day holding a wrinkled purple balloon that had fallen to earth in the yard. "Daddy! Daddy! Look what I found! This is the balloon I let go of when I was three—it came back to me! You never know what's going to fall from the sky." He missed the little girl who had proclaimed with absolute confidence, "Do know what the cure is for the common cold? Cheese."

But he'd gotten used to the young woman who'd replaced her. He'd gotten to know her better the summer before her sophomore year in high school, when she'd proposed they take a trip together. The summer before her *junior* year, she explained, she'd need to study for her SATs, and the summer before her *senior* year she'd need to work on her college applications. So this was the summer when she had to do something, so that she'd have something to write about on those applications. She'd recently finished a book Carl had recommended to her, *Zen and the Art of Motorcycle Maintenance*, a book of philosophy that told the story of a man who takes a trip across the country on his motorcycle with his son, from whom he has become detached, and during the trip he rediscovers both his son and himself. Her idea was to take a cross-country motorcycle trip.

He agreed and did her one better, suggesting they travel all the way to Alaska. She'd always wanted to see where the glaciers calved and chunks fell explosively into the ocean. He'd bought a sidecar for the bike and a helmet for Esme, and a tent. They saw amazing things along the way, fields bursting with wildflowers after a particularly wet summer in Montana, the northern lights above Lake Louise in Banff. They'd roared through British Columbia and up the Yukon Highway, the air getting cooler at night but still warm during the day. They'd rented a two-seat kayak in Juneau and traveled with an outfitter to a lodge in Glacier Bay National Park, and the next day they set out for a place called Taylor Bay, where Brady Glacier was calving.

And there it ended. They'd camped on a small island, just the two of them, ate fish they caught and cooked, talked about Louis and school and Mom, and then they'd set out on a bright sunny morning in the kayak. But after just twenty minutes in the water, the weather changed. Carl had done everything he could afterward to try to comprehend what had happened: a phenomenon called "extratropical cyclogenesis," in which a tropical typhoon, moving poleward, meets a trough of low-pressure air moving south, seeding a sustained squall of gale-force winds generating enormous "trapped-fetch" ocean waves.

They'd seen the weather coming, but they were too far from shore to get back to land. They fought as hard as they could to keep the kayak upright. The wind was so fierce they could hardly hear each other, with Esme in the front and Carl in the back, paddling frantically, summoning strength he didn't know he had, but the storm was stronger than even the two of them paddling together. He heard a voice in his head screaming a kind of mantra, *Cherry on top! Cherry on top!* When the kayak flipped over, the cold of the water took his breath away. They were wearing life vests, but not the cold-water protective suits they would have needed to survive. They were in icy water, the wind and the waves pushing them under, again and again. He'd shouted, "Esme! Esme! ESME!"

When it all went black, he'd prayed to Jesus with his last breath to let it stay black, to bring him to Esme so that they might enter heaven together, hand in hand. But it didn't stay black. He'd opened his eyes and the light struck them, and he realized he was lying on a rocky beach, being attended to by a park ranger. He'd tried to sit up, saying, "Esme," but a hand on his chest pushed him back down and told him to wait until the EMTs arrived.

What happened immediately after that wasn't clear, but he remembered being told that they'd found only Esme's life vest. He remembered being wrapped in a blanket, while a woman wearing an orange hunting jacket told him that in water as cold as Glacier Bay, no one could survive for more than a few minutes, and that he'd probably survived only because of his greater body mass. She'd explained that in cold water the gases that ordinarily formed in the stomach of drowning victims, bringing them to the surface, generally did not build up in sufficient quantity to float a body. The Alaska Coast Guard rescue units rarely recovered drowning victims in waters this cold.

He'd stayed up there two weeks, praying with every bit of his strength, asking Jesus for a miracle while admitting he'd done nothing to deserve special treatment, and that in fact he deserved all the pain he felt, because he should have known better, should have checked the weather report, should have stayed closer to shore, should have . . .

The woman in the orange jacket had visited him, tried to get him to eat, but he wouldn't, couldn't. He was inconsolable. Finally he'd journeyed home, jettisoning the sidecar over a cliff somewhere in the Yukon. What he'd never been able to jettison was the guilt, the shame, the craving for some kind of punishment. Without it, he would never be able to atone. He'd survived and Esme had not, and that was absolutely and eternally unacceptable.

Many nights he thought it was some sort of cosmic joke, where God had told the wise man—the man who'd studied so hard to understand God and sin and resurrection and salvation and all the ways that people had sought to understand God—God had said, "Okay, wise guy—if you think you're so smart, figure this one out."

This was a dangerous place to be, Carl knew, because then the anger he felt toward himself turned into an anger at God—to whom he had pledged his very life, to whom he had promised to teach his lessons and tell others of his infinite love. The anger made him scream, sometimes silently, sometimes out loud, "Where was that love when I needed it? Why did you take the little girl who adored you and honored you in everything she did. Why should *you* have her and not me? How did I ever offend you so, that you would do this to me?"

He refilled his glass, emptying the bottle, and drank, wiping the tears from his cheeks with his sleeve. Everything was blurry and at the same time not blurry enough.

When he saw in the dim light a man sitting in the chair across from him, he knew who it was. Part of him had been expecting this visit for a long time. Part of him, if he was being honest, welcomed it.

"What are you doing here?" Carl said.

"You know what I want," the demon said.

"What?" Carl said, gesturing with his glass to the room, the house, the world. "You want this? You want to take this from me? You don't seem to realize—I don't care."

He drained the last of the bourbon, but instead of making him feel better, the drink only made him feel emptier, until he thought he could hear his heartbeats echoing off the walls of his empty shell of a life. He saw no advantage to living beyond the present moment. He didn't deserve another breath.

"I don't want your possessions," the demon said. "I'm here to give you the pain you've been asking for."

"You want this?" Carl said, laughing, as he poked himself in the chest and threw his glass into the fire, where the alcohol fumes flared. "*This* is what you want? You can have it—give it your best shot!"

With that, the demon overwhelmed him and took command of his body. When he realized what he'd done, Carl tried to resist, but he was too old and too drunk and too tired, and soon he felt the emptiness inside fill with something even worse, though it had been impossible to imagine anything worse. His blood turned black and his skin tightened, choking him. Whatever it was inside him was furious, and hated everything it saw, and wanted to snuff the life from anything that lived.

He went to the mirror in the bathroom and looked at himself. He looked the same. When he pinched his skin, he felt the pinch. He looked into his eyes. Tommy had once asked him a serious question posed with a light heart, "Why is it that you can only look into your own eyes for a minute or less before you start to feel totally weird?" He'd replied that he didn't know, but they'd both tried it, and they'd both burst out laughing.

Now when he looked in his eyes, Carl felt nothing. He saw nothing. He felt that he was looking at someone else, someone who moved when he moved and blinked when he blinked but who was not him.

"I am Carl Thorstein," he said.

But what he heard himself say was, "I am Thadodaho."

16.

Tommy went to George Gardener's place again the next morning, with the same results; the card from the art historian was still tucked beneath the brass hammer of the door knocker.

He decided to find out what Julian Villanegre knew about Gardener, so he drove to the Peter Keeler Inn, where the young woman behind the desk told him that the Englishman was still registered as a guest, though no one answered the phone when she rang his room. When he asked about Ben Whitehorse, her face lit up.

"Mr. Whitehorse went for a walk early this morning."

"What time is early?" Tommy asked.

"Well, my shift starts at five. He was down in the lobby eating blueberry muffins from the breakfast buffet by five thirty."

"That's early."

"He's such a sweet man," she said. "He told me I was an excellent baker. I tried to tell him the muffins come from Sara Lee and all I did was microwave them, but he insisted that nobody could microwave a muffin as good as me."

"If he comes back, could you ask him to call me?"

Walking back to his car, Tommy called his aunt to thank her for letting them use the library the night before. She told him that she'd found the time to bake him a strawberry-rhubarb pie, though if it was more than he thought he could finish, he was free to share it with Carl.

"By the way," she added, "that strange Englishman is back. He asked if Abigail Gardener had left any of her papers to the library."

"I'll be right over," Tommy said.

He found the historian sitting on a couch in the reading room, perusing a week-old copy of the *London Times*. Tommy took a concealed position behind a bookshelf with a view of the reading room and used his RAZ-IR PRO 2 to scan the library. The Englishman appeared to be normal. Well, human at least.

Tommy sat down across from him. On the back page of the newspaper was a story about a cricket match between Warwickshire and Lancashire.

Villanegre lowered his paper and neatly folded it.

"Mr. Gunderson—how are you?" he said. "Would you like a section of the *Times* when I'm finished with it, or do you have something to say to me?"

"How do you know my name?"

"Well, your aunt is enormously proud of you," Villanegre said. "When I asked her if she could tell me anything about Abigail Gardener, she said she knew her quite well and you had been talking about her just last night. She has a picture of you on her desk, you know."

It didn't surprise Tommy to learn that his aunt was entirely without guile.

"We were talking about Abbie," Tommy said. "And I hear you've been asking about her as well."

"Indeed." Villanegre nodded. "Maybe *you* can help me—I'm trying to find her son, George. He left a message at the inn saying that his mother had an art collection he believed may be of value, so he'd hoped I might have a look. I'm afraid if I don't hear from him soon, I will have to leave for home."

"We're not sure where George is," Tommy said. "Last I heard, the police were unable to locate him to tell him about his mom."

"Tell me—when you were watching Dr. Harris and me the other night at Starbucks, you seemed concerned. I can't imagine you'd feel jealous of a withered old prune like me."

"She's a good friend," Tommy said.

"I'm glad to know she has people looking after her, though I doubt she needs much help. Very self-sufficient, as so many American women are. English women try, but too often it's a bluff."

"Do you know if Udo Bauer is planning to buy the Gardener farm?" Tommy said. The idea had occurred to him that morning. Lots of people had tried over the years to buy the place, and had made Abbie offers that were, according to rumor, beyond extravagant. She'd always said no, but now that she was gone, there was no telling what George might say. And for someone as rich as Udo Bauer, no price would be too high for something he wanted.

"I wouldn't know," Villanegre said. "And he's gone back to Germany or I'd ask him for you."

"We'd heard Abbie had an interesting art collection," Tommy said, "but nobody's ever been in the house, so it was never more than a rumor." He stood up. "Well, if I find George, I'll let him know you're looking for him."

"And I will do the same for you," the Englishman said.

Had Tommy waited another ten minutes in the lobby of the Peter Keeler Inn, he would have run into Quinn McKellen, who came down to wait for Dani. Quinn was in a hurry, running late as usual, but when he searched the lobby and then the parking lot, he discovered that this time Dani was the one who was late.

She'd been getting ready to go when she saw a long black Lincoln town car with tinted windows rolling down the driveway toward her house. She watched as a man in a black coat got out of the front passenger seat, while the man behind the wheel stayed put. The man in the black coat opened the rear door and stood aside as an older gentleman in a camel cashmere coat got out of the backseat and looked up at the house. Judging from the body language, it appeared that he told the man holding the door to stay with the car, and the man in the black suit was arguing with him. The older man glanced at a piece of paper in his hand and then approached the house.

Dani opened the door to meet him.

"Dr. Danielle Harris?" he said.

"Yes?"

He smiled warmly.

"I'm Ed Stanley. Your Grandpa Howard's friend. You left a message on my answering machine. Do you mind if I come in?"

Inside, he declined her offer of coffee but accepted her invitation to take his coat off and join her in the living room. He was shorter than she'd imagined, slightly stooped over, with a soft voice and a gentle bearing. He was wearing dark khaki pants and a corduroy jacket over a plaid shirt, but Dani could tell these casual clothes were nevertheless well tailored and expensive. Stanley, who'd worked in Moscow for the State Department for over twenty years, had been enormously helpful when she'd had questions about the Moscow orphanage Amos Kasden had lived in before coming to the United States.

He went straight to a family portrait on the table by the window, a picture of Dani; her sister, Beth; their parents; Grandfather Howard, who was still alive and living in Montana; and Grandmother Ellen, who had passed.

"How's my grandpa?" Dani said.

"He's well," Stanley said as he sat down on her couch. "He's got a porcupine that's been eating holes in his shed, but other than that, he's good."

"When I called you, I thought you were still in Montana," she said. "I didn't expect a visit."

136

"Well, I was in Montana," he said, "but I flew out this morning. Or actually last night, because I had to go regional to catch the redeye from Seattle."

Dani drew a sharp breath. Why had he made such a long trip so suddenly?

"Are you staying?" she said, hoping the Keeler Inn wasn't booked up.

"No, no," he said. "But I had to talk to you. In person."

He began by qualifying that the story he was about to tell her had to remain confidential. It was something he hadn't even told her grandfather. He told Dani that he hadn't really worked for the State Department—he'd been a career CIA officer, rising to the level of station chief before retiring.

"When I heard you mention the name Peter Guryakin," Stanley said, "I knew I had to come as soon as I could. What do you know about him?"

"Very little, really," Dani said. "I met him at an art opening the other night at St. Adrian's Academy."

"He was *here*?" Stanley said, poking the coffee table with his finger. "In this country?"

"Yes. He told me he was in marketing."

"But your message said you'd heard he'd worked in a weapons program for the KGB," Stanley said. "May I ask where you heard that?"

"From a friend," Dani said, reluctant to say more. "Someone who had a job offer from Linz Pharmazeutika. Guryakin works for them, apparently." She wondered if Ed Stanley already had Quinn's name and decided he probably did.

"I'm a friend too, Dani," Stanley said. "That's why I've come. I needed to tell you in person that Dr. Peter Guryakin is not the sort of person you should be dealing with. He's a *very* dangerous individual. If we'd known he was in this country, we might have . . . wanted to talk to him."

"So he did work for the KGB?"

Ed Stanley nodded. "We've been watching him for some time. Until he dropped off the map. No one knew why. One theory was that he'd been the victim of a lab accident."

"What kind of accident?"

"He was developing nerve agents. Not the organic kind, which they were also stockpiling, like weaponized smallpox or ricin or anthrax, but synthetics that targeted the central nervous system. I can't be any more specific than that, except to say we believe his research met with some success. He dropped out of view a few years ago, but when I got your voice message . . . You think he's gone home?"

"I don't know," Dani said. "He didn't act like he was hiding."

"He may not know we're aware of him," Stanley said. "We have reason to believe he could be acting as a kind of biochemical arms dealer. I understand that you may not know why he was at the—what was it? An art exhibit?"

"At St. Adrian's Academy. It's a private boys' school. I was wondering if he might have been connected to the death of a woman in a nursing home who died the night of the exhibition."

"How did she die?" Stanley said.

"Nobody's sure." She was reluctant to tell him what she knew, afraid that he wouldn't believe her or would think she was delusional.

Stanley leaned forward and lowered his voice to let her know he did not mean to sound aggressive, but he was serious all the same. "Dani, I've interrogated a lot of people in my life, and I have a pretty good sense of when somebody isn't telling me everything."

She blushed and looked into his eyes for a long moment, gathering herself. "You're right," she said. "The medical examiner has the body, and—"

Before she could say more, Otto lumbered into the room. He paused for a second and then walked straight to the old man and laid his head in his lap. Ed Stanley scratched him behind the ears.

"That's Otto."

"He's beautiful. How long have you had him?"

"Not too long," she said. She changed her mind—if Stanley knew about Quinn, he would probably have known Quinn owned a bloodhound. "I'm keeping him for a friend. Do you know what kind of nerve agents this man was working on?"

"I really can't say anything more," he said. "I'm sorry."

She could tell from his reaction that he knew, but she said, "I understand."

"The old woman," he said. "It wasn't natural causes?"

"No. You can talk to the ME if you'd like."

"I may," he said, standing up. "I feel like I owe it to your grandfather to look after you. He's a dear friend and a fine fishing companion, by the way. Be careful." He handed her a card with a number on it. "If you spot Guryakin, or find *anything*, call this number. And don't—well, don't eat or drink anything you didn't prepare yourself. Or open any envelopes from an address you don't recognize."

"Okay," she said. She tried not to show how nervous his words were making her.

He picked up his coat. "Dani, you may be chasing questions here you don't want to know the answers to." He offered his hand to shake hers, but then impulsively, awkwardly, gave her a hug. "Be careful. I've got business in Washington. I'm not quite as retired as I may have led you to believe. I'll be in touch."

There was a time when Dani would have said she couldn't imagine a question she didn't wish to know the answer to, but that was no longer true.

⁓⁓⁓

Tommy pulled his Jeep into his garage and was crossing the cobblestone courtyard when he heard Carl's motorcycle coming up the drive. He smiled and waved, then opened a text from Dani.

NEED TO TALK. ED STANLEY HERE THIS A.M. GURYAKIN INVLVD SOVIET NERVE AGENT PROGRAM, POSS A CHEM ARMS DEALR. WILL CALL WHEN I CAN.

He showed the message to Carl.

"Interesting," Carl said, removing his helmet.

"You look terrible," Tommy said.

Carl's eyes were red and his face appeared to have lost color.

"Rough night. Didn't sleep very well. How was your night?"

"I figured out another clue. We were right. Abbie was trying very hard to tell us something. *Don't look back* meant *Look forward*. To the future. Which could mean just about anything, I suppose."

"Let's go inside," Carl said. "You can fill me in."

17.

"So this is where you put the bamboo splinters under their fingernails to pry the truth out of them," Quinn said.

The only free room Dani could find at the DA's office with a computer was Interview 2 in the basement, a windowless cubicle with acoustic tiles on the ceiling and the walls, a desk, and three chairs. The interrogator's chair had wheels, which allowed him to roll forward or back to open or close the distance between himself and the person being interrogated, depending on how much pressure or space he felt was appropriate. The monitor was generally left off because it gave suspects a welcome distraction, but sometimes it was used to show them pictures or videos.

"We don't need to put bamboo splinters under their fingernails," Dani said, typing in her password to log into the system. "Mostly we just bore them until they can't take it anymore and confess." She looked at him. "You think I'm kidding."

He held up his hands in surrender. "I wouldn't last ten seconds. Do you do interrogations?"

"Rarely. I mostly observe," she said, pointing to a video camera mounted at the ceiling in the corner of the room. "For most people, lying generates enormous stress loads. Generally the interrogator leaves the room after an hour or so, sometimes just for ten or fifteen minutes, so that we can watch how the suspect responds to the relief of that pressure. I've seen people so exhausted from lying that they fall asleep in here."

"You don't use lie detectors?"

"Occasionally," she said. "When the suspects don't give themselves away. You do it in three parts. First you're just friendly and nonjudgmental. You say, 'Tell me what happened, in your own words.' The second time, you get them to repeat the story point for point, almost like you forgot what they said the first time or you want to get it straight. Then you compare the two versions, and in the third interview you challenge them and say, 'The first time you said the car was blue, but the second time you said the car was white.' People who tell the truth tell the same story twice. The truth doesn't change. People who lie can't remember what they said the first time they lied. Or they start adding details they think will make the lie more believable."

"And then they crack!"

"Usually," Dani said. "You have to know where to apply the pressure. It's the ones who believe their own lies or who feel nothing that are the scary ones. Which brings us to this guy, Amos Kasden."

She brought up the photograph of the murderer. He was fair-haired and had a fair complexion, a long neck, a prominent Adam's apple, thin lips, an aquiline nose bending slightly to the left, and blank blue eyes. She told Quinn what she knew of Amos's childhood, the abuse at the hands of his alcoholic father, and how Amos had ruthlessly dealt with it. She'd diagnosed him as having a severe dissociative identity disorder, a boy who did not feel real. He could do brutal things to Julie Leonard because he didn't think she was real either. Dani didn't mention any of the supernatural elements that had led her to the conclusion she knew Quinn would never accept. She had pictures of the body taken at the crime scene, and she had Julie's autopsy report, if he wanted to see it, but he didn't.

"Well then, let's get to the good part," he said. "That's why I'm here, right?"

She opened the file containing the proteomic workup Banerjee had ordered. Quinn studied it all quickly.

"No neuroimaging to go with this, I wouldn't suppose?" he asked as he read.

"We have an MRI."

"Oh goody," Quinn said, reading from the report. "*Microtiter plate format*, good, like that. *Antiserum binding sites* . . . blah, blah, blah . . . *peroxidase conjugates*, excellent . . . so on and so forth . . . So we have just two tissue samples, one from the cerebellum and one from the forebrain?"

"This is it," Dani said.

He read a moment. "And you say there was no cytomas?"

"No tumors," Dani said.

"Where'd the dopamine go?" he said to no one in particular. "Probably where the vanillylmandelic acid went. Hmm . . ."

He read in silence for another minute, then asked Dani if the computer had unrestricted Internet access. When she said yes, he told her if she had anything else she needed to do today, now would be a good time, because he was going to need to look at all the numbers for the next hour or so, and he did his best thinking alone. Dani knew that once Quinn was lost in thought, it could be awhile before he found his way back, so she wrote her password on a Post-it, stuck it on the screen, and left.

She took the elevator up to the second floor and found Stuart Metz at his desk, working on his computer.

"Got a sec?"

"Sure," he said as he hit Save and turned toward her.

"Anything on Abbie?"

Metz shook his head. "The LEOs want to call it an FDSTW and punt it back out the Sally port," he said. "Or to paraphrase Sherlock Holmes, 'When you've eliminated the possible, just admit you're too stupid to figure it out and give up.'"

Dani had heard enough cop slang to know that a LEO was a law enforcement officer. The garage where they let prisoners out of the back of a squad car was the Sally port. FDSTW stood for *found dead, stayed that way.*

"Casey's getting the okay today from Irene for a warrant to search the Gardener house," Metz told her. "He's afraid they're going to find George in bed ART."

"Stuart—"

"Assumed room temperature," he said. "Last one, I promise. Casey thinks George might have assisted his mother's suicide and then done himself in."

"I must PMN," Dani said, smiling, as she spun around. As she left she called over her shoulder, "Powder my nose."

She wanted to ask Luisa, the receptionist, if she knew when Detective Casey was expected, but at the front desk she saw a note saying Luisa would be back in five. As she waited, Dani tried to read the cover of a Spanish-language edition of *People*, her attention drawn to a photograph of Cassandra Morton. She appeared to be doing nothing more than walking through an airport. The headline read, in a large red font, *SE LE ROMPIÓ CORAZÓN*, and beneath that, in a smaller font, *Su Lucha Valiente*. When Luisa returned, Dani asked for a translation.

"It says 'He broke her heart.'" Luisa told her, "'*Su lucha valiente*' means 'her brave struggle.' That poor woman. She has such bad luck with men."

"Poor Cassandra," Dani said, "picking 999 bad men in a row. I mean, mathematically, what are the odds that that could possibly be true?"

She stopped when she saw the look on Luisa's face—she couldn't have been more hurt if Dani had told her her baby was ugly.

"I'm sorry," Dani said, feeling like an idiot.

"That's okay," Luisa said. "I bet that's the kind of thing you sometimes wish you could say to your therapy patients."

Dani laughed. "Promise me that will be our little secret?"

The lights above the elevator indicated that someone was on the way up. She waited, hoping it was Tommy, though he didn't know where she was and she had no reason to expect him. When the doors opened she saw Detective Casey, wearing a tan windbreaker and a Boston Red Sox cap.

"You're a brave man to wear that hat around here," she said.

"If you're brave enough to be seen with me," he said, "we're going up to the Gardener place in about an hour. I've got a locksmith meeting us there. What are you doing here, by the way?"

"I brought in a friend," Dani said. "An expert, to consult on the Amos Kasden postmortem. Just in case there's more where that came from."

"More kids like Amos?" Casey said. "I certainly hope not. One was too many. Let me know if you learn anything. I'll be in my office. You'll be in the building?"

"Sure," Dani said. "Do you mind if I bring Tommy?"

"He knew George, right? I mean, well enough to ID him, if it comes to that?"

"He did."

"Yeah, bring him. And, Dani? If your friend figures anything out about Amos Kasden, I'd like to hear it."

"You will."

When she called Tommy's cell, she was surprised that Carl answered.

He said Tommy was out in the chicken coop, getting eggs from the exotics he kept as a hobby. Dani told him about the warrant to get inside the Gardener house and asked him to have Tommy call her.

"My friend Quinn is going over the labs we got back on Amos Kasden," Dani said. "Hopefully between that and the sample we got from whoever left it at Starbucks, we'll know more soon."

"What sample was that?"

"Are you getting forgetful in your senility?" Dani joked. "Anyway, I'll let you know if we learn anything. If Quinn can't figure it out, nobody can."

"Where are you now?"

"At the DA's, in Kisco. Can I ask you a question, Carl? And please don't tell Tommy I asked. But does he ever talk to you about Cassandra Morton? Just guy-to-guy stuff?"

"Guy to guy?" Carl paused, but in the silence, Dani had her answer. A simple no would not have taken any thought. He coughed. "Excuse me. Not since it happened. Why?"

"Her picture was on the cover of a Spanish edition of *People*," Dani said. "Some soccer player just dumped her. I must be a lot more jealous than I'm willing to admit. Jealousy is never really about the other person, you know. It's about your own feelings of inadequacy."

"Well," Carl said, "I suppose it's only human. See you soon."

As Dani pocketed her phone, she was struck by the way Carl had pronounced the word *human*, detecting—though she was probably mistaken—a note approaching scorn. Weird day.

She was passing Detective Casey's office when she heard him call her name. He gestured for her to come in, and when she did, he pointed at his computer monitor.

"Who's this nut job?" He pointed at the video feed from Interview 2 and then clicked to unmute the sound.

"This just . . . well, there you have it," Quinn was saying, leaning forward to stare at the numbers on his screen. "It's ridiculous, but Bob's your uncle. I certainly wouldn't cross the street . . . I don't see . . . Wait a minute . . . No . . ."

"That's the guy I was telling you about," Dani said. "Analyzing the postmortem for Amos Kasden."

From the looks of it, Quinn had already filled multiple pages of a legal pad with notes and scribblings and molecular diagrams.

"Who's he talking to?"

"I'm never sure," Dani said, smiling. "Either himself, or he hasn't realized yet that I left the room an hour ago." On the monitor they saw Quinn push away from the desk and then throw his pen down. "Looks like he's finished."

"Shall we?" Casey said, rising from his desk.

When they reached the hall leading to the interview rooms, they heard a fierce pounding on the door from the inside. Dani rushed forward and opened it. Quinn looked panicked.

"Sorry," she said. "They lock automatically."

"You could have told me," he said, calming down. "I was about ready to confess to something just to get out of there." Only then did he notice the surly-looking man standing beside her.

"Quinn, this is Detective Phillip Casey. We could see you on the monitor. It looked like you'd figured something out."

"May have," he said. "Liquid chromatography has its limitations, even with electrochemical detection. I started looking at kynurenine, glutamate, and GABAergic metabolites—"

"Hold on," Casey said. "If you don't mind, believe it or not, I'm not quite as smart as I look. Can you repeat that using high school English?"

Quinn pointed at the computer screen where the numbers giving the quantitation of isolated bioactive molecules awaited decoding. He sat in the rolling chair and turned the monitor toward Casey and Dani.

"How shall I put this?" Quinn said, nodding in deference to the detective. "Okay. Keeping it simple. Catecholamines are neurotransmitting hormones synthesized from phenylalanine and tyrosine, and they share the same dihydroxybenzene group—"

Casey jerked his head back as if he'd just caught a whiff of something unpleasant. Quinn stopped to regroup.

"Simpler still. In your car's engine," Quinn said, starting over, "you have a variety of fluids that the engine needs to work. You have gasoline and oil and brake fluid and water and antifreeze and power steering fluid and transmission fluid—"

"Not in the engine," Casey said.

"Whatever," Quinn said. "My point is, in a car, each of these fluids has its own system of tubes and reservoirs, and they don't mix. So if your brakes don't work, you know you're out of brake fluid. If the engine stops, you know you're out of gas. All right?"

"With you so far," Casey said.

"Suppose you take all the fluids and mix them in one big tank," Quinn continued. "It isn't a particularly good analogy, but this is something like the fluids in the brain. They're all mixed together, but they all go to specific neurological receptors in the brain."

"Gotcha," Casey said.

"These tests on—what was his name?"

"Amos Kasden," Dani said.

"The tests I did on the cerebrospinal fluids found in Amos Kasden's brain sorted them out and measured how much of each was present, to compare to what we might expect in a normal brain. And sometimes we can say that if you find X amount of this, you can expect to find Y amount of that. Or that when the brain uses substance A, it divides it into B and C, so B plus C should equal A. Or that it divides A into B and C and uses B but not C, so you should find lots of metabolized B but no metabolized C. Okay?"

Casey nodded. Dani could see Quinn was growing frustrated at having to move so slowly.

"Maybe we should get into the details later," she told him. "What's the takeaway?"

"*Trying* to get there," Quinn said. "It's complicated. Catecholamines, meaning epinephrine, norepinephrine, and dopamine, are the chemicals produced by the adrenal glands that sit atop the kidneys, but what they do is help the body respond to stress. You've heard of epinephrine, which is also called adrenaline."

"It gives people superhuman strength," Casey said. "This would be a lot easier to understand if everything didn't have two names, you know."

"I agree," Quinn said. "Anyway, adrenaline almost instantaneously speeds the heart rate, makes enormous stores of energy available to the muscles, and fine-tunes the senses. That's what makes it so valuable to us in stress situations, sometimes providing the superhuman strength you mentioned."

"What does dopamine do?" Casey said. "In a stress situation? I know from working narcotics that drugs like cocaine or methamphetamine flood the brain with it, and that's why those things are so addicting."

"Yes," Quinn said. "Dopamine is, in a sense, a kind of natural pain-killer because it gives pleasure. Dopamine reduces sensitivity to pain by binding the opioid receptors, but it's also how the brain rewards itself. Food can release it. Sex. Narcotics, but also aggression. People who experience an adrenaline rush, rescuing someone from a burning building, feel a very natural and very intoxicating high afterward from the dopamine. It can take hours for it to wear off."

"Which is why guys get addicted to skydiving or rock climbing."

"Yes, and it's also why some people get addicted to violence. What's interesting is that sometimes these people don't really care if they come out on the right or wrong side of that violence. They can kick the stuffing out of somebody, or get the stuffing kicked out of them, and it's all the same, as long as they get the adrenaline rush. These people actually enjoy getting beat up."

Casey leaned back in his chair. "That makes more sense than I wish it did," he said.

Dani slid her chair toward Quinn's to get a better view of the screen. "So how was Amos's brain different from normal brains?"

"If you can bear with me a bit longer," Quinn said, turning again to Casey. "My specialty, at least right now, has been looking at how catecholamines, which also strongly affect mood, function in autistic people. More specifically, what happens to autistics when they reach puberty and become flooded with testosterone and estrogen. I presume you know what happens to normal kids when they hit puberty."

"I used to work juvenile crime," Casey said. "I understand the sudden sex drive, but what I never got is how their IQs go down 50 percent."

"Not quite fifty," Quinn said. "But that has more to do with the dis-inhibition of impulse control in the forebrain." He tapped himself on the forehead, then pointed to the lower back part of his skull. "My work involves the cerebellum, back here. Which is where we find something called the Purkinje cells. Dani?"

"I remember the name," she said. "Aren't they the largest neurons in the brain?"

"Second largest," Quinn said. "But yes, they're quite large. Purkinje cells are also very flat, and they line up in a row like dominos on a two-dimensional X/Y axis, and other cells pass through them on the Z axis."

"In the cerebellum," Casey said.

"Yes," Quinn said. "A part of the brain that hasn't changed much in the last few million years. And we find a significantly reduced number of Purkinje cells in the cerebellums of autistic children. We know that prenatal estrogen promotes the growth of Purkinje cells, so the thinking is that this explains why the vast majority of autistic children are male. The cerebellum also plays a strong role in regulating pleasure or fear. Autistic children have trouble identifying emotions, in themselves and in others. They don't know when to be afraid, and they feel very little pleasure. Now, getting back to our friend Amos here—" Quinn put his hand on the back of his neck and winced briefly from what appeared to be a sudden sharp pain.

"Are you all right?" Dani asked.

"Something I ate," Quinn said, waving off the pain as a minor inconvenience. "Dani told me Amos was taking part in a drug trial and gave me a sample of the drug she thinks he may have been taking."

"Oh, did she?" Casey said, looking at Dani with surprise.

"I was going to tell you about it once we had the results."

"Which we do," Quinn said. "I got an e-mail from my friend at Columbia, who did a fine job, I must say. I think she stayed up all night."

"I didn't know it was a she," Dani teased.

"Illena," Quinn said. "She's the reason I had to dump Otto on you. She's allergic to dogs. Anyway, the medication Amos was on appears to be an SSRI. That's a selective serotonin—"

"Reuptake inhibitor. I know what an SSRI is," Casey said. "It's an antidepressant."

"It's a class of antidepressants," Quinn said. "Including Prozac and Zoloft and Celexa and the like. The drug Amos was testing seems to have been sort of a one-pill-fits-all designer antidepressant. If I had any money and knew what company invented this thing, I'd buy as much stock as I could. Amos should have been flooded with good feelings."

"But he wasn't," Casey said.

"No," Quinn agreed. "His adrenaline and noradrenaline weren't being utilized, and his dopamine levels were nonexistent, except, I suspect, from what Dani told me about his psychopathic behaviors, when he could self-medicate with violence. Remember that catecholamines regulate the fight-flight response. I think the drug he was taking created a craving for that sort of behavior. The fight. Not the flight."

"Well, that ain't good," Casey said.

"It gets worse," Quinn said. "I could be wrong, but here's what I think. If this medication were given to children, or if it were taken by pregnant women, it would create a large population of boys, and some girls too, who would seem to be very happy and content, and they would seem like perfect students and get straight As."

"You could sell a lot of something like that," Dani said.

"Yes, you certainly could," Quinn said.

"Is this the Provivilan everyone is talking about?"

"No," Quinn said. "It's something else. Maybe a beta version. I don't know."

"So what's the problem?" Casey asked.

"The problem is that in that population of boys and girls, the medication would both induce an artificial case of autism and mask it. By inhibiting the Purkinje cells. The kids would seem sweet and slightly robotic."

"Stepford children," Dani said.

Quinn looked puzzled.

"It's an old horror movie," Dani said. "Which I gather you never saw."

"I didn't," Quinn said. "Anyway, for a while you wouldn't know there was a problem."

"Until?" Casey asked.

"Until they hit puberty," Quinn said.

"What would happen then?" Casey said.

"Well, in autistic children, the onset of puberty and the hormonal influx that that involves often result in outbursts of uncontrollable anger."

"What would happen in normal children who take the drug?" Dani said. "Or whose mothers took it when they were pregnant?"

"The girls would be the lucky ones, relatively speaking. They'd have all the usual problems with sexual maturation, multiplied by a factor of maybe ten. Maybe more. The boys would fare much worse."

"How so?" Casey asked.

"It's hard to predict."

"Try."

"I'd say," Quinn said, taking a deep breath, "with a fair amount of certainty, that they would become, rather quickly, emotionally overstimulated beyond their ability to cope."

"Uh-oh," Casey said.

"And then," Quinn continued, "they would become physically and emotionally addicted to the pleasure-giving dopamine released by angry outbursts and violent behavior, without caring about whether or not what they did was self-destructive."

Quinn paused to let his words sink in.

"Assisted by the release of adrenaline and noradrenaline, producing feats of superhuman strength," he concluded. "I, for one, would not want to be around when it happens. I thought of a name for the compound in Amos's brain. Sort of catchy."

"What?" Dani asked.

"I might call it the 'Doomsday Molecule,'" Quinn said.

18.

"Was that my phone?" Tommy said as he set a stainless steel colander with a half dozen large fresh eggs the color of mahogany on the kitchen counter.

"It was Dani," Carl said. "She said they're going over to the Gardener farm with a warrant. She was hoping we could join her."

"How'd she sound?"

"A little tired. She's going over the lab results on Amos Kasden with her ex-fiancé, Quinn Whatshisname."

"Technically, they weren't officially engaged," Tommy said.

"These days, who knows what's official?" Carl said. "Whatever happened to the rock you got Cassandra?"

"It's parked in the garage."

Carl looked confused.

"When she gave the engagement ring back, I sold it on eBay and bought the V-Rod."

"I have to say, I was looking forward to officiating at that wedding."

Tommy was placing the eggs in a tray in his refrigerator.

"You ever think about her?" Carl said.

"Who?"

"Cassandra."

"Not really. I guess when I see her picture in the supermarket checkout line, sometimes I think, 'There but for the grace of God go I.'"

"You dodged a bullet."

"I wouldn't say that, exactly, but it all worked out for the best. And if I hadn't, I wouldn't have met Dani. Everything happens for a reason. Why do you ask?"

"I guess she's on some magazine cover again," Carl said. "Some soccer player broke her heart."

Tommy shrugged. "It's always something. Or someone. I told her she could call me if she ever needed to," he said. "I think we'd just seen *Toy Story*. Whichever one had the song 'You've Got a Home in Me.' That's what I told her. I actually misquoted it. The line is 'You've got a *friend* in me.' I'm glad she hasn't called. She was a lot of work. Hey, I gotta go fill the feed bins."

Once Tommy had returned to the coop, Carl checked out the window to make sure he was busy, then picked up Tommy's cell phone and searched his contacts list. Carl's body ached, a throbbing in his muscles and joints, as if he were coming down with a fever. He tried to tell his hands not to do what they were doing, but the more he tried to resist, the more they hurt. When he found the listing for Cassandra Morton, he scrolled down until he located a mobile number marked as private. He opened the screen to send a text message, tapped in the words REMEMBER—YOU'VE GOT A HOME IN ME. XO, and then put the phone back where he found it. The part of him that was still Carl felt guilty for betraying his friend, but when he thought he needed to warn Tommy, a louder voice in his head said, *You will not!* as an electric charge shot through him and left a sizzling sound in his ears. *That is just a small taste of the pain I can give you—my power over you is complete!*

When his cell phone rang an hour later, Tommy picked up and, sounding surprised, said, "Oh, hey—we were just talking about you . . . All right. See you then."

"Who was that?" Carl asked.

"Dani. Just letting us know she's headed for the farm."

"I wonder if she's bringing Quinn," Carl said. "I'd love to meet him. She tells me he's an absolute genius."

Tommy drove the Jeep, pausing momentarily a mile from his house to move aside a deer carcass lying in the middle of the road, a stag with a full set of antlers and what Tommy took for a frightened look on its face, mouth frozen open, eyes wide. Tommy knew he was probably projecting. It was, after all, rutting season, and deer were everywhere. He used his phone to call a nearby wolf sanctuary where a nonprofit conservancy was trying to raise and eventually restore to the wild endangered populations of Mexican gray and red wolves. He told the director where she could find the carcass, as local roadkill made up a large part of the wolves' diet. Carl stayed in the car while Tommy dragged the buck to the side of the road. Tommy didn't mind, but it was unlike Carl not to volunteer his assistance.

He saw Dani's car parked in front of the Gardener farmhouse, next to a police cruiser and a white panel van with a large gold key painted on the side. Beyond the house the water of Lake Atticus was gray and choppy, waves driven by a cold wind from the north. One of the cops waiting by the car was Tommy's friend, Frank DeGidio, who had his hands deep in the pockets of his uniform jacket for warmth.

"Tomaso!" DeGidio called out. "I wasn't expecting *you*."

"Dr. Harris called and asked us to come by," Tommy said.

"I got a guy says you and her were homecoming king and queen back in the day."

"Don't hold it against me. Or her."

"Wouldn't dream of it. I know how tough it can be to be popular."

"No, ya don't, Frank," Tommy said, patting his friend on the shoulder.

Frank saw Tommy pull something out of his jacket pocket. "What's that?"

"Infrared camera," Tommy said, showing it to him. He pointed it at the house, which registered the same temperature as the air around it. He pointed it at the second cop. "Did you know your partner has chemical hand warmers in his pockets?"

"Are you kiddin' me?" he said. He turned to his partner. "Jimmy, you holding out on me?"

They joined Dani, Detective Casey, and the locksmith on the porch. The locksmith had an old manual he was consulting to research antique locks.

Tommy put his arm around Dani, gave her a hug, and kissed her. "How you holding up? Where's Quinn?"

"He went to walk the dog," she said. "Who is eating me out of house and home. But Arlo loves him. I didn't know cats and dogs could get along so well."

"I thought Quinn was staying at the inn."

"Quinn is. His dog isn't." She looked over her shoulder to the locksmith. "Apparently the lock on the door is straight out of the Middle Ages."

Detective Casey interrupted them, holding a business card between his two fingers like his number had been called at the deli counter.

"Dani says you both met this guy," he said. "His card was under the door knocker."

"George asked him to come by to appraise his mother's art collection," Tommy said.

"Oh yeah?" Casey said. "When did he do this?"

"After his mother died," Tommy said. "Actually, I take that back. He didn't say when George asked him. Just that he left a message."

"Well, then he should be here, shouldn't he?" Casey said. "I'd like to talk to him."

Casey told DeGidio to send someone to pick up Julian Villanegre and invite him to join them. While Casey made arrangements, Dani brought Tommy and Carl up to speed as briefly as possible on the theories and explanations Quinn had laid out after looking at Amos Kasden's pro-teomics. She told them the drug they'd gotten a sample of promised to create walking time bombs, children programmed to explode into anger they'd never be able to control.

"Was the sample you gave him Provivilan?" Carl asked her.

"No way to know."

"Have you figured out who provided it?"

"No. And I don't dare text him because it might give him away," she said. "We haven't had any luck tracing the cell number."

Finally the locksmith got the door open. He then asked Casey if he could take the lock mechanism out of the door and study it because he'd never encountered anything like it. He was clearly disappointed when Casey told him he didn't have the authority to allow that.

Casey opened the door, stepped into the darkness, looked around for a second, then moved aside so the others could enter. Outside the daylight was fading.

Casey noticed the glow of Tommy's handheld infrared. "You looking for ghosts?"

"Demons," Tommy said. "But they're only going to show up if they're standing still."

Casey smiled at what he took for a joke. "Anything?"

"You'll know when I know, Detective," Tommy said, smiling back. He used the scanner to sweep the living room. Carl ducked behind him so as not to get in the way. "All clear."

Casey nodded his head.

DeGidio turned on his flashlight and used it to locate a wall switch, but when he flipped it, nothing happened. Tommy could make out only dimly outlined shapes. The cop with the hand warmers was sent to look for the breaker box. A moment later, he called out from the hall off the back kitchen. "Found it!"

Suddenly the house was filled with light.

"Holy guacamole," Tommy said.

The inside of the home was as elegant and well appointed as the outside was rough and overgrown. Tommy said it reminded him of the Mark Twain House in Hartford that he'd visited on a class trip in middle school. Dani had been on the same trip, different bus, but she agreed. The floors were made of intricate wooden tiles and parquetry; the kitchen floor was polished black-and-white marble. Every room save the kitchen and the parlor had exquisite Persian rugs and Oriental kilims. The interior trim was polished black walnut. Tiffany lamps. The furniture in the living room and library favored Mission and Stickley. The books in the library included leather-bound first editions, Carl noted, of various texts on religion, philosophy, art, history, medicine, and anthropology, as well as works of literature, many in languages other than English, shelved next to their English translations. The walls of the two-story library, where they weren't filled with rosewood bookshelves, were hung with tapestries, one that had to be fifteen by fifteen feet. In the recessed nooks and alcoves were sculptures of ballet dancers in the style of Degas and distended graceful figurines that seemed to be in the style of Giacometti—until Dani took a closer look and announced that as far as she could tell, they weren't works in the *style* of Degas or Giacometti—they were works *by* Degas and Giacometti.

More remarkable than that were the paintings on the walls. The kitchen and the dining room walls were crowded with modernist works by artists ranging from Monet to Picasso to Hammerstein. The rest of the house was decorated with the art of the Old Masters. These tended to have sacred themes, Italian Renaissance Adorations of the Magi and Crucifixions; Annunciations and Assumptions; Stations of the Cross; depictions of St. Jerome with a lion and St. Agnes with a lamb and St. Peter holding keys; Pietàs and scenes from the life of Christ; depictions of dramatic scenes from the Bible, like the fall of Jericho and Moses parting the Red Sea to lead God's people out of captivity. Radiant oils glowing inside their gilt frames against the blood-red wall coverings.

"You looking at these, Carl?" Tommy said to his friend.

"I'm in the library," Carl called from the room adjacent. "Pretty amazing."

What they did not find was anything resembling a telephone, television, or computer. The sole concession to technology was a black, boxy radio on the kitchen table. The other thing they did not find was any sign of George Gardener. His grimy work overalls hung from a hook in the back mudroom, and his splattered work boots sat on a black rubber mat beneath them. The refrigerator was empty, as was the freezer, indicating that wherever George had gone, he'd intended to stay awhile.

In contrast to the classic opulence of the rooms downstairs, the five bedrooms upstairs were sparse to the point of monastic, each containing a simple single bed, a dresser, and a closet. Each had a large cross on the wall, and below it, a desk with a Bible on it. These were places to pray, Tommy thought. He wanted to get Carl's opinion, but his friend seemed content to stay downstairs, examining the books in the library.

After they'd looked in each room in the house, they gathered in the living room.

"Anybody?" Casey said.

"I got nothing," said DeGidio. "Jimmy and I'll check the other buildings."

"Dani?"

"I don't understand how anybody could leave a house like this unprotected," she said.

"I had the same thought," Casey said. "Though if nobody knows about it, I suppose you could imagine it would be safe. But still . . . Tommy?"

"If George took off, he had time to prepare. It wasn't a sudden thing. He was ready."

"Carl?"

"I could spend the rest of my life in that library," he said. "It's practically the essential repository of human knowledge."

"Minus pop culture," Tommy added.

"This might be helpful," Casey said as they all turned toward the headlights coming up the drive. A minute later, a uniformed officer escorted Dr. Julian Villanegre and a man whom Tommy introduced to Casey. "Ben Whitehorse. He's a friend. From the Midwest."

"Nice to meet you," Casey said, shaking the man's hand. "And don't take this the wrong way," he said, turning to the escorting officer, "but what's he doing here? This isn't an open house."

"Dr. Villanegre said—"

"My new friend insisted that I bring him," Villanegre said, looking around the room with deep satisfaction and admiration. "You can make him wait outside, I suppose, but I thought his opinion might be useful. I met him at the inn this morning and we've been talking all day. He knows more about pre-Columbian art than I do. Not my field. Do you mind?"

"Do I mind?" Casey said, still baffled. He looked at Whitehorse, who was smiling placidly. "I guess not, but try not to touch anything. You said George Gardener contacted you about appraising his art collection?"

"He did indeed."

"When was this?"

"Several weeks ago," Villanegre said. "I gathered that he'd seen my name in some sort of press release or newspaper story and knew I'd be in town."

"But you never met him?"

"No," Villanegre said, unable to keep his eyes on the detective. "Do you mind if I have a quick look-see?"

"That's why I wanted you here," Casey said. "Knock yourself out."

"Indeed," Villanegre said. The art historian moved from painting to painting slowly, leaning in close, peering into the corners of some, studying the ways the paint had cracked and flaked, and with two of the paintings, he moved the frames away from the walls to look behind them. Ben Whitehorse accompanied him, keeping out of his way.

When Villanegre was finished, he strolled with his hands behind his back halfway into the library, took a step into the kitchen, glanced up the stairs, then returned to the living room.

"There are a few more on the upstairs landing," Casey said.

"I know it might be difficult to give an estimate," Dani said, "but what would you say, ballpark, the collection might be worth?"

"I could be wrong, of course," Villanegre said, "but I'd say the entire collection might be worth something in the range of one hundred and fifty thousand dollars."

"That's all?" Tommy said.

"Perhaps not that much," Villanegre said. "Every picture in this room is a fake. They're rather good fakes, so I suppose they'd have some value to people who wanted to collect handmade copies. The rug we're standing on has a stamp on the back, under that corner there, that says it was made in a factory in South Carolina. It's a nice enough rug, but it's not worth what the owner wants you to think it's worth."

"But it's a nice house," Ben said. "A house is a place to live, not an investment. It's a good place to live, surrounded by all these beautiful pictures of Jesus and scenes from the Bible."

"Did you look at the books in the library?" Carl asked the Englishman.

Tommy noticed that Carl seemed uncomfortable in Ben's presence, unable to look him in the eye. He wasn't sure how to account for it apart from the general observation that Carl had seemed out of sorts lately, paler, with bags under his eyes, and more often lost in thought.

"I'm not an antiquarian," Villanegre said. "I could recommend one."

"I'm thinking we need to widen our search for George," Casey said. "I talked to Irene. She's ready to call Abbie's death 'cause unknown' and let it go. Anybody here agree with that?"

No one spoke.

"Well, I want to keep looking," Casey said. "I don't like it when people die and I can't figure out why. Maybe George doesn't know either, but he was the last person to talk to her. Does anybody have anything to say?"

There was only silence.

"I'm hungry," Ben said.

Tommy walked Dani to her car. He felt a strong desire to be alone with her, where no one could get between them or hear them talk.

"I really need to see you tonight," he said.

"I need to see you too," she said, leaning into him.

"But I have an errand I have to run first."

"It can't wait?"

"No," he said as he handed her a slip of paper. "I found this on George Gardener's desk. I didn't want the others to see it. It was propped up, like something he needed to remember to do before he disappeared. It's probably nothing."

Dani read the note.

It said *Warn Ruth*.

19.

It would not be a challenge, the beast thought, but perhaps it would afford a diversion. There would be no resistance and so there was no need for haste. The old librarian lived in a small cottage set back from the road, where her screams would not be heard by any nosy neighbors. She could be taken easily—bent and broken—and she would talk. Surprise would not be necessary, though some satisfaction could be derived from the shocked expression on her face as she realized her worst nightmares were coming true.

The thing took form in the woods behind the old woman's cottage, on a hill above it. Feeling no hurry, it pounced on a deer and tore its head off, grasping it by the antlers and snapping and twisting in one brutal, lethal shake. It raised the carcass in the air and drank the blood gushing from the neck, not because it required sustenance, but because it liked the taste of blood, then threw the carcass high into the trees to leave a signature.

Through the kitchen window it could see the librarian at her sink doing the dishes. The oriel window looked out on the small garden she kept in the backyard, with bird feeders filled with suet, and mulch on the perennials. With all the lights on in the kitchen, the librarian would not be able to see very far beyond the reflected glare of her own windowpanes.

The beast moved down the hill, slinking on all fours, its talons ripping the earth as it moved. In the darkness behind the cottage it stood up on its hind legs, trying to decide the best place to enter.

Then, beyond the hill, it heard the whine of an engine. At the top of the hill a single headlight appeared, a man on a motorcycle approaching at great speed. When the motorcycle screeched to a halt in front of the cottage, the thing recognized the rider. Its instructions were to destroy the librarian, but the man on the motorcycle, her nephew, was a future target. The opportunity had presented itself to strike them both down. Would the masters be pleased, the beast wondered, or would they punish? It decided to wait to see what the two humans said to each other first. Perhaps they would divulge the whereabouts of the book. Knowing it could not depend on invisibility, it pressed its back against the cottage, where its light-absorbing armored skin would conceal it well.

Tommy was relieved to see his aunt through the kitchen window. He knocked on the door, and a moment later the light came on in the enclosed porch, where small stained-glass sun catchers hung from varying lengths of fishing line to receive the morning light.

"What a nice surprise!" she said. "Have you eaten? I have a nice lasagna I could heat up."

"No thanks," Tommy said. "How are you?"

"I'm fine. I was trying to finish knitting that sweater I'm making for your father for Christmas."

He smiled and then produced the handheld infrared camera from his pocket and flipped up the screen.

"What in the world is that?"

"Energy audit. This camera detects heat. Or cold."

He stepped back out onto the enclosed porch, opened the door, and quickly scanned the road behind him. Nothing unusual.

"Why do you have it?" she said when he returned to the kitchen. "I don't need an energy audit."

"Yes, you do," he said. "Last winter your heating bills were through the roof. Which was also where all your heat was going."

"Last winter was the coldest in years," she said, still puzzled by his sudden appearance. He left her in the kitchen to quickly scan the living room and the den, and when he pointed it at the ceiling, the images were normal. He returned to the kitchen.

Aunt Ruth was ready for an explanation. "What in the world?"

He put his finger to his lips to shush her. He pointed the scanner at her and saw how beautifully she radiated warmth, a finding he knew was as true figuratively as it was literally. But when he moved the scanner slightly to her left, he saw it—a massive dark blue outline with blurred edges, just on the other side of the kitchen's back wall. His pulse quickened. He gestured for his aunt to come see what his screen was showing him.

"So how are the Thanksgiving plans coming?" he said as she leaned in to look at the screen. Her expression grew more puzzled when she saw the blue shadow on her wall.

"What is—?"

Tommy shushed her again, then made a "keep it coming" gesture with his free hand to get her to keep talking as he approached the wall to take a closer reading.

"Thanksgiving plans are coming along fine," she said. "I made the strawberry-rhubarb pie tonight. That's your favorite, isn't it?"

Tommy put his hand to the wall. It was ice cold.

He noticed that on his aunt's refrigerator she kept a magnetic whiteboard and a marker for reminders. It read, in his aunt's perfect cursive, *Pick up turkey from Bredeson's.* He took the whiteboard from the refrigerator, where it was surrounded by family photographs and artwork the children from the library had drawn for her, erased her message, and wrote: *There is something outside the house.*

She gestured to ask what it was.

Wendigo

She took the pen from him.

Ha ha. Seriously.

"I talked to Dani, and she said she could make the corn bread," he said, writing: *Seriously. We are in danger.*

"That would be lovely," Aunt Ruth said. "I was going to make the cranberry sauce you like."

You are scaring me!!! she wrote.

I'm scared too

"I was thinking of inviting Charlie," Tommy said, raising his voice when he said the name. "I want to say, 'Hey, Charlie—we could use your help right about now.'"

Who is Charlie? she wrote.

Angel

She added a question mark: *Angel?*

He erased the question mark and wrote: *Angel! Will explain later.*

"How many people are you expecting?" he said, taking a large carving knife from the wooden cutlery holder. He opened the door to her broom closet, looking for something else they could use as a weapon. Nothing.

"About a dozen," she said. Tommy crouched low and scuttled across the floor, out of view of whatever might be standing outside the window, and opened the cabinet doors below the sink. Again, nothing.

"I was thinking that there are going to be children here," he said. "I don't suppose you keep any weapons in the house, do you? We want to make sure there isn't anything dangerous that little kids might get their hands on."

"What would a librarian be doing with weapons in her house?" she said, moving to her coat closet, where she reached in and grabbed a twelve-gauge pump-action shotgun. She reached into the closet a second time, grabbed a handful of shells, chambered four shells, and flicked off the safety.

"Whatever happened to that bird gun your grandfather used to hunt ducks with?" she asked as she handed him the gun.

"I don't know," Tommy said. He watched with surprise as his aunt reached back into the closet and pulled out a .45 caliber Colt automatic.

"You know how your grandfather loved guns. Did you know I once dated a policeman?" she said, filling her apron pockets with extra clips. "He used to take me shooting at the target range in Danbury. I quite enjoyed it."

"Are you kidding me?" Tommy said.

"What other stereotypes about librarians would you like me to debunk?" she said, expertly cocking the pistol.

Tommy tried to think. Escape wasn't an option, and standing to fight was not a good idea either. He said a quick prayer but readied the shotgun all the same.

Then the lights went out.

"What happened?" he said.

"Oh, the wind is always knocking the trees down around here," she said. She reached into the closet for a flashlight, but when she turned it on, Tommy covered the beam with his hand and whispered, "No lights!" She turned it off.

Using the scanner, he saw that the thing outside the house was moving. He followed the blue image as it began to slowly circle the house. He kept the shotgun pointed where the scanner told him the demon was. His aunt stayed behind him, holding her weapon with two hands in a way that showed she knew what she was doing.

They backed into the living room and paused as the large silhouette stopped on the other side of the front door. Tommy watched the doorknob turn as it glowed on his screen, bluer and bluer. Then it stopped turning, and the shape began to move again. It was now standing outside the picture window.

Tommy opened up on the demon, firing four thundering shotgun blasts through the glass as fast as he could, shattering the window and splintering the frame. His aunt opened fire a split second after he did, flames spitting from the muzzle of her pistol to make the room flash with light a dozen times.

Tommy reloaded quickly, grabbing shells from his coat pocket, and then moved to the window to scan outside the house.

The screen read blank. The demon was gone. For now.

Aunt Ruth turned on her flashlight to survey the room.

"Maybe we should have Thanksgiving at my house this year?" Tommy said.

"Maybe we should," his aunt said. "Do you think we hurt it?"

"I don't know," Tommy replied. "I think it's more afraid of attracting attention. You'll be safer at my house. I just hope it's not headed that way."

20.

Tommy's cell phone rang on the way to his house at the wheel of his Aunt Ruth's car. He'd retrieve his motorcycle tomorrow, when he met the glass repairman at her house.

The director of the wolf sanctuary was on the other end, asking him again for the location of the deer carcass he'd reported. When Tommy told her, the woman said they'd scoured the exact area he'd described and found nothing.

"Maybe someone from the county or the local police already picked it up," he suggested.

"I've already checked with everyone I could think of. No one's seen it."

"Maybe some of the local wild wolves got to it first," Tommy joked.

When the director told him that the man she'd sent had indeed seen tracks in the dirt on the shoulder of the road, but nothing he could identify, Tommy told her to make sure the gates were locked, because you never knew what might be lurking in the shadows.

She laughed. He didn't.

Tommy carried his aunt's bags into his kitchen, re-armed his security system, and then put her things in his father's room.

When he returned, he watched with a mix of awe and admiration as she tended to her weapons, checked the safeties, reloaded, wiped them down thoroughly with a soft dish towel, and set them carefully on the food island. All the way to Tommy's house, she'd listened as he told her how the investigation into Amos Kasden and the murder of Julie Leonard had led them down a path that was, to say the least, unexpected, but one that was clearer with each passing day. She asked questions when she didn't understand something, but not for a moment did she express any doubt as to his interpretation of events. As he had parked her car in the courtyard, he asked her if she thought he was crazy to be talking about chasing demons.

"Thomas," she said, "when I was younger, I was like most young people—I thought I knew all the answers. Then I thought I knew the questions but not the answers. I stopped going to church for a few years when I realized I didn't even know the questions. But I came back when I realized that even if I didn't know the questions or the answers, Jesus does, and he'd give them to me when I needed them. I don't think you're crazy. I think you'd be foolish not to believe what you believe."

She was puzzled, though, by one thing: why had Abbie suggested that she, Ruth, was "the boy's best chance"?

"I can look things up in books, but anybody can do that," she said. "Why would she single me out? Assuming Ben was right in the first place."

"Ben knows things," Tommy said. "I'm not sure how, but he does."

He'd set his aunt's key chain on the food island, next to the strawberry-rhubarb pie she'd had the presence of mind to grab in case she couldn't get back into her kitchen before Thanksgiving. She promised to make Tommy his favorite, pecan pie, and a traditional pumpkin too, if she had time tomorrow.

He held up the smallest key. "What's this one?"

"That's to the gun chest."

"Gun chest?" Tommy said. "You mean there're more?"

"The policeman was a collector," she said. "He had no one to leave his collection to when he passed on. He thought I might appreciate them." She raised her hand to cut off the question on Tommy's lips. "Don't ask. You didn't know him. It was some time ago. I've moved on."

"Okay then," Tommy said, returning to the key chain. "How about this one? This looks a hundred years old."

"Library attic. It's probably older. As far as I know, it's the same key and the same lock they put in when the library was built 183 years ago."

"What's in the attic?"

"A lot of dusty old books," she said. "Town records. The figurines from the crèche we used to put out front at Christmas before the government said it wasn't allowed. Old newspapers. Now that I think of it, Abigail used to spend quite a bit of time up there before she went to the nursing home."

"Doing what?"

"Research. I didn't pry. A lot of old people come to the library just because they're lonely. Though she didn't mind being alone. I always told her I'd be happy to fetch whatever she needed and bring it downstairs for her, but she said it would be easier if she just stayed up there and didn't make anybody run up and down the stairs. I worried about her on those stairs, but you know how spry she was. She had her own little desk in the corner."

"What kind of research?"

"Town historical stuff, I think. I'm not really sure."

"Can we go have a look tomorrow?"

"We can if Leon has remembered to change the lightbulbs."

"I'll change the lightbulbs," Tommy said. "I think your hunch was right. Abbie knew you were more than just someone who could look things up in books."

His security system alerted him to a visitor at the gate. When he checked the video monitor, he saw Carl's face.

Tommy pressed the intercom. "Come on in."

"I can't. The keypad isn't working."

Tommy remembered that he'd changed the code, just in case, and gave him the new one.

Carl's arrival in the courtyard triggered Tommy's motion-sensor-activated floodlights. He had a large duffel bag thrown across the back of his bike, strapped to the black touring bag he'd slipped over the sissy bar.

Tommy turned from the window to see Ruth scowling at him. "You really need to stop this matchmaking," she said. "I can take care of myself."

"More than I would have guessed," Tommy said, eyeing the guns on the food island. "But I'm not matchmaking. I asked Carl to come over to help keep an eye on things. I don't think it's safe for any of us to fall asleep without someone on watch. Once I get you all settled in, I'm going to go get Dani."

"If we're going to the mattresses, I'm going to need supplies to make spaghetti."

"Going to the mattresses?" Tommy said. "Where'd you learn to talk like that?"

"Isn't that what they called it in *The Godfather*?"

"Yeah, I guess," Tommy said, shaking his head.

Tommy was happy to see his friend, knowing that three heads were better than two. Once he could be sure Dani was safe in his house, it would be five heads better than three, because she was smart enough to count twice.

As Tommy opened the back door for Carl, Ruth got up, saying she needed to go to her room to freshen up, and darted out of the room.

"Glad you could make it," Tommy told Carl. "Let me take that and throw it in the guestroom. You get a nap in?"

"I wish," Carl said.

Tommy knew that after losing his daughter, Carl had been treated for depression, had even undergone electroshock therapy. He claimed that the only thing that really helped him was to ride his motorcycle, because he found he could pray while he rode in a way he couldn't when he was in a quiet place alone with his thoughts. Tommy noticed a scab on the back of Carl's right hand and redness, as if he'd been scratching himself. Where his hair was thin on top, his scalp looked flaky as well. Dani was the mental health expert. He wondered what she'd think.

Carl eyed the guns on the countertop. "What's with the arsenal?"

"They're my aunt's," Tommy said. "She's a lot more dangerous than she looks."

"Apparently. What's that?"

"Strawberry-rhubarb pie."

To Tommy's surprise, Carl wrinkled his nose. Had he only been acting polite when he'd said he liked it?

"If the landline rings, would you pick it up? It might be Dani. If it is, please tell her to throw some clothes in a bag, because I'm on my way to get her."

"Will do," Carl said.

Tommy was worried. Dani hadn't called. When he reached her house, he rapped on the back door and was greeted by the barking of a dog that, viewed through the window, appeared to be the size of a water buffalo. Dani had inherited the house after losing her parents in a plane crash, but after being attacked by Amos Kasden in her own kitchen, and watching him die there when Tommy saved her, she was leaning toward selling it. Her memories of her parents were intact, but the house no longer contained them. Tommy saw a For Sale by Owner sign on her back porch, leaning against the railing, but it was still on the porch and not in the front yard.

He turned to see Dani's car pull into the driveway. She climbed out of her car and smiled to see him. When she reached the back steps, he took her in his arms and kissed her. She had a bag over her shoulder and shopping bags dangling from her arms, making it hard for her to reciprocate.

"Better," he said.

"Much better. I've been meaning to tell you I think we need to kiss more."

"Why didn't you say something?"

"I *was* saying it by batting my eyelashes."

"Is that what that was?" he said. "I thought you had allergies."

"There's a fifty-pound bag of dog food in the trunk, Romeo," she said. "Otto's probably hungry. Would you mind?"

"Maybe you should leave it in the car," Tommy said. "You didn't get my message? I think you should stay at my house for a while. Otto and Arlo too."

He quickly told her what had happened at his aunt's house, and when he'd finished she agreed that they needed to stay close together and be on constant alert.

"So Ruth knows?" Dani said.

"I couldn't exactly pretend it was just my imagination after blowing a giant hole in her house. She's on board. Not thrilled about having a demon on her trail, but she's in."

"Why was she attacked? Because Abbie mentioned her?"

"That's all I can think of."

"How do they know what Abbie said?"

"I don't know. Where's Quinn?"

"Good question," Dani said. "He seems to have disappeared. Okay, 'disappeared' makes it sound ominous. He's still checked in at the inn, but he asked the young woman at the front desk for a cab to the station in Katonah. I assume he's gone back to the city."

"Is he coming back?" Tommy said. Otto barked again.

"He'd better. I can't afford to feed that eating machine much longer."

"Grab everything you need," Tommy said, taking the keys from her hand and opening the door for her, "but make it quick. I don't like leaving Carl alone with my aunt for too long."

"Do you think they can't protect themselves?"

"I'm worried we're going to catch them making out when we get back."

"Speaking of which . . ." She grabbed him by the head and kissed him with all the passion she felt inside of her. "Who knows when we're going to get another chance?" she said when she finally pulled her lips from his.

"Yeah, who knows?" he said, throwing his arms around her. "Oh, look—here's another chance now." They kissed again and he lifted her off her feet for a long minute. Then he set her down. "I'll put the food back in the car, and then I'll help you pack. Tell me what to get. And don't forget your computer."

<hr />

His friends had told him when he'd closed on the mansion—with its ten bedrooms, high-tech security system, exterior walls built from stone and solid as those of a castle; the land marking the highest elevation in Westchester County, surrounded by a stone wall topped with a deer fence rising ten feet, with a hedgerow between the wall and the road that completely blocked any view of his house from the street—that he'd bought himself a fortress of solitude. He agreed with them completely.

Tommy had decorated the house according to his taste, which gave it a distinctly masculine feel, but he had a pair of guestrooms decorated with female guests in mind, with bedspreads and curtains more floral and pastel, and bathrooms stocked with shampoos and skin-care products that, he had to admit, he'd hired a female personal shopper to pick out for him. He put Dani in what he referred to as Chick Room 1.

Over a late dinner, Tommy, Dani, and Carl gave Ruth a more thorough debriefing. Dani broke down for her what Quinn had learned about the drug they'd been given at Starbucks, and his explanation for Amos Kasden's psychotic break. When Carl referred to Quinn as Dani's ex-fiancé, Dani awkwardly corrected him, saying he was just a friend.

"Well, either way," Carl said, "he seems to be a genius. We're lucky he's working for the good guys."

When everyone started yawning, Carl agreed to stay up for the first watch. His job was to watch the security monitors, both the night-vision cameras and the FLIR monitors, and wake everybody if he saw anything.

"As I understand it," Tommy said, "they might scare us, but they can't physically harm us unless they take material form. And when they do that, they're vulnerable. I don't know if that thing we saw at Ruth's house is still out there, but when we shot at it, it definitely didn't like the attention. They feel pain when they're corporeal. And I, for one, intend to cause as much of that as I can."

Dani got ready for bed, then went down to the kitchen in her flannel pajamas because she'd forgotten to fill Otto's water dish. She didn't ask Carl to do it because for some reason Otto had growled at Carl. Until then Otto seemed to like everybody he met.

They'd decided that since the property was walled in, it was safe to let the dog sleep on the back porch where he'd be sheltered from the wind and cold by an old denim duvet cover Tommy found in the garage and stuffed with straw from the chicken coop. Otto seemed content with the plan.

Dani set down his dish of water, which he'd nearly finished by the time she was done rubbing his ears and wishing him good night.

In the kitchen she told Carl she felt ever so slightly safer with the dog on the porch.

"I'm not sure it will mean much if push comes to shove," Carl said. "Though he is a big one."

"Carl," Dani said, "if you don't mind, please don't tell Tommy I was asking about Cassandra. It's none of my business and I know it's over—there was really no point in my bringing it up. Just forget I said anything."

"You have my word," Carl said. "But it's tough to be around someone else's ex, knowing that somewhere in the past they loved the other person as much as they love you now. Has Tommy said anything to you about Quinn?"

"No," Dani said. She found it hard to believe Tommy would be jealous of Quinn. "Has he said anything to you?"

"No," Carl said. "Though I imagine he wouldn't mind getting your friend in an arm-wrestling contest or something similarly macho."

"Really? He said that?"

"No," Carl said. "He didn't say that. Actually, I think he learned his lesson on jealousy with Cassandra. I couldn't count the number of times he got upset when she'd have her picture in one of the tabloids and the headline said she was cheating on him. I told him they were just trying to get readers, but it was hard for him not to take it seriously. He was heartbroken when she finally left him."

"That's not the way he told it to me," Dani said.

"Well, I'm sure that with twenty-twenty hindsight he can see it more clearly," Carl said. "Time and perspective and all that."

"Good night, Carl," Dani said.

"He loves you very much, you know."

"I know," she said. But inwardly she thought, *If he loved Cassandra but played it down when I asked about it, what's he saying now that we're involved? Does he even know what being in love means?* "You going to be okay down here?"

"All good," he said. "Can't fall asleep on my first watch."

"No, but when you're done, warm milk really can do the trick. It's not just an old wives' tale."

"I'm good," he said. "You go to bed. Otto and I will be fine."

⁂

Alone in the kitchen, Carl fought back tears. He'd thought there was no hell greater than the one he'd been in, but now that he was leading the people he loved down a path toward destruction, he wished only to die. He felt beyond redemption, and yet he knew if he could just ask for it . . . He tried to bring his hands together in prayer, but it was as if he were holding powerful magnets with opposing poles, his hands repelling each other, no matter how hard he pressed.

His hands gripped the armrests of his chair and he leaned forward, gritting his teeth, squeezing his eyes closed as he fought to say the words.

"Our Father . . . who . . . art . . . in heaven!"

He heard himself growling, his throat constricting to cut off the flow of air. He grunted and pushed harder to make his mouth obey his will, but his will was failing.

"Hallowed . . . ," he managed to say, but he could go no further. The harder he struggled, the more he was trapped, like in one of those straw finger puzzles he'd loved as a child.

"Help me, Jesus," he mumbled. "Please . . ."

He was crying, weeping tears of anguish and profound regret. He wanted to die and he wanted to kill simultaneously. If only he could kill himself, he thought, but when he tried to move his arm to pick up the Colt automatic sitting on the counter not five feet away, he couldn't do it.

Then the thing inside him noticed that Tommy had left his cell phone on the food island to recharge.

He picked up Tommy's phone, searched his contacts, and found the private cell phone number for Cassandra Morton.

Using Tommy's phone, he dialed her number, made sure it went to voice mail, then hung up.

When she called back, Carl didn't answer. A moment later, he listened to the message she'd left him, or rather, the message she thought she was leaving Tommy: "It's good just to know you're still there. You've got a home in me too." He deleted the voice mail and put the phone back where he'd found it.

21.

"This place is like an optical illusion," Tommy told his aunt. "It's bigger on the inside than it is on the outside. Has anyone ever gone through all this stuff?"

"I wish we could hire someone," Ruth said. "Who knows what they'd find in the far corners."

They were in the library attic. They'd brought flashlights and light-bulbs, as well as an electric camp lantern Tommy kept in his garage in case of power failures. Carl had volunteered to come along, but Tommy asked him to stay with Dani, who was still trying to track down Quinn. Ruth illuminated the room with her flashlight while Tommy replaced the overhead bulbs. Ruth said she was going to speak to Leon again about the squirrels.

"It's hard to keep up when half of your staff are unpaid volunteers. If we could pay them, we could fire them," she told Tommy. "When they're volunteers and you ask them not to come in, they say, 'Oh, that's all right,' and they come anyway."

"There's what you probably smelled," he said, pointing his flashlight beam at the carcass of a dead pigeon.

"How did that get in here?" she said.

"You must have a hole under the eaves somewhere."

They pushed farther into the labyrinth, the shadows getting longer behind them as Tommy carried the lantern forward.

"Hel-lo," he said when they found the old oak desk in the northeast corner of the room.

Ruth looked at him, puzzled. "Who are you saying hello to?"

"I don't know, but that's what Sherlock Holmes always says when he finds something." He set the lantern on the desk and pulled on the chain of the old gooseneck desk lamp. It did not light up. He screwed the lightbulb in tighter and tried again, had no luck, then replaced it with a 100-watt bulb from his pocket.

"*Fiat lux*," Ruth said as she turned off her flashlight and sat down in the folding chair beside the desk. The surface was covered with a layer of dust thick enough for Tommy to write his name in with his fingertip. The desk had a matching captain's chair on wheels. He sat down in it and opened all the drawers, but found only pencils and blank pads of yellow legal paper, a small dictionary, a box of paper clips, a hole punch, rubber bands, note cards, Post-it notes, an eraser, and a box of brass roundhead fasteners.

"I can't believe you let Abbie work up here in all this dust," Tommy said. "You could have at least given her a feather duster."

"She insisted on being up here, now that I think of it," Ruth said. "I offered to make her a place downstairs, but she said she liked the quiet up here."

"Yeah," Tommy said. "Everybody knows how deafening it can get in a *library*. Did she carry a briefcase or a book bag?"

"She always carried a large straw bag. Almost like a beach bag. With handles. I don't know what was in it."

Tommy turned on his flashlight and swung the beam around the attic, a cone of light illuminating the dust in the air. Close by, he saw shelves stacked with copies of the *East Salem Chronicle* dating back to before the Civil War. Below that, massive volumes, two feet high and four inches thick, labeled *Plots and Titles*, shelved in chronological order.

"If she wanted to hide something," Tommy said, "this would be a good place."

He shone the light on the floor, hoping to see some indication of where she might have walked, or a sign that anything might have been recently disturbed.

Everywhere he looked he saw only cardboard or paper or leather-bound book spines. A collection of Shakespeare that appeared about to crumble; a bundle of Mickey Spillane paperbacks, tied with twine; string-bound bundles of *Colliers* magazines.

"Do you think there's a loose floorboard?" Tommy said.

"I can virtually guarantee you there's a loose floorboard," Ruth said. "But where to start? We'd have to move everything, and there's nowhere to put it."

"If that's true for us, it was true for Abbie too, and she was a little old lady. She's not going to be shoving heavy boxes around. She would have kept it simple. Given that we don't even know what we're looking for, whatever it is could be the size of a matchbox or larger. Probably small enough to carry in her straw bag. The desk is easy to get to, but we've already searched it."

"No, we haven't," Ruth said, moving the gooseneck lamp to the front corner of the desk. "Your grandfather had one of these desks. In his day people used old typewriters, but they didn't want them cluttering their desktops when they weren't using them. So they had a foldaway drawer, and they'd mount the typewriter there. I used to play with it—it was like a magical hidden compartment. It's this middle part here."

She bent the light over the edge of the desktop. Tommy now saw the groove cut into the bottom of the front edge.

"Pull that forward and flip it back," she said.

The center portion of the desktop rotated backward as the hidden drawer tilted up and forward. On it they saw a wooden box about the size of a small briefcase, perhaps 16 x 12 x 4 inches. Made from rosewood, Tommy guessed, or perhaps a dark mahogany. The box had a striking inlay, a Celtic cross about a foot tall and eight inches across, made of gold, atop a smaller circle of what Tommy guessed was silver, because it had tarnished while the gold had not. Centered along each of the four sides on the top of the box was a smaller Celtic cross made of silver, each one about the size of a nickel. When Tommy turned the box over, he saw identical small Celtic crosses in the same four locations.

"Hel-lo," Ruth said.

When Tommy tried to lift the box, it was heavier than he had expected, and when he shook it, nothing inside moved. When he rapped on it with first his knuckles and then with the end of his flashlight, it sounded solid. He examined it from every direction but could not find anything resembling a hinge or door. He pried and pressed from all angles but could not open it.

He rotated the center portion of the desktop back into position and set the box on it, then moved the lamp down to throw more light on the object. He pressed every part of the inlay, in varying combinations, thinking there might be some kind of hidden latch or button.

"I give up," he finally said. "What do you think is in it?"

"I've seen similar boxes that held Bibles," Ruth said. "Though that was when I was in Europe. It might be a chasse."

"A chasse?"

"A reliquary," she said. "Containing a relic from a saint or holy person."

"You mean bones?"

"Sometimes."

"Abbie wanted us to find this. She knew you'd lead me to it. Let's get it back to the house." He rolled his chair back from the desk. "But make sure Otto doesn't bury the bones in the backyard."

At the house, Dani studied the box from every angle and pronounced it lovely and mysterious.

"Thanks," Tommy said, "but we already knew that."

She thought it might be one of those ancient puzzle boxes that opened by sliding and pressing and rotating hidden panels and knobs and levers.

"Could be. I also have a table saw in the garage in my shop that could expedite matters."

Dani advised against it. She'd seen a show once about medieval puzzle boxes on the History Channel and learned that the makers often booby-trapped them with vials of acid or ink that destroyed whatever was inside if someone tampered with it.

"How about an MRI?" Ruth said.

"You can't put metal in a magnetic imager," Dani said. "But maybe an X-ray or an ultrasound would work."

"Maybe Quinn could use his incredible psychic powers," Tommy mocked. "It's a joke," he added when he saw Dani scowl.

Dani had finally heard from Quinn—he'd sent a text to say he was coming back with news she would find interesting. She needed to pick him up at the station in Katonah at 4:40 that afternoon.

"We should probably wake Carl up from his nap," Tommy said. "Why don't we ask him to pick Quinn up?"

"Carl couldn't sleep," Dani said. "He left twenty minutes ago. He said he had an errand to run."

"He left you here alone?" Tommy said, irritated. "What happened to the buddy system?"

"I told him I'd be fine with Otto on guard and your aunt's arsenal close at hand. Carl seems a little off. Maybe he's fighting something. My sister called to ask me if I thought she should get her girls flu shots. She keeps thinking I'm a pediatrician."

"I think he's still thinking about Esme," Tommy said. "He can't stop blaming himself."

Too late he realized his thoughtlessness. He knew Dani blamed herself for letting her parents book a flight home with a bush pilot who was a known smuggler after they had visited her in Africa. She'd left them at the airport because she'd wanted to stay to say good-bye to Quinn instead of going with them. If she'd stayed with them, she would have insisted they find another pilot. And they'd still be alive.

"Did your folks ever meet Quinn?" Tommy said, knowing she was thinking about them.

"No. He was supposed to join us in Kumasi, but something came up. But that's just the way it is in Africa. You can plan a trip, but if the gas station is out of gas or somebody stole the train tracks and sold them for scrap, you gotta adjust."

"Like the old line, 'If you want to make God laugh, tell him your plans.'"

"I wish they'd met you," Dani said.

"They did," Tommy said. "Or your dad did. He used to give me my sports physicals."

"I mean now."

She thought about how often Quinn had disappointed her, stood her up, or canceled on her. She remembered her mother saying, after she'd learned Dani was homecoming queen to Tommy's king, "He's such a nice boy." Her mother would approve. Her dad would too.

"Just promise me one thing," she said. "Promise you won't break my heart."

"Don't worry," he said. "Not gonna happen." He kissed her.

Dani spent the day online catching up on the latest developments in psychotropic pharmaceuticals. A colleague had once commented that the untold billions of dollars spent developing drugs to treat the symptoms of depression would be better spent fighting the causes of it, war, poverty, hunger . . . and sometimes Dani was inclined to agree. Linz, the German pharmaceutical giant, was clearly poised to dominate the marketplace, the way Microsoft dominated the computer industry. When it was time for her to leave for the train station, Tommy walked her to her car and made sure her Beretta was in working order.

The gates opened as she headed down Tommy's driveway. She'd gone half a mile when she saw a cab coming in the opposite direction. It occurred to her that Quinn might have taken an earlier train, so she turned around to follow the cab, thinking he might be in it. As she got closer, she saw that it was a New York City taxi. She knew it was at least a $150 cab ride from Manhattan to East Salem, and she was sure Quinn didn't have that kind of money. And come to think of it, how would Quinn know where Tommy's house was, or that she was staying there?

When the cab turned into Tommy's drive, pausing at the gate, Dani pulled over, fifty yards behind it. There was nowhere for her to hide, she realized, but there was also no reason to hide. She started making her three-point turn to head back to the train station when she saw a figure get out of the back of the cab and walk to the intercom on Tommy's gate. It was a woman wearing sunglasses and a baseball cap, with her blond ponytail looped through the hole in the back of the cap, but Dani knew from the way the ponytail bounced, and the way the woman bounced when she walked, and the way she smiled to the cabbie as she asked him to wait, that it was Cassandra Morton.

Dani stopped in the middle of the road, shocked, then jerked her steering wheel hard to get pointed in the right direction and stomped on the gas.

⌘

"Surprise!" Cassandra said. "What's that?"

"This?" Tommy said. "Nothing." He lowered the RAZ-IR PRO 2 he'd been pointing at his ex, closed the screen, and turned it off. Cassandra was still trouble, he knew, but according to the scanner, not of the supernatural kind. "What brings you here?" he said, trying to sound welcoming.

185

"You've got a home in me," she said. "That's what you said."

"I did indeed," he said, smiling gamely. "*If you ever need a place to stay, or to hide, I'm your man*," he'd vowed—a long time ago. Usually people don't take you up on offers like that. "Come in," he said as he reached for her suitcase. "Here, let me get that."

He lifted her bag and grimaced a bit for comic effect. As they stepped into the kitchen, Tommy congratulated himself for remembering to put Aunt Ruth's guns back in the broom closet as the cab pulled up.

She looked around. "I like what you've done to the place."

"You mean, cleaned it?"

"Tom, if this is inconvenient, tell me," she said. "I know I should have called first, but it would have ruined the surprise. At least I knew when you called me and hung up last night that I wasn't completely off your radar."

"I called you? I didn't call you."

"Your private number is on my call log," she said, confused.

"I must have pocket-dialed. Seriously, Cass—I didn't call you."

"Oh no," she said, her mouth turning down. "I thought—"

"It's okay, though," Tommy said. "It's all good. Don't worry about it."

"Is this a bad time?"

He couldn't help laughing.

"Oh dear," she said. "It *is* a bad time, isn't it? Let me call the cabbie back before he gets too far."

"Cass, it's all right," he said. "But yeah, it's not a good time. It's too much to explain right now. But it's obviously not a good time for you either, is it?"

Cassandra was, generally speaking, a loving, caring person, but she was also accustomed to being the center of attention. Tommy had figured out early in their relationship how easy it was to change the subject, any subject, by putting the spotlight back on the actress who'd always been the prettiest woman in the room no matter how big the room was.

"You've heard?" she said.

"Only what I try not to read in the tabloids."

"I thought you didn't read the tabs."

"Actually, Carl told me," Tommy said. "He was one of those one-named Brazilian soccer guys, right? Like Kaka, or Poo-poo . . ."

"His name shall not be spoken," she said.

Tommy nodded in agreement. "I thought you were in LA."

"I'm going to be on Broadway," she said. "I'm doing a month in *South Pacific* as Nellie Forbush. My agent says it's something all us Hollywood types have to do these days. We're required to go on all the talk shows and say how much we love the theater."

"You don't?"

"Right now, I'm terrified. Not just about what the critics might say. I've never sung in public."

"You have a beautiful voice."

"Well, that's very nice of you to say. You are one of the few people who've heard it." Her eyes fell on a woman's purse on the counter. "Do you have a guest?" she said. "I really should have called. I'm so sorry."

"That's my aunt's," Tommy said. "But yes, I do have some people staying for a few days. You remember Carl?"

"I do. How is he?"

"He's good. At least that's what he wants us to think. He still has a few . . ."

"Demons? Don't we all?" Cassandra said. "But I'm working on mine. I wanted to tell you I've taken a great many new steps since we last spoke. Apart from a One-a-Day Flintstones gummy vitamin, I am completely pill-free. I sleep like a baby and I exercise and I eat much better too. The tabloids hate me—they have nothing to say about me anymore. I'm completely boring."

"That's good, Cass. Really good."

"I've started going to church again too," she said. "With my schedule I can't go every Sunday, but I go when I can. I like it. I still have a lot of questions, but I'm back on track, you might say. And I have you to thank for all of it."

"You're the one who made the changes."

"Well, you never preached," she said. "And I appreciate that. Unlike all the other men who've tried to tell me how to live. You just set a good example and trusted me to decide for myself."

"I'm glad to hear it," he said. An awkward silence followed.

"I was thinking I might stay the weekend and we could catch up," she finally said. "But I guess that's a no-go. I still might stay the weekend somewhere. You wouldn't believe how good it feels to get out of the city."

"I can take you over to the Peter Keeler, if you'd like."

Cassandra saw the wooden box with the inlaid Celtic cross on the food island. "That's beautiful," she said. She moved to have a closer look and traced the cross and the circle with her little finger. "Where'd you get it? What kind of wood is it?"

"Tag sale," he said. "Not sure what it's made of. Let me get my coat and I'll drive you."

Trying not to rouse Cassandra's curiosity, he casually picked up the box along with a stack of newspapers and brought them into the study. With a glance over his shoulder to make sure she hadn't followed him, he moved a mirror on the wall to reveal a hidden safe. The man who'd built the house had been running a Ponzi scheme, but ended up swindling a Mexican drug cartel that was using him to launder their money, or so they thought. The Ponzi schemer had multiple reasons to be nervous, so in addition to the security system, he'd installed a large wall safe to hold his ill-gotten gains. Tommy's friends had laughed when he'd showed it to them, and asked him if he had any revolving bookcases hiding secret passageways.

The safe had two dials, one with letters and the other with numbers. He'd had the combination changed to Bond 007. The safe contained his Super Bowl rings, a folder of legal documents including his will, his mother's diary, his high school yearbook with the embarrassing heart drawn around Dani's picture with a red Sharpie, and a book of poems he'd written in middle school that he should have burned a long time ago but couldn't. He put Abbie's box in the safe, which he no longer thought of as safe, given the adversaries he was up against, but was sa*fer* than anywhere else he could think of.

He grabbed a coat and walked back to the kitchen where he could hear his aunt talking to his ex.

"I'd introduce you, but I see you've met," he said.

"Your aunt was just telling me about Dani," Cassandra said. Tommy flinched, but then realized he was glad that Aunt Ruth had broken the news for him. "She sounds great. Are you going to let me meet her?"

"I don't know," Tommy said. "She's been really busy lately. Maybe. Sure."

"Well, then you must tell me *everything* about her on our way to the inn," she said, grabbing her suitcase. "Your father is in Texas? How's he doing?"

On the way to the inn they talked mostly about Dani. Taking care not to violate anything Dani might have told him in confidence, and steering clear of any issues she might consider nobody's business but hers, or theirs, Tommy told Cassandra that he'd met the right woman and knew she was the best thing that had ever happened to him, or ever could.

"I'm happy for you, Tom," Cassandra said, and sounded like she meant it. "You know what they say. Everyone has a purpose, even if it's only to set a bad example. I do what I can."

Despite the joke, Tommy knew Cassandra was glad for him. She hadn't come hoping to rekindle a dead romance, but rather in the spirit of friendship, at a time when she really needed a "home." By the time she'd finished describing the soccer star who'd dumped her, it was abundantly clear to both of them that she was much better off without him.

"Gosh," she said. "Just talking to you about him makes me see how stupid I was. What was I thinking? It's amazing how things can seem so clear when you have to explain them to someone else. I guess that's what therapy is all about. Well, duh."

"Just give it a rest before you fall in love again," Tommy said. "Most people wait more than a few days for the smoke to clear."

"That is most excellent advice," she said. "I shall not rebound."

"But don't pass up any slam dunks either," Tommy said.

At the Peter Keeler he checked her in under the fake name she always used, Tess Tosterone. It was the name of the first character she'd ever played, in a movie about women's roller derby called *When Girls Collide*. While she used her cell phone to get a rental car delivered to the inn, Tommy asked the desk clerk if Julian Villanegre was in. It occurred to him that the art historian might know something about Abbie's mysterious box.

When he was told that Villanegre had stepped out, Tommy asked her to give the Englishman a message, that they'd found an art object Abbie had left behind. Then he asked for Ben Whitehorse. The clerk at the reception desk typed that name in and then scrolled up and down before telling him that there was no one named Ben Whitehorse registered. He asked her to check again, and said he knew Ben was staying there because he'd helped him check in.

She searched again. "No one by that name. Sorry."

He spelled it for her. "You said he was a sweet man," he reminded her. "He thought you'd baked the Sara Lee muffins at the breakfast buffet."

It didn't ring a bell. She checked again. "Nope. Sorry. You're sure he was here?"

"Well, I was," Tommy said. "But now I'm not so sure about anything."

22.

At the train station, Dani checked her phone and saw a text from Quinn:
MISSED TRAIN. NEXT ONE IN 30. I PROMISE WAIT WILL BE WORTH IT.

"Typical," she said.

She called her office, Ralston-Foley Behavioral Consulting. The receptionist, a young woman named Kelly, told Dani that a trial at which she was scheduled to testify had been postponed again and another, involving a battered mother of four, had been settled with the husband pleading guilty. Dani asked to be connected to her office voice mail.

"Oh—before I do," Kelly said, "you also got a letter. I mean an actual letter, on paper, with handwriting on the envelope. I've never seen one of those before."

"Who's it from?"

"Doesn't say. The return address just says Starbucks Guy."

Dani looked at her watch. If the traffic was with her, she could race to her office, pick up the envelope, and get back to the train station in time.

"Hold on to it, Kell. I'll be there in ten."

As Dani drove to her office, she asked herself again the question she'd been asking herself for the last four days—if someone was going to betray her, who would it be? She'd never suspected Tommy, but of all the people she needed to count on, he was the most important, and thus a betrayal

191

from him would hurt the most. She ran the syllogism through her head: 1) Cassandra came to see him; 2) it was highly unlikely that she'd come to see him if he hadn't invited her; 3) he didn't tell her Cassandra was coming; 4) therefore he had lied, by omission if not by commission.

She would not be in a relationship with someone who lied to her. It was that simple.

At her office, she took the letter from Kelly, thanked her, apologized for letting the work back up, promised she'd be in soon, and ran back to her car. She opened the envelope as she drove and shook out a single SD card, eight megabytes, black with no label. She stuffed it into her coat pocket as she pulled into the train station parking lot.

Quinn was already there, full of apologies for having fallen asleep in Grand Central Station. When Dani asked how he—or anybody—could fall asleep amid the cacophony of Grand Central, he said he'd been up all night with Illena.

"I don't want to hear about it," she said.

"I think you do."

"I know I don't," Dani said, her tone sharp and angry and certainly nothing he deserved, she realized immediately. But she wasn't in the mood for apologizing. He gave her a minute and then asked if something was bothering her.

"A lot," she said. "I'm sorry for barking at you. It's not your fault. I just can't—I can't really tell you what's going on."

"Do you mean with Tommy?"

"Actually, that's the part I can tell you," Dani said, surprised at Quinn's perceptiveness. "I think he's been seeing—let me rephrase that. Today, his ex showed up. He said he wasn't in touch with her, but apparently he has been. Cassandra Morton."

"The actress?"

"That's the one."

"I *love* her! Oh, I'm sorry. That was insensitive."

"Ya think?"

He waited a moment. "Where are we going?"

"I don't know," she said as she considered her options. "I think maybe you should go back to New York."

"Dani—"

"I got you involved in something I never should have involved you in. It's too . . . much. And I can't tell you why, but I think you need to get your dog and your stuff—where is your stuff? Is it still at the inn?"

He nodded.

"I think maybe the best thing for you and for me and maybe for everybody, but definitely for you, would be to go back and pretend all this never happened. While you still can. I know that's confusing and annoyingly mysterious, but just trust me."

They rode in silence for a few minutes.

"I don't have very much to go back to," he said.

"Don't say that."

"You say there's something I don't understand. Well, you should know there's something *you* don't understand."

"Illena—"

"Is a very nice person, but I don't love her and she's not part of my life," Quinn said. "This . . . whatever *this* is—whatever you're doing—feels rather important to me. More than anything else I'm doing. Or have ever done. And I need to do something important. It's not just because I'm curious. So if you're giving me a choice between in or out, I'm in. All the way. If you want me."

She pulled over to the side of the road and looked at him.

"This isn't a joke, Quinn. This makes whatever we were doing in Africa look like a game of hopscotch. This is really big. So much bigger than I can even explain right now. It could be dangerous . . . really, seriously dangerous. And it requires a certain suspension of disbelief. And actual belief too. I'm not sure you're going to be on board when you get the full picture."

"Try me."

"We have to get your things," she said, putting the car in gear and pulling back into traffic. "We're going to the inn first, and then to Tommy's house."

"Yikes," Quinn said. "Tommy's house? Really? Do you want me to punch him for you?"

Dani looked at him and laughed. It felt good to laugh. "Quinn—have you *ever* hit anyone?"

"No," he said. "But how hard could it be? Has Tommy ever hit anyone?"

"For a living," she said. "They used to give him trophies for hitting people."

At the inn Dani waited in the car while Quinn went inside to pack his suitcase. She took the SD card from her pocket and looked at it, as if she could learn something just by staring at it. She wondered if she was doing the right thing, bringing Quinn into this. She knew she was doing the wrong thing by bringing him in without consulting Tommy and the others, but Tommy hadn't exactly consulted with her when he invited Cassandra Morton up for a visit.

No sooner had she thought of the actress than a blonde with long, stylish bedhead bangs came out the back door of the inn and stopped. She extended her arm and aimed a car-key remote in the general direction of the parking lot, sweeping from left to right and back again. Dani had to admit that she was even prettier in person than she was in movies, and she had a lot of help when she appeared in movies. She appeared to be frustrated. Dani would have left well enough alone if the actress hadn't approached her car. Dani rolled down her window.

"Excuse me," Cassandra said. "Do you know what a Maxima is?"

"It's a car."

"I know it's a car," the actress said with a self-deprecating laugh. "The rental company dropped it off but they didn't say where they put it. They said it's silver, but half the cars out here are silver, and I don't know what a Maxima looks like."

"Press the red button," Dani said. "I think you were pressing the door unlock."

Cassandra pressed the red button, and a silver Maxima three rows back began to honk and flash its lights. She frantically pressed the button again to get the alarm to stop, but nothing happened.

"You have to put the key in the ignition," Dani advised.

Cassandra ran to the car, unlocked it, and turned the key in the ignition, silencing the alarm, then returned to where Dani was.

"Thank you *so* much," the actress said, catching her breath. "That was so kind of you. I obviously don't drive much. I'm sorry I bothered you, but can I ask one more favor? Is there a decent place I can get something to eat?"

"You're Cassandra Morton," Dani said. She realized immediately what a stupid thing it was to say. Then she wondered why Cassandra was dining alone. Was Tommy going to keep her hidden, make some excuse, and go to her later? Could he be that devious?

"I am," the actress said matter-of-factly but without any apparent ego. "You're not hungry, are you? I'll buy you dinner. I'd love the company. Unless you think that's weird."

"You don't know anyone in town?"

"I have one friend but he's busy tonight, so I'm on my own."

"Who's your friend?" Dani said. "I know just about everybody here."

"I'm sure you know him," she said, "but I shouldn't say. Are you sure you won't join me?"

"Thank you, but I'm waiting for someone. Try the Pub. Across the green, about halfway down. Or the Miss Salem Diner, but the Pub is nicer."

"Thanks again," Cassandra said, smiling brightly as she headed back to her rental car.

Dani was left to wonder whether she'd just been fooled by an accomplished actress, but she found herself liking the woman despite how much she wanted not to. She seemed genuine and friendly and all those things you want to believe about actresses who portray plucky, likable characters. Dani didn't think of herself as the kind of person who was impressed by celebrities, but perhaps she was, more than she wanted to admit.

She was startled when Quinn opened the passenger side door and threw his suitcase in the backseat.

"Should we check on Otto?" he said as he plopped in beside her.

"He's already there," Dani said. "Arlo too."

At the house, Dani introduced Quinn to Tommy and Ruth, then asked where Carl was. Tommy said he still wasn't back and that he was getting worried—Carl wasn't answering his phone.

"Dani, can I speak to you for a moment in private?"

"I need to check something on my laptop first."

Tommy could sense she was bristling with anger. He desperately needed to address whatever it was that was bothering her.

"Quinn needs to know the whole story," Dani said. "He knows about Amos but not the rest of it. Why don't you fill him in while I have a look at this." She held up the SD card.

"What's that?" Tommy said.

"I won't know until I see what's on it, will I? Our friend from St. Adrian's mailed it to my office."

"Use my desktop in the study," he said. "That card reader is on the right."

Dani went into the study, closing the door behind her. Ruth went upstairs to finish turning down the beds.

Tommy looked at Quinn and said, "Can somebody tell me what's going on?"

"I was going to ask you the same question," Quinn said. "She thinks you should have told her Cassandra Morton was here."

"I just tried to," Tommy said. "That's why I wanted to talk to her in private."

"I don't want to get between the two of you," Quinn said, "but if it were me, I'd give her awhile to cool down. She usually does."

Tommy nodded, then went to his study. He hesitated at the closed door, thought for a second that he should open it, then decided he should knock, and then decided Quinn was right. It occurred to him at that moment that perhaps Quinn was right in any number of ways—a better match for Dani, more tuned in to the things Dani had studied and cared about. Perhaps the fantasy he'd been entertaining, that God and fate had brought her back to him for a higher purpose, was just that, a fantasy, a self-composed delusion.

"Will you excuse me for a minute?" he said to Quinn. In the kitchen, he put on his barn coat and then stepped out the back door.

He went out into the yard and walked to an Adirondack-style bench set beneath a weeping willow tree overlooking the pond. The late November air was cold, the moon well on the wane, the sky overhead bright with stars. He pulled his collar up, buttoned it closed at the top button, kept his hands in his pockets for warmth, and closed his eyes. He breathed deeply through his nose three times, more slowly each time, and then he prayed silently.

Jesus, I'm sorry. I think I'm letting you down. You called on me to do something for you, and I think I'm failing you. You sent Dani to me, but I'm losing her and I don't know why. Something changed. I'm confused, Lord. If you could help me understand what she's feeling right now, I might be able to figure the rest out. I don't want to lose her, but if that's your will, please make that clear to me because otherwise I'm only going to waste her time. I've never felt this way before, and I'm scared . . .

He stopped when he realized he was putting his own needs and desires ahead of something of far greater importance. He'd lost focus. This wasn't about him. He'd forgotten the lesson his father had taught him a long time ago after reading a book called *I Am Third*. "God comes first," Arnie had said, "and others come second. You're third, but I think you'll find if you take care of the first two, you won't need to worry too much about yourself."

When Tommy stepped back into the kitchen, Ruth was telling Quinn about Amos Kasden and the party the night Julie Leonard was killed.

"Don't let me interrupt," Tommy said, glancing toward the door of his den, which was still closed.

"Please do," Ruth said. "You know these matters far better than I do, and this young man needs to understand everything if he's going to help us."

Dani wanted to climb out the window, get in her car, hit the interstate, stomp on the gas, and drive until she couldn't drive any longer, and then sleep for a few hours, wake up, and drive some more, and perhaps by the time she reached Alaska, or Mexico, or both, she'd be able to breathe again.

Stupid, stupid woman! In over your head. Trust your instincts. Why didn't you know better? You ran away from him in high school—you knew then that this would happen. He's a player. He was always a player. You should have taken better care of your heart. You should have proceeded with caution. You weren't ready for this. You made a bad decision. You're smarter than this. Take it slow—that's what your better judgment was screaming at you. Why didn't you listen?

When will you ever listen?

She closed her eyes, and for a second she gave in, gave up, gave herself over to the tears. A small cry seemed appropriate. Not a big one. She let it out, then pulled herself together. She took a deep breath, and another, sniffed, and used a tissue from the box on the desk to blow her nose and dry her eyes.

She rose from the desk to look in the mirror and wipe at her mascara where it had smeared. She blew her nose again and threw the tissue in the wastebasket, regarding herself in the mirror again. Maybe it was wrong to feel this way. Maybe Cassandra Morton was exactly the sort of woman Tommy needed—pretty and shallow and submissive. Maybe he'd be extremely happy with her. It was his decision, not hers, after all. All she could do was take care of herself.

She returned to the laptop and clicked on the icon to open the one file on the SD card.

When she did, she saw a long list of names, 662 of them, in alphabetical order, beginning with *Abbot, James 1829* and ending with *Zachary, William 1927*. The earliest date she could find was 1816. The most recent was just a year ago. When she found *Bauer, Udo 1977*, she was certain she was looking at a list of boys who'd graduated from St. Adrian's Academy.

Bauer's was the only name she recognized, so she randomly picked names and Googled them, searching for—she didn't know for what. She skipped names that were too generic, like *Smith, Martin 1901* or *Jones, David 1958* and concentrated on those that were less likely to produce multiple search hits. She read a few results and saw nothing of interest. She was about to give up when the results popped up for *Druitt, William H. 1863*. He was, according to Google, an English barrister and the assistant headmaster of a school in Blackheath, England; but more intriguing, he was the older brother of Montague John Druitt, the man Scotland Yard inspectors at the time suspected of being Jack the Ripper. Montague J. Druitt was murdered and his body found floating in the Thames in 1888. William had said his younger brother was "profoundly insane" and acknowledged that he'd found a woman's arm in his brother's possession, a limb that may have matched a dismembered body found in Whitechapel, but, William said, he'd thrown the arm away. No conclusive proof was ever found to connect Montague Druitt to the crimes.

Dani tried another name: *von Königsberg, Karl Francis 1842*. He'd been a German educational reformer and a friend of Friedrich Fröebel, the man credited with inventing kindergarten. Karl Francis von Königsberg's perverse claim to fame, however, was that he'd been a teacher in a school in Fischlham, Germany, where he'd given a picture book on the Franco-Prussian War to a seven-year-old boy named Adolf Schicklgruber, who later changed his name to Adolf Hitler. It was said that the boy became fixated on warfare because of that book.

She tried other names on the list. Before the existence of the near-limitless capacities of Google's Booleian engines, it would have been impossible to perform the kinds of searches she was now executing, but the more she looked, the more she discovered about the names on the list. They were not the names of famous mass murderers or serial killers, but they were the names of the babysitters, the next-door neighbors, and the childhood tormentors of mass murderers and serial killers—the accomplices and abettors, provocateurs and progenitors and behind-the-scenes agents.

Her heart pounded. She tried one more name: *Gitchell, Albert 1917.* His biography said that after attending "a private school in New York," Gitchell had gone home to Haskell County, Kansas, to enlist in the army. He'd reported to Fort Riley, Kansas, where he'd worked as a company cook, preparing food for thousands of soldiers on their way to the Western Front. On March 4, 1918, Gitchell reported in sick with the flu. Within days, 552 other men at the camp were stricken. Thousands of other soldiers from Fort Riley had already deployed. Gitchell was believed to have been the source of the 1918 Flu Pandemic that killed perhaps as many as a hundred million people before it was contained, many of them strong young adults who were overwhelmed with what the doctors were calling a "cytokine storm," killed by their own immune systems overreacting to the virus.

Not every name Dani checked came with some gruesome connection, but she believed each name would if she had enough time to put the pieces of the puzzle together. She understood now, with a horrible certainty, that St. Adrian's was the source of this litany of evil. And then she contemplated the long list of boys who'd graduated in the last twenty years, the St. Adrian's graduates who had yet to "distinguish" themselves as their predecessors had. They were out there somewhere, waiting to spread death and mayhem.

And Udo Bauer was one of them. She thought of that horrific painting, *The Garden of Earthly Delights*, and of the enlargement Julian Villanegre had focused on in the lower right-hand corner of the center panel: a man was emerging from a cave, but next to him, hidden and barely visible, a second man was whispering in his ear. He was like St. Adrian's Academy, influencing history without appearing at the forefront of it. Evil once removed.

23.

"You have failed us."

Carl Thorstein knelt on the floor at Headmaster John Adams Wharton's feet, in the library adjacent to his office. The demon inside him had relaxed its grip enough to let Carl respond to the questions Wharton and Ghieri put to him, though like a torturer wielding an electric cattle prod, the demon could still inflict pain if Carl resisted or refused to answer. The pain was unbearable, like a heart attack, sharp and internal and anguishing. Worse was the feeling of being utterly alone, like a lone miner trapped miles under the earth by a cave-in, knowing there was no way back, no way to even get an SOS out.

"You're telling us nothing we didn't know already," the headmaster said sternly.

"They have a technology—"

"I have no interest in what technology they have," Wharton said. "We sent you to bring us information. You can go where we cannot."

"I'm trying," Carl said, pleading.

"Let me," Ghieri interrupted, holding back Wharton with his hand. He moved to the chair next to Carl. "Look at me, Carl."

Carl, temporarily able to command his body again, turned his head but dared not lift his eyes.

"Look at me!" Ghieri commanded. "I know what you're going through. You want it to end. We can end it for you, but you have to find out what we need to know first. Do you understand?"

"Yes."

"I'm not sure you do," Ghieri said. "We need to know where the book is. We need to know what they know, and who they've told. Can you get us that information?"

"Yes."

"Can you, Carl? Or will you forget about us, the way you forgot about Esme and swam to shore to save yourself and let her die?"

"I didn't swim—"

"Shut up!" Ghieri said. "You know you did. Do you want your torment to end, Carl?"

"Yes."

"Then get us what we need. Go back. You have one more chance. Ask more questions while they still trust you. Go. Now."

Carl stood up and scurried for the door. When he was gone, Wharton moved to the window and watched as Carl sped away on his motorcycle.

"I shouldn't have listened to you," he said to the psychologist. "If we'd destroyed them when we had the chance, it wouldn't have spread this far."

"It is not as bad as you think," Ghieri said. "Once we start a fracture among them, it will spread and disperse them. We just need to give it time."

"You may be right," Wharton said. "But sometimes a holy fire can spread from a few sparks. My inclination is not to wait."

"We might be close to finding the book," Ghieri said. "That is worth the risk. The old woman had to give it to someone."

"She gave it to the son."

"We don't know that. She may have seen the son as another dead end. It would make more sense for her to pass it along to someone younger. It wasn't in the girl's house, and if it was, it's burned to ashes."

"Perhaps."

"I think we should wait one more day," Ghieri said. "If we still have nothing, we'll destroy the ones we know about and take our chances."

"Agreed," Wharton said. From the window he caught a brief glimpse of the motorcycle's taillights as Carl drove through the school's gates. "I don't like to wait."

"We've waited for a thousand years," Ghieri said. "What's one more day?"

24.

"Where's Tommy?"

Dani had come back into the kitchen braced for an awkward conversation, but Tommy wasn't there.

"He went to look for Carl," Ruth said. "He thinks Carl has been acting odd."

"I agree," Dani said.

"Do you think Carl might . . . do something to himself?"

"Is that what Tommy's worried about?"

"It's a hard time of year," Ruth said. "The days are so short, and with the holidays coming . . . Carl's always had a problem in the fall since he lost his daughter. I believe her birthday was around this time of year."

Dani called Tommy's mobile. She heard it ring in the back hall, where she found Tommy's barn coat with the phone in its pocket.

"He forgot his cell," she said, waving it as she returned to the kitchen. She looked out the window and across the courtyard to the garage, where one door of the six garage bays was open and the light was on inside. She saw that one of his motorcycles was gone, the big black one with the fat tires.

She struggled for a moment, thinking. What she was about to do was wrong, but she had to know. She turned her back to make sure neither Ruth nor Quinn could see her, then scrolled through Tommy's phone, checking his voice mail. There were no messages from Cassandra, but her name and phone number were on Tommy's contact list. She checked his call log and saw that he'd called her the night before, at 1:22. Finally, she checked his text records and found the message he'd sent Cassandra: YOU'VE GOT A HOME IN ME.

She put the phone back in the pocket of his barn coat when she heard someone behind her.

"You look like you've seen a ghost," Quinn said.

"I'm all right."

"Are you hungry?" Ruth said. "I made soup."

"It's really good," Quinn said.

"No thanks," Dani said. "I'm not hungry. They told you what's going on?"

"They did."

"So? Do you think we're all nuts?"

"I might have, a year ago," he said.

"But not now?"

"No," he said. "I've been opening my mind to many things lately. And given the facts before you, I think you've reached the proper conclusions."

"You believe in angels?" she said. "You think God has given us a task to complete?"

"I do."

She was relieved but puzzled by Quinn's easy, well, *conversion*. She'd anticipated resistance and had already mapped out her argument to convince him that St. Adrian's was a school teaching and exporting evil. The names on the SD card, and the horrors attached to them, could not be explained any other way.

"You must be exhausted after being up all night," Dani said.

"I am," Quinn said. "Can I tell you now what I was doing?"

"Why is it so important for you to tell me what you were doing all night with your *girl*friend?"

"She's not my *girl*friend," Quinn said. "For the last time. She's a colleague, and we were in the lab all night. That's what I've been trying to tell you."

"Doing what?"

"I told you I had a job offer with Linz, right?"

"Right."

"Well, so did Illena. And she accepted. She started a month ago."

"And?"

"And she knows people there."

"And?"

"She stole something. I needed to test a sample of Provivilan. I needed to know that what Linz is about to market as the wonder drug of the next century and a vaccine against depression is not the same Doomsday Molecule we found in that little blue capsule you gave me. Illena shared my concerns. She doesn't know anything about the school or its test group, but she did the assay and reached the same conclusions I did. And the good news is: it's not. All the scary side effects we discussed seem to have been addressed. Provivilan, which by the way has already gone out to doctors and clinics as free samples, is missing a couple of the nasty psychoactive components I found in that blue capsule. I don't see the monoamine transporters conflicting with gonadal steroids the way we predicted with the Doomsday Molecule."

"That's a relief," Dani said.

"I agree," Quinn said. "Maybe the drug you were given was a beta version."

"Or something posing as one," she said. "I don't think the boys they were giving it to were a test group, and I think the people giving it to them knew all about the scary side effects."

"You think they were knowingly dosing students?"

"Yes," she said, and pulled out the SD card. "And I've got proof that they've been doing some version of it for a long time. This list shows—"

207

Ruth cut Dani off. "I think Tommy found him!" she said, looking out the kitchen window.

Dani joined her and saw a pair of motorcycle headlights coming up the drive. She checked the thermal scan on the security monitor to confirm it was two humans, riding two very hot motorcycles.

Otto began to growl, a deep, ominous rumble from the back of his throat.

25.

Tommy had found Carl sitting on his motorcycle by the side of the road near the turn that led to the Gardener farm. Carl told Tommy he needed to think, and he did his best thinking while riding. Tommy said he didn't need an explanation, but that his friends back at the house were worried about him.

They parked their bikes in the garage bay closest to the house and closed the door behind them. Tommy wore a down vest beneath his leathers and a fleece face shield beneath his helmet, but he was still cold to the bone from the icy wind. When he used his handheld infrared scanner to check the courtyard, he saw that Carl, who was walking ahead of him, registered several degrees colder than normal.

"You need to get inside and warm up," Tommy said, worried for his friend. He turned off the scanner to save the batteries. "It's too cold for you to be riding without more protection."

"You're probably right," Carl said, though he seemed unaffected by the chill.

"Has anybody seen my phone?" Tommy said once he was inside, taking off his coat and hanging it on a hook. "I tried to call you, but I couldn't find it."

"It's in your barn coat," Dani said.

She seemed oddly unemotional, Tommy thought, or maybe indifferent. He'd hoped for a sign that she was glad to see him.

"Quinn, this is my friend Carl Thorstein," Tommy said. "He's been looking forward to meeting you."

"Your hand is freezing," Quinn said as he shook Carl's hand.

"I left my warmer gloves at home," Carl said. He turned and walked to the sink, where he held his hands under hot water as Tommy checked his security monitors, visual and infrared.

"I want to show you something," Dani told the others. "But I need the computer in the study."

"You can use this one," Tommy said. He brought the laptop and the wireless mouse over and set them up on the food island in front of Dani. She did not say thank you or even look at him. She plugged the SD card into the laptop and waited.

"This is the file I found on the SD card mailed to my office," she said. "We have someone inside St. Adrian's helping us."

"A student?" Carl said. "Do you know his name?"

"I don't," Dani said.

"How do you know he's giving you reliable information?" Carl said. "It could be disinformation meant to lead you away from the truth."

Tommy noticed that Carl had said *you*, not *us*.

"I thought of that," Dani said, "but usually when someone is lying"—she looked briefly at Tommy—"they tend to check in to see if you believe the lie. It's hard to lie and just trust that the lie is going to work. We interrogate people who are lying at the police station or the DA's office and we know they're lying when they start asking us questions because they want to know how much we know. They'd probably get away with it if they could just shut up, but they never do."

She showed them the long list of students, then clicked on the shorter list she'd compiled from her Google searches—William H. Druitt, class of 1863; Karl Francis von Königsberg, class of 1842; Albert Gitchell, class of 1917; and the others. Each name came with a story, until it became clear to everyone what the school had been teaching for over a century.

"I was thinking that at some point, not now, but at some point we might want to pass this list on to someone like my friend Ed Stanley," Dani said. "The recent graduates are still out there."

"How many kids have they graduated since the school started?" Tommy said.

"This list has 662 names," Dani said, "but I couldn't find out how many they've graduated overall. And I was surprised by how little is really known about the school's history. I Googled it and came up with almost nothing. Ruth, do you know much about it?"

"I know it was a fort during the Revolutionary War," Ruth said. "Congress consolidated its military training facilities at West Point prior to the War of 1812, and the garrisons were converted into a private school after that. I'm pretty sure they graduate over a hundred boys a year today. Enrollment was much smaller when the school started."

"Whoever sent us this list picked these names for a reason," Dani said. "Or copied a list of selected names. It can't be true that every graduate of St. Adrian's went on to mentor a mass murderer or a serial killer. I'm thinking these men are a subgroup, like the Skull and Bones Club at Yale. All private schools have secret clubs."

"Mine didn't," Quinn said. "Or if it did, no one told me about it."

"Which proves how secret it was," Dani said, smiling.

Tommy found his old resentments rising, having grown up a townie with an elite private school nearby. His jock friends had called the St. Adrian boys *Addies* and took pleasure in spray-painting taunts and curse words on the private school's high stone walls. He also realized he resented that Dani was making jokes with Quinn but not with him.

"But how is any of this related to Abbie Gardener?" Carl said.

"Wait here," Tommy said. "I might be able to answer that."

He went to the den and opened the safe behind the mirror. Abbie's box was right where he'd left it. He brought it into the kitchen and set it on the food island, and the others gathered around.

"We found this in a secret compartment in the desk Abbie was using up in the library archives," Tommy said.

"It wasn't a secret compartment," Ruth said. "It was where secretaries used to keep their typewriters."

"What's a typewriter?" Tommy said.

"It's beautiful," Carl said, reaching his hand out toward the box, but reluctant to touch it.

"The problem is, we can't figure out how to open it."

"It may be a Himitsu-Bako box," Ruth said.

Tommy looked at her with surprise.

"Well, I *am* a research librarian," she said. "I'm going to need to do more than just sit around making sandwiches. They were popular in nineteenth-century Japan for keeping personal secrets. They open with a sequence of twists and turns and squeezes. Some take two moves, but others can take up to three hundred. In Europe in the eighteenth century they were called burr puzzles because the interlocking pieces were thought to resemble a seed burr."

"Or Lemarchand's boxes," Quinn said, taking the box in his hands and turning it over. "Believed to be portals to other planes of existence."

"You believe in that?" Dani said.

"No," Quinn said. "I read it in a horror novel."

"The inlay may be a version of *yosegi-zaiku*," Ruth said. "Japanese parquetry from the Edo period. Himitsu-Bako boxes were decorated with it, but the mosaic tiles were sometimes used as a key to open the box. Like those plastic puzzles where you slide the pieces around to make a picture."

"I saw Bobby Fischer on the *Tonight Show* once, and he unscrambled one of those in about ten seconds," Carl said.

"The chess master could do it," Dani said. "Quinn, you wanna give it a shot?"

Tommy felt insulted again, even though he saw the logic of asking Quinn and not him. Quinn pressed on various pieces of the inlay for no more than thirty seconds, then set the box down.

"I don't see how the pieces move if there's not a free space to move the first one into," he said.

"You wanna try, Carl?" Tommy said.

Carl shied away. "If Quinn can't figure it out, I'm sure I can't," he said. "Why don't you give it a try?"

"I have," Tommy said, puzzled by Carl's reluctance—it was the kind of challenge he would ordinarily be drawn to. "No luck."

"Try again," Dani said, the hostility in her voice cutting. "You're good with secrets."

Tommy closed his eyes, took a deep breath, and counted to ten, or tried, getting as far as three.

"Excuse us for a second," he said. "Dani, can I talk to you for a minute in the study?"

26.

"What's going on, Dani? You're furious at me and I have no idea why."

He leaned against his desk. She stood at the window, staring out into the darkness. She tried to collect her thoughts, to breathe deeply, to calm down and tell herself that the task at hand was more important than their relationship. For a moment she wondered if she could convince Tommy to postpone this conversation, but when she turned and saw the look on his face, she knew it couldn't wait.

"When were you planning to tell me Cassandra Morton was here?" she said.

"The second you walked in the door," he said. "When were you going to tell me you intended to bring Quinn into the circle? That decision should have been discussed first."

"There are a lot of things that should have been discussed first," she said. "Things that should have been discussed before you and I ever decided to . . . get involved."

"Getting involved with you wasn't something I 'decided,'" he told her. "I won't speak for you, but for me, it wasn't something I could have either planned or prevented. An army couldn't have stopped me from falling in love with you."

"Don't say another word," she said. "You're just digging the hole deeper."

"What hole?" he said, lowering his voice so that the people in the other room wouldn't hear him. "What hole are you talking about?"

"The hole of distrust," Dani said. "All right, I'll give you a chance. Tell me why Cassandra Morton is here."

"I don't know why she's here," Tommy said. "She just broke up with some Brazilian soccer dude and she needed a friend. I guess that's why."

"You didn't call her?"

"No," Tommy said. "As far as I knew, she was still in Los Angeles."

Dani moved toward the door.

"Wait," Tommy said. "Did you talk to her?"

"I ran into her in the parking lot at the inn," Dani said. "She couldn't find her rental car. Which was about twenty feet away in plain sight, by the way."

"She *thinks* I called her," Tommy said. "Apparently I pocket-dialed or something. She thought I was reaching out to her. I wouldn't do that."

"You never told her, 'You have a home in me'?" Dani asked. "And by the way, it's not 'You've Got a Home in Me.' It's 'You've Got a *Friend* in Me.'"

"I know," Tommy said. "It was a reference to something she said once. Her parents had just sold the house she grew up in, so she said to me, 'You're my home now.' And when we broke up, I told her she'd always have a home in me. It was just one of those things you say to soften the blow."

"You're saying you didn't invite her here," Dani said. "That you pocket-dialed her?"

"Apparently."

Dani was too hurt to laugh. "Let me see your phone."

"My phone?"

"Let. Me. See. Your. Phone."

He handed it to her. She scrolled through his text messages and found the one she'd seen earlier. She showed it to him.

He looked at it, stunned.

"That's one heckuva pocket-dial," she said.

He read the message three times, then checked the time it was sent.

"I was asleep when this was sent," Tommy said.

"You were asleep? Now you're trying to say you sleep-texted? No, wait—you sleep-pocket-texted?"

"Dani—"

"I was told you were going to betray me," she said. "That's why I'm kicking myself. Got it from a highly reliable source."

Tommy's eyes opened wide as he recalled that the angel had told him exactly the same thing.

"Someone you trust will betray you. How you handle it will make all the difference," he said. "Charlie told me the same thing."

"Why didn't you tell me?"

"I'm not sure. Why didn't *you* tell *me*?"

"I thought . . . Were you worried that I'd betray you?"

Tommy thought about it. "I think so," he said, "and it made me afraid. There's nothing I'm more afraid of than losing you."

"Then why did you lie to me?"

"I didn't lie to you. I'm not lying to you now."

She stared at him for a long moment, then said, "Well, when Cassandra gets here, we can ask her what happened."

"What do you mean, when Cassandra gets here? You invited her?"

"I borrowed your phone while you were out looking for Carl."

"You read my private texts *and* sent her a message from my phone, pretending to be me?"

"I did," she said. She felt deeply ashamed. At the time, she'd thought what she was doing fell under the rubric of "All's fair in love and war." She was fighting back, striking a blow against all the pretty little flirts who'd ever batted their phony eyelashes and stolen guys away from the smart girls who didn't know how to play that game. She now felt ashamed for a number of reasons, but chief among them was allowing herself to be reduced to an insecure fourteen-year-old again. "It was wrong, but I did it."

"When can we expect her to show up?"

"I don't know," Dani said. "Any minute. Unless she has trouble finding her car again."

"She's not stupid," Tommy said. He stepped closer to her. He wanted to take her hands in his, put his arms around her, kiss her, but he didn't know what was allowed anymore, and he didn't know what she wanted anymore.

"What's happening to us?" Dani said, tears welling.

"I don't know," he said. "I truly do not know."

They were interrupted by a knock on the door to the study. When Tommy answered it, his aunt was at the door, announcing that they had a visitor—a woman had buzzed the intercom at the gate.

"It's Cassandra," Ruth said. "Should I tell her you're not home?"

"No," Tommy said. "No lying. Open the gates and let her in. I'll be right out."

27.

When the silver Nissan Maxima eased to a stop in the courtyard, Tommy was surprised to see that Cassandra wasn't alone. She'd brought Julian Villanegre and Ben Whitehorse with her.

"What the heck did you tell her?" Tommy said.

"I said we were having a party," Dani said. "Or that you were, since she thought I was you."

"Cass tends to believe what people tell her," Tommy said.

"Cassandra Morton? The actress?" Quinn said, joining them at the window. "She's here?"

"I didn't know you were impressed by celebrities," Dani said.

"I'm not," Quinn said. "How do I look? Do I have anything stuck in my teeth?"

Tommy picked up the wooden box. There wasn't time to put it in the safe, so he hid it in the oven just as Cassandra knocked on his back door.

"Hello," she sang out with a bright smile as she entered. "Hello, everybody. I'd say let me introduce you to my new friends, but you already know—"

She stopped where she stood when she saw Dani.

"You're the woman from the parking lot," she said.

"I am," Dani said. "Or I was."

Cassandra smiled. "Well, I found someone to have dinner with at the pub you recommended."

"We saw her eating all by herself," Ben said. "Seeing people eating alone makes me sad. First I saw Professor Villanegre eating alone and then her, so I suggested we all eat together. It turned out we all know you, Tommy."

"Small town," Tommy said.

Cassandra looked cheerfully around the room. "So where's the party?"

"This is it," Tommy said. "Can I get you anything?"

"I would love a root beer float," Ben said. "Why do you have a Himitsu-Bako box in your oven?"

"I do?" Tommy said, unable to come up with anything better.

"Yes. It's right there," Ben said, pointing.

"Oh, *that* Himitsu-Bako box," Tommy said, while Ruth just looked at Quinn, who shrugged in reply.

"Is it like the bento boxes you get at sushi restaurants?" Cassandra said.

"No," Tommy said. "It's—"

"May I see it?" Villanegre said. "The young lady at the inn gave me your message that you'd found something of Abigail's. I got a later flight when I heard—may I?"

Tommy took the box from the oven and placed it once more on the food island where the art historian examined it from every angle before speaking.

"Napoleon had one of these," the Englishman said. "He used it to hold his war plans. They say it required an exact sequence of over one hundred moves to open it." He ran his fingers along the edges and traced the inlays, pressing and prodding gently, like a pediatrician examining a child with a stomachache. "You've obviously tried to open it."

"Many times," Tommy said.

"I thought we might bring it to the hospital and X-ray it," Dani said. "We were worried that it could be booby-trapped."

"Yes," Villanegre said. "That is a possibility. Have you shown it to anyone else?"

"No," Tommy said. "We just found it yesterday, in the desk Abbie Gardener was using in the library archives."

"Ah," Villanegre said. "I strongly suspected that this was part of the Gardener collection. I have something here that we might be able to use to open it."

He reached into the inside pocket of his coat and pulled out a brass cross, six inches by three, holding it out in front of him like a shield. He tucked the box under his arm and said, *"Qui faceret opera Diaboli—ut ejiciant vos invoco Angeli ex domo! Abire iubeo!"*

Tommy and Dani and the others looked at each other. Carl, who was standing behind the Englishman, took a step for the door, as if Villanegre had brandished a hand grenade.

"Gesundheit," Tommy said. "What do you think we are—vampires or something?"

Villanegre lowered his hand. "Oh, dear Lord," he said. "You don't know. You genuinely don't know, do you? It appears we are all on the same side." He lowered the cross.

"All on the same side of what?" Cassandra said frantically. "Will some-body *please* tell me what's going on here? Oh, wait a minute—I get it. This is one of those practical joke shows, isn't it? Where are the hidden cameras? Are you punking me, Tommy?"

Nobody moved or spoke.

"You're not, are you?" she said, now frightened.

Tommy shook his head.

"This is the worst party I've ever been to," Cassandra said as she plopped down on one of the high chairs beside the food island. "And I've been to some really bad ones."

"If you let me," Villanegre said, "I can explain."

"I think we'll all be more comfortable in the living room," Tommy said. "I'll throw a few logs in the fireplace."

28.

Villanegre promised to tell them what he knew about the box, but first he wanted to hear what they had to say. He'd produced the cross, he told them, because it was known that demons were discomforted by sacred icons, and in the obverse, his wielding it proved he himself could be trusted.

"I believe him," Tommy said. "I think he could be helpful to us."

"I certainly hope so," Villanegre said. "The fact that you have the box is testament to the gravity of the situation."

They took turns telling their story one more time for the benefit of Ben and Villanegre and Cassandra, Tommy filling in the details Dani left out and Dani doing the same when Tommy spoke. Quinn laid out the medical questions raised by the pill Dani had gotten from the Starbucks source and the "Doomsday Molecule"; two separate compounds, but they had to be related somehow. Dani ran through the list of names she'd received, and Ben recited what was understood about Hiawatha and the ancient demons that had somehow reappeared in America a thousand years ago. Tommy finished by noting that the murder of Julie Leonard had presented them with a mystery that opened into greater and greater mysteries, but each step of the way they'd been given signs to help them along the path, torches to light the way through a labyrinth where nothing was familiar and forms and "facts" constantly shifted.

Two important questions remained—what was Abbie Gardener trying to say to them, and what was the evil entity at St. Adrian's Academy planning? Given what the school's graduates had already accomplished, Tommy pointed out that there was a third question: how could they stop it?

"I believe I can help with the second question," Villanegre said. "You're quite right, young man, about the smaller mysteries opening doors to the larger ones. You know, Dr. Harris, it was no accident when I ran into you at Starbucks. I knew there was something about you when I looked into your eyes at the opening. I sensed our missions might converge, but I had to find out where your allegiances were. It is not accidental, either, that I've arrived in your town at this date and hour. This is something I've been pursuing for a long time."

He leaned forward and gently brushed a fleck of dust from the box Abbie had left behind, examining it for a moment.

"What I am about to tell you is going to sound rather fantastic," he said. "They say those who fail to understand history are condemned to repeat it. Understanding pre-history is even trickier, since it is by definition unrecorded. We can get only glimpses, intimations from various sources—cave paintings, stone monoliths, occasionally archaeological artifacts.

"When God sent his only Son, Jesus Christ, to die for us on the cross two thousand years ago, the world was a desperate place. As Dani's research demonstrates, there is evil in the world. It is here now, and it was walking the earth two thousand years ago. As you all understand, Lucifer was cast out of heaven, but he was not destroyed. He survived to influence men and to send his representatives to torment us and lead us astray. There is an unseen war raging between good and evil. I would not say mortal men are the pawns or foot soldiers in this war, because there are many on the side of evil who are very much willing volunteers, just as there are those on this side, on my side—on *our* side—who believe in God Almighty and who have trusted in Jesus Christ as Savior. Men and women who will take up arms and lay down their lives, as I would—as you would—for the cause of righteousness. We are not pawns. We participate. We *must* participate.

"But I'm a historian, not a theologian," he said.

A log in the fireplace popped loudly, causing Arlo the cat to jump up from the sofa where he'd been lying. Otto, dozing before the fire, wuffled in his sleep and his paws twitched, while Villanegre continued. He spoke of a time when the world had been ready for change, when the pagan Egyptian and Greek and Roman and Aztec and Incan civilizations had all failed, but had prepared mankind for the coming of a brand-new idea, the message Christ brought in a narrative that began in a manger in Bethlehem and ended on a cross at Golgotha. But that was a false ending—the true ending to the narrative came when the stone was rolled away and it was learned that Christ had defeated death, and that he'd shown us all the way that we too could find everlasting life.

"But as Christ's message began to spread, Satan and his forces redoubled their efforts. He sent his demons out to attack mankind and to teach them the ways of black magic and sorcery. In the ancient world one of these heathen pagan groups was called the Oak-Worshippers, or People of the Oak. The proto-Indo-European word for them was *deru-weid*, which Latinized as *druides*. The Welsh root *dryw* means 'seer,' but the meaning is more that of sorcerer or fortune-teller than visionary."

"Druids?" Dani said. "Are you saying East Salem has a *Druid* problem?"

"There go the real estate values," Tommy said.

"I warned you it was going to sound fantastical," Villanegre said. He explained that the Druids, who worshipped Satan and practiced his dark arts and engaged in cannibalism and human sacrifice, established themselves in Gaul, which at the time spread across most of modern-day France, Belgium, Luxembourg, Switzerland, and parts of Holland and Germany. They were driven out by the Romans, as one pagan civilization replaced another, but they always knew that Christianity was the true threat.

"As of about the second century AD, the Druids were pushed from the

223

continent and had relocated mainly in England and Ireland, where they managed to hang on by keeping a lower profile. As Christianity gradually transformed the Roman Empire—"

"Into the Holy Roman Empire?" Tommy guessed.

"Not quite," Villanegre said. "The HRE was a German affiliation of royal houses. But the word of Christ could not be stopped by artificial boundaries drawn on a map by man. By the end of the first millennium, the pagans had been essentially crushed in England and Ireland too."

"St. Adrian," Carl said. "The man who drove the last Druids from Great Britain."

"With the help of Charles the Black," Villanegre said. "Very effectively, it seemed. The name makes him sound a bit evil, but it refers to the color of the armor he chose, matte black, which allowed him to make stealthy attacks at night. His war horses were black as well. Charles was as ruthless as any warrior who'd ever drawn a broadsword, but he also fancied himself a rather clever chap and thought of a way to slip a spy behind enemy lines. He sent a fellow named Tibald into the Druid camp, where he pretended to worship with them. Tibald convinced the Druids he was one of them. Funny thing, though—"

"They turned him into a double agent," Quinn said. "Just a guess."

"Quite a good one," Villanegre said. "The Druids managed to flip poor Tibald. Some think Satan tempted him with a female demon. A succubus. Tibald, under the control of Satan, told Charles the Black precisely where the Druids were, and Charles and his men rode in on their mighty war horses and slayed them all. Two hundred and eight men and women. Brought their heads back to Adrian on pikes. The skulls are still at the abbey, buried in a sealed vault in the basement. And that, they thought, was that."

"Except?" Dani said.

"Except the 208 souls Charles slaughtered were not the last of the Druids. They weren't even Druids. They were Picts dressed as Druids. He'd been duped. I don't know what manner of sorcery got them to carry out that fatal masquerade, but it isn't hard to imagine."

"What happened to the real Druids?" Ruth asked. "They obviously wanted Charles to think he'd killed them all."

"And by the way, has anybody bought the film rights to this story?" Cassandra said.

"The real Druids," Villanegre said, smiling politely to Cassandra, "boarded two ships and sailed from the English shore."

"I didn't know the Druids were seafarers," Quinn said.

"They weren't. But they'd formed an alliance with some people who were very capable seafarers."

"Vikings," Ruth said. "Who else could it be?"

"Our people," Tommy said. "Sorry about that, guys."

"The same," Villanegre said. "The remaining Druids divided into two groups to better their chances of surviving. One ship sailed to the south and turned east at the Strait of Gibraltar to circle back through the Mediterranean and land in southern France. I should add that by this time—"

"When was this?"

"End of the eighth century," Villanegre said. "By this time the Druids who'd survived had learned their lesson. They'd learned that you can't hope to lie low and be undiscovered if you build massive stone monuments that are visible for miles."

"Stonehenge," Quinn said.

Villanegre nodded. "So they went underground. Literally. They worshipped only in caves. And they blended in with society and lived rather normal lives, except when they'd congregate to practice their black magic. But we tracked them down, eventually, after one poor fellow ended up on a rack and had the truth stretched out of him. We killed as many of them as we could find in what history has recorded as witch hunts. You may recall."

"There were a lot more than 104 people killed as witches," Dani said, recalling a figure from a women's studies class that said as many as six million women in Europe may have been executed for practicing witchcraft.

"Yes," Villanegre said. His tone became somber. "Much of that was Satan's doing, but some of it was ours, I'm afraid. We started a terrible mania that we hadn't anticipated. And we learned, from a very hard lesson, to play our cards much closer to the vest."

"You've been saying *we*," Carl said. "Who is this we?"

Villanegre studied him for a moment.

"People like you, Carl. People who've given their lives to God and pledged to renounce Satan and to defeat him. Originally we were the descendants of the soldiers who fought with Charles the Black. Some of us chose to wear the vestments and serve God in a public capacity. Others saw a greater wisdom in staying hidden and operating surreptitiously. It was a game of cat and mouse. We knew we hadn't found them all. We only rooted the last of them out of Europe after we saw that painting."

"*The Garden of Earthly Delights*?" Dani said. "The Duke of Ghent?"

Villanegre nodded. "He was merely a pawn. His oldest—and I dare say rottenest—son was a Druid high priest. They claimed they were an Adamite cult, trying to use sexuality to return to the state of grace man had originally known in the Garden of Eden. But they were just another hedonistic cult of charisma, of the sort we've seen many times over the millennia. The two figures emerging from the cave—"

"In the lower right-hand corner of the center panel of the painting," Tommy said.

"One is the Prince of Ghent, and the one whispering in his ear is a demon."

"What happened to the second ship?" Tommy said. "You said there were two."

"We never found out. But we received a prophecy. An angel told us that someday they would send for their painting, and when they were reunited with it, their powers would multiply."

"I know where the second ship went," Ben Whitehorse said. "Tommy, do you remember when I told you that Leif Ericson sailed for America with thirty-five men but returned with only thirty-four?"

"The Man of the North," Tommy said.

"Leif Ericson wasn't the first Viking to sail to America," Ben said. "When Ericson sailed, he was using a map that another man had drawn. That other man was the one the Druids hired to bring them to America. We don't know his name, but in Indian lore he's just called The Sailor."

"Does Indian lore say where he landed?"

"He is said to have sailed up the Hudson River as far as he could go and dropped them off," Ben said. "That would have been around Albany. Not so far from here. The Iroquois called it Muhheakantuck, which meant 'the river that flows two ways.'"

"Where'd they go from there?" Dani said.

"They went to the region of New York you call the Finger Lakes," Whitehorse said. "It was there that the Druids corrupted the people and taught them to be cannibals who practiced human sacrifice. They brought Thadodaho and the Wendigo to America."

"We had our theories, but until recently we had no proof," Villanegre said.

"How many 'we's' are there?" Tommy said.

"It's a very small and very secret group. There are twelve of us—like the twelve disciples. We call ourselves the Curatoriat. None of us knows who the others are, but we have ways of staying in contact with each other."

"If you don't know who the others are, you can't reveal the names if you're questioned," Dani said.

"Precisely," the Englishman said. "We are, in a fashion, the curators of that painting. Our task, since wiping out the last of the fiends in Europe, has been to find out what happened to the second ship. The painting currently hanging in the gallery at St. Adrian's originally hung in a cave in northern France, where it was used in what one might laughingly call worship. We're the ones who moved it to the chapel in the Duke of Ghent's

227

palace. We had to get it into the public view, despite its atrocious message, because we needed to use it as bait. We've been waiting over five hundred years. And now it's here."

"How are the members of the Curatoriat chosen?" Carl said.

"We are each responsible for selecting and training a successor," Villanegre said. "That is also a secret we keep. But we are ever vigilant, because we know that when the painting is reunited with Satan's vulgar acolytes, it will be a sign that time is short."

"Time is short?" Quinn said. "Short for what?"

Villanegre looked at him somberly but didn't answer.

"I'm still not clear what this has to do with Abbie Gardener," Dani said, resting her hand on the box. "Or with this."

"Ah, yes," Villanegre said. "As I said, there are twelve of us. Once there were thirteen. For a while, when we were unable to establish contact with the thirteenth, we assumed Satan had somehow found him and destroyed him. Then we heard from him. He was a wise man who had received a vision from God that to keep us all safe, only one should know who the other twelve were. The Guardian would be protected. God had blessed him and his successors. Or her—the Guardian is not necessarily male. We learned where the second ship had landed, and that the Guardian was there, fighting them alone but protected. Abbie Gardener was the Guardian, the last in a long line."

"She couldn't have been too protected," Tommy said. "They killed her."

"I don't know how they managed that," Villanegre said. "It worries me greatly. We think the forces of darkness are gaining strength. We don't know how or why."

"How do you know Abbie was the last?" Dani said. "I mean, how do you know she didn't pass the torch on to someone else?"

"I dearly hope she did," Villanegre said. "The Guardian was the coordinator. I and my fellow curators passed our messages through her, and we received our instructions from her. But the line went dead, so to speak. Mind you, we did not know her identity. We don't know each other's identities either. She knew ours, but neither man nor demon could put us into enough pain to get us to reveal her name because we didn't know it. I came here following the painting. And hoping."

"Is it George?"

"There's no right of primogeniture. That would be too easily defeated," he said. "By the way, those paintings in the house weren't fakes. I had no choice but to lie about them, or there'd be headlines from here to Singapore about the astonishing hidden art collection with a value well into the billions of dollars. The Curatoriat put it together over the centuries, piece by piece, and shipped it to the Guardian by various methods to keep the destination secret. We are to sell them when the time comes to raise funds."

"Funds for what?" Cassandra asked.

"It's a defense fund," Villanegre said. "The money raised can be spent only after a vote by the Curatoriat. We have the power of Jesus behind us, but to get things done here on earth, it helps to have financial resources."

"The question remains, what's in this, and how do we get it open?" Tommy said. He put his finger on the box and traced the inlays. "There might be a key we need. Though there's no hole to put a key into."

Dani pressed the central inlay in various places, then pressed the four smaller Celtic crosses.

"I already tried that," Tommy said.

"Maybe it takes a special kind of touch," Dani said. "Or combination. Like the keypad that opens the gate at the end of your driveway."

"It wouldn't take much pressure," Villanegre said. "The masters of marquetry during the Renaissance could work in incredibly small tolerances."

"I think if there are buttons that can be pushed, it would be those smaller crosses," Ben suggested. "Remember that demons can't overcome their physical aversion to sacred icons. They wouldn't be able to touch the crosses."

Tommy took up the box and pressed his fingers against the Celtic inlays.

"There are eight inlays," he said. "Four on the front and four on the back. But because of . . . this . . ." He stretched his hand as wide as he could. "Because of the distance between them, one person can only push four at a time, in corresponding pairs, one on the front and one on the back. So how many possible combinations are there?"

"For one person?" Quinn asked. "You need a factorial equation. Pascal's triangle. If AB and BA are the same, there are 120 combinations. If the order you press them in matters and AB is not the same as BA, then there are 392 ways to do it."

"What if it requires three sets of combinations?" Ruth asked. "Or four?"

"Then it's exponential," Quinn said. "Pascal's triangle becomes Pascal's pyramid. One hundred twenty cubed is 1,728,000. Three hundred ninety-two cubed is 60,236,228. To the fourth power—"

"In other words, a lot," Tommy said.

"Maybe it takes two to open it," Dani said. The others looked at her. "Simultaneously. If this is something one Guardian passes on to another, that would make sense."

"That would require harmony and cooperation," Villanegre added.

"Consistent with the Christian message," Dani said. "I think I'm starting to get the hang of this faith thing. Just hear me out—God wants us to love one another, right? He doesn't want us fighting amongst ourselves."

She looked Tommy in the eye long enough for him to get the message meant just for him.

"I think the box can only be opened by two people," she said. "Like the launch boxes on nuclear submarines where two people have to put their keys in the locks in order to fire the missiles. It's a fail-safe, in case one person goes crazy and tries to fire them on his own."

"That sounds reasonable," Ruth said.

"But what's the pattern?" Dani said. "The combination? Quinn, how many possibilities with two people at the same time? Never mind. Too many."

"Or not," Tommy said. Now all eyes were on him.

"What do you mean?" Dani asked.

"Whoever made this box wanted the good guys to open it and the bad guys to keep out," Tommy explained. "Maybe the combination is something else a demon can't do—like make the sign of the cross. Top, bottom, left, right. Head, navel, left shoulder, right shoulder. The buttons are already arranged in a cross-like pattern."

"*In nomine Patris, et Filii, et Spiritus Sancti.* Amen," Villanegre said. "It's certainly worth a try."

"Tommy," Dani said, "hold the end of the box just the way you were, with your thumbs on the top and your fingers on the bottom. Okay— bring it this way."

Tommy extended the box, and Dani held the opposite end in both hands, pressing the top inlays with her thumbs and the bottom ones with her fingers.

"Now press the pair at the top," she said. Tommy did as she instructed. "Hold them in, and I'll press the pair at the bottom. Okay, so now, Tommy, press the inlays on the left side . . ."

"Got it," he said.

"And I'll press here . . ."

Dani and Tommy pressed, then pulled. The box slid open.

29.

Nested inside the box was a book, about twelve inches by eight, and three inches thick. On the cover were the words *Vademecum Absconditus* embossed in gold leaf.

"A *Vademecum* is a reference," Villanegre said. "The Oxford Vademecum lists phone numbers of the colleges and local restaurants and such. *Absconditus . . .*"

"Means secret," Ruth said. "Or concealed."

"Yes," Villanegre said. "I'd suppose it means it's a reference of secret things."

"That's so weird," Cassandra said to Tommy. "I had a dream in which you were looking at a book."

Tommy was startled and tried hard not to show it as he looked at Dani. He could see by her reaction that she too had immediately grasped the implications of what Cassandra had said. If Cassandra had had a prophetic dream about Tommy, with such specific imagery, it signified more than just a random reconfiguration of preexisting memes. It meant the mosaic of God's design included her.

"Dreams are one way we've been getting messages," Tommy told her. "Some of us have found connections in our dreams." He looked at Dani again. "Carl," he said, offering his friend the first chance to open it. "You wanna go first?"

"No, no," Carl said, waving him off and stepping back, holding his hands up in refusal. "All yours."

While Tommy carefully lifted the book from the box, Carl cleared the magazines from the coffee table and spread a polar fleece throw on the table to protect the book.

Tommy set the book down and gently ran his hand across the surface, feeling the ridges and depressions of the leather and the indentations of the embossed title. He couldn't begin to guess how old it was. He carefully opened it, placing the tip of his little finger beneath the upper corner of the cover and gently folding it back.

The title page was only that—the same words that were on the cover, but hand lettered and surrounded by a colorful decorated border of leafy vines bearing fruits and flowers.

"I do know a bit about these as works of art," Villanegre said. "May I?" He reached in to feel the paper. "I believe that's calf vellum. It's rare to find such a well-preserved example. Too dry and it turns brittle, and above 40 percent humidity, it gelatinizes. Or else mold destroys it."

"The library attic would be a good place to put it, in that case," Ruth said.

"The *rinceaux*," he explained, "that's the decorative border—and the script, which is *insular majuscule*, were commonly found in Psalters and Books of Hours in medieval Britain and Ireland. The black-letter gothic script didn't come into favor until the thirteenth century, so this most likely predates that. I'd be willing to bet the red ink is insect-based. The yellow is probably from tumeric or saffron."

Tommy carefully turned the page. The facing page seemed to have been written in a different hand from the title page. Tommy turned the book so that Villanegre and Carl could have a better look. It read:

TU TITULARI SACRO TEXTU VOS HAEC CUSTOS,
HAEC VOBIS IN MANUS CONFREGI CATENAS
TU TENENTES ET ABSCONDITUS ES POSSESSIO IMPETUM

CUM SANCTO MUNERE USQUE AD ULTIMUM SPIRITUM
TUUM ET ANIMAM TUAM ADVERSUS OMNES SATANAE
ET OMNIBUS OPERIBUS EIUS VIRTUTEM,
OMNEM GLORIAM DEI,
ET PUERUM EIUS CUSTODIO.

HAEC MANDO VOBIS,
UT ERAT DICTUM,
IN NOMINE PATRIS ET FILII ET SPIRITUS SANCTI.
EXCEPTEUR SINT RENATI,
ET ACCIPE VOCATIONEM SACRAM,
HABEBIS PROMISSUM CAELI IN ALTERA VITA,
ET HOC IN CUSTODIA ANGELORUM.

ET AMARE EIUS HUMILIS ANCILLA,
ADRIANI
ABBATIS IN ABBATIA SANCTI AUGUSTINI
CANTUARIENSIS

"Oh dear," the Englishman said. "I may be wrong, but I believe this is Middle Latin, or what was called Church Latin. Not the Latin of Cicero or Caesar that I'm familiar with."

"Do you mind if I try?" Ben said. Tommy was doubtful but moved aside so that Ben could sit in front of the book. He settled into his chair, aligned the book, and then leaned in to study the text. "That's funny-looking writing."

"Can you read it?" Tommy said.

"You, the holder of this sacred text," Ben read slowly, studying the words carefully. *"You, the keeper of these words, you whose hands have broken this lock, you hold the secret. And you are charged by this*—oh, wait; make that

by the fact of your possession—with a holy task to give until . . . Sorry, can't make that out . . . *to offer your last breath, your life, and all your strength to the battle against Satan and his works, and to glorify God and to keep safe his every child.* That's this part here."

He pointed to a passage.

"*This I ask*—no, I think it says command—*this I command of you, to keep this promise, in the name of the Father, the Son, and the Holy Ghost. If you are born again, and accept this sacred calling, and keep his command-ments, you will have the certain promise of heaven in the next life, and the protection of angels in this one.*"

He leaned back and smiled. "That's good to know. It explains some-thing I was wondering about," he said.

"What did you need to know?" Cassandra asked.

"It explains why I'm here," Ben said. "What my purpose is."

"What's the last line?" Dani said. "I recognize the name Adrian there."

"The last line is just the signature of the guy who wrote this," Ben said. "*His humble and loving servant, Adrian, Archbishop of Canterbury.*"

"The man himself," Ruth said.

"Scholars of the day believed Latin was a language that would never die," Villanegre said. "Like English today, I suppose. He must have given the book, or part of it, to Charles the Black. This page was his commission."

"*Sic transit gloria,*" Dani said.

"The keeper of the book is protected by angels," Tommy said, looking at Carl. "So where were they the night Abbie died?"

"She was no longer the keeper of the book," Dani said. "But why did she hide this in the library?"

"She wasn't thinking too straight toward the end," Tommy said. "If she was being protected, she was still over a hundred years old. Nobody beats the clock."

"If it takes two people to open it, what was she doing in the attic alone?" Ruth said.

"It takes two to open it," Tommy said, "but it only took one to hide it. She brought it there. Probably from her home."

He turned to the next page, which had, rather than words, a parade of runes and glyphs drawn across the page in sequences that reminded Dani of ancient Egyptian hieroglyphics. They were executed in the same style as the pictographs found in Leatherman's Cave. Ben put his finger on the first rune, then the second, then the third. He turned the next page, then the next, then skipped ahead a dozen pages, and a dozen more.

"I know what this is," he said. "It's rather remarkable. It's an Algonquin Bible. A translation of the main stories, not a complete, word-for-word rendering. This canoe with two bears in it and a man and his family is Noah and the flood. The bear was the symbol for all animal life. And this drawing . . ." He quickly flipped through the pages to find what he was looking for. "Here—what would you think that is?"

He pointed at a grouping of feathers surrounding a child, with a deer or elk standing next to him and three men who appeared to be chiefs.

"That's the Nativity," Tommy said.

"Here's the Star of David," Ben said, pointing. He smiled. "The man who wrote this wouldn't have used donkeys because the people who lived here wouldn't have known what he was referring to, so he drew an elk."

He leafed through more pages, letting them reveal their narratives. On the last page of runes Tommy saw, though it took a bit of effort to decode the images precisely, a trial and a crucifixion and a cave, and a man rising into the stars.

"Who drew it?" Villanegre said.

"Hiawatha," Ben said. "This white canoe here was the mark he made. Deganawida—"

"The Man of the North," Dani explained to Cassandra. "He was a Christian Viking who stayed behind when Leif Ericson sailed back to Iceland. Sort of the first missionary in the Western Hemisphere."

"Deganawida told Hiawatha the stories, and Hiawatha translated them," Ben said. "Deganawida must have brought this calf vellum with him."

Ben then turned the page again, and showed that the closing images of the Algonquin Bible were not the final pages of the book. After the last page of runes there was a blank page, and then a page upon which something was written in a script none of them could recognize or parse. Without being able to translate this text, they were still able to conclude that the pages contained a series of letters. As they turned the pages of these letters, they were gradually able to read and understand them, because they were written in a language that grew closer and closer to modern-day English. The first letter they could fully understand began:

Dear Robert,

As thou holdest this book and letter, it shall indicate that thou hast been chosen not only by me but by the Lord God Himself, who hast told me thou art a Good Christian and worthy of carrying out this Sacred mission. This is a secret thou art commanded to keep, for in the forfeit of such, shalt thou surely fail. When the day cometh that thou must choose a successor, thou shalt copy this letter to him.

A great evil hath come onto this land. That evil is nothing less than Satan himself and the fallen angels who do his bidding. They will seek to find you out and destroy you if they can. Thou shalt be safe as long as this book is kept close and these words live in thine heart. In our Lord and Saviour Jesus Christ, from Whom all blessings flow and in Whom only salvation and the promise of Eternal Life may be found, shalt thou find guidance and surety in the wisdom of His Holy Might . . .

"Can we go back for a moment?" Villanegre said. "I'd like to see the first letter again."

He read it several times.

"You said that Hiawatha and Deganawida defeated Thadodaho, but that they were in turn visited by an affliction?" he asked Ben.

"Yes," Ben said. "The people who lived here enjoyed an abundance difficult to imagine today. Before the Europeans arrived in great numbers, a squirrel from Massachusetts could travel from tree limb to tree limb and reach the Mississippi River without ever touching the ground. The skies turned black from flocks of passenger pigeons so numerous they blotted out the sun. You know about the buffalo. Because there was so much food to eat, the people had no need to grow crops or keep livestock. But the Europeans came from lands where they'd learned to live with animals the people who already lived in America would have considered unclean."

"And those domesticated animals exposed the early Europeans and cultures from the Mesopotamian regions to all kinds of diseases. The Europeans had built up strong immunities. The Native Americans had none," Dani said.

Ben nodded.

"I've read estimates by pandemiologists," Quinn said, "that as much as 95 percent of the indigenous American population died off due to exposure to diseases to which the European settlers had acquired immunities in childhood. Measles, the flu, all sorts of things."

"So many people died," Ben said. "It was germ warfare. That's the affliction the demon-worshippers gave to Hiawatha and Deganawida."

"And Hiawatha and Deganawida knew what would happen," Dani said. "They knew they would infect the others, so they quarantined themselves. At the time it would have been the only way to stop the infection from spreading."

"The Black Death was around then," Quinn said. "And don't forget our boy Albert Gitchell and the Spanish flu epidemic of 1918. I wonder how long Satan has been using biological weapons."

"So they put what they knew in a book," Tommy said.

"How did the book get from there to Abbie?" Dani asked. "Not to Abbie, but to the first Guardian?"

"Either the Guardian found them or they found the Guardian," Villanegre said. "I'd love to know that provenance. It's probably in this first letter. The one we can't translate."

Villanegre turned to the second-to-the-last letter, a loose-leaf insert that began, *Dear Abigail.*

```
I have chosen you as my successor, Abigail. I'm writing
this letter to you, and when it's your turn to choose a
successor, you will need to write a letter to him or her
in your own words. I can tell by your fine good manners
and deportment that you are a shining model of feminine
grace and charm, and have in you a keen intelligence,
and by means of this alone you will prosper and do well.
However, as you will see, I have chosen you according to
the direction of our Lord and Savior Jesus Christ, and by
his guidance through prayer. I know you love and worship
him and that your heart is filled with piety, charity, and
humility. In the task I am about to describe, Abigail, you
will need to use all your God-given talents, and be both
humble and bold . . .
```

It was signed by a man named Julius Leominster.

Quinn pointed at the font. "That's a typewriter," he said to Tommy. "You asked."

"I know that name," Ruth said. "He was on the library board when they built the extension. He was a banker. Had a reputation as a meanie."

"I think the Guardians do what they can to keep the town at bay," Tommy said. "Which is why Abbie cultivated the image of an eccentric. This is the letter that recruited her."

"Go to the last letter," Dani said anxiously.

Tommy turned the page. The final letter was signed by Abbie Gardener, and it began, *Dear Jerome*.

The room was silent.

"Well, I have to say I didn't see that one coming," Tommy finally said. "Who's Jerome?"

"Read the letter," Dani said to Dr. Villanegre. "Maybe it will tell us."

The historian read:

The fact that you hold this book in your hands means that you have been chosen both by me and by God, to whom I have prayed for guidance. He has told me that you are pure of heart and have the courage and strength to carry out this sacred mission. I knew when I visited your class when you were in fourth grade, and you were all excited that "the Witch Lady" was coming to speak (Oh dear!). But you were not afraid of me. You spoke up, asking good questions about witches and ghosts, when the others sat in silence or perhaps even made fun of you and your faith in Jesus Christ.

You must never tell another soul about this letter and the contents of this book, for telling others will place them in great danger. There may be times when you feel this to be a burden, but it is indeed a sacred calling from which you cannot turn away. There is no way that I can overstate the importance, except to say that there are many in this place where you live who would kill you and everyone you love to get their hands on this book, for once they have it in their possession, the knowledge of their existence will disappear with it.

Jerome, you need to know a story that will probably

240

surprise you. Hundreds of years before the Pilgrims landed at Plymouth Rock, a great evil came to this land. I have spent my life researching that evil, trying to understand it . . .

Her letter went on to describe how St. Adrian drove the pagans from the English shores but learned later that he'd been deceived, and how he'd commissioned Charles the Black to find out where they'd gone. Charles had created a society of pious men, scholars and historians who knew the battle against evil had not been won. She described how they'd been able to discover a group of pagans in France, but not all of them. The remainder of the group had sailed west across the Atlantic, where no one of that day could follow. Some so-called "wise men" believed the ship had sailed off the edge of the world. Some held out hope the ship had been lost in a storm. Others feared it had succeeded and made landfall.

The men charged by Charles the Black, and the descendants of those men, watched and read, studied and researched, until they learned of an account written in Norway of a Holy Man who'd traveled to America, where he encountered a group of brutal savages who practiced witchcraft, human sacrifice, and cannibalism.

Abbie's account told the story of Hiawatha and Deganawida and how they were able to defeat Thadodaho. Villanegre read the rest of the letter out loud.

But all they were able to do was drive the Druids into hiding. They knew that if they surfaced again, they would be destroyed outright by the angels of the Lord. Then one day more ships arrived, carrying people who looked like them. Finally, enough Europeans migrated to the New World to allow the evil ones to blend back in, and then it became even more difficult to find them.

241

At the time of the American Revolution, the place we know as St. Adrian's Academy was called Fort Atticus. It had barracks for the troops of the great generals, first George Washington and then Horatio Gates, who turned it into a military training facility. After the war was over, the new government moved all their training facilities to West Point across the Hudson. Fort Atticus was sold to a group of so-called academics who claimed they wanted to turn it into a college to rival Harvard or William and Mary. They proposed to name their school after St. Adrian, the medieval Archbishop of Canterbury credited with driving the darkness out of England.

Posing as an institution of higher learning, it became a school for depravity. In the name of academic freedom, they resisted governmental oversight and refused to open their rolls for review. The walls of the old fortress, fallen into disrepair, were restored and refortified. Boys from the highest ranks of society, from all over the world, were recruited and tested. Some were found lacking, and they passed through the school with a standard education without ever suspecting there were others among them receiving a second, more subversive education. Yet in all graduates the mandate for secrecy surpassed all other bonds uniting them. They were charged to aid and assist each other as they made their way in the world. St. Adrian's graduates were to hire other St. Adrian's graduates without question; they were to assist each other and they were to tell no one, ever, what went on inside those walls. It was always a simple choice for any St. Adrian's graduate: follow the rules and keep the secrets, and you will become wealthy and prosper; break the rules, and you will perish and go unrecorded in the annals of time.

Jerome, please understand that these are not merely the evil deeds of bad men. The evil at St. Adrian's Academy is the work of Satan and the fallen angels who do his bidding. They will seek to find you out and destroy you. They will destroy not only you but all who know and love you, because they seek to erase you and delete the memory of you.

You will be safe as long as you hold this book close and keep these words in your heart. I know that God will keep you safe from harm, but you must pray to him daily for guidance. And when you feel you are ready, you must choose someone to succeed you, and pass this book and the box that holds it on to him or her, along with your own letter.

But, Jerome, always remember how the devil works, by making you uncertain of all the things you think you know and believe, by sowing confusion and by planting doubt, by deceiving and inveigling. The truth is not uncertain, Jerome. The message of Jesus Christ is not ambiguous or unclear. If you learn how to practice your faith, the faith you voiced with such strength and confidence even as a child, you will see that the Lord shines a light on the truth, a special kind of light that you will begin to notice.

Villanegre stopped. The room fell silent.

"Okay," Dani said. "That didn't help. Who's Jerome?"

"She talks about visiting a fourth-grade class," Quinn noted.

"Yeah, but she'd been doing that for fifty years. Maybe longer," Tommy said.

"Is the letter dated?" Ruth asked.

"None of them are," Villanegre said, turning the page.

"Jerome is obviously the person she chose as her successor," Dani

243

said. "I think if we find him, we can find the rest of the answers we're looking for."

"Perhaps this will help," Villanegre said. He held between two fingers a small envelope he'd found tucked into the pages of the book after Abbie's letter. The envelope was plain, cream-colored paper, without postage, the size of a thank-you note. He lifted the closing flap and removed a piece of paper from the envelope. Villanegre read the words written on the page, raised his eyebrows, and said only, "Indeed."

He handed the paper to Dani to read.

Dear Ms. Gardener,

My name is Julie Leonard and I am a freshman at East Salem High. My father, Jerome Louis Leonard, abandoned my mother and sister and me ten years ago, but it doesn't make sense to me because that was not the kind of father he was. I was looking for him and finally found him a year ago with the help of Google and some other stuff, and he was living in Portland, Maine. I got a ride from a friend and we went to the address. No one was there, so I left a letter under his door. In my letter I told him I wasn't mad at him and that I hadn't told anybody I'd come to see him but I just wanted to talk to him. About a month later I got a letter from him that said I could ask you and to stay away from St. Adrian's Academy. So I am asking. I don't know what I'm supposed to ask, but if you have anything you could tell me that might help explain, please let me know.

Yours truly,
Julie Leonard

The letter ended with her cell phone number and e-mail address.

"That explains what Julie was doing at the party," Tommy said. "The surest way to get teenagers to do something is to tell them not to."

"She saw Amos as her way in," Dani said. "She was trying to find out what happened to her father. Do we know if she ever talked to Abbie?"

"We can ask at the nursing home," Tommy said. "She might have visited."

"The question is, how much could Abbie have told her? How much was Abbie even capable of telling her?"

"Something must have gone wrong," Quinn said. "She chose her successor, but her successor didn't step up."

"That's why I'm here," Villanegre said. "We hadn't heard from the Guardian in some time. The last thing we heard was a cryptic message: 'St. Adrian's is moving.' We didn't know what it meant."

He turned several blank pages and came to the third section of the book, separated from the first two sections with a title page that read *Curatoria*. He read a bit of the next page, then shut the book.

"This is what I feared," he said. "The Guardian has always been the keeper of the names. I imagine my name is on that list toward the end. I can't read it because I don't want to know. Only the Guardian can know the names of the Curatoriat. You can imagine how eager the fiends would be to get their hands on such a list."

"When was the last time Abbie visited the archives at the library?" Tommy asked his aunt, who paused to think.

"I'm not sure of the exact date," Ruth said. "But I know it was the day before George took her to High Ridge Manor. I know because I said to one of my volunteers, 'I don't believe it—she was just here yesterday, fit as a fiddle.'"

"Now we know why Amos Kasden killed Julie Leonard," Tommy said. "The question is, how did they know? Did Julie do something to give herself away? We didn't think Julie fit some sort of demented fantasy Amos was having, but we didn't think she was chosen at random either."

"Tommy thought somebody had put Amos up to it," Dani said.

"Like the mystery man in the cave," Villanegre said. "The dark conspirator who whispers 'murder' in the madman's ear."

"I'll call Casey and see if he can find anything out about Jerome Leonard, recently of Portland, Maine," Dani said.

"We really need to find George Gardener," Tommy said.

"Why don't you just track him?" Ben said.

"I appreciate the suggestion, Ben," Tommy said, "but this isn't one of those Westerns where the outlaws ride horses that leave hoofprints on the riverbank."

"No, it's not," Ben said. "These days it's even easier to track somebody because they drive cars that leave prints that never stop. I told you before, I'm a really good tracker. And unless I miss my guess, that wonderful creature sleeping in front of the fire is an even better tracker than I am."

"Otto?" Quinn said. The dog raised his head at the sound of his name.

"Do you think he could do it?" Tommy said.

"I've been training him," Quinn said, "but I've never actually tried to track with him. It's worth a shot."

"He's a smart dog," Ben said. "Big one too."

"We'll go first thing in the morning," Tommy said. "I've got NVGs and some Luminol that'll show blood, if there is any. And a metal detector. Now that there are eight of us, I think we should keep watch in pairs."

"Why don't I take the first watch alone, and then two of you can relieve me?" Carl said.

"You need some rest," Tommy said. "You and Dr. Villanegre can go last."

"I'll take the first watch," Dani said.

"I'll take it with you," Cassandra said. "My body is still on LA time anyway."

"I thought you said you're doing a show on Broadway," Tommy said. The idea of Cassandra and Dani talking into the wee hours, just when he and Dani were on the mend, made him uncomfortable. Then again, he had nothing to fear from the truth. Maybe they'd sort it out, whatever it was, and things would be better in the morning.

"I am," Cassandra said. "But rehearsals don't start for another week."

"Okay, then," Tommy said. "Everyone get a good night's sleep, because . . ."

"Because what?" Ruth said.

"I don't know," Tommy said. "That's just what people say at times like this."

"He's right," Cassandra said. "I've said it in three movies. Once with a British accent."

"Which was quite good," Villanegre said.

"Thank you," Cassandra said, putting on a British accent. "I should have been born the Queen of England. I would *so* rock those hats."

"One thing," Tommy said to all of them. "Abbie was right when she said the more people who know about the book, the greater the danger. That just multiplied times eight."

"Can I make a suggestion?" Ben said. "You should let your chickens out of the coop. They're very sensitive creatures. If the power goes out, they'll make a good alarm system."

30.

Dani pulled a book off a shelf in Tommy's library, a collection of passages by Carl Gustav Jung. He was the founder of analytic psychology, but he'd also been a bit of a mystic, a man of science who nevertheless believed that man's fundamental nature was spiritual and religious. His quest for knowledge was never-ending and as open-minded as any intellect she'd ever encountered, which is why he'd long been a personal hero of hers. After a brief search, she found the passage that had convinced her she needed to go to Africa to work for Doctors Without Borders:

Anyone who wants to know the human psyche will learn next to nothing from experimental psychology. He would be better advised to abandon exact science, put away his scholar's gown, bid farewell to his study, and wander with a human heart throughout the world. There in the horrors of prisons, lunatic asylums and hospitals, in drab suburban pubs, in brothels and gambling-halls, in the salons of the elegant, the Stock Exchanges, socialist meetings, churches, revivalist gatherings and ecstatic sects, through love and hate, through the experience of passion in every form in his own body, he would reap richer stores of

knowledge than text-books a foot thick could give him, and he
will know how to doctor the sick with a real knowledge of the
human soul . . .

Cassandra was standing in the doorway, holding a copy of *People* magazine she'd found in what Tommy told her was Chick Room 2.

"What are you reading?" Cassandra said. "It's gotta be more interesting than this stuff."

"A collection of quotes from Carl Jung," Dani said. "He was a Swiss
psychiatrist."

"I know you think I'm just a silly actress, but I know who Carl Jung
was," Cassandra said.

Dani put her book down. "I'm so sorry. You're right. Will you accept
my apology?"

"I will," she said. "I could also name a dozen actresses who, if you asked
them, 'Who was Carl Jung?' would probably say, 'The same guy before he
was Carl Old.' You're a psychiatrist, aren't you?"

"I am."

"Why didn't you tell me you knew Tommy when I spoke to you in the
parking lot?"

"I didn't think it would matter to you."

"It was kind of like lying to me."

"You're right."

"And why did you tell me there was a party? Tommy told me it was you
who sent the invitation, not him. That was a lie too."

"It was," Dani said. "I'm sorry. I'm not handling this very well."

She recalled Charlie's admonition: "*How you handle it will make all
the difference.*" At the time she'd sent Cassandra the e-mail, Dani had convinced herself that she was confronting the situation head-on and acting
with integrity. She could see now that she'd lied and she'd gotten someone
involved who might not be prepared for what was ahead.

"I guess I was just hoping we could all have a nice little chat and find out what's going on," she said.

"Well, we've certainly had that," Cassandra said. "One minute I'm looking forward to a nice holiday in the country, and the next minute I'm fighting a vast satanic conspiracy to destroy the earth. I've seen that movie. I was *in* that movie. But this isn't a movie and it isn't funny."

"No," Dani said. "It isn't. Tommy says he must have pocket-dialed you. He says he never told you, 'You have a home in me.'"

"If Tommy says he didn't do it, he didn't do it," Cassandra said. "He's the most honest person I've ever met."

"You can't pocket-dial an entire text message," Dani said.

"Well, then one of these Satan's people must have done it," Cassandra said. "With all the weird things you've all been talking about tonight, a mysterious text message doesn't seem so implausible, does it?"

They looked at each other for a moment, wondering which way the conversation was going to turn. Were they going to be friends or enemies?

Cassandra smiled. "As long as we're being honest," she said, "I was always jealous of you."

Dani guffawed. "Are you kidding? *You* jealous of *me*? That's the most ridiculous . . ."

But she could see Cassandra wasn't joking.

"I find that hard to believe," Dani said, "coming from 'one of the most intensely beautiful actresses on the American screen,' as I recall reading in *Entertainment Weekly*."

"I don't ordinarily read anything written about myself," Cassandra said. "Which sounds like I'm so above it all, but I'm so not. The good stuff is just silly, but the bad stuff *kills* me. I am *not* thick-skinned. Even when there's a mostly positive article, it might have one bad little sentence like, 'Morton was miscast in the part and yet . . .' I never finish the sentence to see what the 'and yet' is because I'm too upset. If people who dream of being famous only knew how awful it is to pick up a magazine or a news-paper and see where someone . . . I mean, I know it's part of the deal. Just don't be jealous of me. Pretty girls in Hollywood—well, you know all the clichés. And I'll be completely honest with you—you know what's going to happen in ten years to pretty girls in Hollywood?"

"What?"

"Unemployment," Cassandra said. "One hundred percent, because in ten years you won't be able to tell the difference between a real woman and CGI, and computer-generated women will be prettier and they won't grow old or gain weight or ask to be paid what they're worth." She set her magazine on the desk. "I was jealous of you because you were the one who got away. He was too much of a gentleman to talk about you, but I knew what you meant to him."

"You didn't think he was trying to get back with you when he sent you the text message?"

"Assuming he sent it," Cassandra said, "which I don't think is the case. But at the time that I thought he had sent it, no. Not at all. Do you want to know what he said when we broke up?"

"I don't know," Dani said. "Do I?"

"He said, 'Cass, the thing that was there inside of you, that I fell in love with, will always be there, and I will always love that part of you, because that was the piece of the puzzle where we interlocked. But you know, there's a lot more than two pieces to a puzzle, and the rest of them don't fit. That doesn't make them good or bad pieces. They just don't fit.'"

"Wasn't that a line you used in your last movie?" Dani said.

"It was," Cassandra said. "I stole it from Tommy. But when he said it, I knew how I'd been trying to force the pieces to fit, like when you're doing a picture puzzle and you try to jam it in and hit it with a hammer and then pretend the whole thing works. But *you* fit him. I knew that then, and I can see that now."

"Wow," Dani said. "You really are America's sweetheart."

"Oh no, I'm not," Cassandra said. "I'm a BC. Basket Case. Some people fake their own deaths. I just learned at an early age how to fake my own life."

"There's a kind of therapy based on that idea," Dani said. "It's called behavioral modification. Sort of like the longer you act normal, the closer you get to being normal. Fake it till you make it."

"I must have missed that one," Cassandra said. "I've tried all the others. Being with Tommy put me on the right track in so many ways. I'd be lying if I said I wasn't still jealous, seeing the way he looks at you. I wanted that to be me, but it's not and it never will be."

"Knowing him has put me on the right track too."

"Let's bake the boys cookies," Cassandra said. "Or is that too wholesome? Darn. I've been trying to be edgier."

"That's not the problem," Dani said. "I'm not exactly handy in the kitchen."

"The kitchen!" Cassandra exclaimed. "See? I *knew* you'd know the best place to make cookies."

"What kind?"

"Depends on what we can find in the cupboards," Cassandra said. "I have an app on my phone where you put in the ingredients and it tells you what you can make."

31.

Tommy and Quinn took the second watch. As they changed shifts, the women mentioned that there was a plate of cookies on the counter. When they'd left, Tommy took a bite of one.

"What kind are they?" Quinn asked.

"I'm not sure," Tommy said. "It's like a fried oatmeal patty with either Craisins or Gummi Bears in it."

"Is it good?"

"*Good* isn't the word I'd use."

"What is?"

"Words fail me. Maybe chewy. What are you looking for?"

Quinn had asked if he might plug in his laptop because he wanted to follow up on some of the research he'd been doing. The computer screen in front of him was a jumble of numbers.

"I don't know," he said. "It would certainly expedite things if I did."

"Well, in that case, what aren't you looking for?" Tommy said. "Maybe that would narrow it down."

"Well, I'm not looking for miracles," Quinn said. "I just don't understand something about Provivilan. We know Linz is making it. We know Bauer is a graduate of St. Adrian's, and we know his name is on Dani's list, but I can't figure out how the drug counter-indicates, which is a soft way

253

of saying it ought to be the same poison Amos was taking, because that would make sense, but it's not. I heard a colleague call it 'world peace in a bottle.'"

"Can you get other samples to test?"

"Don't need other samples," Quinn said. "We broke it down. Which I suppose is something I should have done when I started taking it, but I had no reason to suspect."

"Wait a minute," Tommy said. "You're taking it?"

Quinn looked up from his laptop. "I am. It's a dirty little secret among big pharm workers. When we discover a drug that works, we sometimes cadge a sample or two for ourselves."

"Your friend Illena didn't get it for you?"

"She helped. Please don't tell Dani."

"I think she knows about Illena," Tommy said.

"No—don't tell her I'm taking Provivilan. I once spouted off, back when I thought I knew everything, how the only thing keeping half the known world from slaughtering the other half is the pharmaceutical industry. I'd look like a hypocrite if she knew."

"Okay," Tommy said. "But why are you taking it? Or is that too personal?"

"It is," Quinn said. "But I can't see why one wouldn't. As far as I can tell, there is absolutely nothing a full-grown human being has to fear from this drug. I would say, from personal experience, it could be the wonder drug they say it is."

"I thought it was developed to treat autistic kids," Tommy said.

"Ten years ago, when the research and the development work first started, yes, that was true," Quinn explained. "But it's often the case that a drug developed for one purpose can serve another. They just learned that a fairly common sleeping pill can rouse patients from their comas who were believed to be brain-dead. No one would have thought. And if Provivilan can help adults, Linz is going to sell a lot more of it than if it just helped autistic kids. Look at me. Living proof. Haven't you noticed how full of good cheer I am?"

"I've seen you trying, but it comes off a little phony. No offense."

"Don't worry," Quinn said. "You can't hurt my feelings. I'm taking the feel-good wonder drug, remember?"

"Maybe there's another way to look at it," Tommy said.

"Well," Quinn replied, "as I said, I can't find any reason to be alarmed by the interactions of Provivilan with gonadal steroids. The other drug, whatever Amos was on, absolutely, but this just won't do it. I mean, maybe if you took massive doses . . ."

Tommy thought a moment. He remembered the riddle of the light-bulb and the three switches. The fourth dimension was time. Look forward in time.

"Maybe you don't have to be grown at all," he said.

"What do you mean?"

"I don't know. Just thinking out loud . . ."

"No—tell me—*what*?"

"Well, the clue Abbie gave us was *Don't look back*, which I took to mean *Look ahead—look to the future*. So then I thought of the Groucho Marx joke, 'I'd save the world for future generations, but what have future generations ever done for us?'"

"That's funny," Quinn said.

"So I was thinking that from conception on, anywhere along the line, we could be poisoned, right?"

"Right," Quinn said. "They've done studies with various endocrine disrupters that affect cognitive development in utero."

"I was on a talk show once on ESPN, where the topic was Title Nine. Funding sports for girls in college," Tommy said. "And one of my team-mates at the time said they need sports for boys to channel all that testosterone—"

"A popular premise."

"Yeah, but this guy was a moron," Tommy said. "He accidentally shampooed his hair with BenGay. Twice. So I called a doctor friend and found out that everybody thinks little boys are full of testosterone, but in fact, they don't have any more than girls do. Boys start getting testosterone again when they hit puberty, but before that, the embryo gets a dose when it's only been in the womb for a day or two and that's about it."

"When sexual differentiation begins," Quinn said. "The stage at which the embryo becomes either male or female."

"So what if Provivilan does something to the embryo?" Tommy said. "When it's only a day old, and it changes it so that when it grows up, if it's a boy, it turns into Amos Kasden? Times ten. On steroids. Literally."

"Well, for that to happen . . ." Quinn stared at his computer screen for a second, then punched a few keys and called up a molecular diagram. "Unless . . . No, that won't do . . . But maybe . . ."

Tommy let him work. He went to his security monitors to make sure everything was okay. He saw the chickens nesting peacefully in the yard, and his rooster, Elvis, perched on the Adirondack love seat beneath the willow tree. He noticed, closer at hand, that the dishes Dani and Cassandra had used to make the cookies had been washed and put away, which ran contrary to what he knew about them.

A minute later Quinn looked up. "I think you might be right," he said. "It's going to take me awhile because there are a number of variables I need to look at, but what you said is brilliant."

"What *I* said is *brilliant*?" Tommy said. "As my dad likes to say, even a stopped clock is right twice a day."

"You are far too self-deprecating," Quinn said. "But that's coming from somebody who's not self-deprecating enough. Or at least I didn't used to be, but I've been humbled a bit lately. You strike me as the sort of person who's always known himself. I'm still getting the hang of it."

"You know, I was feeling really intimidated by you," Tommy said. "I know I'm not stupid, but I also know I don't have the kind of smarts you do."

"Well, I subscribe to the multiple intelligence theory," Quinn said. "I have one kind, at the expense of others. Trust me—my brain is not something anybody should envy."

Tommy heard something in Quinn's voice that reminded him of a game he'd played in college when his team was down by four touchdowns at the half, and his teammates acted like the game was over. "What part of *half* don't you guys understand?" he'd screamed at them. "We have just as many minutes as they had to score four touchdowns. As far as I can tell, right now, we're even. We just let them start first." They won that game, and Tommy had understood from that point on that it was his job as team captain to recognize what defeat sounded like and throw water on it. He recognized it now.

"What's going on, Quinn?" he said. "Something's bothering you."

"Something is," he said. "Something deep inside me. Have a look."

He pulled an image up on his screen of a cross section of a skull. Tommy knew what he was looking at without really knowing and said nothing.

Quinn looked him in the eye. "That, even though you have the good manners not to ask, is a midgrade infiltrating multiforme glioblastoma of the pons reticular formation—right about here," he said, pointing to the lower rear part of his skull. "Near the cerebral peduncle." He pointed at a spot on the screen. "This little guy right here. Right there in the middle where one simply cannot operate."

"You've tried—?"

"I went for one course of chemo," he said. "That was enough. I shouldn't have let them talk me into that much. Do you want to go first, pointing out the abundant ironies, or should I? I am a neuroscientist who is well aware of the most minute biochemical processes inside my brain that nevertheless cannot be stopped or even slowed. I could break it down into its smallest components to tell you in great detail what's happening, but that's not the same thing as saying *why* it's happening. Why me? So I don't think about that all that much. I really don't. But I think about what

I've done with my life so far, and I don't think it's very much. And I know I don't have much time left to make up for it. So when Dani called, I thought it was a sign from God that someone needed me. That's the thing—you want to know that the work you do, in the lab or in the field, will have an effect. Benefit mankind. All those future generations who've never lifted a finger for us. You want to serve somebody."

"Do you have a . . . time line?"

"Thanks for not saying deadline, but that's what it is," Quinn said. "I'll make this deadline, even if it kills me. Ha-ha. No, it's growing rather slowly, but it could always speed up. If you notice me . . . changing, will you tell me?"

"I promise."

"Thanks. Some people wouldn't. They'd just pretend everything is okay."

"I won't tell Dani," Tommy said, "but I think you should."

"I agree," Quinn said. "I just don't want her to . . . After she lost her parents, I didn't want to pile on, so to speak."

"Would you mind if I prayed for you?"

"Actually, I was hoping you could show me how," Quinn said. "I wasn't raised in any religious tradition. One of those other intelligences where I come up short."

"Prayer is just a conversation with God," Tommy said. "You don't even have to use thee's and thou's or get on your knees—though it's okay if you do."

Tommy said a short prayer thanking God for Quinn and asking for healing and for peace for his new friend.

"I know I have a lot to learn," Quinn said.

"You'll get it," Tommy said. "You're a quick study."

"Speaking of which," Quinn said, gesturing to the computer and changing the screen back to the molecular model. "I should get to work on your theory. Tick-tick-tick, after all."

32.

Ben and Julian took the third shift, from four to six, but by five o'clock Tommy, Carl, and Quinn were up too, and soon Ruth was preparing omelets with eggs from Tommy's coop. When she offered Carl a slice of strawberry-rhubarb pie to go with his breakfast, he politely declined, and Tommy saw the air leak out of her just a little bit. She took up her knitting and sat quietly apart from the others.

When they were done eating, Tommy armed himself with his automatic and gave Quinn Ruth's handgun, along with a brief lesson on how to use it. He gave Carl the shotgun and asked him to stay behind to hold down the fort. "You're in charge," Tommy told his friend, "so remember—do everything Dani tells you to do."

"Gotcha," he said, which disappointed Tommy. Carl had once told him the secret to a happy marriage: "The man makes all the big decisions, and the woman makes all the little decisions—and in all the years we were married, there was never a big decision." He made the joke every time the subject of marriage and the so-called Battle of the Sexes came up. *Every* time—that was what made it funny. How could Carl have missed such an obvious setup?

Dani was still in bed when Tommy, Quinn, and Ben loaded Otto into the back of Tommy's Wrangler Sahara. Ben sat in the backseat with Otto, who instantly took a strong liking to his traveling companion. Ben talked to the dog as if he could understand English. The sky was just beginning to lighten in the east when they reached the Gardener farm.

Ben asked Tommy to park short of the end of the driveway so that their footprints wouldn't contaminate the area. Tommy tried to tell him that as far as they could tell, George had left in a 2004 navy blue Honda CRV. Regardless of how skilled the tracker was or how sensitive the dog's nose, Tommy didn't think a man and a dog could track a man in a car.

Ben shrugged. "You never know unless you try." He asked Tommy to remind him how many people had been walking around the house the day they'd used the locksmith to gain entrance.

"As best as I can recall, only Frank DeGidio and his partner looked in the barn or the machine shed."

Ben borrowed one of Tommy's headlamps, tightened the straps, and stretched it around the toe and heel of his right cowboy boot, explaining that a light source low to the ground would give greater definition to any footprints in the dirt and gravel between the house and the barn. "They call the trackers down on the Arizona-Mexico border shadow walkers, because they do their work at sunup and sundown."

Tommy and Quinn stood back with the dog while Ben circled from the house to the barn and back twice. He opened the barn's great door and looked at the floor of the barn, bending low twice to brush away the dirt, pausing to think. He looked up at the hayloft doors. When he returned to them, he raised his eyebrows.

"I've got some good news and some bad news," he said. "The good news is, I don't think George took the car."

"But it's not there," Tommy said.

"I won't argue with you about that, but I found a set of footprints from the same shoes George was wearing when he got in the car—and I found them on top of the tire tracks."

"I'm confused," Tommy said. "How could he leave his footprints on top of the tire tracks while he's driving the car?"

260

"That would be a good trick," Ben agreed.

"Then what happened?"

"He drove the car somewhere and walked back," Quinn said. "Maybe he moved it out of the barn, then got out to close the door, then got back in."

"I thought of that, but that's not what the tracks are saying," Ben said.

"You said you had good news and bad news," Tommy said. "What's the bad news?"

"The bad news is that the Wendigo was here," he said. "Do you have your gun with you?"

"I do," Tommy said, patting his jacket pocket. "I have the scanner too. And the cookies Dani and Cass made, if we want to give it a stomachache."

"Good. I don't think you can kill it with a gun, but it might buy us some time."

"Time to do what?" Quinn said.

"Say our prayers," Ben said. "Let's see what that dog of yours can do, Quinn. I found one of George's T-shirts in the shed. That ought to have his scent on it. To be honest, it smells so bad I think I could track the man who was wearing it."

"He had to have left over a week ago," Tommy said. "Does that matter? Plus, there are scents from other people. Me, Dani, you, Casey, the cops . . ."

"Not to this dog," Quinn said. "I've been practicing with him in Central Park. Just for fun. I had a friend try to lose herself in the middle of a huge crowd at a Paul McCartney concert on the Great Lawn, and Otto went right to her."

Quinn explained that when he put the chest harness and leash on the dog, Otto knew it was time for work and not play. Ruth had given him a baggie of bacon scraps from breakfast to reward the dog. He made Otto sit, then took the T-shirt from Ben and pushed it up against Otto's snout, saying, "Get it, boy! Get it! Go get it!"

Otto was on a twenty-foot lead. Quinn held the looped end, wrapped around his wrist several times, as Otto circled the yard.

"It can take him a minute or two to get a sense of direction," Quinn said. "The tracking books say they don't know how the dog knows to follow the freshest trail. Once he gets it, he tends to—"

Quinn was nearly yanked off his feet as the huge bloodhound found the scent, his tail sticking straight up to indicate he was on the job. They followed him at a pace faster than a walk but not quite a jog. Tommy worried that Ben might not be able to keep up, but soon realized the old man was as fit as guys half his age who worked out in Tommy's gym.

Otto led them to the shore of Lake Atticus, then west on a footpath to where the Gardener property abutted The Pastures, a private country club where the sixteenth and seventeenth fairways hugged the water before heading up to the clubhouse for the eighteenth. They scrambled over the stone wall and made better time on the groomed golf course, where the grass was turning brown, the pins from the greens already in storage for the winter. They could see in the distance the grand clubhouse that had been the home of Andrew Siemans. Siemans was a nineteenth-century robber baron who'd tried to establish a leisure community of super-wealthy New Yorkers in East Salem—similar to the great camps in the Adirondacks built by the East Coast railroad and shipping magnates, financiers, and oil tycoons, but closer to the city. Siemans and his investors had created Lake Atticus by building a massive earthen dam at the far end of the lake. He'd stocked it with rainbow and speckled trout shipped all the way from Montana, and he had nearly two dozen families ready to move in until the Johnstown flood of 1889 in Pennsylvania killed over two thousand people when a dam just like the one Siemans had built burst. His investors pulled out. He ended up selling the property north of the lake to the county, and his home was turned into a golf course.

The dog worked around the edge of the lake until he brought them to the gravel road leading across the top of the earthen dam, dead-ending at a set of concrete Jersey barriers. They climbed over, lifting Otto's hindquarters up by hand. They crossed a bridge over the overflow sluice and continued until, in the middle of the dam, the dog stopped. He sniffed forward a ways, then turned around and sat, waiting for his treat. Quinn reached into his pocket and gave Otto a few pieces of bacon.

"Here?" Tommy said. "He stopped here?" Tommy looked out across the water, then turned around to look in the other direction, where a rocky slope led down to the valley below—a few farms, the campus of St. Adrian's, and beyond that the town of East Salem, where he could make out the church steeple and the roof of the Grange Hall.

"Do you think he climbed down and went into town?" Tommy said.

"Otto wouldn't have stopped if the trail continued," Quinn said. "He only gets a reward if he finds the person or if he finds the end of the scent."

Ben was twenty feet down the road, squatting on his haunches. He gestured for Tommy and Quinn to join him, then pointed at the gravel.

"Do you see this tire tread?" he said. "This is the same one I saw in the barn. It goes off the edge here, and here." He pointed into the water, ten feet below. Tommy and Quinn looked but saw nothing.

"Hold on," Tommy said. "This is going to be cold."

He quickly stripped to his underwear, grabbed his Maglite, which was waterproof to fifty feet, took three deep breaths, and dived into the lake. He'd swum in the same waters, at the same place on the dam, dozens of times as a teenager. Twenty feet below the surface, he found what he was looking for—a navy blue 2004 Honda CRV. He used the flashlight to quickly search the interior before swimming to the surface. Quinn used the dog's twenty-foot lead to help pull Tommy back to the top of the dam, where he quickly dressed.

"The car is down there," he said, shivering and gasping. He shook his head to cast the water from his hair and smoothed it back with his fingers. "No sign of George." He remembered what Carl had told him about bodies not floating when the water was cold. "He should come up sooner or later, but we might have to get some divers."

"You're too pessimistic," Ben said. "Let's keep going. This is a lovely lake, even if it is man-made."

It was a shorter distance back to the Jeep and the farmhouse if they made a complete loop around the lake rather than retracing their steps. A hundred yards from where George Gardener docked his boats, the dog got excited again, his tail straight up and his nose and ears dragging along the ground, leading away from the house. Ben knelt to look at the ground, then asked Quinn to stop the dog for a moment.

"Here's what I think happened," he said. "I don't think George's body is in the lake. I think he drove to the dam and pushed his car over the edge. I saw some footprints there in the gravel that I think were his. Then he walked back around the lake the long way, the way we came, across the golf course, to avoid running into anyone who might have seen his car. The tracks on the other side of the lake were of a man who weighs maybe a hundred and forty pounds. But these tracks"—he pointed to the ground—"are the same shoes, but now the man weighs about two hundred pounds. They're deeper. I think he went back to the barn and got some supplies, maybe a backpack, and then headed this way." He pointed in the direction the dog wanted to take them. "Do you know what's in that direction?"

"Route 35," Tommy said.

"And what's beyond that? What's on the other side of Route 35?"

"Town park," Tommy said. "Picnic grounds, the town pool, a baseball field and some bleachers and a couple of tennis courts."

"And beyond that?"

"The Ward Pound Ridge Reservation," Tommy said. "It's a state park. About five miles across and ten miles from north to south."

"I think that's where he went," Ben said. "Let's see what Otto thinks."

Quinn took the dirty T-shirt and once more gave the dog his instructions. They were off. As Ben predicted, the dog led them across the highway to the town park and then to the parking lot above the baseball field, at the bottom of what was once a ski hill, now grown over with trees and underbrush. The local kids believed that the machine shed housing the rusted remnants of an old lift pulley at the top of the hill was haunted. Tommy recalled making twenty bucks by going into it on a bet one Halloween night.

They followed Otto up the abandoned ski slope and into the woods, stepping over fallen trees and rotting stumps, frost still riming the leaves underfoot. They continued for about a mile until they came to a trail. The dog went left, swept the ground with his nose, then circled to the right.

"I know where we are," Tommy said. "And I think I know where George is."

The trail was the same one he'd run when he'd competed in the 10K race called the Leatherman's Loop. Leatherman's Cave, near the southwest edge of the park, was where anthropologists had found the Indian pictographs portraying the founding of the Iroquois League of Nations.

The cave was at the base of a massive granite outcropping, facing south where the towns of Pound Ridge and Bedford, New York, and New Canaan, Connecticut, were still waking up. Tommy stopped at the bottom of the hill, where the cave's location was marked by a white arrow painted on a rock. "Why don't you tie Otto up and we'll leave him here?"

Quinn gave Otto the rest of the bacon and a command to lie down.

The three men walked cautiously up the trail, which grew steeper and more difficult toward the top. The footing became treacherous, a mattress of soggy leaves covering loose rocks and crumbling gravel, until they had to pull themselves upward tree to tree. The Leatherman's Cave, formed where a black diamond-shaped boulder had cleaved from the granite rock face to lodge on the talus below, was shielded from view by a large boulder. Tommy quickly scanned the area while Ben read the trail.

"Lots of people in running shoes," Ben said.

"No signs of the Wendigo?" Tommy asked.

Ben shook his head. "He leaves a trail of destruction. Sometimes dead animals."

Tommy thought of the dead deer he'd called the wolf sanctuary about.

He went first around the left side of the boulder and waited at the top for Ben and Quinn. When he shone his flashlight high on the left-hand wall, he saw the pictograph Ben had told them about at the library. Tommy studied it for a moment, then held his hand out to quiet the others.

"George?" he called out. "George Gardener?"

They moved into the cave, crouching to duck under an overhang before entering a chamber where Tommy saw a small cookstove, a sleeping bag on a foam mat, a backpack, and, wedged into the rear crevice, making himself small, an old man holding a gold cross on a chain in front of him. The cross caught the light of Tommy's flashlight and glinted brightly.

"I believe in God, the Father Almighty, maker of heaven and earth," George muttered, barely audible. He was clearly terrified. "And in Jesus Christ, his only Son, our Lord, who was conceived by the Holy Spirit, and born of the virgin Mary, suffered under Pontius Pilate, was crucified, died, and was buried."

Tommy fished the cross he wore on a chain around his neck out from beneath his T-shirt and shone his flashlight on it for George to see.

"He descended into hell. On the third day he rose again from the dead," Tommy said softly. Ben joined him.

"He ascended into heaven, and sitteth at the right hand of God the Father Almighty. From thence he will come to judge the living and the dead," they said in unison. "I believe in the Holy Spirit, the holy catholic church, the communion of saints, the forgiveness of sins, the resurrection of the body, and the life everlasting."

The look on George's face changed from abject fear to something less.

"Amen," Quinn said.

"I knew you were a quick study," Tommy said. "George, we're not going to hurt you. You're safe with us. We have the book."

"You found the book?" George said.

"Yes," Tommy said.

"You're not safe," George said, alarmed. "If you have the book, they'll find you. They'll kill you all. Every last one of you!"

33.

When Dani came downstairs a little after seven o'clock, she saw Villanegre and Ruth sitting at Tommy's kitchen computer. They'd spent about an hour researching the names from the SD card Dani had been given, and told her they'd found two more disturbing hits—a St. Adrian's alum who'd been on one of the planes that hit the World Trade Center, and another who'd owned radio stations in Uganda used to urge Hutus to kill Tutsis in the atrocities that took place there in 1994.

"This is horrible," Ruth said. "I find it . . ."

"It leaves one speechless," Villanegre said.

"I nearly forgot," Ruth said to Dani. "Quinn left you a note on his laptop."

She found a folded piece of paper with her name on it and a hand-written message that said:

Thanks for the cookies. They were really chewy! Open the file on the desktop labeled Dani.

She opened the file and read:

First of all, I apologize for surreptitiously uploading the postmortem for Amos Kasden. You were quite clear when you told me

267

we were not allowed to take the information off campus, but I had a feeling it would be important. Given what we now understand to be at stake, I think you'll agree that I was correct in that assumption.

Second, I was hoping you could review my work. Last night while Tommy and I were standing watch, I had some time to review the numbers. It seemed rather obvious to me, as I'm sure it did to you, that, knowing the track records of other St. Adrian's graduates, the drug Provivilan in production by Linz, owned by Udo Bauer, had to have something wrong with it that we were overlooking. I had to be missing something, and as you know, I can't sleep when I know I'm close to solving a puzzle.

Tommy led me in the right direction. When I said I couldn't find any way that Provivilan, taken in proper dosage, could damage a fully grown human being, he suggested that perhaps, in smaller concentrations, it might alter cognitive development in the prenatal environment.

You probably know how waste-water effluents have been damaging the prenatal environment. Right now the main offenders are citalopram, sertraline, and fluoxetine, which biodegrade slowly, and the numbers are going up as more and more people take antidepressants. Some data suggests that transplacental migration of SSRI metaboloids stimulates steroidogenesis and causes genetic alterations.

I think Tommy is right. In the prenatal environment, Provivilan could possibly produce genetic alterations that might result in the same catastrophic time-bomb scenario of hormonally crazed psychopaths with impaired judgment on adrenaline. I can't really give you an educated guess as to what a significant dosage might be, but if we're talking about zygotes at the two- or four- or eight-cell level, it could be as little as one part per trillion. Provivilan has the precursors anyway.

It would have to combine with something else. But we could be on the right track. Need to do more tests.

I'm eager to hear what you think about all this. All my files are on my desktop if you want to look at any of them.

On a considerably less grave note, you need to know something. Tommy loves you. You should have no doubt about that. He told me. He strikes me as a really great guy. I don't know what's going on between you two, but whatever it is, stop it!

Dani was inclined to believe him about Tommy, but it was still difficult to reconcile that with the evidence she'd seen that he'd lied to her. She got up, poured herself a cup of coffee, and then sat back down in front of Quinn's computer. She studied the analysis he'd drafted. As far as she could tell, his conclusions were sound. Something wasn't making sense. Linz Pharmazeutika was releasing Provivilan, which was harmless to adults but potentially dangerous to fetuses, but only if it combined with something else to become the Doomsday Molecule. Combined with what? How? What was the mechanism?

She was mulling this over when Cassandra came down the stairs, yawning and walking with her eyes half closed and one arm extended like a zombie, saying, "Coffee . . . coffee . . ." After she'd had a sip, she wandered over to where Dani was sitting.

"Do you seriously just roll out of bed looking that good?" Dani said. "That's so unfair." Cassandra was wearing sweatpants and an old hooded sweatshirt, no makeup, and hair that seemed artfully mussed.

"Oh, please," Cassandra said, waving away the compliment. "Where is everybody?" She looked around the kitchen, slurping her coffee. "Where are the boys?"

"They're out trying to track down George," Dani said. "With Otto."

"Did Carl go with them?"

"I don't think so," Dani said. "Ruth—do you know where Carl is?"

269

Ruth looked up, then surveyed the kitchen. "I thought he was still here. But wherever he went, he took the shotgun."

Dani moved to the kitchen computer and clicked on the surveillance monitors. She could find no trace of Carl either inside or outside the house.

Carl wasn't visible on the monitors because he was behind the chicken coop with the barrel of the shotgun in his mouth and the stock braced between his feet, his left hand pressing the muzzle to his lips, his right thumb hovering over the trigger guard. Yet as hard as he pressed, he could not force his thumb to pull the trigger. The thing inside him controlled his body, but his mind was not entirely disconnected. He'd hoped that one final burst of will could overcome the evil within, an evil he understood in ways he couldn't have dreamed before—the desire to own and abuse, to conquer and dominate, to tear apart and burn down and destroy, and to cause pain for the pleasure of seeing someone else suffer. He felt an absence, a giant hole, a darkness inside where he'd once known what it felt like to love and be loved in return, by his wife, by his daughter, by the Father and the Son he'd sworn to serve and love and fear and respect. The feeling wasn't there anymore.

In its place was a small vessel he could only fill with pleasure by committing acts of cruelty, and he had to keep that vessel filled or the pain would become too much. It was almost a chemical dependency. He was a prisoner, forced to witness his crimes with eyes wide open, helpless. He was hypnotized and could not snap his fingers to wake himself up. He'd taken the gun with the hope that he could end it, but his body wouldn't let him.

He heard a voice calling his name. "Carl?" It took him a few seconds to realize it was Dani.

"I'm back here," he said, taking the gun from his mouth and pointing it in the direction of her voice. "Behind the coop."

"What are you doing?" she called out, getting closer. "Are you okay?"

"I'm good," he said. He heard a car approaching and saw Tommy's Jeep at the front gates.

"There you are," Dani said, rounding the corner. "I was worried. You should let people know if you're going somewhere."

On the ground between them she saw a dismembered chicken, the head torn off, legs and wings ripped from it and scattered. She felt a wave of nausea flutter through her and stepped back.

"I thought I heard something," Carl said. "Must have been a fox."

"The guys are back," Dani said. "Tommy texted. They found George."

"I'll be right there," Carl said. "Let me just clean this up."

When she was gone, he nudged the pieces of flesh under a bush with the toe of his boot and kicked dirt to disperse the blood. A fox had not done this. A coyote had not done this. He had done it—or rather the evil thing now inside him had commanded him to pick the poor bird up, stroke it gently, and then . . .

It had been a demonstration.

This is what I can make you do, the demon had said to him. *It's just a taste of what's to come . . .*

34.

There were twenty-one of them gathered at St. Adrian's, and they were aware of each other, but they'd been taken from their rooms blindfolded and told not to speak, so they did not speak. They understood that they'd been chosen. They would go on to do great things, and soon they would be told what those great things were. They waited together, forbidden to fall asleep, until they could not tell how long they'd been waiting, or if the thoughts that passed through them were waking thoughts or dreams.

Then they heard a door open and a voice say, "Rise." They were instructed to line up, and then each boy was told to put his left hand on the shoulder of the boy in front of him and to follow. They marched, they couldn't tell how far, but judging from the acoustics and the echoes, they went through a large room and down a hall and then down a set of stairs. The walls got closer and the air more humid and cooler; then they passed into another chamber where the air was dank and thick.

"You may take off your blindfolds," the voice said.

This was the room they'd heard of, in whispered, dangerous rumors. The only light came from a pair of candles on the central altar, a massive piece of black marble carved in the shape of a bull. Dr. Wharton stood behind it, and Dr. Ghieri stood next to him. They were wearing academic robes, each in a black surplice with red tippets. Wharton looked each boy in the eye, one by one, as if he were still making up his mind about them.

After what seemed like an eternity, he spoke.

"You are the select," he said. "Others have been rejected. Do not ask why, or where they've gone. You have succeeded, but each of you still has a task to complete. If anyone feels that for any reason he will not be able to complete his assignment, speak now."

No one spoke.

"Andrew."

"Yes, sir."

"You have a pet you keep in your room."

"Yes, sir."

"What is it?"

"It's a rabbit, sir."

"Bilal—what animal do you keep?"

"A cat, sir."

"Carlos?"

"A dog. His name is—"

"I do not care what his name is," Wharton said. He turned to Ghieri, who handed him a small wooden container, the size of a small shoe box. "Each of you will receive one of these," Wharton said, lifting the box for all to see. "It will contain the ashes of your pet. Tonight you will write a letter to your parents telling them how sad you are. If you need help with this, we can help you. Each of you lives near a significant body of water. Edmond?"

"King George's Reservoir. North of London."

"Sidney?"

"Lake Michigan."

"Han?"

"The Yangtze."

"In your letter you will explain that when you come home for break, you want to spread the ashes of your pet into that body of water. You will each receive more specific instructions as to how and when to do that. Are there any questions?"

"Will there be any problems at the airport?" a boy asked.

"No," Wharton said. "The boxes will go into your carry-on bags, but if the security people have any questions, you will simply explain what it is you're doing. Act upset if they say they want to examine the boxes. Cry if you think it will be persuasive. The name of your pet will be on the box."

Andrew raised his hand. Wharton nodded to him.

"I didn't name mine," he said.

Ghieri found the appropriate box. "It will be more believable if you give your pets names. Andrew, you are to say your pet's name was . . . Bugs," he read.

The other boys laughed.

"You will not open your boxes until it's time to dump the ashes in the water," Wharton said. "You will not ask any questions about your assignment, and you will not fail to complete it. You understand what will happen if you fail."

The laughter gave way to a reverberating silence.

"Put your blindfolds back on," Wharton commanded.

When they were alone, Wharton spoke to Ghieri. "The priest," he said. "The minister, whatever he is—do we still have use for him?"

"He's found the book," Ghieri said. "That is significant. It's been a long time since we even knew where it was."

"Yes, but can he get it?"

"He thinks he can."

"He *thinks* he can?"

"He should be given the chance to try."

"No," Wharton said decisively. "The priest has had enough time. What's the name the Indian has given him?"

"Thadodaho," Ghieri said.

"Oh yes," Wharton said. "Well, he's failed. I see no reason not to send the other."

"The Wendigo," Ghieri said.

"Yes," Wharton said. "Use him. Wait until after dark. We can sort through the rubbish when he's finished."

"I think—"

"Do *not* think," Wharton said.

"Yes."

"And blow out the candles."

"Yes," Ghieri said.

35.

"Do you know where you are?"

George Gardener looked confused. When Dani shone a small flashlight in his eyes, his pupils dilated normally, indicating, though not
conclusively, that he probably wasn't under the influence of any drugs. He
sat in Tommy's kitchen, a comforter wrapped around his shoulders. The
others gathered around him, though Dani had advised them to stay back
and give the frightened man time to adjust to their presence.

"George—do you know where you are?" she said again.

"No."

"Do you know what day it is?"

"No."

"Can you tell me what month it is?"

"November."

"Do you remember Tommy? You met him in the hardware store a few
weeks ago. He had a question about how to stop raccoons from getting in
the garbage."

"No."

"You don't have to be scared, George," Dani said. "You're among
friends, and we have the book. When was the last time you slept, George?"

"I don't know."

"You can't remember?"

"Can't sleep," he said. "They come to take you when you're sleeping."

"Have you slept at all since your mother died?"

"I killed her," he said.

"You killed your mother?"

"No."

"Then who did you kill, George?"

"The girl. I killed the girl."

"What girl?"

"Julie."

"No, George. A boy named Amos Kasden killed Julie."

"I killed her," he said, suddenly focused and angry. "I went to her house. My mother . . . I thought it was time. I couldn't tell. I went to her house. They must have followed me. That's how they knew."

"George, you couldn't have known—"

"They burned down the house," he said. "They burned it down! With her mother and her sister in it. Because of me. I killed them all." He started sobbing.

Dani pulled a chair up next to him and held him, pressing his head against her shoulder and stroking his back. Ruth moved her chair to the other side of him, ready to take over when Dani got tired.

After a few minutes George stopped crying. Dani stood and crossed to where Tommy and Quinn stood.

"I don't think he's slept in a week," she said. "People who go without sleep that long start dreaming while they're wide awake. I don't think we're going to get much out of him until he's had a chance to recover."

She opened Tommy's refrigerator, searched for a moment, and pulled out a container of vanilla yogurt, a bottle of ranch dressing, and a bottle of Worcestershire sauce. She mixed those ingredients in a cup, along with some ground ginger from Tommy's spice cupboard. She tasted it, winced, stirred in a big spoonful of brown sugar, then took the concoction and a tablespoon from the cutlery drawer to where George was sitting.

"This medicine is going to let you sleep," she told him. "You're safe now, George. We're going to watch over you, so take this and sleep."

She gave him one tablespoon of her "medicine," then another. Carl offered to escort George to one of the guestrooms, but Ruth said she wouldn't mind doing it.

"Where did you learn to make a home remedy sleeping potion?" Tommy asked.

"I didn't," she said. "I gave him a placebo. I just wanted to make sure it didn't taste like anything he'd ever had before. If he thinks it's going to work, it will."

Ruth returned a moment later and gave Dani a thumbs-up.

"Out like a light," she said.

<hr />

Ruth and Villanegre spent the day researching names. Quinn and Dani worked on the computer, testing theories about the drug. Ben taught Cassandra to play chess. Tommy tried to talk to Carl, but Carl didn't want to talk and kept to himself.

"Tommy," Carl said finally, "would you mind getting the book out of the safe and setting it up for me on the coffee table? I'd like to have a look at some of the earlier letters from Abbie's predecessors. Might be able to learn something."

"Good idea," Tommy said. "Do you want the combination?"

"No, no, that's okay," he said. "If you could just set it up for me. And put the blanket down so it doesn't get scratched."

"All right," Tommy said. "Just give me a second."

Dani leaned against the kitchen counter near the sink, talking to Julian Villanegre about the painting. Looking past them out the window, Tommy saw that the sun was already going down, leaving behind a blood-red sunset.

"Dani—I'm going to need your help in a second," he said. "Carl wants to look at the book, but I can't open the box without you."

"Okay," she said.

Once he left the room, she saw the Englishman raise an eyebrow.

"I gather there's some sort of lovers' quarrel going on between you two," he said. "Can I help?"

"We'll work it out," Dani said. "The course of true love never did run smooth. Isn't that what your boy Shakespeare once said?"

"Lysander, in *A Midsummer Night's Dream*, act 1, scene 1," Villanegre said. "Poor Lysander. He loved Hermia, but Hermia's father wanted her to marry Demetrius. Shakespeare wrote a great deal about lovers who were preordained, and all the obstacles they had to overcome."

"Do you believe in soul mates, Dr. Villanegre?"

"I do. I lost mine years ago, but I shall see her again soon enough. If you don't mind an old man's interference, I think there's another Shakespeare quote you might want to heed."

"Please."

"Beware the green-eyed monster, which doth mock the meat it feeds on."

"*Othello*," Dani said.

"Indeed. But the irony, of course, is that Iago is the one who says it to Othello, right after Othello compliments him on being so honest. And Iago's the one who's been whispering in Othello's ear to make him jealous. It's as if he's saying, 'Here's what I'm going to do to you, and you know it, and I know it, and there's nothing you can do to stop me.'"

"You think that's relevant now?"

"I think it's odd," the Englishman said, "that both your old flame and Tommy's old flame are here. Don't you?"

"*Odd* is one word for it. *Excruciating* is another."

"Everything happens for a reason, I suppose," Villanegre said. "But if this lovers' quarrel you're having has anything to do with jealousy, just remember how easily the joy of having something can turn into the fear of losing it."

"Thank you," she said. "I have a question—why did the box open when Tommy and I touched it?"

"I think you know the answer," Villanegre said. "Ben read it to us. 'You, the holder of this sacred text, the keeper of these words, whose hands have broken this lock, you hold the secret, and you are charged by the fact of possession with a holy task.' You've been chosen."

"But we weren't intended to hold the book," Dani said. "Julie Leonard's father was."

"And after that?" Villanegre said. "You don't think God would have left it all to chance, do you? I will tell you one thing. The fact that you can put your hands on the box together certainly proves one thing—you're not demons in human form. We have learned over the centuries that demons are incapable of making contact with sacred objects or icons. Because it shames them, I suppose. Tells them how fallen their stature is. That's why so many of the figures in *The Garden of Earthly Delights* are chimerical hybrids. The intended viewers would have been unable to look at a conventional rendering."

"The statue of St. Adrian's in the museum atrium," Dani said. "Tommy noticed he wasn't wearing a cross. He thought that was odd. He thought a cross would have made the St. Adrian's student body uncomfortable. To say the least."

"You know, at Oxford, when we teach art history, we give students a slide or a print of a painting and we say, 'Tell me what you see.' In America it's the reverse; you sit in a big dark auditorium and a slide of a famous painting comes up and the instructor tells you what he sees. And what you ought to see. And half the students are so bored that by the third slide, they're sound asleep. I've had a number of American graduate students who are very book-smart and can regurgitate what their professors told them word for word. But Tommy has the other kind of intelligence. He can look at something and see it. And that kind of intelligence is rare. You may want to compliment him on it. I think he feels just a bit intimidated by Quinn."

Villanegre smiled, then turned to Ruth, who offered him the last of the strawberry-rhubarb pie.

In the study, Tommy picked up the box and held it toward Dani. Together they pressed on the cross inlays in the correct sequence, and once again the box slid open.

"Pretty cool how it does that," Tommy said. "Did you worry at all that this was going to be some kind of Pandora's box? That once we opened it, we'd wish we hadn't?"

"No," she said. She grabbed his hand and held on to it. "Tommy—we have to talk."

"Uh-oh," he said. "Those are four words no man likes to hear."

"It's not one of *those* talks," Dani said.

"You want to talk?" he said.

She nodded.

"Then we can talk."

"The angel told us both, 'How you handle it is going to make all the difference,' right?"

"Right."

"Well, I have not handled this well," she said. "The problem from the very start is that we've stopped really communicating with each other. I should have come straight to you as soon as I started feeling the least bit jealous."

"I agree with you about communication," he said.

"Honesty is what matters," Dani said. "So if you tell me you sent

Cassandra that text because you were feeling insecure, or because you wanted to fight fire with fire, or even that you were thinking you could fix her up with Quinn—whatever—I don't care . . . just as long as you don't try to tell me you didn't send it. Just tell me what happened."

He looked her in the eye for a moment. "I didn't send it."

Dani turned and stormed out of the room.

Tommy followed, passing Carl in the doorway on his way out.

"Is it okay if I look at the book?" Carl said.

"Yeah, yeah," Tommy said. "It's all set up for you. Knock yourself out."

Carl closed the door behind him.

Tommy caught up to Dani in the living room, where he grabbed her hand. She shook it loose.

"Dani—"

"You *really* need to stop talking right now," she said.

"Dani, we just agreed that not talking was the wrong way to handle things. Talking is the way to handle things. We just said that, right?"

She looked at him, feeling hurt and a little ashamed for being so gullible, but she didn't say anything.

"Just listen," Tommy said. "Dani, I checked with Ben. I'm not denying that there's a record of the text message on my phone, okay? And I'm not denying that Cassandra received it. But I was sound asleep when it happened. I can't prove that, but it's the truth. Ben said a demon could only send a text message if he took on some sort of physical form, and that didn't happen, because when I went to bed, I left my phone on the food island to recharge, right in the middle of a completely lit kitchen. If any demon materialized in the kitchen, Carl would have seen it, because he was on watch."

Both Tommy and Dani realized what he'd said as soon as the words were out of his mouth.

"Carl!" Dani said.

Tommy ran from the room and burst through the door of his study,

Dani right behind him. They rushed into the room. On the floor next to the coffee table, Tommy saw the wooden box. It was empty.

He looked around. The window facing the front yard was open, and the screen had been punched out. The book, and the blanket it had been resting on, were gone. As was Carl.

36.

Tommy ran into the kitchen.

"Has anyone seen Carl?"

They heard an unmistakable, deep-throated growl, the roar of Carl's motorcycle. Through the kitchen window he saw Carl speed away, heading for the front gate.

Tommy ran to his kitchen computer and punched up his security screen. He saw Carl fishtailing down the driveway and clicked to the camera covering his gate. The gate was open. When he tried to close it, the program asked him if he was the system administrator. He clicked yes, and the computer asked him for the password. When he typed it in, the computer told him it was the wrong password. He tried one more time, carefully, but got the same response.

"Carl changed the password," Tommy said.

He reached for the hook where he kept his keys and grabbed his leather jacket. Before he could put it on, Dani stopped him, kissed him quickly, and handed him his .45 caliber Taurus automatic. They both knew Carl was not Carl anymore, and that the book could not be allowed to fall into the wrong hands.

Tommy ran to the garage and threw open the last bay door. He put the key in the ignition of his Harley-Davidson Night Rod, squeezed the clutch with his left hand, and said a little prayer as he pressed the ignition. The bike roared to life on the first try. He throttled up once, throttled down and let the clutch out, leaning hard to the right as he screeched out of the garage, already in third gear by the time he was on the straightaway leading to the gates.

Once he was on the street, he whipped his head left and right, left and then right again, looking for a taillight. Had Carl gone north, toward the countryside, or south, toward town? He saw a single red taillight cresting a far hill, jerked his bike to the right, and hit the gas. He had a fair idea of where Carl was headed.

Tommy had driven this road many times, and driven it too fast too many times. He held the throttle full back and toed the bike into its highest gear, downshifting into the curves but leaning so far into the turns that his knee was a foot off the black asphalt. The Michelin "Scorcher" tires were as fat as an automobile's, built for racing, as was the 1250-cubic-centimeter liquid-cooled V-twin engine that kicked out 122 horsepower, capable of flinging the 900 pounds of bike and rider down the road at 150 miles an hour. At the first hill, Tommy's bike sailed two feet above the ground before landing rear tire first on the downslope.

Tommy knew he was a better rider than Carl. They'd even joked about it, and they'd had a few races on empty back-country roads where there was no traffic and the possibility of endangering other drivers was negligible.

Tommy had never tried too hard to understand why, but the simple fact was that he was good at every sport he'd ever tried. He could pick up a bowling ball, roll a gutter ball his first ball, knock down nine on his second, and end up rolling a 284 the first time he tried bowling. He'd been a three-sport All-American in high school, but had dropped basketball in college to concentrate on football and baseball. Even so, in addition to being a first-round draft pick in the NFL and heavily recruited by a half dozen professional baseball teams, he'd also been a third-round pick by the Boston Celtics. His physical gifts, which he could only think of as

God-given, extended to the operation of mechanical devices and motor vehicles. Skateboarding and snowboarding came naturally to him, as did mountain biking and motocross. There were faster motorcycles in the world, but there wasn't a faster motorcycle in Westchester County that night, and there wasn't a better rider.

Tommy knew he was going to catch the older rider. And Carl knew it too.

Carl had snatched the book off the coffee table by wrapping it in the blanket and carrying it in a sling. He was unable to touch the book—or rather the beast inside of him, the one controlling him, could not touch it—but he managed to get it out the window and into the touring bag strapped to the sissy bar above his rear fender. He'd sped off on his motorcycle thinking only that he had to deliver the book to the school, where Wharton or Ghieri would know what to do with it. Then he'd be free of the demon inside him.

Yet as he rode, he felt something return to him, a kind of control or autonomy that had been absent since the demon had entered him. He could tell the bike where to go and how fast, and the faster he went, the more in control he felt. Before, when his thoughts troubled him and he needed to rebalance, Carl had discovered that with the wind in his face and the rumble of the road and the thundering machine beneath him, he could enter a kind of consciousness some might have called contemplative or meditative; he knew it as a state of constant prayer, a kind of worship in motion that at times approached religious ecstasy. It wasn't that riding relaxed him, which was what he told people, but more that with his body fully engaged in the operation of the machine, his mind was free to engage in the kind of deep prayer other people needed quiet chapels and stained-glass windows to achieve.

When he slowed down, he felt the thing take hold of him again, but when he sped up, it let go, as if it were afraid of the speed and the violence the motorcycle created.

He looked in his rearview mirror and saw a lone halogen headlight, a bright bluish white that he knew was Tommy's. "Come on, man!" he shouted. "Catch me!"

It was the first time since he'd been so careless as to invite the demon in that he'd spoken words completely of his own choosing.

Tommy had never seen Carl ride so fast. It was as if he had a death wish. He'd catch him, he knew, but it wasn't going to be easy. And one or both of them might be killed.

Coming down a hill, Tommy slowed. Carl was no longer on the road in front of him. Tommy lifted the visor of his helmet to see better. It was possible Carl had gone into a ditch somewhere.

Then he saw him speeding cross-country, or more accurately, cross-country-club. He'd turned from the road onto the tenth fairway of The Pastures. Tommy kicked down into second gear, used a roadside hummock as a ramp, and launched himself over the hedgerow; he landed in a sand trap on the left side of the twelfth fairway, then cut across the wide swath of manicured grass to intercept Carl.

Tommy ducked to miss the low-hanging branches of the red pines lining the other side of the twelfth and dug a deep groove in the turf as he leaned hard left to keep pace with Carl, who'd moved over to the next fairway. Tommy had worked there as a caddy in high school, so he knew that Carl was speeding down and then up the hill of the par three sixteenth, which was a dead end. Tommy was now just fifty yards behind him and closing fast.

Carl nearly wiped out when he hit the green and came close to laying down the bike. Tommy jumped his bike off the slope of a bunker and landed on the green just as Carl accelerated again, ripping into the rough and through the underbrush.

Tommy followed. Neither bike was built for off-road travel, with low ground clearances and stiff suspensions. If either one of them were to hit a log buried in the fallen leaves, he was sure to launch over the handlebars.

Getting traction was difficult. Tommy's wheels were slipping, and he threw a rooster-tail of leaves in the air behind him. Under these conditions the massive power of his engine worked against him, like a Corvette on an inch of snow.

He kept up the chase, the bike beneath him bouncing off unseen rocks hard enough to jar him off the seat. He wrestled the handlebars, fighting to keep the bike upright while Carl slashed through the woods, now thirty feet ahead of him.

Carl burst out of the woods, bouncing onto a paved road. Tommy followed. He'd nearly caught the larger bike when Carl braked suddenly and turned hard. Tommy overshot him and skidded to a stop, yanking his handlebars to execute a U-turn as he kicked down into first, screeching rubber against the pavement as he sped up again and followed Carl.

He recognized where they were. It was the path Amos Kasden had taken the night he'd brought Julie Leonard up to kill her on Bull's Rock Hill. He knew the way intimately, having made it part of his training runs in high school, and he still ran it from time to time. It would widen and flatten into a gravel road a hundred yards short of the top of the hill. The path was relatively straight and wide and free of fallen trees, but laced with thick roots that slowed them both down.

When Carl picked up speed, Tommy knew in an instant what he was going to do. He was headed for the top of the hill and the cliff where, beyond the precipice, Lake Atticus lay more than one hundred feet below.

Tommy's gift, his physical intelligence, had allowed him to make instantaneous decisions on the football field. If he could visualize what he wanted to do, his body could do it.

He visualized what he wanted to do now.

He glanced at the speedometer and closed the distance between his motorcycle and Carl's. Seventy miles an hour, eighty . . . ninety . . . Tommy could see the cliff and the darkness beyond. He was just thirty feet behind Carl, then twenty, then ten and no way to stop now—

Carl hit the edge of the cliff at ninety miles an hour, sailing out into the black abyss.

Tommy hit the cliff at ninety-two miles an hour, flying right behind Carl but diving off his bike, pushing it down.

He caught Carl's bike in midair before it began to drop and ripped the touring bag from the sissy bar, grabbing it with both hands and rotating with as much torque as he could wield. As he descended toward the lake, he saw Carl.

He reached out his hand, hoping to grab hold of his friend, falling and falling . . .

Tommy knew of two boys who, over the last hundred years, had believed they could survive a dive into the lake from Bull's Rock Hill. Both of them had been wrong.

As Tommy fell, he believed something far greater, that Jesus and the angels he commanded would save him. He believed it because the first page of the book had promised that whoever held the book would be protected.

Instead of hitting the surface of the water, which at that velocity and from that height would have been like hitting solid concrete, he felt two arms encircle him in midair and carry him to the near shore, where he turned to see two motorcycles—and one man—smash into the water with a horrific splash.

Tommy rose to save his friend, but the angel put a hand on him to quiet him, then said, "I'll get him."

Tommy watched as the angel Charlie carried Carl from the water and set him down gently. Tommy pulled his helmet off, his hair drenched with sweat despite the cold night air.

"I'm glad you understood," Charlie said.

"I'm glad I did too," Tommy said.

He knelt beside his friend. He undid the chinstrap of Carl's helmet, pulling it off him. Carl coughed. Tommy looked to the angel for instruction.

"The demon that attacked him is gone," Charlie said. "It left as you fell. But your friend is gravely hurt. His body won't survive the damage that's been done to it."

"Carl?" Tommy said, cradling Carl in his arms. "Come on, man—talk to me."

Carl looked up at him and smiled. "Hey, Tommy," he said. "That was some ride."

"Best one ever," Tommy said. "The book is safe, Carl. I've got it. You did good. You're free."

"Feels great," he said. "It's my own fault. I messed up. So tired . . ."

"Shh," Tommy said.

"I invited it in. I wanted to die. Can you forgive me?"

"Absolutely," Tommy said.

"I thought maybe if I could split you and Dani up, they wouldn't see you as such a threat. I know how they think, Tommy. You must be doing something right because they're scared of you. Wherever two or more of you are gathered in his name . . ."

Carl coughed, spitting up blood. He wiped his mouth with his sleeve.

"I was supposed to bring them the book," he said. "After that you'd be expendable. You have to be careful. You have no idea how strong they are. How strong it is. The demon that attacked me."

"Shh," Tommy said. "Don't try to talk."

"You can't understand what it's like," Carl said. "To touch evil like that."

"Do you know what they're doing?" Tommy asked. "What's going on at St. Adrian's?"

But he couldn't be sure Carl had heard him. Carl coughed again, and blood bubbled out from between his lips. Carl wiped it with the back of his hand, then looked up and saw the angel.

"This is Charlie," Tommy said. "The one I was telling you about."

Carl smiled broadly through his pain. "I've always wanted to meet an angel," he said.

Charlie reached out his hand and put it gently on Carl's forehead. "It's nice to meet you too, Carl. Jesus is waiting for you. Esme too. You can go now."

Carl closed his eyes and breathed his last.

Tommy held him for a moment, then laid his friend's head on the ground and stood. He stared at the crumpled, lifeless body, and a tear rolled down his cheek.

"So the demon that attacked Carl," Tommy said. "Was that the Wendigo?"

"No," Charlie said. "The one that attacked Carl won't be back, but it wasn't the Wendigo."

"Well then, where's the Wendigo?" Tommy said, turning to address the angel, but when he did, he saw that he was alone.

Tommy put Carl's touring bag on his back like a pack, took a few steps, then began to sprint. The others back at the house were in great danger. There were two demons, not one, in their midst. And the one that remained had a mission.

37.

Tommy ran hard, on hiking paths and bridle lanes, taking the same short-cuts he'd discovered as a boy. He'd walked or run through these woods for miles to get to friends' houses or to meet the guys downtown at the diner. He knew the way. He also knew he had a long way to go. Carrying the touring bag wasn't a problem. He'd once, on a bet, run up to Bull's Rock carrying a teammate on his back. This was nothing.

He cut through some heavy brush that put him on a trail under the power line just beyond the southern edge of his property and scaled the ten-foot deer fence to enter the woods, approaching his house from the other side of the pond. He paused on the edge of the two-acre pond. The house was ablaze with light. He rounded the greenhouse and saw what appeared to be a bloody shirt or rag. Moving closer—startled briefly when the motion-detector turned on the floodlights in the courtyard—he saw it was a dead chicken. He turned to see the courtyard and the lawn beyond littered with dead chickens, his white-tufted Sultans and his green-black Sumatras and his French Marans, all dead. Near the gate to the chicken coop, he found the body of Elvis, his twelve-pound French Maran rooster.

"Hey, buddy. I'll bet you put up quite a fight," Tommy said, kneeling to lay a hand on the body. "Good boy."

He drew his gun and entered the house.

In the empty kitchen he called out but got no response. He went to the intercom, pressed the all-call button, and asked again if anyone was home. There was a cup of tea on the counter. When he felt the cup, it was still warm.

At his kitchen computer he clicked through the video feeds of his surveillance cameras, but saw nothing moving. He was about to call up the events log when a message box signaled an intruder alert.

On the monitor he now saw something registering dark blue, growing clearer in the middle of the courtyard.

He cocked his automatic, removed Abbie's book from the touring bag, tucked it under his arm, and stepped out into the courtyard.

The demon had the neck and face of a lizard, but the body seemed more like that of an oversized humanoid with a tail, like the hybrid creatures in the painting hanging in the museum at St. Adrian's. Its dark skin was shiny with slime, and the odor coming off it was worse than anything Tommy had ever smelled. As the demon materialized, Tommy guessed it was perhaps twenty feet tall and, judging from the way the patio tiles beneath its feet were cracking, as heavy as an elephant. Tommy could see shriveled wings on its back, and thought that a thousand years ago this demon might have been called a dragon or a gargoyle.

If there was any good news, he decided, it was that dragons could be slain. More to the point, he held in his hand something the demon could not defend itself from, and he wasn't thinking of the gun. The book contained the Word of the Lord and the power of Christ. He held it in front of him like a shield.

"Go!" Tommy shouted at the beast. "Leave us alone."

The thing cringed at the sight of the book and then, with a shriek that hurt Tommy's ears, grabbed a rake and swung it at him. Tommy turned quickly to dodge the rake, but not quickly enough. He instinctively dropped the book to protect himself, just as the rake caught the book flush and sent it flying, pages fluttering to the ground.

Tommy was puzzled, and then scared.

"Charlie?" he said as the demon took a step toward him, lowering its head as if ready to pounce. "You wanna explain that?"

Tommy fired his gun at close range, gripping the automatic with both hands to steady his aim. Each time he fired, the Wendigo moved its head, dodging the bullets quicker than Tommy would have thought possible. Tommy was distressed that he had been unable to hit the beast, but if it was bothering to dodge his bullets, it must be vulnerable. It could be hurt. Maybe it could be killed. How many shots had he fired? He'd lost count, but he believed he had one bullet left.

He backed toward the greenhouse and the garden shed, looking left and right for anything he might use as a weapon. He saw on a shelf a can of insecticide capable of shooting a jet of the toxic chemical thirty feet to destroy the nests wasps built under the eaves of a house. He popped the top off the can, gave the can a shake, and sprayed it directly at the face of the Wendigo from point-blank range just as the creature approached. The beast took a step back at first, grimacing as the spray hit it in the eyes, then rose up, wiped the fluid from its eyes with one hand, and licked its fingers, savoring the deadly chemical.

Note to self, Tommy thought. *Buy stronger insecticide.*

Tommy ducked under the grape arbor, but the demon slashed through it, uprooting the trellis from the ground and flinging it aside as if it were made of toothpicks. Tommy ran for the tool shed and flipped on the lights.

The Wendigo ripped the door from the shed just as Tommy pulled the starter cord to his chain saw and slashed at the beast. This time he made contact, slicing into the Wendigo's right arm. It pulled its arm back and howled in pain, spun around, and leapt from the shed.

Tommy went on the offense, chasing after it, but he was careless and got too close. The demon spun around and lashed him with its tail, snapping it like a whip. Tommy had been blindsided by 350-pound linemen. He'd taken a skull-ringer from a bull in the streets of Pamplona, and he'd belly-flopped from a trestle bridge once as a kid and nearly lost consciousness when he hit the water, but he'd never been hit this hard.

The chain saw flew from his hands as he rolled across the courtyard, bouncing against the chicken coop. He jumped to his feet and dived to his right, just as the Wendigo slashed at him with its talons.

Tommy ran toward the patio, which was more like an outdoor kitchen set up with commercial restaurant equipment. He wondered how many ribs he'd cracked. More than two.

At his barbecue grill he picked up a pair of hamburger tongs in one hand and a long metal spatula in the other; he slashed at the creature with the spatula, a weak defense but the best he could come up with. The creature lashed out and knocked him back again. He was thrown across his patio thirty feet, but again jumped to his feet and glanced around frantically, trying to think of something that would stop the beast. It looked at him, in no hurry to finish the job.

Then he saw it.

Tommy took the gun from his pocket and pointed it at the Wendigo.

"Okay, you nasty freak," Tommy said. "I'm going to give you one more chance to surrender, and if you don't, it's no more Mr. Nice Guy."

For a second, the Wendigo seemed almost amused as it rose up on its hind legs to tower over him.

"Have it your way," Tommy said, raising the gun.

He lowered the gun and fired a bullet between the creature's legs, penetrating the stainless steel door behind which sat the 200-gallon propane tank attached to his grilling equipment—which included a stove with a burning pilot light. The explosion knocked Tommy off his feet, and the ball of fire singed his hair and eyebrows. For a second he thought he was going to black out. He shook it off, waiting for the sparklies in the air to burn away and his ears to stop ringing, and got to his feet. As the smoke cleared, he saw that the thing was gone.

Then he heard someone shouting. "Tommy—we're over here!"

The others had heard the warning the chickens put up and had taken refuge in the greenhouse, fleeing out the back of the house as the creature approached from the front. Tommy took Dani in his arms and held her close, relieved to know she was okay.

"You got it?" Dani said, raising the shotgun she was carrying and gazing out into the night. "You have the book?"

"I had it," Tommy said, looking over his shoulder. Dani lowered the gun. "Until that thing knocked it out of my hands."

"How did you get it?"

"Leap of faith."

"Where's Carl?"

Tommy shook his head.

He looked inside the greenhouse and saw that Villanegre had been mauled by the beast. Quinn was ministering to him as best he could, using a stack of white terry-cloth towels to stanch the flow of blood from the Englishman's chest. Cassandra stood guard at the window, Ruth's .45 Colt automatic in her hands.

"Julian was trying to cover for us when we ran for the greenhouse," Dani said.

"Is he going to make it?"

"Maybe," Dani said. "A man his age, it's hard to say."

Tommy walked into the greenhouse and knelt beside the fallen Englishman. He leaned close to speak to him. "Can you hang on, Julian?" he said. "We need you with us."

Villanegre looked at him, then at Ruth and Quinn, then back to Tommy. "I shall try my utmost," he said. "I'm afraid I'm of no use to you at present."

"Just rest." Tommy stood. "Is everybody else okay?"

They nodded.

Ben spoke up from where he stood near the greenhouse door, looking out to the courtyard. "Tommy?"

"Are you okay, Benjamin?"

"I'm quite well, thank you. But I think you'd better have a look at this."

Tommy went to see what Ben was pointing at and saw the Wendigo reconfiguring in the courtyard, apparently as strong and as dangerous as before.

"What's it going to take?" he asked.

"I told you it was a terrible demon," Ben said.

Tommy felt a sinking sensation, a moment not of doubt but dismay. He'd tried everything he could think of to kill the beast. He looked around the yard for anything he could use as a weapon and grabbed a baseball bat from a rack near the batting cage. His Taurus was out of ammunition. He took a deep breath. The others gathered around him.

"Okay," he began. "Here's the plan . . ."

The Wendigo raised itself up to its full height, leaned back, and roared. It was angry, and in a hurry this time.

"You said you had a plan?" Dani said.

"Right," Tommy said. He reached into his pocket and handed Dani his keys, isolating one of them. "I'll see how far I can lure it away from the house. As soon as you can, pick up the pages of the book and then get in the van and drive. Head into town, where there might be people. I don't know if that will stop it, but it might."

"Bad plan," Dani said, hoisting the shotgun and handing the keys to Quinn. "I'm coming with you. Don't even try to talk me out of it."

"All right," Tommy said. "Quinn, you drive. Cass, help him. Are you ready, Dani?"

She smiled bravely. "Not really," she said. "But I don't think it's going to wait until I am."

Together, Tommy and Dani walked toward the demon, Tommy with the Luger in one hand and a baseball bat in the other, Dani wielding the shotgun. They'd gone ten paces when they realized Ben was walking beside them.

"I told you I was here to help you, remember?"

Tommy saw there was no point arguing with him. "How many shells do you have left?" he asked Dani.

"How would I know?" she said, keeping her eye on the creature. "I'm not a librarian."

"How many did you fire?"

"Two."

"You have two left," he told her. He closed his eyes to pray. "Jesus, please watch over us and give us the courage we need," he said. There wasn't time for more.

The Wendigo approached them more warily this time, sizing them up.

"Spread out," Tommy said. "Get as close as you can before you fire. Ben, I don't suppose you have any hand grenades, do you?"

"No," Ben said, "but I have faith."

"So do I," Tommy said.

"Good," Ben said. "Your faith has been tested. It's stronger because of that."

The monster took another step toward them.

"Yeah," Tommy said. "But is it enough?"

"I also have this," Ben said. He reached into his pocket to show Tommy what he was holding.

"A Swiss Army knife?" Dani said.

"It has attachments," Ben said.

In an instant the pocketknife began to glow in his hand, extending until it became a brilliant flaming sword ten feet long, held by a magnificent angel standing where Ben had stood. The angel was no longer disguised in human form nor limited by it. He was almost too beautiful to look at directly, the way looking at the sun hurts your eyes. He was nearly thirty feet tall and perfectly proportioned, draped in satiny silver robes, and when he spread the massive wings on his back, the light that shone from them flooded the woods in a warm, white glow, illuminating the yard, the courtyard, the house, the garage.

"This is the form you're probably more familiar with," the angel said to Tommy.

Then a second angel appeared. It was Charlie, dressed in his familiar motorcycle garb. He too held a small pocketknife in his hand, and then both he and the knife transformed. The knife became a fiery blade, the kind Tommy had been thrilled to read about in the Bible as a child. The biker shed his earthly disguise and took his place beside the Angel Benjamin, both of them equally magnificent yet distinct from each other.

"That's . . . ," Tommy began.

"Is *awesome* the word you're looking for?" Dani said.

"Awesome doesn't come close," Tommy said.

Confronted by the pair of angelic warriors, now revealed in their full heavenly raiments, the demon cowered and slunk to the side, head low to the ground like a whipped dog, lips curled back in fear. He snarled and held up a claw, talons extended, in petulant but futile defiance. The Angel Benjamin smiled, raised his sword, and swung it over the demon's head. The wind from the angel's sword bent the willow tree at the end of the driveway and sent its branches swaying. The Wendigo swung around to face its foes as Benjamin moved to one side and Charles to the other, cutting off any possibility of escape. The battle, Tommy thought, resembled a bullfight where the angels were matadors, dignified and regal against a senseless beast.

The demon tried to run. The Angel Benjamin flew forward in the blink of an eye to cut off its retreat. When the demon tried to run a second time, the Angel Charles leapt in front and spun to deliver a blow to the head that sent the demon sprawling. The angel bounced on his toes like a boxer, circling and cutting the demon off until he had it backed up against the side of the garage, where it cringed, shielding its eyes from the white-hot heavenly light.

The Angel Benjamin lifted his sword high above his head.

The demon sprang forward, lunging for the Angel Benjamin's throat.

The angel jumped to one side with the grace of a martial arts master and swung his sword down and through, neatly decapitating the monster. At the same time, Charles swung his mighty sword to split the body in half, as easily as splitting a piece of dry wood with an ax, and then, perhaps to hasten the process of decomposition, Tommy guessed, he split the halves in half before stepping away from the putrid corpse. He looked down on the slain demon as its corrupted fluids drained into the dirt, exchanging a brief but satisfied glance with his heavenly counterpart. A moment later the demon's body parts seemed to calcify, then turned to ash, crumbled, and blew away.

In an instant the night grew dark again and the angels transformed back into Ben and Charlie. As Ben walked toward Tommy and Dani, he folded his knife and put it back in his pocket.

"We told you it had attachments," he said.

"Will the demon be back?" Dani asked.

"No," Charlie said. "This is permanent. He's gone forever."

"You were here all along," Tommy said.

"You can trust in Christ," Charlie said, nodding. "All our power comes from him. The things you see in this world, the forms and frames, don't last. The love of Jesus is eternal. Everything else will fade away."

Quinn, Cassandra, and Ruth came cautiously from the greenhouse. They all gathered around the angels. Charlie let Ben speak for both of them.

"I took this form to tell you something you needed to understand," he said. "When I arrived, I didn't know what my task was until you found the book." He held out his hand to Cassandra. "Do you have it?"

Cassandra had picked up the book and gathered up the loose, unpaginated sheets of calf vellum, now pressed between her two hands.

She handed all of it to Ben, who took the book and the loose pages and then handed the book back to her, bound and collated and protected again by its cover. Cassandra looked at the restored book in her hands, slack-jawed.

"If you ever want a job at the library, let me know," Ruth said.

"Do you know what's coming?" Dani said to Ben.

"No, we don't know the future," the angel said. "But we'll be there. And there are many more where we came from. Many who are far more powerful than either of us. We can't tell you what to do, but use what you've learned. The strongest faith is the kind forged by challenge. Sometimes you just don't know how strong your faith can be until it's tested."

"'Then I looked, and I heard the voice of many angels around the throne, and the living creatures and the elders,'" Tommy quoted. "'The number of them was myriads of myraids, and thousands of thousands.'"

"There's a reckoning coming," Ben said. "You've been chosen to do the Lord's work. Failure is not an option."

They heard a noise behind them and turned to see Otto crawling out from under the porch.

"You're not very brave," Quinn said to his dog, "but you are smart."

When they turned around again, Ben was there, and Charlie was there, and then both faded from view.

38.

At St. Adrian's Academy, twenty-one boys waited in the rotunda of the commons. Above them a mural, a 360-degree panorama, depicted the history of civilization, conceiving it as an unbroken sequence of wars and battles led by kings and generals, with a few scientists and thinkers (all male) and a handful of mechanical inventions added to the composition. Closer scrutiny by anyone trained in historical analysis would reveal that the inventions, suits of armor, rifles and airplanes and missiles, all had military applications or were developed in response to military needs. Close examination would also discover that next to each king or general or thinker there was a second man, smaller but in close proximity, ready to give advice.

The twenty-one boys who'd assembled wore winter clothing, coats and hats and gloves, and each boy had a suitcase. Each suitcase contained a small wooden box holding the cremated remains of a small animal. Mixed in with the ashes, something else.

The boys spoke quietly to each other, waiting. At the appointed time they were told by the porter that the vans to take them to the Westchester County Airport in White Plains had arrived. Dr. John Adams Wharton and Dr. Adolf Ghieri stood at the door as the boys filed out, each boy shaking the hand of the headmaster and the school psychologist. No words were spoken, no wishes for happy holidays or merry Christmases. The semester was over. The other boys on campus had already departed for home and the six-week-long winter break between semesters.

In the distance, work had begun on the new science center, bulldozers and caterpillars moving earth and digging holes.

Dr. Ghieri smiled. At the very same time, a motorcycle chase and a battle between good and evil were taking place. He'd sent the demon to the house where the athlete and the girl and the others had taken refuge to inflict as much damage as possible, but mainly to create a diversion. The ploy had worked. The boys were safely on their way.

Shortly after the scene in Tommy Gunderson's courtyard ended, a lone unmarked police car pulled up to the gates and Detective Phillip Casey asked over the intercom if Tommy was home. Tommy recognized Casey's voice and told the detective to drive on through, then pressed the button to open the gates.

The detective parked on the cobblestones and got out of the car, walking with a stiffness that made him seem older than he was. Tommy and Dani greeted him on the back steps.

"Are you all right?" Tommy said.

"My knees don't like the cold," Casey said. "My nephew ain't crazy about it either."

"Hello, Detective," Dani said.

"Dr. Harris. They told me I might find you here."

Dani and Tommy looked at each other.

"I didn't mean that to come out the way it sounded."

"My house is being fumigated, so Tommy told me I could stay in his guestroom for a few days," Dani explained. She hated lying, but at the moment she couldn't think of any way to explain to Casey what was really going on.

She glanced over her shoulder to where Quinn, Cassandra, and Ruth were clearly visible through the kitchen windows. Villanegre had recovered enough to walk under his own power to a bed in a downstairs guestroom. Dani hadn't had a chance to call an ambulance, but he seemed to be stable and not as seriously injured as they'd first thought.

"Their houses being fumigated too?" Casey asked. "Look, this is none of my business. All I ask is that if you have a Super Bowl party, you invite me, because my wife says we can't get a flat-screen TV until the old TV breaks."

"Would you like to come in for coffee?" Tommy said. He saw Casey eyeing the barbecue pit where the propane explosion had singed the grape arbor. The expression on Casey's face grew even more puzzled.

"I think I've had enough caffeine for the day," Casey said. "Looks like maybe you have too. Is there someplace we can talk? The three of us?"

Tommy led him to the greenhouse. The air outside was cold and dry, but the temperature inside the greenhouse was over eighty, the air humid and fragrant with the aromas of hothouse tomatoes and marigolds. There were benches in the center of the greenhouse, but when Tommy suggested they sit, Casey declined.

"I've just got a minute," he said. "Dani, I looked into Jerome Leonard, last seen in Portland, Maine, like you asked. I'm afraid it's not good."

"What happened?" she asked.

"That's why I wanted to talk to you in private," Casey said. "You remember the condition of the body when they found Abbie Gardener? How she seemed to have been crushed, like those submarines that dive too deep and implode? That was how they found Jerry Leonard. Same COD: not yet determined. Same sort of crime scene, except this time, the guy was inside a locked room."

"When was this?" Dani asked.

"About six months ago," Casey said. "Jerry Leonard was Julie's father. That makes the whole family either killed or dead under suspicious circumstances. Any thoughts?"

The way Casey eyed her, Dani understood that he suspected she knew more than she was saying.

"What do the Portland police say?"

"They don't say much," Casey said. "He was living alone in a crummy apartment by the waterfront. Using a fake name. They just called it cause of death unknown and closed the case."

"Huh," Dani said.

"Huh?"

"You're thinking someone might be going after the whole family?" Tommy asked.

"It certainly looks that way," Casey said. He looked at each of them again before realizing they weren't going to tell him anything.

"Okay, look," Casey said. "I like you both. I don't know what's going on here, but right now, since there apparently aren't any other members of the Leonard family we need to worry about, I'm going to put this aside and move on. I don't know you very well, Tommy, but you seem like a straight-up guy, so if you have your reasons not to talk to me right now, I'm going to respect that. But I want you to know I'm on your side and I can work with you on this if you want my help. Meanwhile, I got your backs. Okay?"

"Okay," Dani said.

"And I meant what I said about the Super Bowl party," he told Tommy, opening the door to his car. "My brother-in-law Vinnie runs a pasta tailgate at Foxborough where guys pay $20 a head for all they can eat, and I know all his recipes."

"We'll definitely invite you if we have a Super Bowl party," Tommy said.

After he left, Tommy turned to Dani. "How much do you think he really knows?"

"He's like an iceberg," Dani said. "What he lets you know he knows is just the tip. He's really smart."

"He'd be good to have on the team," Tommy said.

"We might need to include him, eventually," Dani said. "You realize that the more people we bring on board, the more we're going to look like a bunch of kooks. Radical religious extremists, predicting the end times."

"It crossed my mind," Tommy said. "We should be careful."

"You can say that again."

"We should be careful."

39.

The next two days were quiet. They regrouped and discussed how to proceed. The immediate danger had passed, but the greater danger had not. Villanegre was taken to North Westchester Hospital, where he was treated for a punctured lung, broken ribs, and a bruised kidney. He smiled through the pain and tried to dismiss his condition, adding that his belief in the eternal life palliated any concerns as to his immediate future. "I'll be all right," he told Dani. "But I won't mind a few days in a hospital. Stay calm and carry on, as they say."

Ruth went back to her house to collect the small arsenal she'd inherited from the policeman. Cassandra called her agent and told him she was entering rehab, and that she couldn't tell him where she was because she didn't want the paparazzi to find her, hanging up before he could protest. Quinn spent the time developing a pair of simple colorimetric protein assays using dyes that would bind with the compounds they'd found in the pill Dani had taken from Starbucks and with the Provivilan sample. The first dye test would turn a glass of water blue if it contained Provivilan. The second dye test would turn a sample red if it contained the Doomsday Molecule. Quinn's work gave them the ability to detect the presence of a threat. It was a good start.

Knowing Carl had betrayed them ("death by drowning" was the

official version of events), they looked back and wondered why they'd failed to notice something that should have been obvious. The way he'd failed to translate simple Latin words or make jokes from obvious setup lines, or turned down Ruth's strawberry-rhubarb pie after saying it was his favorite—they'd known he'd been acting odd, but they hadn't put it together, even when they'd been explicitly warned. The message was clear: think the unthinkable. They were fighting an enemy that would stop at nothing to defeat them. It was agreed that they would monitor each other and speak freely if they noticed any aberrations.

"They're evil and we're not," Tommy said. "We need to try to understand how they think. 'Be wise as serpents but harmless as doves.' So says Scripture."

"Good advice," Dani agreed.

Detective Casey told Dani that the case on Abbie Gardener was closed. As far as Irene Scotto was concerned, a 102-year-old woman had died alone in her room of unknown causes. The papers said only that Abbie had died of "old age." Casey told her the report on the reptile scale Banerjee had sent to the FBI came back marked *Cannot identify*.

"I think I'm going to have trouble sleeping over this one," Casey said. "I might call you for a prescription. I'm going to call my guy in Portland and see if they found any reptile scales near Jerome Leonard. You never know."

"Try warm milk," Dani told him. "It really does work."

George Gardener came down from the bedroom after sleeping for nearly forty-eight straight hours and asked what he'd slept through.

Tommy laughed. "Not much."

George ate three cheeseburgers, a large bag of chips, and half a pie, and drank four cups of coffee before Dani and Tommy questioned him.

He said he hadn't known his mother was some kind of warrior for Christ until a year ago. Before that he merely thought her to be a somewhat distracted and distant woman who was always busy with what she told him were "her books." He'd been resentful of the neglect he'd endured, but stayed on the farm because she told him she needed him to run things. She had written him a letter, he said, once she'd realized her mind was slipping, but she'd asked him not to open it until after she'd passed. He didn't wait—he opened it the day he came home from putting her in the nursing home, which he said was the worst day of his life. The letter explained her mission in life, that she'd been chosen by her predecessor, a banker named Leominster, George recalled, and told to carry forward a sacred duty.

"At first I thought she was crazy," he said. "All that nonsense about witches in East Salem. But then I realized the people she'd named as witches had all been affiliated with the school. They really were evil. She wasn't crazy after all. She was watching the school. Getting names. Finding out where people went."

Tommy put his hand on George's shoulder. "When we found you, you said that you'd killed Julie Leonard."

"She came to the house," George said. "She wanted to talk to my mother, but she wouldn't tell me what it was about. I should have scared her off. They were watching me. They wouldn't have known about her if they hadn't been following me. I'm not smart enough. I got her killed."

"You didn't know," Tommy said. "They already knew about her, George. They killed her father six months ago. He was the one your mother chose, but he didn't want the job. He was too afraid."

"It's up to you now," George said. "You and Dr. Harris."

"We're going to carry on your mother's work," Dani said. "We promise."

"I'm sorry," George said. "I let her down. I can't go home. They're going to kill me. I figured if everybody thought I was dead already, they'd leave me alone."

"You can stay here," Tommy said.

"Thank you," George said. "My mother's letter said they're getting bolder. They think . . ." He was unable to finish the thought.

"It doesn't matter what they think," Tommy told him. "They're wrong."

George moved into the room Carl had occupied and joined them for Thanksgiving dinner. Tommy and his aunt tried to make the occasion as normal as possible, cooking a large turkey and preparing stuffing and sweet potatoes and corn and cranberry relish. Ruth made four pies, two pumpkin, one pecan, and a strawberry-rhubarb in memory of Carl. They sang the doxology before they ate, and Tommy led them in giving thanks—for the friends they had, for the friends they'd lost, for the new friendships still forming, for all the blessings the Lord had showered upon them, and for his love, which still burned strongly in their hearts.

After dinner they all watched football on the television, and Tommy tried to explain, for Quinn's benefit, what was happening on the field. Dani sat next to Cassandra on the couch. Ruth adamantly refused to let any of them help her clean up in the kitchen.

George kept himself apart and said little. He was brooding at the thought that his mother's body was still unburied, but it was not safe to do so yet.

After the football game ended in the early evening, Tommy and Dani called a meeting. They sat at the dining room table, pie plates pushed away from them.

"We need to talk this through," Dani said. "Tommy and I are committed. We've been called. It's that simple. But the rest of you still have a choice. Even George has a choice. I know you all understand what's at stake, but we need to get it on the table. If you want to walk away to take care of yourselves or your families, or for any reason, you can do that. You don't have to explain, and nobody will think any less of you."

She waited.

"Well, I'll go first," Ruth finally said. "I'm in. Period. You're my only family, Tommy. You and your dad. He'd be in if he could be. Whatever you need."

"I'm in," Quinn said. "I've got nothing better to do." He glanced briefly at Tommy.

"Well, don't look at me," Cassandra said. "I'm not bailing. Do you really think I'm going to go back to Hollywood and make more idiotic movies about spunky young women who just gotta make it on their own? I mean, seriously? I'll help any way I can. And I might know other people who can help."

"George?" Dani said.

"I don't know what good I'd be," he said. "But I'm with you."

Tommy looked each person in the eye to make sure, then poked the table with his finger. "Done," he said. "Just remember whose side we're on. It's not just us."

Dani jumped in. "That said, we still need to do what we can. We've been called to action. Evil triumphs when good people do nothing. So if anybody has any ideas, now would be a good time to share."

"I was thinking," Quinn said. "I might just take that job they offered me at Linz Pharmazeutika. See what I can learn from the inside."

"There's a good chance they know who you are," Tommy said. "We don't know what Carl told them."

"That's true," Quinn said. "But from what you've said, I don't think he would have told them anything more than he had to. And even if they think I'm a spy, they might want to figure out what I know. They might even try to turn me into a double agent, like old Tibald. In which case I'd pretend to agree, and then I'd be a triple agent. How many microbiologists get to do that?"

"I was talking to Dani about Udo Bauer," Cassandra said. "Dani's impression was that he fancies himself quite a ladies' man. I think I could make myself into quite a lady."

"Cass, that's too much to ask," Tommy said.

Cassandra touched him on the arm to stop him. "I'm a good actress," she said. "It would be nice to do something that's actually important with the one thing I can do really well. Role of a lifetime."

When Cassandra had finished, Ruth spoke up. "I'm a research

librarian," she said. "And a gun collector. I will do research. And shoot people when asked."

"Okay then," Dani said. "I think that's enough for tonight. Let's get some sleep, and then in the morning we can start making plans."

Tommy asked Dani if she wanted to go for a walk before bed. They bundled up and Tommy took her by the hand, leading her out beneath a sky filled with stars. They strolled the grounds with Otto keeping them company and finally sat on the Adirondack bench beneath the willow tree overlooking the pond, where Tommy put his arm around her, then his other arm, and kissed her. When the kiss ended, a good while later, he smiled at her, their faces a few inches apart.

"I am so sorry I doubted you," Dani said. "I will never do that again."

"I won't give you any reason to," Tommy promised. "But if it happens, and we get confused, either of us, we talk to each other, openly and honestly, and figure it out together. We're much better together than we are apart."

Dani remembered what Villanegre had said about the two kinds of art history students. She and Tommy had different approaches, but they always arrived at the same conclusions, taking different routes.

She kissed him again, letting her passion flow, and for a moment she could block out everything else and bask in this glow of good feelings she hoped would last forever. She wanted to do everything for this man and everything with this man.

"I don't know when we'll get the chance," he said, "but when I can, I have to do something. Carl told me a long time ago, before any of this happened, that he wanted to be cremated. I promised I'd take his ashes up to Alaska, to a place called Taylor Bay. I'd like you to come with me when I go."

"I'd like that," Dani said. "I'd like to do an autopsy on him first. If he had a demon inside him, I'd like to see if there's any physical evidence left behind. We might be able to learn something."

"Science can't answer everything," Tommy said, "but I'd be interested to know what you find out."

"I was thinking I'd send that list of names to Ed Stanley," she said. "He said Guryakin's name was on a list. Maybe some other names will mean something to him."

"Good idea," Tommy said. "Are you going to tell him where you got them?"

"I will if he asks."

With all the leaves down, the view was spectacular, and they could see the lights of the town in the distance. When she commented on how lovely the view was, Tommy told her he'd been lucky when he bought the property.

"This is the highest elevation in Westchester County," he said.

"Really?" she said. "Higher than Bull's Rock?"

"Oh yeah. By maybe fifty feet or so. Which is another way of saying it's all downhill from here."

Dani turned and looked at him, eyes alerted. "What did you just say?"

"It's all downhill from here," he said. "Joke. Figure of speech. Dani? Earth to Dani—are you okay?"

She was lost in her thoughts, waving her hand at Tommy to give her a second. After a moment, she rose from the bench, excited. She had it— everything became clear.

She'd assumed that Provivilan was part of some kind of plot, but there was no way to distribute enough of it to cause any real harm. It wasn't a virus or a living microorganism that could reproduce itself, and it wasn't an infectious agent that could spread through contagion.

"Wait here a second," she told Tommy, running to the house.

When she returned she was carrying a glass jar, which she filled with water from the pond. She then hurried back into the house, and Tommy followed. She set the jar of pond water on the food island, went to his cupboard, grabbed a coffee filter, and poured the water through it from the first glass jar into a second. The water in the second jar retained a slightly brownish-green hue, but it was clearer than it had been.

Quinn looked on as Dani held the jar up to the light, examining it.

313

She turned to him. "I want to test something—how long would it take you to get another sample of Provivilan?"

Quinn hesitated. "Less than a minute," he finally said.

"You have more?" she said.

"I got some from Illena. But I lied. She didn't steal it so we could test it. I've been on it for about six months. Sort of a test group."

"Why?"

"I have a tumor, Dani. Cass, I was going to tell you too."

At first Dani thought she'd heard him wrong. It took her a moment to realize he wasn't joking.

"Provivilan treats cancer?" Cassandra asked.

"No, but it treats the sadness that comes with it," Quinn said. He pointed to the base of his skull. "My oncologist thinks it's all in my head. You know me. Once I get something in my head, it's hard to get it out."

"Oh, Quinn . . . ," Dani said. "When—what can they do?"

"Inoperable," he said. "And right now—and I'm choosing my words carefully, Dani—it's also inconsequential. Let me get you that sample."

He went upstairs and returned a moment later with a small plastic orange bottle. He opened it and poured a handful of pills into Dani's hand. She told him she needed the reagents he'd prepared. Quinn went to Tommy's study, where he had set up a place to work in the corner, and returned with a pair of bottles, one marked *Provivilan Reagent/Blue*, the other labeled *Doomsday Molecule Reagent/Red*. Dani filled two drinking glasses with clean springwater from a bottle in the refrigerator and brought them to the food island.

"Two glasses," she said, "both with nothing but clean water in them. Okay? Tommy, I need some drinking straws."

He brought her a box of straws from the cupboard. She took one, dipped it into the bottle of Provivilan reagent, and placed her thumb over the top of the straw, using it as a pipette. She moved the straw to the first glass of spring water and lifted her thumb to drop the contents into it.

"If this works," she said, cracking open one of the capsules of the drug, "when I dump Provivilan into the glass containing the assay, it's going to react, right?"

"The anionic form is blue," Quinn said.

"It will turn blue if what's in these capsules is really Provivilan. So . . ."

She dropped the contents of the Provivilan capsule into the first glass of water, and it indeed turned a pale shade of blue. She swished the water around to mix the contents.

"But this isn't going to hurt anyone," she said, raising the glass. "This is just Provivilan. It lacks the molecular components needed to turn into the Doomsday Molecule, right?"

"Right," Quinn said. "It needs to combine with a number of other components."

"This reagent," she said, using another straw to draw a sample from the second bottle and dump it into the second glass of clean bottled spring-water, "will react to the presence of the Doomsday Molecule. What will happen if this glass has any of the Doomsday Molecule in it—the drug they were testing on Amos Kasden and the others?"

"It should turn red," Quinn said. "I modified the Bradford assay. But we don't have any more samples of the Doomsday Molecule."

She dropped the reagent into the second glass. Nothing happened. She dumped the contents into the sink and rinsed the glass.

"We don't," she said. "Doomsday Molecule reagent red plus clean bottled water equals nothing." She refilled the second glass with bottled water, added a capsule of Provivilan, swished it around, then added the Doomsday reagent. Again, nothing happened. "This did not turn red. This means Provivilan is not the Doomsday Molecule. Now watch."

She again emptied the second glass and rinsed it. This time she filled it halfway with the filtered pond water she got from Tommy's backyard pond. She added a capsule of Provivilan to the pond water.

"Now we have something entirely different," she said. "Bear with me—when people take antidepressants, their brains don't utilize 100 percent of the drug. The brain utilizes what it needs, and the rest passes through the kidneys and gets flushed. And these days, there are so many people taking so many different kinds of antidepressants that our waste-water effluents contain a virtual cocktail of psychotropic compounds, like a big SSRI smoothie."

"I got in trouble when I asked for only bottled water on the set," Cassandra said. "I got called a diva because I didn't want to poison myself."

"I thought sewage treatment plants cleaned up the drinking water," Tommy said.

"Waste water is indeed recycled," Dani said. "But treatment plants can't strain out the catecholamine metaboloids. It stays in the water."

"In concentrations too small to worry about," Tommy said.

"Just because we *don't* worry about it doesn't mean we *shouldn't* worry about it," Dani said. "It's there, in our drinking water. It's in the ground and in the clouds and it comes down with the rain. A small portion bio-degrades, but the larger portion doesn't."

"Okay," Ruth said.

"And so, in this glass," Dani said, holding up the glass combining pond water and Provivilan, "that smoothie of psychoactive compounds is pres-ent. This is water from the pond out back. To which we added Provivilan." She swirled the water around again. "So if we add the red Doomsday reagent . . ."

She used a straw to add the Doomsday Molecule reagent into the sec-ond glass.

They watched. Cassandra crossed her fingers. Ruth rubbed her nephew's back. Quinn's face registered an increasing concern as the liquid took on a pinkish hue, then a deeper magenta, and finally a bright red.

"Lord, help us," Ruth said.

"That's how they're going to do it," Dani said. "As Quinn said, Provivilan has to combine with something. Provivilan is going to pass every test every

FDA scientist ever performs on it. The new wonder drug is going to go on the market, people are going to take it, it's going to pass through their systems and enter the effluents and eventually the drinking water supply. And then, in miniscule concentrations, one part per trillion, it's going to combine with metaboloids already in the environment and turn into the Doomsday Molecule, and then it will impair the cognitive development of boys by polluting the womb environment. A few girls too, but mostly boys. They're going to grow up lacking Purkinje cells, and they'll seem like wonderful, happy, intelligent, productive little boys, but then when they hit puberty, they will *all* turn into homicidal, suicidal, raging monsters craving the adrenaline rush that comes from inflicting pain and committing violent acts. They'll be addicted to it. It's . . ."

"It's the end of the world," Ruth said.

Dani went to sit in front of the fireplace in the living room to think. She reviewed the steps in her thinking to see if she might have missed a step, or if her reasoning was flawed, but she kept arriving at the same conclusion. She talked it over with Quinn, who helped her see it from every conceivable angle. Nothing new occurred to them. They'd thought of everything.

A few minutes later, Tommy came in, leaned down from behind, and kissed her on the forehead.

"Come here," he whispered, so that Quinn couldn't hear. "I want to show you something."

She followed him into the kitchen. Quinn said good night and disappeared up the stairs. The others had gone to bed. Tommy and Dani had the first watch. The half-empty jar of pond water sat on the food island.

"The night Abbie Gardener came to visit me—the night Julie was killed—we found her by the pond," Tommy reminded her. "But I didn't turn my security system on every night. It was kind of a fluke that it was on the night she came. I have a ten-foot-high deer fence around my property. That's a pretty high fence for a 102-year-old woman to jump over. I don't know how she got through, but she was motivated. Do you remember what she said to me at the pond, when she was holding the dead frog?"

"These are the first to go. You'll be the last."

"I couldn't tell if she meant 'you, Tommy Gunderson,' or just 'you,' people in general. But she didn't come to my house by accident."

"God sent her," Dani said.

"Well, yeah," Tommy said. "But she didn't know who I was. She didn't leave the nursing home thinking, 'I think I'll go see that has-been football player.'"

"She was trying to get to her house," Dani said. "She wanted to go home. Your house is on a line between the nursing home and the farm."

"And we thought that's why she ended up in my yard. But after your little demonstration tonight, I thought—wait a minute. That's not why she came to my house. She came to my house because it's the highest point in Westchester County. If you were going to poison the drinking water for New York City, where would you go? Where are all the drinking water reservoirs?"

"Westchester County," Dani said.

"And if you wanted to poison one body of water in Westchester, knowing that sooner or later, the water in it would run into all the other drinking water reservoirs, where would you go?"

"I'd go to the highest point in Westchester County," Dani said.

"That pond out back drains from a little stream that empties into Lake Atticus," Tommy said, "and from there it passes through the Katonah reservoir, the Cross River reservoir, the Croton reservoir, the whole shebang."

"Okay," Dani said. She felt her whole body begin to shake, because she knew where this was going. "So we need to guard your pond."

"Watch," Tommy said. He took a drinking straw, plunged it into the bottle of Doomsday Molecule reagent, then emptied it into the jar containing the remainder of the pond water. The water in the jar turned bright red, the color of blood.

"You dropped a capsule of Provivilan into the pond water, added the reagent, and it turned red. I didn't add a capsule. I just dropped the reagent into the pond water, and it turned red. Provivilan is already in the drinking water supply," he told her. "Combining to form the Doomsday Molecule. They poisoned my pond. I don't know how or when, but some night when the security system wasn't on. Abbie must have figured that out. That's why she came to my house. That's what your dreams about water and blood were telling you. They're not waiting until Provivilan goes on the market. It's already too late."

Dani was too stunned to speak. She thought of all the children she'd seen playing on the town green. She thought of Emily and Isabelle, her nieces.

Tommy held her hands and pushed his forehead against hers. "Have faith," he said. "God isn't going to let this happen."

"Can I have faith and still be scared?" she said. "Terrible things have already happened. You saw that list of names. Those evil people . . ."

"We'll figure it out," he said. "You and me. Together. We'll figure it out. Something will turn up, I promise you. Do you believe me?"

"I believe you."

"Say it with me," he said, taking her hands in his and closing his eyes. "Our Father, who art in heaven, hallowed be thy name . . ."

"Amen," they finished, just as the intercom buzzed to indicate someone was at the gate.

Tommy jumped up, grabbed his gun and stuck it in the back of his waistband, and punched up the security monitor.

Dani joined him. On the monitor they saw a boy of about fifteen with neatly combed hair, a white shirt, gray slacks, a black blazer with the St. Adrian's crest on the breast pocket, and a necktie striped in the school colors of purple and red.

"Can I come in?" the boy said. He held up a Bible and placed his hand on it to show them he was telling the truth. "My name is Reese. I'm the one who sent you the pill and the SD card. Please let me in. They're going to kill me."

Dani and Tommy exchanged glances, and then Tommy reached for the keypad to open the gate. Dani stayed his hand.

"What if it's a trick?" she said.

"Fool me once, shame on you," Tommy said. "Fool me twice . . . how's it go?"

"Shame on me," Dani said. "I just want to err on the side of caution— but he's holding a Bible. I don't think it's a trick."

"Good enough for me."

"Open the gate."

READING GROUP GUIDE

1. Why do angels choose to conceal their activities from man?

2. What obstacles do you think the first Christian missionaries in continental North America faced?

3. What actions might humans take to fight demons and their activities? What actions should be left to God?

4. Find a copy of Hieronymus Bosch's painting *The Garden of Earthly Delights* in a book or on the Internet and study it closely. How would you interpret the imagery in the three panels?

5. Dani and Tommy are driven apart in *Darkness Rising* by jealousy. Where does it come from?

6. What leads to Carl's capitulation to the forces of darkness?

7. Quinn begins as a man of pure science but finds himself opening his mind to larger thoughts and beliefs. What causes Quinn to change?

8. What was the nature of Tommy's relationship with Cassandra, and how is his relationship with Dani different?

9. How do you think microorganisms fit into God's plan?

ACKNOWLEDGMENTS

Conceiving of and writing a book takes a leap of faith. Thank you to all the readers of the East Salem novels who have taken that leap of faith with me. I am humbled and inspired.

Thank you, O'Reilly, from Wiehl. And Roger Ailes, who took a chance on hiring a certain legal analyst. And Dianne Brandi, whose judgment is infallible.

Thank you to Pete's lovely wife, Jen, and son, Jack, for all their patience. And to Bob Roe, for his keen eye and pen.

Thank you to the amazing team at Thomas Nelson, including Daisy Hutton, senior vice president and publisher (a true visionary); Ami McConnell, senior acquisitions editor (and compatriot); L.B. Norton (so appreciate your work and sense of humor); Amanda Bostic, acquisitions editor ("brilliant" should be added to her title); Natalie Hanemann, senior editor; Becky Monds, associate editor (and a stellar human being); Jodi Hughes, editorial assistant. In marketing, thank you, Eric Mullett, marketing director; Ashley Schneider, marketing specialist; Ruthie Dean, publicity coordinator; Katie Bond, publicity manager (and one of the finest people I know); and Kristen Vasgaard, packaging manager (who is a creative genius). Your spirit and enthusiasm is wonderfully infectious. And a special thank-you to the awe-inspiring Allen Arnold, my friend always.

Thank you to our book agents, Todd Shuster and Lane Zachary of the Zachary, Shuster, and Harmsworth Literary Agency. We couldn't have done this without you!

All of the mistakes are ours. All the credit is theirs. Thank you!

Dᴏɴ'ᴛ ᴍɪss ᴛʜᴇ sᴛᴜɴɴɪɴɢ ᴄᴏɴᴄʟᴜsɪᴏɴ
ᴏf ᴛʜᴇ Eᴀsᴛ Sᴀʟᴇᴍ Tʀɪʟᴏɢʏ ɪɴ . . .

FINAL
TIDE

Aᴠᴀɪʟᴀʙʟᴇ Sᴇᴘᴛᴇᴍʙᴇʀ 2013

AN EXCERPT FROM *FACE OF BETRAYAL*

NORTHWEST PORTLAND
December 13

Come on, Jalapeño!"

Katie Converse jerked the dog's leash. Reluctantly, the black Lab mix lifted his nose and followed her. Katie wanted to hurry, but everything seemed to invite Jalapeño to stop, sniff, and lift his leg. And there was no time for that now. Not today.

She had grown up less than two miles from here, but this afternoon everything looked different. It was winter, for one thing, nearly Christmas. And she wasn't the same person she had been the last time she was here, not a month earlier. Then she had been a little girl playing at being a grown-up. Now she was a woman.

Finally, she reached the agreed-upon spot. She was still shaking from what she had said less than two hours earlier. What she had demanded.

Now there was nothing to do but wait. Not an easy task for an impatient seventeen-year-old.

She heard the scuff of footsteps behind her. Unable to suppress a grin, Katie called his name as she turned around.

At the sight of the face, contorted with rage, Jalapeño growled.

MARK O. HATFIELD UNITED STATES COURTHOUSE
December 14

As she walked to the courtroom podium, federal prosecutor Allison Pierce touched the tiny silver cross she wore on a fine chain. The cross was hidden under her cream-colored silk blouse, but it was always there, close to Allison's heart. Her father had given it to her for her sixteenth birthday.

Allison was dressed in what she thought of as her "court uniform," a navy blue suit with a skirt that, even on her long legs, hit below the knee. This morning she had tamed her curly brown hair into a low bun and put on small silver hoops. She was thirty-three, but in court she wanted to make sure no one thought of her as young or unseasoned.

She took a deep breath and looked up at Judge Fitzpatrick. "Your Honor, I ask for the maximum sentence for Frank Archer. He coldly, calculatedly, and callously plotted his wife's murder. If Mr. Archer had been dealing with a real hired killer instead of an FBI agent, Toni Archer would be dead today. Instead, she is in hiding and in fear for her life."

A year earlier Frank Archer had had what he told friends was a five-foot-four problem. Toni. She wanted a divorce. Archer was an engineer, and he was good at math. A divorce meant splitting all their worldly goods and paying for child support. But if Toni were to die? Then not only would Archer avoid a divorce settlement, but he would benefit from Toni's $300,000 life insurance policy.

Archer asked an old friend from high school—who also happened to be an ex-con—if he knew anyone who could help. The old friend found Rod Emerick, but Rod wasn't a hired killer—he was an FBI agent. Archer agreed to meet Rod in a hotel room, which the FBI bugged. In a window-less van parked outside, Allison monitored the grainy black-and-white feed, all shadows and snow, waiting until they had enough to make an arrest before she gave the order. With gritted teeth, she had watched Ar-cher hand over a snapshot of Toni, her license number, her work schedule, and $5,000 in fifties and hundreds. She sometimes understood those who killed from passion—but killers motivated by greed left her cold.

Given the strength of the evidence, Archer had had no choice but to plead guilty. Now, as Allison advocated for the maximum possible sentence, she didn't look over at him once. He was a small man, with thinning blonde hair and glasses. He looked nothing like a killer. But after five years as a federal prosecutor, Allison had learned that few killers did.

After she finished, she rejoined Rod at the prosecutor's table and listened to the defense attorney's sad litany of excuses. Archer hadn't known what he was doing, he was distraught, he was under a lot of stress, he wasn't sleeping well, and he never intended to go through with it—lies that everyone in the crowded courtroom could see through.

"Do you have anything you would like to say to the court before sentencing?" Judge Fitzpatrick asked Archer.

Archer got to his feet, eyes brimming with crocodile tears. "I'm very, very sorry. Words cannot describe how I feel. It was all a huge mistake. I love Toni very much."

Allison didn't realize she was shaking her head until she felt Rod's size 12 loafer squishing the toe of her sensible navy blue pump.

They all rose for the sentence.

"Frank Archer, you have pled guilty to the cowardly and despicable act of plotting to have your spouse murdered." Judge Fitzpatrick's face was like a stone. "Today's sentence should send a strong message to cowards who think they can hide by hiring a stranger to commit an act of violence. I hereby sentence you to ten years for attempted capital murder-for-hire, to be followed by two years of supervised release."

Allison felt a sense of relief. She had an excellent track record, but the previous case she had prosecuted had shaken her confidence. The date rapist had been pronounced innocent, which had left his victim stunned, fearful, and angry—and left Allison feeling guilty that she hadn't been able to put him away for years. Today, at least, she had made the world a safer place.

A second later, her mood was shattered.

"It's all your fault!" Archer shouted. He wasn't yelling at Toni—his ex-wife was too afraid to be in the courtroom. Instead, he was pointing at Allison and Rod. "You set me up!"

Archer was dragged from the courtroom, and Rod patted Allison's arm. "Don't worry," he said. "We'll keep an eye on him."

She nodded and managed a smile. Still, she felt a pulse of fear. Ten years from now, would the man come back to take his revenge?

Shaking off the feeling of foreboding, Allison walked out of the courthouse—known to Portlanders as the "Schick Razor Building" because of its curved, overhanging roof—while she called Toni with the good news. In the parking lot, she pressed the fob on her key chain, unlocked her car door, and slid behind the wheel, still talking.

Only after she had accepted Toni's thanks and said good-bye did she see the folded paper underneath her windshield wiper. Muttering under her breath about junk advertising, she got back out of the car and tugged the paper free.

Then she unfolded it.

The professional part of Allison immediately began to take notes. For one thing, except in a movie, she had never actually seen a threat written in letters cut from a magazine. For another, were her own fingerprints obscuring those of the person who had done this?

329

But the human side of Allison couldn't help trembling. For all her detachment, she couldn't tamp down her horror as she read the message.

I'M GOING TO RAPE YOU. AND YOU'RE GOING TO LIKE IT. AND THEN I'M GOING TO CUT YOU INTO LITTLE PIECES. AND I'M GOING TO LIKE IT.

Better Not Let Me Talk to Boys

September 5

Hi! I'm a Senate page on Capitol Hill. This blog will tell about my experiences here in Pageland.

Washington DC is all tall buildings, honking cabs & humidity that feels like someone wrapped you up in a blanket of steam. Plus it smells funky. Like hot garbage.

It turns out that the Vietnam Memorial & the Washington Monument & the statue of Lincoln are all a couple of blocks apart. My stepmom V has been trying to get me to all the famous sites, even though there will be trips every other weekend just for the pages. (Now she's asleep & I'm writing this in the bathroom of the hotel, which has free wireless.)

I can't believe that the whole time we've been here it's been raining. For some reason, I never thought it would rain in DC. Luckily some guy on the street was selling umbrellas.

After all the sightseeing, we went out to dinner with Senator X. He got me this internship, but I probably won't see him very much. I'll be working for all the senators, especially the 50 Republicans, not just him. (Working in the Senate is better than working in the House. I hear they have to stare at hundreds of photos so they can memorize all the faces & names in their party. Compared to that, 50 is a piece of cake.)

We ate at an elegant Japanese restaurant, where I had many things that I can't pronounce. Not only are the Japanese people good at anime, but they know how to cook.

Before our food came, V told these people at the next table to keep their toddler under control. He had a cup of Cheerios & was throwing some on the floor. So of course she had to boss them around. Then V started telling the senator that he had better keep an eye on me & not let me talk to boys. I just wanted to crawl under the table, even though they both pretended she was joking.

Doesn't she realize that I'm not a little kid anymore? In eight days, I'm going to be seventeen!

Allison set the pregnancy test on the edge of the tub. Marshall was in the living room, stretching in front of the TV news, getting ready to go for a run.

All afternoon, this moment had been in the back of her mind, providing a welcome distraction from her anxiety whenever she thought about the threatening note. Rod had come as soon as she called and had taken the document away as evidence. He asked her if she had any enemies, but they both knew the question was a joke.

Of course Allison had made enemies, most recently Archer. She was a third-generation prosecutor, so she knew it came with the territory.

The so-called blue-collar criminals—bank robbers and drug dealers—weren't so bad to deal with. For them, getting caught and doing time was an accepted risk, a cost of doing business. They were professionals, like she was. In a weird way, they understood that Allison was just doing her job.

It was the other ones, the ones who had been fairly upstanding citizens until they snapped at dinner and stabbed their spouse or decided that bank robbery was a perfect way to balance the family budget. Those were the ones you needed to watch out for. Their feelings for Allison were personal. Personal—and dangerous. For now, she would be extra careful, and Rod had alerted the Portland police to make additional patrols past her house.

Her watch said 6:21. She told herself that she wouldn't pick up the white stick again until 6:30. The test only took three minutes, but she wanted to be sure. How many times had she watched one of these stupid tests, willing two crossed lines to show up in the results window but seeing only one?

"I'll be back in about forty minutes, honey," Marshall called from the living room. She heard the sound of the front door closing.

Allison hadn't told him she was going to take the test today. She was four days late, but she had been four days late before. After so many failed tests, so many months in which being even a day late had filled her with feverish speculation, Marshall no longer inquired too closely into the details.

When they started this journey two years ago, she had been sure that she and Marshall would conceive easily. Any teenager could have a baby. How hard could it be? She and Marshall had always been scrupulous about birth control. Now it seemed like a bitter joke. She had wasted hundreds of dollars preventing something that would never have happened anyway.

They had started trying a month after her thirty-first birthday, giddy to be "playing without a net." At the end of the first month, Allison was sure she was pregnant: her breasts felt different, the taste of food changed, and she often felt dizzy when she stood up. But then her period arrived on schedule.

As the months passed she got more serious, tracked her temperature, made charts. Even though she had read all the statistics about how fertility declined with every passing year, it hadn't seemed like they applied to her.

How many crime victims had she met who had never believed that anything bad could happen to *them*? Because they were special?

"It's in your hands, Lord," she murmured. The idea was one she struggled with every day, at home and at work. How much was she responsible for? How much was out of her control? She had never been good at letting go.

To distract herself, Allison turned on the small TV they kept in the bedroom on top of an oak highboy. After a Subaru commercial, the Channel Four news anchor said, "And now we have a special bulletin from our crime reporter, Cassidy Shaw. Cassidy?"

Allison's old friend stood in front of a beautiful white Victorian house. She wore a coral suit that set off her blonde shoulder-length hair. Her blue eyes looked startlingly topaz—either she was wearing colored contacts or the TV set needed to be adjusted.

"A family is asking for your help in finding a teenager who has been missing from Northwest Portland since yesterday afternoon," Cassidy said, wearing the expression reporters reserved for serious events. "Seventeen-year-old Katie Converse left her parents a note saying she was taking the family dog for a walk—and she has not been seen since. Here's a recent photo of Katie, who is on winter break from the United States Senate's page program."

The camera cut to a photograph of a pretty blonde girl with a snub nose and a dusting of freckles. Allison caught her breath. Even though Katie was blonde and Lindsay had dark hair, it was almost like looking at her sister when she was Katie's age. The nose was the same, the shape of her eyes, even the same shy half smile. Lindsay, back when she was young and innocent and full of life.

Cassidy continued, "Katie is five feet, two inches tall and weighs 105 pounds. She has blue eyes, blonde hair, and freckles. She was last seen wearing a black sweater, blue jeans, a navy blue Columbia parka, and Nike tennis shoes. The dog, named Jalapeño, is a black Lab mix.

"Authorities are investigating. The family asks that if you have seen Katie, to please call the number on your screen. This is Cassidy Shaw, reporting from Northwest Portland."

Allison said a quick prayer that the girl would be safe. But a young woman like that would have no reason to run away, not if she was already living away from home. Nor was she likely to be out partying. Allison knew a little bit about the page program. It was fiercely competitive, attracting smart, serious, college-bound students whose idea of fun was the mock state legislature. The kind of kid Allison had been, back when she and Cassidy were in high school.

She looked at her watch and was surprised to see it was already 6:29. She made herself wait until the clock clicked over to 6:30, then reached for the pregnancy test. The first time she had bought only one, sure that was all she would need. Now, two years later, she bought them in multipacks at Costco.

In the control window was a pink horizontal line. And in the other window, the results window, were pink crosshairs.

Not single pink lines in both windows.

She was pregnant.

The words popped up on FBI special agent Nicole Hedges's screen.

PDXer: Whats ur favorite subject?

Nic—using the screen name BubbleBeth—and some guy going by the name PDXer were in a private area of a chat room called Younger Girls/Older Men.

BubbleBeth: Lunch

It was what Nic always answered. She could disconnect from her fingers, from the reality behind her keyboard and the words that appeared on her screen. Which was good. Because if she thought about it too much, she would go crazy.

At first, working for Innocent Images, the FBI's cyber-crime squad's effort to take down online predators, had seemed like a perfect fit. Regular hours, which were kind of a must when you were a single parent. The downside was that she spent all day exposed to vile men eager to have sex with a girl who barely qualified as a teen.

Most people were surprised that it wasn't the creepy guy in the raincoat who went online trolling for young girls. If only. In real life it was the teacher, the doctor, the grandpa, the restaurant manager. The average offender was a professional white male aged twenty-five to forty-five.

PDXer: How old R U?

BubbleBeth: 13

In Oregon, eighteen was the age of consent. But prosecutors preferred to keep it clear-cut to make it easier for the jury to convict. So Nic told the guys she met online that she was thirteen or fourteen, never older. Some typed L8R—later—as soon as Nic told them her imaginary age. For the rest, it was like throwing a piece of raw meat into a dog kennel.

PDXer: KEWL

Surveys had shown that one in seven kids had received an online sexual solicitation in the past year. It was Nic's job to find the places where the chances weren't one in seven, but 100 percent, which meant going to chat rooms.

Sure, that kind of thing happened on MySpace, but the FBI didn't have the time to put together pages that would fool anyone. They never looked as good as the real thing. Real kids spent hours on their MySpaces, tweaking them with photos and music and blogs. Real predators went there, too, but it was hard to catch them without some kind of tip.

But there were plenty of chat rooms. Nic's being there was predicated on the chat room name (Not Too Young to Have Fun, for example) or a kid's report of having been solicited.

Sometimes she took over from a true victim, but usually she just started out fresh—went into a chat room and announced her presence. The first thing you noticed upon entering a chat room was the absence of any actual chat. The point of being there was to start up a private conversation. It never took longer than five or ten minutes before someone approached her.

PDXer: R UR PARENTS TOGETHER?

BubbleBeth: No. I LIVE W/MY MOM. ONLY C DAD SOMETIMES.

It was what she always said. Guys like PDXer loved kids with one parent and unfettered access to the Internet. It was like that line in *Casablanca*. *"This could be the beginning of a beautiful friendship."*

PDXer: DO YOU HAVE ANY BROTHERS OR SISTERS?

BubbleBeth: 1. SHES 3.

Young enough that Nicole's imaginary mom would have her hands full.

Nic let Makayla play Neopets online. But only when she was in the room with her. And her daughter knew that at any time her mom could come to her and ask to see what she was typing, and Makayla would have to show her right away.

PDXer: R U A COP?

Nic smiled. *Got ya.*

BubbleBeth: No!

Nic went on answering PDXer's questions, not even paying that much attention. It was better if she didn't. Didn't think about this sick jerk sinking his hooks into a girl. Grooming her. Better if she didn't wonder how many there had been before her. Girls who really *were* thirteen or fourteen.

PDXer: CAN U SEND ME A PIC?

Since they never used pictures of real kids, Nic would send him a picture of herself, morphed back to look like she was thirteen. The morphing wasn't accurate because it didn't take into account three years of braces and four pulled teeth. When she had really been BubbleBeth's age, everyone had made fun of her buckteeth.

PDXer: WANT 2 GO 2 A MOVIE SOMETIME?

BubbleBeth: SURE, THAT WOULD BE COOL.

Nic had to backspace and retype the last words, changing them to B KEWL.

PDXer: ANYTHING U REALLY WANT TO C?

BubbleBeth: MEAT MARKET.

It was rated R, which meant technically she couldn't get in. Well, BubbleBeth couldn't. Sometimes Nic forgot to distance herself. She wasn't thirteen, she wasn't going to school, she didn't fight with her mom.

PDXer: GR8. R U WEARING ANY UNDIES RIGHT NOW?

Bingo.

It all starts with
a phone call
from the dead.

Available March 2013

ABOUT THE AUTHORS

Lɪs Wɪᴇʜʟ is a *New York Times* best-selling author, Harvard Law School graduate, and former federal prosecutor. A popular legal analyst and commentator for the Fox News Channel, Wiehl appears on *The O'Reilly Factor* and was cohost with Bill O'Reilly on the radio for seven years.

Pᴇᴛᴇ Nᴇʟsᴏɴ is the coauthor of Waking Hours as well as the author of *Left for Dead*, which won the 2003 Christopher Award. He was listed in the Esquire Register of Best American Writers and nominated for an Edgar Award.